Praise For Wi

I think this story is a experienced hardships and suffering and yet proceed with life. In this story the path takes each one to Willow Bend, where the process of healing and hope comes through acceptance and faith in God. I think Sarah is one of my favorite characters because she is unafraid (ha!) and even though she has to make a change by coming to Willow Bend, calmly approaches her destiny. If there was anything I would improve, I would like to see more complexity and diversity between the characters.

Dee Perry

"Loved the book! Can't wait for next book! Actually, it would be hard to pick just a few characters to follow because their lives are all connected in one way or another. Want to see what happens in next book. Great job!"

Ruth Forward Smith

"The perfect combination of heartfelt romance, action and drama. Franklin and Sarah being the two most compelling characters touched my heart the most. Many will enjoy this book for it's relatable characters and light hearted tones in some of the scenes. As a teenage boy (19), I usually don't find book like this interesting but this one appealed to me greatly. This book is a great read for all, since it touches on so many genres."

Isaac Morey

Diane has a penchant for pulling on heart strings, as well as providing delicious food for thought. She captivates by stirring just about every possible emotion in a person with the obvious hopes of enrichment and conviction of better ways of living more fully, while inducing deep longing to improve one's own life. Keep Kleenex handy and plan on some sit-and-ponder time after each chapter. Sometimes the questions dangle for a number of chapters before you get the satisfaction of answers - oh, but the answers are satisfying! So glad I got a sneak peek! Feelin' privileged haha! I know you're gonna love her book and you will get to know her charm, humor and beautiful heart of love thru this read. I HIGHLY RECOMMEND!"

Billie Korstad

I found this book to be a refreshingly and uniquely written drama. I enjoyed the feeling it gave me, as a reminder that acts of kindness and friendship are the core of a community. Especially when it takes place in the Civil War era, where hardship and emotional turmoil were prevalent. When you call a town a home, you can be provided so much more than a roof over your head.

The centralized common gathering place was the hotel, which housed it's residents but provided so much more, as in support, a listening ear and just a comforting atmosphere. It reminded me that kindness doesn't have to cost a thing, and actions can be priceless.

The war affected so many people besides the soldiers. It traumatized the country on a personal level and a regional level. It was places like Willow Bend that helped heal both the soldiers and the people who welcomed them home.

I enjoyed the interactions of the residents and the uplifting emotions that go along with relationships, both professional and personal, and their varying individual faith journeys.

Throughout the book I found myself being easily able to visualize the surroundings, like the hotel, and the places of business and the ranch settings. Through that ability, I enjoyed each of the individual characteristics that the main and secondary characters exhibited, and found them to be realistically interesting.

I was glad to know that the book was part of a series, as I look forward to following the future relationships and endeavors of the characters.

Cindy Arnold

WILLOW BEND

Welcoming Our Soldiers Home

Diane Metzger

WILLOW BEND

Welcoming Our Soldiers Home

By Diane Metzger

Published By
Positive Imaging, LLC
http://positive-imaging.com
bill@positive-imaging.com

Cover Art by Dusan Arsenic

ISBN   9781944071363

I would like to thank the following people for their support in helping me to complete my first book:

Kevin Farmer who asked me one day why I hadn't started writing my book and that prompted something inside of me to actually begin.

Julia Farmer (8) who helped me to make a map of Willow Bend and name some of the animals

My son Billy and his wife Bethany for believing in my writing and encouraging me

My daughter Susan who has spent countless hours praying for me

My friend Cynthia who has helped me with research of the area I now call 'Willow Bend' and who has encouraged me in countless ways through phone calls and emails and writing an article about my book.

My friend Marcus who has received dozens of calls from me, asking if he would listen to something that I'd just written. He always laughed in the right places.

My friends Billie, Dee, Isaac, Cheryl, Kendra and my cousin Ruthie for editing my book and reading it to write a review.

My niece Tracey who calls me often and prays a lot for everything I've needed prayer for

My publisher, A. William Benitez, of Positive Imaging, LLC, who has led me through the steps to actually hold a copy of my first book in my hand.

My Heart Feels Their Pain

Walking all over this battlefield,
sends my thoughts back so many years.
What happened on this spot where I'm standing?
What were they thinking; what were their fears?

Was someone's son lying here by himself,
left all alone to die?
Did his voice call out for his mother or sweetheart,
with no one to hear his sad cry?

Maybe someone was wounded right here,
and his best friend carried him away.
But others had to remain behind,
with no choice but to stay.

I seem to have no trouble imagining,
so many young men with futures no more.
The wounded and dying lying in every direction,
where there were beautiful trees and meadows before.

Nothing could have ever prepared them,
for the horrors of what they saw as they fought.
Fighting for your cause should be honorable;
this was like nothing they'd ever been taught.

Oh, to be back in their homes once again,
for even one single night.
Just to have the knowledge and peace,
that their loved ones were safe and alright.

Some men had dreamed of being doctors;
others would have spent their life behind a plow.
But now thousands of men would not return home,
their families must find a way to go on, but how?

I'll never tire of reading the history books,
that tell of all their gallant fights.
Knowing they were about to die,
as the enemy had them in their sights.

Today as I walk this path by myself,
I'm so glad that no one else is around.
I need this time to be alone,
in this special place that I've found.

Although I did not know these brave boys,
my heart feels like that is not true.
I wish I could have been there to help them,
but what could just one woman do?

By Diane Metzger

Pvt. George Philo Smith
Fought at Gettysburg
Wounded July 1st, 1863

11th Corp, 3rd Division,
1st Brigade
157th NY Infantry

Born: July 22, 1840 Williamstown, VT
Died: Oct. 6, 1929 Tekonsha, MI

Picture of George in a suit was taken on Aug. 5, 1913
(aged 73)

Contents

1
MAY 1865

So Many Lives Intertwined

"Chaplain Rogers" yelled the orderly, "Doc said to get to the hospital tent fast! A soldier has been wounded in the face and isn't expected to live." The Chaplain was almost tripping over his own feet in his haste to get there quickly. At times like this he felt like he had nothing to offer any of the men; he felt so empty inside after four years of this brutal war. As he ran, he prayed silently to God, asking for words of comfort for this soldier. He entered the tent and Doc motioned him over to the far corner. He knelt down on his knees and took the young boys hands. It was a shock when he realized who it was and then he said, "Tommy, it is Chaplain Rogers; I'm here son. Please tell me what I can do."

Tommy had apparently been given morphine and his voice sounded strange. "Tell my ma and pa that I was a brave soldier. They woulda' been proud of me. I never ran from a fight. Tell them I'm sorry that I won't see them again 'til we meet in heaven but I love them dearly. My special girl, Susan, we was to be married when I made it home. Tell her I want her ta find a fine young man and have some sweet children, like we planned to do. Tell her I spoke her name at my last breath." Tommy's body went limp and Chaplain Rogers fought back a sob. He had never felt so helpless in his entire life.

His best friend, Doc, came over to him and said, "I'm so sorry James. I know how special he was to you. I just got word a few minutes ago that General Lee has surrendered. You and I are to leave in a few days to go home to Willow Bend on the train. It may take at least a week to get there, but we are going home, my friend." Chaplain Rogers had nothing to say. He stood up but his shoulders were stooped over, and he looked a lot older than his true age of 35. He walked out of the tent and kept going, until he found a path into the woods. It was almost dusk and he could barely follow the path. He found a place where a large tree had fallen and he went around to the backside of it and hid under a limb full of leaves, where no one would see him. Finally, the sobs came out in a rush and the noise that he was making was nothing like he'd ever heard before. His fists kept hitting the ground, over and over. It felt like huge amounts of grief were coming out, like waves in the ocean. One sob and cry after another, until he lay exhausted on the ground.

When he finally sat up, he started talking to the God that he loved and served with his whole heart. "Lord, I am a broken man who has watched countless men die or suffer wounds. I'm heading home soon, to a village full of hurting people. Some of our men are coming home with missing limbs and some aren't coming home at all. Many of those returning will have emotional scars that no one can see. I've prayed before, asking you to send me a wife of your choosing. Lord, I just feel in my heart that I can't wait much longer. I need a woman who will love me and will help me to take care of the people in my new church. I can't do it alone Lord! Your word says that you know our needs even before we ask, and Lord; I'm asking and desperately need an answer soon. Amen!"

The following morning Doc and Pastor sat down together, away from everyone else. They were about to face an emotional farewell to one of the dearest soldiers either of them had ever met. Over a month ago, a young man had been brought in to them and what they saw, broke their hearts. A cannon had blown up and burned this soldier all over his face, chest, and arms. His name was Franklin Jefferson, and even through his intense pain, something about him touched both of them. They sat together and asked God for the strength they would need when they had to say goodbye to Franklin.

'Lord, we lift up our friend Franklin to you and ask your greatest blessings over him as he leaves this battlefield. You are the only one who can understand what he is going through right now, both physically and emotionally. We believe that you still have plans for his life and we ask you to lead him step by step. Surround him with people who will become his friends and treat him kindly. Please give us the strength that we need to say goodbye to him this morning. Let him not see pity in our eyes; only your love and affection. Amen!

Pastor and Doc went to the tent, dreading this moment, but knowing that they had to face it. *'Lord, please don't let us break down.'*

Doc was the first to speak as he said, "Good morning Franklin. We just stopped by to see you off and to find out what we could do to help you. Do you have any particular destination in mind? I know you've told us that you lost your parents years ago."

Franklin replied, "I have no earthly idea Doc. I don't think God invented a place that would accept me now. I've thought of taking my life, but I just can't do it. I'm still young and strong. Maybe the good Lord can show me ways for me to help people in secret."

Doc had taken out a piece of paper and written down his name and the name of his village. He said, "Franklin, if you ever need anything at all, come to Willow Bend and find me or write to me, and I promise that I will do anything I can to help you. I'm going to leave you two jars of my special salve to take with you. I want to hear from you son, and I mean that sincerely." Franklin knew that Doc meant what he said, and he knew that he and the Chaplain could be counted on.

Chaplain Rogers went right over to Franklin. He had helped Doc put up hanging blankets all around Franklin's cot, for privacy. "Hello Franklin, I understand that you have been discharged. I came by to give you a few things to take with you."

"Franklin said, "I don't have a horse anymore, unfortunately. I guess these two feet will manage to get me to where I'm going."

Chaplain Rogers said, "We have that problem solved. One of my friends offered me an extra horse for you when he found out about your accident. She's right outside! I also have a bag of food for you and a canteen full of water, a blanket and a tent and a few other items that I thought might come in handy. I know you will have a hard road to go down in the future but always believe that the good Lord has a plan for your life. He knew when He created you that you would have this tragedy to deal with, but He still has a plan for you. Has the doc given you the name of the village we are both going back to?"

Their kindness was making it hard for him to speak for a moment. Now he said, "Yes, Doc gave me the name of Willow Bend and offered to help me if I ever needed anything. I'll do my best to stay in touch from time to time. I plan to travel at night because of my face. Thank you both for all that you've done for me. I didn't expect anything." Chaplain knelt down by Franklin's cot and held his hand as he prayed.

Franklin's face was badly scarred, so he would have to travel at night. If anyone saw his face, they would either be repulsed or terrified, and he just couldn't handle going through that again. Even his closest friends in the Civil War couldn't look at him after the accident. While he was working on a cannon, it had blown up, and Franklin's life was close to being over. The medics were kind to him, but even they had to force themselves to look at him from time to time and he could see in their eyes that he was probably very ugly looking now. Even after a couple of months, he still didn't have the courage to look in a mirror or see his reflection in a window. The only two people who had looked him straight in the face were the doctor and chaplain that had watched over him constantly. As he was riding along the first night, he reflected back on the two men who were so good to him.

At first he had been out of his mind with pain but they gave him laudanum, which knocked him out for several hours at a time. The doctor had put a salve all over his face that was soothing and actually reduced the pain. He explained to Franklin that it was a salve that he had made himself back in his village of Willow Bend. One night Franklin asked the doctor to tell him about his village back home. Doc said, "I've been in a lot of places in my life, but nothing has ever compared to Willow Bend, in my opinion. There is just a special feeling when you come around the bend. Most of the villagers are very happy to welcome strangers. Some people are just passing through, and others were looking for some place to settle down and ended up staying. There are woods on three sides of the village. I've camped out there a few times in my younger days. There is a stream that runs through the woods, right behind the hotel. I've caught a few fish in that pond and nothing smells better than frying fish that you caught yourself."

It had taken four days for Doc and Chaplain Rogers to find a train that had room, but they were finally on their way home. "Can't this train move any faster?", said Chaplain Rogers? "I need to get home to meet the veterans. I'm not helping anyone by just pacing here." Doc shook his head and decided to speak the obvious. "Maybe you can cheer up some of the men on this train, instead of thinking about how slow this train is moving." Chaplain Rogers looked shocked! "Why hadn't he thought of that?" He turned and held onto the back of the seat to steady himself. He walked towards the back of the filthy, smoky car and almost missed a soldier that was slumped over, head against the window. Chaplain stopped and said, "Danny, is that really you? How is your hand doing?"

Danny opened his eyes and recognized the chaplain who had prayed for him when he was injured a few weeks ago. "Hello, Chaplain Rogers, I'm mighty happy to see you. My hand is useless, but I still have it. The doctors were determined that I was going to lose it but I had other ideas. I'm on my way home to see my girl Mandie."

Chaplain sat down beside Danny and took his injured hand and began to pray. "Lord, we thank you for sparing Danny's life. We ask that you be with him when he meets his girl Mandie soon. Please watch over him as he makes the adjustments to being home again. Amen!" Pastor took a piece of paper and a pencil out of his pocket and wrote down his name and the location of the small village where he lived. "Danny, if you ever need anything, please be sure to write me. I look forward to hearing from you."

He spent the next couple of hours going from one soldier to another, giving out words of encouragement, handshakes, prayer and even holding one young boy in his arms as he cried. The young man had lost an arm and was so afraid of what life would be like for him from now on. Pastor had passed out his name and the name of Willow Bend on dozens of little slips of paper and he felt so much better now. His feelings of frustration were gone and he knew he had done the right thing by getting up and checking on these men.

Sarah Waters stood in front of the mirror over her dresser and sighed. Looking at herself in a mirror always made her wonder how she looked to other people. What she saw was a young woman with deep brown eyes and long, reddish brown wavy hair that was the color of a copper penny. The freckles across her face still hadn't disappeared. She had been such a tomboy when she was younger, much to her mother's dismay. She could ride bareback on her horse and could shoot a gun as well as her brothers. Now she was almost 20 years old; the age of a spinster if you believed some of the gossip in town.

When she was a small child, she had given her heart to the Lord, but not in church. She wanted it to be a very private moment between her and God, so she had walked down a path behind her home, following the fence line beside the pastures. When she knelt down in the meadow filled with yellow wildflowers, she had felt such a warmth and a peace wash over her entire body. She had spoken out loud to God, as she usually did when she was alone.

After finishing school, she threw her whole heart into teaching. Even the students who were quite a challenge, eventually made some changes in their attitude when Sarah gave them so much individual attention. She loved to see that dull look in their eyes gradually turn to show some interest. It was a challenge that she enjoyed. She had lost her mother when she was only six years old and her father and older brothers had done their best to raise her. The result was a young girl who was happiest wearing her brother's overalls, helping to clean out the stalls and taking care of all of their animals. Her idea of a good bath was jumping into the creek with most of her clothes still on. Sarah was a hard worker and always full of energy. When she was old enough to start attending school, she finally found something that piqued her interest. Because she was a student in a one-room schoolhouse, she picked up on subjects ahead of her age group. Sarah was indeed a unique young lady, but delightful, just the same.

Becoming a schoolteacher was what she had enjoyed immensely for the past three years, but she was feeling restless. Working with children was wonderful but she had recently felt like she was trapped. Teaching the children about life outside of their small community gave Sarah a strong desire to travel. What other opportunities were out there? She had written a letter to a friend of hers who was living in another state. Her friend's name was Maude and she lived and worked in a hotel. Before the war, Sarah and her family were visiting relatives in Michigan and had stayed at a nice hotel in Willow Bend. Something drew Sarah to Maude, who lived in that hotel, and worked the front desk. They became fast friends, even though there was a great difference in age between them. They had written to each other several times a year during the war. She knew that she was more than welcome to stay with her as long as she wanted to, but she asked her permission as a courtesy.

Instead of writing a letter, Maude sent a telegram to let Sarah know she could visit her and that there was an opening for a schoolteacher in their village. Now they were going to be reunited and Sarah was so eager to see her old friend in person. School would be out next week and she sent a telegram to Maude that she would leave the day after school was dismissed. A few days later, she purchased her ticket for Willow Bend and started packing. Sarah didn't have any fancy dresses except a nice one that she wore to church. Her trunk was packed with a few dresses and lots of books and school supplies. She wanted to be prepared if she were to be hired to be their new schoolteacher.

After several long and tiring days on the train, Doc and Chaplain arrived in Willow Bend. This was a wonderful village to raise your children or to live, surrounded by caring friends. Life wasn't necessarily easy but you didn't have to shoulder your problems by yourself. Even the eldest residents could be counted on to bring a meal to someone sick or injured. The men often got together to build barns, tear up stumps, or help to plant a crop. At the train station on the north edge of the village, Doc had asked if someone could spare a few minutes to take them into the village, and the slow ride was enjoyable. As they looked at the wonderful sight of their small village, they were pleased to see that not much had changed. The elm and maple trees lining Main Street had grown taller and fuller and there were several stores that weren't here four years ago. One of them was a blacksmith's shop, which was greatly needed and another was a café. Several people stopped to wave to them and a few of the children looked like they had grown a foot. By the time they arrived at Doc's office, someone had already alerted Maude at the hotel. She was standing outside just beaming. Chaplain nudged Doc in the ribs and said, "You shouldn't waste any time letting her know how much you missed her."

Doc growled back, "I don't need your advice Chaplain. Come to think of it, I need to start remembering to call you Pastor James, now that you are resuming being the pastor of our Baptist Church again. According to Maude, the young pastor that has been filling in the past four years, has done a splendid job."

Maude waited for them to get down from the carriage and then she gave them both a warm hug and said, "My, you two look a little worse for wear but it is so good to see that you are back home safe and sound. Are you hungry? Charlie has cooked up a fine dinner for the last two days, not knowing for sure what day you would arrive."

Doc and Pastor both wanted to clean up and change clothes. "Maude, tell Charlie that we'll definitely be there for the evening meal tonight," said Pastor James. We will expect you to join us too. By the way, thank you for the letters that you wrote to us. That meant a lot to hear about how the village was doing while we were away."

Doc just stood there, not knowing what to say. He finally managed to get a few words out, "Yes, thanks for the letters, Maude. It was very thoughtful of you." Both men went their separate ways and Maude walked back over to the hotel to tell Charlie the news. She was a little disappointed in Doc's reaction to seeing her, but maybe he was just tired.

In truth, Doc was completely exhausted, mentally and physically. He had seen so many men die from being shot, who might have survived if the medical conditions had been better. In the beginning of the war, the doctors had no idea how much the unclean surgical tools were doing to cause infection and death. Doc was one of the first to figure out how keeping their instruments clean would give many of the wounded a fighting chance to survive. He would never be able to erase some of the worst memories; of hearing the men screaming for mercy, for water, for their mothers. Those horrible memories could never be erased.

Doc had summoned the Chaplain too many times to count. Doc had silently watched how he spoke softly and kindly to the soldiers. He asked how he could pray for them and always wrote down their family's names and addresses. Sometimes he wrote letters that were dictated by the dying men. Doc never saw any signs of shock on the pastor's face as he looked directly at the men and their wounds.

Doc and Pastor James were the backbone of this village. Dr. Thomas had lived here so long that he knew every resident by name. He had treated most of them for one thing or the other over the years. He would often give out medicine at no charge, asking them to drop off some of their delicious jam or their wonderful apples. Doc always made sure to suggest they give him something in return so that they wouldn't feel like they were receiving charity. Some of the families lived on farms or ranches on the outskirts of Willow Bend and he would try to make it out to their homes at least once a month, if time permitted. Both men were in a line of work that suited them perfectly. Doc was a handsome man who didn't seem to have a clue that he was. His ears were a little large but somehow seemed to fit right in with his square jaw. He rarely looked in a mirror because memories of his childhood came back to him way too swiftly. His father had never managed to say a kind or positive thing to him. All he could remember hearing was *"You dress like you come from a poor family, son. Go change your clothes right now!"* or *"There you go slouching again. Put your shoulders back and stand straight. How many times do I have to tell you that?"* How he ever managed to make it through medical school was a wonder. The change must have happened when he was many miles away from his father. Once he received his medical degree, he had no thoughts of opening up a practice back home. A small inexpensive ad in a local paper had caught his eye. A small village in Michigan, called Willow Bend, needed a family doctor. He answered the ad and was accepted and built up his practice slowly but steadily, and that's where he met Pastor James. Both of them were still single, but hopefully that might change now that the war was over. Doc had a special lady in his life named Maude, who hadn't been given much encouragement about how he felt. He had done little to encourage the relationship to go much past being good friends, but he had changed his way of thinking since the war. Yes, Maude was such a unique woman, who was probably running out of patience.

The Yankee sharpshooter shifted his weight around on the strong limb of an old oak tree. He absentmindedly stroked the scar on his face with his thumb. A painful memory flooded back to the night he had received that scar. He tried to shake off those feelings of anger and struggled to think about something else. While riding down this dirt road, covered with huge oak trees on each side, he had a feeling that someone was following him. The hair had stood up on the back of his neck, so he made a decision. He rode his horse into the brush and climbed up into this big, sturdy tree, where he was well hidden. Even if someone looked up in that tree, they wouldn't be able to find him. He was an expert at concealing himself, not to mention a crack shot with his rifle and pistols. He had decided to stay where he was for another hour or so, to see who exactly was traveling down this road behind him.

His name was Johnny Anderson and he was exhausted from spending four years shooting at men he was ordered to kill. When he signed up to fight in the war, word spread quickly that he was one of the best marksmen in their unit and he was ordered to join the Sharpshooters. He took no pride in the number of men he had killed or wounded. Getting through the war in one piece was his only concern and he had only been wounded once, in the right leg, and he had recovered quickly. Now that the war had mercifully ended, he had no idea where he would go. His parents had passed away during the war from malaria and his two brothers were hopefully alive - but where? No wife or sweetheart was waiting for him to return. He had believed that he had found the right woman but the joke was on him. He had surrendered his heart, but the woman turned out to be quite different from what he had first thought he'd seen in her. He was never going to let any woman make a fool out of him again. Shortly after they were married, he had casually mentioned to his wife, Carolyn, that he was eager to have children. The shocked look on her face stunned him. His wife had just found out that she was going to have a baby and she couldn't accept it. He had come in from the fields the next day to find a note from her.

'Johnny, I wired my father for money to take the train home. I will not be returning and I am not proud of what I am about to do. I found out that I am with child. When you told me that you were looking forward to being a father, I realized with great fear that I am not the motherly type. You have already figured out that my parents spoiled me and I do not want to see my life changed by becoming a parent. I promise to find a safe, loving home for your child so please don't worry

about the care it will receive. My parents have located a wonderful orphanage for when the time comes. I know I am disappointing you and making you angry but I refuse to pretend that I can become a loving mother. Please don't try to contact me. I want to put this all behind me. I do hope that you will find the right woman who can live up to what you need and want in a wife.'
   Carolyn

   Johnny wasn't even given the choice to raise the child himself. Now that he was discharged, he was determined to find his missing child. It made no difference to him if the child was a boy or girl. He would love that child with all of his heart and would try his best to be a good father. If he thought about it too much, he would feel sick inside. Most of the time during the war he had been too busy or too tired to think about his child but these hours up in the tree, gave him way too much time to think. Johnny was the kind of man who stood out in a crowd. He was about 5' 8" tall and slight of build but he was stronger than he looked. His hair was black and wavy and his moustache was thick and always neat. Something about his dark brown eyes reminded you of pieces of coal. There was a 3" scar across his left cheek that wasn't ugly but very noticeable. He never talked about it and so far, no man was foolish enough to ask him. The way he carried himself spoke of a lot of confidence and of someone who had been through a lot in his life. He never smoked and rarely drank more than one beer. No matter where he was, he always made sure that he was very aware of his surroundings and who was close by. Johnny never acted cocky but it was easy to tell that you would have your hands full if you started a fight with him. Growing up with an older brother had given him a lot of practice at defending himself.

When the war had ended, he started traveling from Kentucky on a train. It was filled to the brim with wounded, homesick soldiers, and those who were just sick at heart. No one had expected this war to last so long or to be so brutal. Since he had no idea where his brothers were, he was going to look up his best friend in Indiana. The train ride would end in Cincinnati, and from there he would have to buy a horse. In Cincinnati, he asked around and found a man whom he felt was honest and he bought a sturdy horse from him; a gelding who looked like a horse he'd had back home.

All of a sudden, he saw a soldier in a tattered uniform, on an old horse, coming down the road towards his hiding place. The soldier was being followed by a man on a faster horse, who was about to overtake him. Johnny could tell that the man being chased was weak and unarmed. He kept quiet, trying to figure out what was going on. The man catching up to him was scraggly looking but riding on a horse of good quality, which meant he must be stolen.

"Hey, Yank. Stop right there. I think you must have stolen that ole nag. I might have to hang you for that." The man rode up to the wounded soldier and grabbed a rope off of his saddle. At that moment, Johnny decided this was enough. He couldn't stomach watching a man who was hurt and apparently not able to defend himself, being picked on. His rifle dropped silently into the bushes. Now he moved as swiftly and quietly as a cat as he swung himself down from the limb and kicked out at the man with the rope. He hit him hard on the head with his boots and knocked him off his horse.

The man he had hit had silently pulled a small pistol out of his boot and was aiming at the injured man. Diving through the air Johnny reached the injured man and pulled him out of the saddle, and tried to break his fall by putting himself underneath him.

He had no sooner hit the ground hard, then he felt a bullet rip through his shoulder. Pinned beneath this man, he couldn't reach for his pistol. Before he knew it, the man he had saved grabbed Johnny's pistol and shot the other man in the chest. This guy might be injured but he sure reacted quickly. He asked the man if he was all right and was assured that he was.

He said, "The other guy is dead. I didn't intend to kill him. My name is Samuel and I was a medic in the war; I'll bind up your wound enough to stop the bleeding." He was trying hard not to pass out from the pain and loss of blood. Samuel was doing a good job of bandaging his shoulder. Samuel explained that he was on his way home to his wife and son in Willow Bend, Michigan. Johnny managed to tell Samuel his name and got out the words, "Get my horse behind those trees!" and then he passed out.

When Johnny came to, he had no idea where he was but he didn't sense that he was in any danger. He carefully let his eyes roam the room he was in, but his head didn't move. He could feel a bandage around his shoulder and quite a bit of pain radiating from it. The room was small but clean and neat. He was lying in a single bed and there was a bedside table with a pitcher of water and a glass, on his right side. *"Where was Samuel?"* Now Johnny was starting to remember what had happened to them. *"How had he gotten to this place?"*

He heard light footsteps coming towards his room. As he watched the open doorway, in walked a woman who resembled an angel in his mind. Her blond hair was curly and pinned back in a bun. She looked quite young; maybe in her late 20's and she smiled slightly when she saw that he was awake. "Hello, my name is Elizabeth and I am your nurse. The doctor just happened to be going down the road where you and your friend were lying hurt on the ground. Luckily, he had his larger carriage, which had room for both of you. Can you tell me your name and what happened?"

"My name is Johnny Anderson and I was a sharpshooter for a Yankee regiment. I didn't know the other man but when I saw someone trying to hurt him, I stepped in to help him. He looked like he wasn't in any shape to defend himself. Where is Samuel? Is he hurt bad?"

"Your friend is in a room down the hall and he is doing well. He was very hungry and weak and his old wound had opened up, but Doc cleaned it up and took good care of him. He has been a good patient and has been asking about you. I'll help him walk down here to see you, if you would like that. I don't think you are ready to get out of this bed just yet." She handed him a glass of water and helped keep it steady with her hand. It tasted wonderful and made him forget the pain for a minute. Elizabeth handed him a spoon full of medicine for the pain and helped him take some more water. She set the glass down on the side table and turned and left the room.

Pretty soon he heard her footsteps again but they were slower this time and the other steps were more like shuffling. Samuel peeked his head into the room and gave Johnny a big grin. "I'm so glad to see that you are alive. I hardly know how to thank you for saving me from that ruffian. I managed to stop the blood from flowing from your wound, Johnny, but they will take better care of you here."

"Samuel, it's so good to see you doing so well. I owe you my thanks for saving my hide too. I think that about makes us even. Maybe in a day or so, I can make it outside to get some fresh air and we can spend some time talking. I want to take you back to where your wife and son are waiting for you. Can you can give me a few more days to heal up?"

"I'll give you all the time you need Johnny. I look forward to sitting outside and getting to know you better. You rest easy now and I'll be back to check on you again." He closed his eyes and fell asleep quickly.

The following day, he saw two young faces staring at him when he woke up from his nap. A young girl and a smaller boy were studying his face intently. He asked them their names.

The girl spoke right up and said, "My name is Julia and I'm eight and this is my brother Timothy and he's five. Our mother is your nurse. We lost our papa in the war so we need a papa really bad. Are you married?" It was amazing how bold Julia was.

He said, "No, I'm not married. I'm sorry to hear about you losing your papa." He recognized Elizabeth's footsteps and when she came into the room the kids looked guilty.

Elizabeth said, "Have they been bothering you? I apologize for them coming into your room uninvited like this. It won't happen again, will it children?" They both shook their heads and ducked out of the room.

Elizabeth had explained that he had been in and out of consciousness for two days because of a high fever caused by an infection. He tried to get her to talk about herself during the days and weeks that she took care of him, but he learned very little. He had heard more from listening to her children. He hadn't been around a lot of children in his life but he felt drawn to Julia and Timothy. They never missed a day of coming into his room to tell him about their day. Elizabeth did her best to keep them away from him but her efforts were futile.

One night Elizabeth heard someone call out and she jumped out of bed, thinking it might be one of her children. When she tiptoed down the hall, she looked into Timothy's room and his bed was empty. She wasn't too alarmed, thinking he might have been thirsty or something. She kept walking down the hall and she looked in on Johnny and found Timothy curled up in bed with him. He was snuggled as close as he could get to Johnny and was holding one of his hands. Both of them looked so peaceful and it put a lump in her throat. She knew her children missed having a father and Timothy had such a big heart. He must have heard him crying out in his sleep. She decided not to wake either of them up and turned and left the room.

When Johnny woke up the next morning, he was surprised but touched to see Timothy cuddled up next to him. It made his heart ache, wondering if his child was a boy or a girl. *'This child is the same age as my child. How long is it going to take to find this child? I've already suffered four years, wondering what kind of an orphanage he is being raised in.'*

Every day that Elizabeth took care of Johnny, she could feel her heart melting and it scared her. He would be leaving soon and life would have to go on for her and her children. Elizabeth couldn't remember the last time she had laughed or felt relaxed. Since her husband's death, she felt such a heavy weight of responsibility to insure her children were taken care of. Thankfully she was a nurse and earned decent wages for a woman. In a few minutes, she would be cleaning his wound and she had to brace herself not to show any of her growing feelings for him. She felt sure that he was a decent man and he was wonderful around her children. She'd never seen him get upset with them and they could wear out anyone with their constant questions.

Elizabeth walked into his room and tried to act as professional as she could. "You have taken excellent care of Samuel and I."

Elizabeth started unwrapping his bandages and kept her eyes down. She could feel her body tensing up and hoped that he didn't notice. "Your wound is healing nicely, now that we have gotten rid of the infection. Are you in very much pain?"

"I'm not in much pain or discomfort any longer, and I'll soon be leaving to take Samuel back home. I'll miss your children coming in to see me every day."

Since he obviously wasn't going to miss her, it was better that she face that fact. "I'm glad you're doing much better. If you'll excuse me, I have some other patients to check on."

Johnny and Samuel had now been here for almost a month. Samuel had gained weight and looked like a different man. Johnny was now able to go outside and walk around the beautiful backyard. He and Samuel had decided to leave for Samuel's hometown, Willow Bend, in a day or so. While they were sitting on a bench in the backyard, Samuel said, "It's not hard to notice that those two kids think you've hung the moon. I heard Julia ask you if you were married. She is going to be a handful to raise but she is so cute. They would make a nice family for you."

Johnny just shook his head and replied, "They are a great family; you are right about that, but I'm not interested in getting married. It's been my experience that it is hard to find a woman that you can trust."

Elizabeth stood inside the house, with just the screen door between her and the men. She heard that conversation quite clearly and knew that she had to get her and the children out of here quickly. The doctor had told her only yesterday that an old friend of his had written him a letter. He lived in a small town in Michigan in a farming community and they were searching for a nurse. She would ask the doctor today if he would be kind enough to send a telegram to his friend and ask if he would be willing to hire her. She would also have to mention that she had two young children. It would take too long to send a letter and wait for a reply. She had to know quickly. She dreaded telling the children that they might be leaving but it would be easier on them this way. At least we would be the ones leaving; not standing there waving goodbye to Johnny. Right then she made the decision to just leave without speaking to him, if she was offered the job. She was afraid that he would guess her feelings if she had to face him.

The doctor that Elizabeth worked for said he would be sorry to lose her, but he sent the telegram right away. That same afternoon he received a reply. Dr. Stone would hire her on his recommendation. Besides her salary, she would also be provided with a room at the hotel for her and the children. Elizabeth didn't like the idea of leaving without saying goodbye, but she just couldn't face Johnny. Her feelings were becoming too obvious and because he was a sensitive man, he would be able to read her like a book. She told the children that she had news and tried her best to stir up the idea of this being something exciting. That afternoon, she went down and bought tickets on the stage for the three of them. She waited until that evening to tell the children exactly what was going to happen. The stage would be leaving around nine o'clock tomorrow morning; just enough time to get the kids dressed and fed and to leave the doctor's home. The children both asked to say goodbye to Johnny but she told them that it would be too upsetting to him. It didn't make them happy but they obeyed her.

Today was the day to begin Sarah's new adventure. The stagecoach was going to be full this run. As Sarah stood outside near her trunk, she looked the other passengers over. There was a very pretty nurse named Elizabeth and her young son, Timothy, and daughter, Julia.

31

When they were getting ready to start boarding the stage, a tall, handsome man with a black patch over his left eye walked up and started helping the ladies into the coach. He said, "Good morning ladies, my name is Will Baker and I will be traveling with you." He reached down and lifted the young boy and girl up into the coach. When everyone else was seated, he climbed in beside Timothy.

Worley, the stagecoach driver, hopped down to check to make sure the doors were shut tight and secure. He was anxious to get to Willow Bend to see his sweetheart, Daisy. Just thinking about her put a big smile on his face. She worked in the saloon and Worley had met her when he went in to have a beer, after his run. She had flaming red hair and a temper to match, but all it took was one glance and he couldn't come up with even one intelligent word to say to her. Somehow, she took his shyness as something she liked and she paid special attention to him all evening. Their relationship had gone on for several months now, and it made Worley feel sad inside that he had nothing to offer her. He just couldn't come up with a way to make a decent wage at this stage of his life. He was 40 and he felt like life had kind of passed him by. Today the stage had supplied a guard named Gus Nelson to accompany Worley because they were carrying a load of gold in the strong box. Gus didn't have a special girl but Worley was determined to find him someone.

As Danny got closer to home, he started feeling nervous. He had told the chaplain on the train that his girl Mandie knew about his withered hand and said that she could accept it. What if she was wrong? She hadn't seen him in person since his injury. He had started to get used to it but he had several months to adjust to having the use of only one arm. She would be seeing his wounded hand for the first time.

Thankfully it was his left hand, so he still had the total use of his right hand; the strongest one.

Danny certainly couldn't blame her for being uncomfortable around him or embarrassed to be seen with him. Well, in another mile or so he would have his answer. His mood lifted just seeing the familiar trees and fences outlining the fields. There were no signs of any battle in this ranching community. He noticed that some of the neighbor's ranches were more run down than when he was last here. Danny supposed that things would start improving now that the young men were returning. He realized that a lot of them wouldn't be. Maybe he could find a rancher or two who needed help getting their crops in. He wouldn't take any pay for what he planned to do. He wasn't paid a lot while he was a soldier but he had been very frugal and had saved the majority of his pay.

He had only one more road to turn down and he would be at Mandie's home. He had written her from a town he had passed through three weeks ago, letting her know that he was not too far away. As he rounded the bend, he saw her sitting on her front porch with her mother and father. She stood up as soon as she recognized Danny but she didn't make a move to come closer to him. Danny slowed down his pace, trying to get up the courage to face her. She looked very uncomfortable but was making a point of not looking down at his hands. Now they were only a few feet apart, looking each other in the eyes. Danny's eyes were full of hope that she would do something to show him that everything was going to be all right. Now he knew what was about to happen. Her lip was quivering and she looked pale and her eyes were sad. She forced herself to look down at his left hand and she shook her head slowly back and forth without speaking. All of Danny's hopes were shattered. He looked over at

Mandie's parents. Her mother was silently crying and her father was hanging his head.

Danny held his head up high and slowly turned around and walked back down the road where he had just come from. Although it was his hometown also, he couldn't live here, where he wouldn't be able to avoid seeing Mandie. His parents had passed away before the war and he had never made any close friends. He could feel the pain but somehow, he managed to shove it down. He needed time alone and there was only one place that he knew to go for the night. For years he had a special hideout in the woods surrounding the ranches. He had spent many a night in those woods and no one would ever find him if he didn't want to be found. Later tonight he would let the tears fall but not yet. Danny tried to shift his thoughts to all of the parents and young ladies who would not be seeing their soldier return. That kind of pain would take a lot longer to heal. The pain in Danny's heart would eventually ease up some and he would not let it make him bitter. He had to go on with his life and just face each day, one at a time. Chaplain Rogers had given him a piece of paper, where he had written down the village called Willow Bend, which was about 100 miles from his hometown. That would be far enough away from Mandie where they wouldn't run into each other. Nothing could hold him back now.

It was getting close to dusk and Danny needed to stop for the night and rest. He started following a path off to the right, avoiding some bramble bushes. What was that strange sound? He stopped to listen and it sounded like an animal whimpering. He moved towards the sound cautiously, with his pistol ready to shoot if necessary. The moon was bright enough so that he could see a few feet in front of him. Now he could see that it was a dog laying down and in a lot of pain. Danny saw that his left paw was caught in a trap.

As he moved slowly toward it, his tail started wagging and his eyes were begging for help. He lifted the trapped paw and supported it with his leg. He strained to get the trap open and finally he gently backed up enough for the paw to be free. He examined the injured paw and saw that it had been mangled. He reached back in his pack and pulled out an old rag, which he tore into strips. He wrapped the paw carefully and tied it in a secure knot.

This dog looked like it was quite a mixture; part sheep dog and part mutt. Danny stroked his matted fur and the dog licked his hand in gratitude. He wondered when he had last eaten or had any water. Danny had a hard cracker in his pack, so he fed it to this poor dog. He had water in his canteen but needed to find a way to get it into the dog. Danny finally decided to pour some into his hat and the dog eagerly lapped it up. Now he got licked in the face and he laughed. This was as good a spot as any to rest for the night. He figured it would take him at least four days to get to Willow Bend. Now with the dog to carry, it would add on another day. That was all right; he wasn't in any big hurry anyway. He decided to give the dog a name. Several names came to mind but were quickly rejected. His best friend from the Civil War was named Roscoe and so he decided to honor his friend by giving him that name. Now he felt a lift in his steps as he carried Roscoe around his shoulders. Carrying a dog like this wasn't the easiest way to walk all day long, but now Danny didn't feel so lonesome. He and Roscoe needed each other. "Your left paw and my left arm are both in bad shape my new friend, but we're not going to feel sorry for ourselves, are we? I promise to take good care of you and you can stay with me wherever I end up. I'm sure glad that we found each other."

Riding on the stage was not very comfortable, but having two attractive women as passengers took his mind off of the discomfort. Will was a man who always knew how to make decisions quickly. When he entered a room, the ladies definitely took notice. He didn't consider himself a handsome man by any means but there was something about the confident look in his eye and the way he held himself that made him stand out. He was a stocky man, with dark brown wavy hair and high cheekbones. He had been hired by the stagecoach line to accompany this stage to Willow Bend and beyond. They were carrying a strongbox full of gold and the bank didn't want to take any chances on losing this to stagecoach robbers. Will was fast with a gun but never tried to kill anyone. He had recently been released from the war and he had experienced enough killing to last a lifetime. As a Yankee scout, he had always had the men's admiration in his regiment. Several times he had led his men out of danger because of how alert he was.

During the war, he had cared deeply for a sweet girl, who lived in Knoxville, Tn. Being assigned to that city for several months, gave them plenty of time to get to know each other. She had always made him feel as if he was special and he in turn looked forward to every moment they could spend together. When his regiment had been sent out of town, they were both faithful to write to each other. Then last year he had received a letter from her mother, telling him the sad news that she had died from scarlet fever. His world came crashing down around him and he stopped caring about the future.

Now those days were behind him and his uncle had recommended him for a job with the stagecoach line. The bank in Willow Bend also had an opening and he was able to handle both jobs. He wasn't sure how long he would be working for the stage line, but it was interesting and exciting. Today's assignment was to ride the stage as a passenger but to also back up the guard. Their shipment of gold was too tempting to possible gangs that tried their hand at robbing stages. Since he was the only male passenger, it was his job to protect these two women and two small children. That in itself was a huge responsibility. From his experience as a scout during the war, Will had an uneasy feeling that they were going to be in danger on this run and he must stay extremely alert.

2

MAY 1865

From Hopeless to Heartwarming

When they had been back in the village for a week, Pastor decided to have a serious talk about Maude needing some encouragement. He decided to stop by Doc's office.

"Can you spare a few minutes Doc? I've got something important to discuss with you."

Doc finished writing something and then laid his pen down. "Of course, James; what is on your mind?"

"It wasn't hard to notice how excited Maude was when she first saw you the day we came home. Since you hardly spoke more than two sentences to her, I saw the look of disappointment on her face. You two have known each other for several years and you couldn't ask for anyone more faithful or loving than Maude. You need to start courting her or you just might lose her."

"What in the heck does courting mean, anyway? I've heard the word before but never understood it."

"It means bringing a lady flowers or taking her for a ride in the country in a buggy. Maybe bring along a blanket and a picnic basket. Women love that sort of thing."

"Where on earth would I find any flowers, for petes sake?"

"You just happen to be in luck Doc. I have a beautiful field of wildflowers right behind my house and there are all different colors and they are free. I know how you like to pinch pennies."

"Well, I'll think about it. Since when are you an expert on women? I don't see any of them hanging onto your arm, as a matter of fact."

"I haven't found the perfect woman for me like you have. She hasn't been staring me in the face for several years, like Maude has you. You mark my word Doc, she'll be one happy lady when she sees that you are finally showing some interest." Pastor turned around and walked out the door; quite pleased with himself.

The next morning, Pastor was making coffee in the kitchen and happened to glance out the back window. Lo and behold, Doc himself was out there. He was bent over, picking some wildflowers. Pastor quietly opened the back door and crept down the steps and across the yard. Doc was so intent on what he was doing, he didn't hear Pastor behind him. All of a sudden a young voice said, "Look at Doc, fellas. He's out here pickin' posies for a lady friend." Doc lifted up his head and froze on the spot, as the blood was rushing into his neck and face. He knew those youngsters would enjoy spreading the word all over the village at how foolish he was. He slowly turned around, trying to act dignified and who was standing there bent over laughing, but Pastor James. He was holding his side with one hand and wiping tears from his eyes with the other. Doc was fuming and saw nothing humorous in the teasing.

"James, you have a strange sense of humor and I don't appreciate it one bit."

"Aw Doc, I didn't mean to upset you. I just couldn't resist the opportunity to tease you. Let's go inside and have a cup of coffee and I'll put your posies in water so they won't wilt."

Doc grudgingly went into the kitchen but he was still upset. By the time he had drunk his coffee, he hadn't calmed down much. As he left the house, he figured he'd better get the posies over to Maude before he lost his nerve or they wilted. He stood in front of the hotel and almost backed out. Finally, he walked up the steps and went inside and there was Maude behind the front desk. He walked over to her and thrust the posies into her hands and said, "These are for you Maude. I just ran across them in a field while I was out taking a walk. Don't let them die!"

Maude's face lit up and her eyes were sparkling. "Oh Doc, they are lovely. Thank you for going to so much trouble. I'll take good care of them." Right then, two of the maids walked by and Maude said, "Girls, come see what Doc brought me. He picked them himself." The two girls oohed and aahed over the bouquet and Doc wanted to disappear into the floor. He quickly turned around and practically ran out of the front door. *'What an idiot I am. I've never felt so foolish in my life.'*

As soon as Maude saw the look on Doc's face, she knew that she had made a grave mistake. This should have been a private moment between them. It had taken Doc years to get the courage to do something and she had undone it within minutes. She excused herself and went to her room and silently let the tears flow.

'I've hurt him so deeply and it wasn't my intention at all. I was just so excited after waiting so many years for him to show that he cares about me, like I do him. How will I ever be able to make this up to him?'

Only one thing was missing in Pastor James's life and that was a Godly wife. Pastor often thought about this woman, hoping she would come into his life soon. He was anxious to get married and have a partner in his various duties of being the village pastor. Several women were determined to set him up with their daughters, but he had his sights set a lot higher than that. He only wanted to be married once and this woman had to be God's first choice. Pastor was not going to settle on second best. First of all, this woman would need to understand that his priorities were to serve God and then be as good a husband as he could possibly be.

Sometimes on his daily walks, he found himself daydreaming about this woman. She would fix him a big delicious breakfast each morning, and would go on visits with him to the various church member's homes. Their house would always be clean and ready to welcome guests, even the unexpected ones. They would eat all of their meals together and at night they would sit side by side in the parlor. He would be reading or working on his sermon and she might be knitting or darning socks. Every so often they would both look up and smile at each other and maybe speak about their day. He sometimes wondered what was taking the good Lord so long to bring this woman into his life. One thought crossed Pastor's mind, *'Maybe the Lord is expecting me to do something to cause this to happen, but what could that be? I'm certainly not going to make an announcement in church that I'm looking for a wife. And I can't put an ad in the paper, so what else is there to do but wait as patiently as possible?'* His home wasn't anything fancy but it had extra bedrooms for any children the Lord might bless them with. What pleased him the most was the big wrap-around-porch, with two rocking chairs sitting side by side, with a small white wicker table between the chairs.

Pastor James had a great sense of humor but not everyone appreciated it. Some of the ladies in his church expected him to be prim and proper but he couldn't have changed if he wanted to. His mother used to tell people that he could tell jokes at a very young age and enjoyed making others laugh. His style of dress didn't resemble any other pastor that they'd ever seen or heard of. His stocky frame wasn't fat, just muscle; but he must have inherited this because his walks were his only exercise. His dark brown wavy hair was usually in need of a haircut, but he had more important things on his mind. Since most of his congregation lived on a ranch or farm, he was usually seen in overalls and a flannel shirt. On Sundays, he did wear a coat and pants, but nothing very fancy. As long as it was clean and didn't have too many wrinkles, he was happy. The ladies, on the other hand, could be heard clucking to themselves and shaking their heads. Pastor James just gave them his biggest smile and kept on going. He was hoping that the woman God had chosen for him wouldn't be too disappointed when she first laid eyes on him.

He had a very personal walk with the Lord and if he was pleasing the Lord, that is all that mattered to him. Every day, weather permitting, he took a long walk early in the morning, out towards the railroad, where he wouldn't run into very many people. A long piece of straw was usually dangling out of his mouth, which helped him to think. His favorite sermons were the ones where he had studied hard all week long but never spoke a word of what he had written. That is when the Holy Spirit took over and he looked forward to those times. It was almost as if he were listening to someone else talk. The words coming out of his mouth clearly were nothing he had written down or even thought about. After church, someone often came up to him and told him that he had said just the perfect thing that they needed to hear that morning. He couldn't take any credit for that except having the sense to give the Holy Spirit the freedom it needed so the right words would flow out.

Pastor had a variety of people in his small church and it kept him very busy. He made a point of visiting everyone in their home, if he was welcome. Some of the men didn't accompany their wives to church, so Pastor sought them out where they were working, the majority of them on their ranch or farm. So far, they didn't seem to mind, especially when Pastor walked up to them dressed just like they were. He always asked about their crops and animals and that was a subject that any rancher or farmer wanted to talk about. Pastor knew how to ask a question that would keep the conversation going. If an opportunity arose where he could pitch in and help a little bit, he would. Sometimes he would hand them a tool or help to push a wagon out of a rut. They always appreciated his being willing to help and get his hands dirty. When he had a wife, she could help him on his visits.

He had made a list of men that he needed to visit, and all of them were returning soldiers. Today he would spend time with Jacob Jenkins, who had lost an arm. He and his mother were waiting anxiously for news of his father, Samuel. He was currently working any job that he could find, in order to take care of his mother. His dream was to be a rancher with his father. Pastor found him at the general store, boxing up orders.

"Good morning, Jacob. I wanted to see how you were adjusting to being back home."

"Hello Pastor, I am doing just fine, but we'd sure like to see my father walk in the door. We received a note from a friend of his, who said he is weak, but on his way home. My mother is trying to be brave, but I know it is hard on her. My parents have a wonderful marriage and they are miserable when they are apart."

"You seem to be managing just fine with one arm and I'm pleased to see that."

"It has taken time but, yes, I have adjusted to my loss. I can still do a lot of things with just one arm. One thing I've noticed is that I don't have too much pride, trying to pretend that I can do everything by myself. I am well aware that I could have lost my life, so I am very thankful that my life was spared."

"Is there anything that I can do for you or your mother? I've been praying for Samuel to return home safely but is there anything else? I plan to stop by this week to pay a call on your mother. It is a joy to see you both in church each Sunday."

"I can't think of anything else at the moment. Mother would welcome a visit from you. She enjoys working at the hotel in the dining room. I need to deliver these boxes but it was good of you to stop by. I know that you are looking out for all of the soldiers that have returned. The hardest part must be going to see the widows and their children. You are a good man, Pastor. I'm glad that we can count on your support."

When Jacob was by himself again, he couldn't stop thinking about the day he had been wounded. During a battle, he had been focused on aiming at a soldier, unaware of someone who was aiming at him. Before he got off his shot, he knew that he had been wounded in the left shoulder. He dropped his rifle and put his right hand over his wound. One of his friends had yelled for a medic and Jacob had seen the blood dripping from where he had been shot. *Lord, please let me make it back home to my family and protect my father, wherever he is.'* God had answered part of his prayer. He had lost his arm but he wasn't going to be bitter over that. He would gladly spend the rest of his life helping out his parents. Just seeing his father again was the second part of his prayer. When his father came home, together they would find a way to have a place to farm. If God chose to send Jacob a woman to fall in love with and marry, he couldn't imagine needing anything more to make him happy.

The Village Hotel was about to have new owners and some of the employees were a bit nervous about this. What if they wanted to hire their own employees? Many of the people currently working at this hotel had been given a free room as long as they worked for the hotel. The majority of people who worked here had eventually wound up feeling as though they were a part of a loving family. Maude ran the front desk and knew almost everyone living in the village. She was the friendly face that greeted each person coming in the door. She was also in charge of hiring the maids and waitresses and so far, had never had to fire anyone. Maude felt like a mother to many of the young employees and tried hard to keep the peace, if there were any disagreements.

The kitchen was one area that Maude never had to worry about. Charlie ran the place like he owned it and no one ever gave him a hard time. He knew how to make a delicious meal out of very little and they rarely had any complaints. He had a sweetheart named Martha, who was a waitress in the hotel restaurant. If anyone even thought about giving her a hard time about anything, Charlie would find a reason to leave the kitchen to check on the situation and suddenly everything was calm again. He was a big man with a broad chest and thick arms and he wore whiskers and a beard. They were secretly talking about getting married, but didn't have anywhere to live as man and wife. Charlie slept on a cot in a tiny room right beside the kitchen. Martha shared a room in the hotel with a widowed lady named Florence. From the moment they had first met each other in the kitchen, something happened to both of them at the same time. She looked at Charlie like he was someone she could trust and she made him feel important for the first time in his life. Martha had never had someone to take care of her and this gave her hope that she had found a very special man. As time went on, they drew closer to each other but lack of money was the only drawback to getting married.

As Jennie Tucker was bouncing along in their old wagon, she glanced over at Richard and felt so much affection in her heart. Their marriage had always been a struggle, financially and health wise, but never for a moment had they ever doubted their love for each other. Richard understood her like no one else had or ever would, except for the good Lord above. In one small area, she was concerned about Richard. He pushed himself constantly and would never turn down a chance to work. She had tried to suggest that he slow down and had even resorted to begging him, but he would always turn a deaf ear. Richard was determined to provide for his family, no matter the cost. During the war, he had been wounded in the leg, and he would be limping for the rest of his life. This added to her worries but she tried to hide it. Jennie would happily go without a new dress or shoes if he would turn down a job now and then and rest. They never argued but he knew how she felt and she understood him just as well. This was an area that Jennie prayed about most often. She had been asking God to provide an income for them that only He could do. She had been praying for months, when a letter showed up from her distant uncle. His sister, her Aunt Emma, had passed away in her sleep recently. According to the letter, she had left Jennie a hotel in a small village in Michigan. A letter from an attorney stated that the hotel was paid for free and clear and also money for taxes for up to 20 years had been set up in a separate account. A second letter gave information regarding the hotel and some of the residents.

At the present time, there were some boarders in several of the rooms, which would generate income. There was plenty of room for Jennie and her family to live comfortably. The cook had been with the hotel for several years and he had no intention of leaving, according to what Maude had told her in a letter. Maude had written Jennie several letters, filling her in on the village and the hotel. Her job was to work the front desk, but it sounded like she kept on top of everything going on in the hotel too.

When Richard and Jennie pulled into Willow Bend, it was not difficult to find the village hotel. It stood out, proud and tall among all of the smaller buildings. It was three stories high and had a wonderful view of the countryside. As Richard steered the wagon down the road, he was wondering what he would do in a hotel all day long. He knew that this was an answer to prayer for his wife Jennie and he wouldn't do anything to hurt her, but he was a creative man. He had a talent for creating furniture and often coming up with original ideas. Working with his hands gave him joy and peace like nothing else ever had. He would try not to be too hasty in feeling confined. Surely the good Lord hadn't given him this special talent to waste. He would try to be more patient from now on.

The woman behind the desk gave them a welcoming smile and she had already figured out who they were. This must be Maude and she was the perfect person for that job. She asked them to follow her down the hall and she led them to the two rooms that had been set aside for them. The first room was a beautiful sitting room, with solid oak furniture, which Richard quickly went over to admire and inspect. The second room was to be their bedroom and the bed was obviously an antique oak frame. He ran his hands over the furniture in both rooms and clearly approved of the workmanship. He felt that strong pull inside of him to create something, but where could he work? Some of his tools were in the wagon but they would have to be kept in a spare room that Maude had saved for him.

The next day, Pastor James and Doc came by to welcome them. Jennie was just getting ready to get a tour of the kitchen with Maude, so Richard invited Doc and Pastor into the dining room for coffee. Doc said, "We are so happy to have another loving family take over this hotel. Jennie's aunt and uncle were kind to everyone and took such good care of this beautiful hotel. Now you and your wife will breathe new life into it."

"I know that it is a blessing, that we have inherited this hotel and I am very thankful. I am hoping to find a small shop that I can rent out, so that I can start my own carpentry shop. I can't stay cooped up in this hotel all day long. God has blessed me with a love of creating things out of wood. Would you happen to know of a place nearby that is available?"

Pastor looked over at Doc and smiled and they seemed to agree on something. Pastor said, "Doc and I have been discussing what we can do with an abandoned building right down the street from this hotel. It was originally built to be used as a harness shop, but then the man fell on hard times and had to let it go. We would be willing to let you use it for three months' rent free if you would just clean it up and help it look more presentable. After that time, we can meet again and see if you are happy with the building. I'm sure that we can work out some agreeable terms." Richard's face was changed instantly to a man with big plans who was about to see a dream come true.

"I'll be over bright and early to start cleaning it up, whenever you can give me a key."

Doc produced one from his key ring and handed it over to Richard. "Can you give us some idea of what you like to build? We know everyone in the village and the outlying farms and ranches. We could help drum up some business for you once we know what you can do."

Richard said, "I can build just about anything; tables, chairs, cabinets, dressers, bed frames, and work tables. I've never had a complaint about anything that I built myself."

Doc asked Could we place an order for a cradle for a woman in town who is due in the fall?"

Richard almost jumped up out of his chair when he said, "I can get started the day after tomorrow and you are welcome to stop by any time to see how I am doing. Thank you for such a wonderful welcome and for offering me the building temporarily." When Richard found Jennie in the kitchen, she knew something had happened to lift her husband's spirits. Even though he would never complain, she knew him well and even she couldn't picture him shut up in this hotel every day. When he explained about his good news, she was happy for him and silently thanked the Lord for this additional blessing. *'What a wonderful answer to my prayers.'*

Jennie asked Maude to set aside a couple of hours that afternoon, so that she could learn about how the hotel was being run and to know what each employee was responsible for. As they were going over Maude's lists, Jennie said," I've noticed that Charlie and Martha seem to care very much for each other." This pleased Maude to find out that the new owner was so sensitive.

"Charlie and Martha are engaged, at least their hearts feel that way. They can't get married until they can find a way to rent a room that they can afford. As you can imagine, neither of them makes a lot in wages, but they are both extremely hard workers. We were hoping that you would continue to allow Charlie to sleep in a cot in a small room off the kitchen. Martha shares a room with Florence, an elderly widow."

Jennie spoke up right away and said, "Maude, we inherited this hotel and it is paid for. My husband and I both agree that we want to use this hotel to help others, as much as possible. With your help, I would like to organize a small wedding for Charlie and Martha and I intend to offer them a room on the ground floor, rent free, as long as they are employees. Would you help me?"

Maude was so delighted that she jumped up and clapped her hands. "Yes, of course I will help you Jennie. When can we tell them?" Jennie said, "I'm not one to waste time, as I'm sure you'll pick up on quickly. Just let me discuss this with my husband and we can tell Charlie and Martha in a day or so.

Martha was a slim lady with pretty dark brown hair that she always wore in a tight bun. Her eyes were light brown and she often had a timid look about her. The only exception was when Charlie was nearby and then she relaxed and changed into a different person. He could make her smile and blush and feel like a young school girl. She had never had a relationship with a man. Maude felt very protective of her, but she knew that she was in good hands with Charlie. Martha had a way of looking at him that made him feel like he could do anything. She only wished that they could be man and wife. They were both very down to earth and didn't require a lot. While they were waiting, they tried to keep up a cheerful attitude.

Maude was uncomfortable about needing to talk to Doc about Martha and Charlie's wedding, but she felt as though she didn't have any other choice. This village was far too small, and they would be running into each other often, so she might as well make the first move. She braced herself and walked into his office. He was saying goodbye to one of his patients, so Maude stood by quietly. When they were alone she said, "Doc, I have some good news to tell you. Charlie and Martha are getting married next week in the hotel. Jennie and Richard have offered them a free room in the hotel. Isn't that exciting?"

Doc was even more uncomfortable than Maude, but he managed to respond with, "I'm very happy for both of them. They deserve to be married and not have to worry about the money for a place to stay. How can I help?"

"I'm glad that you asked me that because I know that Martha doesn't have any nice dresses. I was hoping that you and I could go in together and hire Emily to make her a pretty dress to be married in."

"You can count on me to help with that. It is a great idea. I need to get back to my work now. I'm trying to come up with a new batch of medicine. Thanks for including me in this Maude."

"I know that you have a generous heart Doc and I wanted to be sure that you were included. I'll let you go now."

As she walked down the steps, she thought to herself, *'Well, I made the first step and I'm glad that I found the courage. I'm pretty sure that Doc wouldn't have been able to get past his pride. I'm happy for Martha and Charlie but I know that I'm feeling sorry for myself. I've got to shake this off and go on with my life as best I can.'*

Doc watched her walk away through the window and thought, *'She's a bigger person than I will ever be. I know that wasn't easy for her to come over and ask me to help with the dress. I'm not very proud of myself right now.'*

The next day Richard and Jennie and Maude walked into the kitchen with a look on their faces that couldn't hide their excitement. They asked Charlie and Martha to take a break and sit down to meet the new owners. After Maude had made the introductions, Jennie said, "We have heard glowing reports about what a good cook you are Charlie and that you are a hard worker Martha. We were also told that you were in need of a place to live after you get married. My husband and I would like to offer you a room for free on the ground floor, which will be yours on the day of your marriage. How does that sound?"

Charlie and Martha looked at each other, completely stunned. Charlie was speechless, but Martha burst into tears and said, "I can hardly believe this. We didn't know what we were going to do."

Richard looked at Charlie and said, "Are you still wanting to get married Charlie?"

Charlie finally found his voice and said, "As soon as possible sir; now that we will have a place of our own. I don't know how to thank you for your generosity."

Maude felt that now was the time for her to speak up. "Jennie and I have been talking and we would like to arrange for your wedding to be here in the hotel dining room, and we are going to provide the meal afterwards. Just tell us the date that you've decided on and we'll do all the work." Martha's face changed into a deep sadness and no one could figure out why at first. Maude put her arm around Martha and said, "Honey, what is making you so sad all of a sudden?"

Martha was trying to hold herself together and she said, "I don't have a pretty dress to wear for my wedding."

Maude gave her a big hug and said, "That is not a problem. We asked Emily to come over to the hotel this afternoon to get your measurements. It is a gift from Doc and I."

Now Martha was dancing around in a circle with a huge smile on her face and tears of joy were streaming down her face. "Oh Charlie, we are really going to be married soon."

Charlie looked like he was close to tears so he said gruffly, "Well, it's about time Martha." Everyone started laughing and Richard patted Charlie on the back. "Now get back to work so we can plan your wedding."

Emily was the young widowed seamstress hired by Maude. She came over later that afternoon and got all of the measurements that she needed. She promised to get started on the dress that very evening. Maude and Jennie sat down with Martha and they decided to invite everyone who lived in the hotel, along with several other people who lived in the village that Martha and Charlie considered friends. The wedding was going to be held in one week, on a Saturday afternoon. Pastor James had set up an appointment to meet them at his church, since he was performing the ceremony. Charlie was not comfortable being married in the church since he and Martha didn't attend. Pastor said that he was fine with marrying them in the hotel, so that took away their concern.

Pastor James walked over to the general store to see if he could spend a few minutes checking on Emily. When he entered the store, he walked to the back, where she was usually found working on a sewing project. "Good morning Emily. I was wondering if you could spare a few minutes from your work, to sit down and talk to me."

"I'd be happy to sit down with you, Pastor. It's so nice of you to come by to see me."

"I wanted you to know that I'm available if you ever need prayer or someone to talk to. I was so sorry to hear about the loss of your husband, Emily. I know he was a fine soldier."

"He was always very good to me and I miss him dearly. Thankfully, I'll have our child to raise soon and that gives me much comfort. I treasure the short time he was sent back to me after his first injury."

"I won't keep you from your work any longer. I understand that you are busy making a dress for Martha to wear at her wedding. Maude said she is so excited because she has never had a new dress before. Please don't hesitate to let me know if you ever need anything, Emily."

"I promise that I will get word to you if something comes up that troubles me. Thank you for taking the time to visit with me. I want you to know that it means a lot."

As Pastor left the store, he had a fleeting thought of Jacob. Rebecca had told him recently how she would love to see him get married. *'Oh well, Lord, I'll leave that up to you, but please don't forget about my request for a wife.'*

The day of their wedding arrived, and Charlie was pacing all over the kitchen. Richard had loaned him some clothes to wear for the wedding and he looked like a new man. Maude had everything under control, as usual, with Jennie's help. They had both enjoyed arranging this day. Charlie and Martha were shocked to be told that they would have Saturday and

Sunday off. Charlie was not allowed to cook the entire weekend. Maude and Jennie had found volunteers to do the cooking. Everyone was seated in the hotel lobby and Charlie had asked Doc to be his best man. Martha had chosen Maude to stand with her. No one had seen Martha that morning, except for Maude and Jennie. When the music started, the door opened and out came Maude and a few seconds later, there stood Martha. One of the ladies had fixed her hair in a becoming style and the pale blue dress she was wearing made everyone ooh and aah. Martha held a bouquet of wildflowers and she was absolutely beaming. Charlie looked at her as though he had never seen her before. For a second, it looked like he might pass out. Then Martha walked slowly to where Charlie stood and they both looked at each other shyly. Pastor asked them to repeat the vows after him and then he said, "I would now like to introduce Mr. and Mrs. Charlie Thompson." Everyone clapped and cheered, and it was now official. The bride and groom were seated in the middle of the long dining room table and everyone ate a delicious meal. Even Charlie had to admit that it tasted pretty good.

The dishes were cleared away quickly and suddenly presents were being piled up on the table in front of Charlie and Martha. Obviously, they were not expecting any gifts, so this made it even more special. One by one they opened the gifts and you could tell by the expression on their faces that they appreciated every single gift. Finally, it was time to show them to their new room. They walked down the hall behind Maude and Jennie and then Charlie was handed the key. When he opened the door, Maude and Jennie left them alone. Charlie and Martha walked into the room, hand in hand, and they both felt like they had stepped into a palace. They would never forget this special day, as long as they lived.

3

JUNE 1865

Lives In Danger

Danny and Roscoe seemed like old friends after just a few days. He had wrapped his injured foot up in part of a sheet. That dog looked at him like he knew something that he didn't. He wondered how he had been treated in the past and how he got separated from his owners. Danny had caught some fish and smoked them, and he and Roscoe nibbled on that during the day. He had his arm around the dog's neck and Roscoe looked quite comfortable sleeping close beside him. Every person should have a dog, in his opinion. With any luck, they should arrive in Willow Bend sometime tomorrow. Danny needed some new boots. Once he earned some money, that was one of the first things he would purchase. From somewhere behind him, he heard a wagon coming slowly, so he moved off to the right side of the road. When the wagon stopped beside him, he turned and saw a friendly farmer smiling back at him. He asked Danny where he was headed, and it turned out this man was from Willow Bend. He told Danny to hop into the wagon with his dog and he offered them both some water. The man introduced himself as Jonas Whitestone. He and his wife and children lived on a farm right outside Willow Bend. His oldest son had just returned home from the war recently. He offered to give Danny shelter, and he knew his wife would invite him in for supper. "Son, I could use an extra hand if you are willing to work on my farm. There is always plenty to do and we never manage to get caught up."

It meant the world to Danny that he was being offered a chance to work and a place to sleep. He knew Jonas must have noticed his bad wrist. For the first time since he was shot, he felt some hope rising up inside him.

As they pulled into the lane leading to his farm, Danny took a good look and liked what he saw. None of the fields were overgrown with weeds and tall, stately sunflowers stood up so proudly. The gate to Jonas' farm was well built and swung open at the slightest touch of his hand. He could see off in the distance a farm house that you could tell was built with care. On the front porch were two dogs laying in the shade resting, until they heard the creak of the wagon wheels. Now Roscoe was trying to sit up and his tail was wagging in a friendly greeting. Danny was afraid for a moment that the other two dogs might be too rough for Roscoe but Jonas anticipated his concern. "My two dogs look forward to company and they won't harm your dog in any way. This here is Molly and she's a sweetheart and this one is Smiley, because she always looks like she is trying to smile."

A woman opened the screen door with a big welcoming smile on her face. She was a little overweight, but it didn't take away from her delightful overall appearance. The blue flowered calico dress she wore was very pretty and her apron had not one stain on it. Her dark brown hair was streaked with gray but it was very becoming. She walked up to the wagon and held out her hand in a friendly welcome and then reached over and stroked Roscoe's head. "Hello, welcome to our home. I am Jonas' wife, Dora. You'll meet our children at supper tonight." Danny couldn't believe how welcome they made him feel already. Compared to the way Mandie had greeted him, this was a nice surprise indeed.

Jonas showed him where he would be sleeping, along with his dog. The barn was as clean and neat as the outside of the farm house. He was given a blanket and pillow and a lantern. He could have fallen asleep right there on the spot but he had been invited for supper, so he asked where he could wash up. Afterwards, Jonas led him into the kitchen and they sat down at a long oak table that looked as though it were a prized piece of furniture. It just gleamed from the constant polishing it had been given and white daisies were in an old jar in the center. Some delicious smells were coming from behind him on the old cook stove. Dora brought over a large pot, just brimming with a roast and a large assortment of vegetables from their garden. Biscuits that were just waiting to be slathered with butter and honey were piled high on a platter. Danny was offered the first serving of everything and he tried hard to hold back and not take too much, but Dora chided him gently and put more on his plate.

One by one, Jonas introduced Danny to their children. "Danny, this is our son Billy and he has recently returned from the war." He had a noticeable limp, probably from a wound during the war. "He has now taken over as the foreman of the farm and loves every minute of it. He will be taking over the farm some day because it is a tradition for the eldest son to have it passed on down to him."

Dora broke in with a sly comment for her son. "We are hoping that the good Lord will bring Billy a loving wife someday soon, so we can get started on the grandchildren."

Billy blushed but took the comment good-naturedly. He was extremely shy, especially around the ladies. *'I don't want to disappoint my mother, but I can barely say 'hello' when I see a lady, so how am I supposed to actually spend time with one? This is going to have to be put at the top of my prayers, because I need help in a big way.'*

Sadie was the next in line and she had just turned 18 and was working at the General Store and also helped out her mother on the ranch. She had beautiful blonde hair that was tied back with a blue ribbon that matched her dress. Her smile just lit up the room. "We are so happy to have you join us. You won't leave this table hungry, I can guarantee that." Dora noticed that her daughter's cheeks were getting a little pink.

Nellie was 16 and had a job cooking in the village cafe and also helped her mother as often as she could. She was not as outgoing as her sister but still managed to smile and make him feel welcome. Her hair was light brown and one thick braid was hanging down her back. "Please make yourself to home and make sure you keep up with Billy. He isn't bashful about eating a lot and you'll be lucky to see any crumbs left over when he is around."

Danny noticed that all three of the children were not ashamed to show the love and respect that they had for their parents. Danny came from a family that rarely showed any affection and smiling was almost unheard of. He had grown up feeling so lonely and unloved and could never figure out why his parents were so cold.

Danny was 26 years old and he wondered if it were even possible for a woman to want to marry him with his deformed hand. Tonight, not one person in this family had stared at his hand or acted like anything was unusual. He wasn't going to kid himself into thinking that most people would be reacting that way, so he tried to prepare his heart for the pain that was going to be coming soon. Danny wanted nothing to do with receiving any sympathy or charity. He was going to earn his own way and make a success of his life. He knew that it wouldn't be easy, but he wasn't afraid of hard work. He told Dora how much he had enjoyed the delicious meal and excused himself to get settled in the barn. Roscoe had been given a bone and he acted so pleased with it. Danny picked him up and carried him out to the barn. They were both asleep within minutes in their comfortable new dwelling place.

Pastor James woke up this morning with someone special on his heart. Hank Hawkins was the village blacksmith and one of the men that didn't attend church. He didn't hide his bitterness very well. As Pastor approached the blacksmith shop, he took a good look at Hank. His whole body was extremely muscular, because of the hard-physical labor he performed each day. Pastor had heard only good things about the quality of his work but very little about his personality. Hank rarely smiled and could be intimidating. In the beginning, Pastor had only brought up safe subjects to talk about. Today he had decided to try and find out more about Hank's personal life to see if he could learn where his bitterness came from. "Good morning Hank. I've never come by your shop without seeing you hard at work."

"Mornin' Pastor, if I don't keep busy, I'll never be able to keep up with all of the business comin' my way.

I'm the only blacksmith within 40 miles of Willow Bend."

"I've forgotten, how long have you lived in Willow Bend, Hank?"

"I moved here about eight years ago." Pastor was trying to figure out how to find out more without making Hank shut down.

"Have you always been a blacksmith?" Hank was starting to wonder why the Pastor even cared but he liked the man and decided to answer his question.

"No, I used to be a farmer, but I can't do that anymore, so I took up a new trade. My neighbor back home was a blacksmith and I used to help with small jobs, so I could learn the trade."

"Hank, I'll be honest with you. I've noticed that you seem angry about something and I was hoping that we could talk about whatever it is. Keeping things inside is not good and I would keep our conversation confidential; I can promise you that."

"Pastor, I appreciate your honesty. I was wondering why you was asking me the questions that you were. I don't feel comfortable talking here at the shop 'cause I never know who is going to come by. If it's not too much trouble, could you come by my house tonight around seven o'clock?" The pastor was very encouraged to be invited to Hank's home and he agreed to see him.

Pastor knew that Hank lived in a house on the edge of town that used to belong to an elderly couple. When they passed on, the house had been abandoned for several years. Obviously, Hank had taken pride in fixing it and the roof had been patched up neatly, the porch stairs were no longer creaky and a new coat of paint had done wonders for the old house. When he walked up to the front of the house, Hank was waiting on the front porch in one of the rocking chairs. There was a small table between the chairs, with a pitcher of lemonade and two glasses. Hank invited him to sit down and poured each of them a glass. Pastor took a big drink and enjoyed the freshly squeezed lemonade cooling his throat. He wanted Hank to start the conversation so he just sat there and rocked for a few minutes. Presently, Hank spoke up.

"I used to have a farm when I was married, and we had a little boy named Jefferson. He would follow me around everywhere like he was my shadow. One day my little boy took sick and the doctor said it was diphtheria. He passed away a few days later. It was like a nightmare and I couldn't stop blamin' myself for not being able to protect him."

"I can't even begin to imagine the pain that you and your wife must have felt."

"My wife grieved somethin' fierce Pastor and when she looked at me, she was looking right through me. I tried to comfort her but she wouldn't let me touch her; not even to hold her. She stopped eating except for a few spoonsful of soup that our neighbor could get down her. Between my guilt and my wife putting up such a wall between us and missing my son so dearly, I was just dyin' inside. A few months later my wife just slipped away from me. The doctor said she died of a broken heart. The two people that I loved the most in this whole world were gone and I was still alive but wanted to die.

Somehow, I managed to get the crops in with the help of friends and neighbors and then I sold the farm. I couldn't stand to be there any longer. The memories were eating me alive. A friend had told me that when he was travelin' through Willow Bend, he noticed that they didn't have a blacksmith and that was all I needed to hear. I was desperate to get away and start my life over; what was left of it, and here I am. I ain't talked to God since 'cause I'm afraid of what might come out. I want nothin' to do with Him anymore."

Pastor had hoped that Hank would open up to him but this was more than he had expected to hear. He prayed silently for the right words to come. "Hank, I am so sorry for the loss of your wife and son. No one can ever explain why some people have to experience this kind of pain and loss. I can tell you this; God understands why you are angry with Him and that will never stop Him from loving you. I am going to start praying for you today, that God will help your heart to heal."

"Pastor, I don't mean no disrespect, but I don't want you to pray for me. I thought I made myself clear that I want nothin' to do with God anymore." Pastor knew that he had to step carefully here but he was not about to let Hank believe that he was not going to pray for him."

"Hank, you may not want my prayers, but I intend to pray for you anyway. I try my best to serve God with my whole heart and I will not turn my back on you. I promise you that. I appreciate your telling me about your past and it will go no further. May I stop by and see you from time to time?"

"I can't stop you from prayin' I suppose, but it won't do no good. There is a lot of anger inside of me and I don't want it to come out against you. I think it's best for you to leave now. I have nothin' against you comin' by once in awhile but don't go gettin' your hopes up." Pastor walked up to Hank and shook his hand and patted him on the back and left.

As soon as he started walking home, he lifted Hank up to the Lord. "Lord, I lift Hank and his pain and bitterness up to you. I know that you aren't shocked at how he feels about you. I want with all of my heart to see you bring him to his knees and help him to let go of this terrible pain and guilt. Someday soon I hope to see him in my church. Amen!"

While waiting for the stage to leave, Sarah had learned that Elizabeth was on her way to Willow Bend to work with a Dr. Thomas. How interesting this was turning out to be already. Sarah was an old friend of Maude's and Dr. Thomas was a dear friend of Maude's. Sarah had once asked Maude if she were interested in the doctor and she had replied that he was a good man but showed no interest in her. Sarah noticed that Will was wearing a gun and he looked very at ease. His clothes were not fancy but well cared for, and his dark moustache was very becoming; at least the ladies seemed to think so. He wore a gun and holster that looked like it was part of his clothing. Once everyone was seated, the stage started up with a lurch and they were finally on their way. Timothy was immediately full of questions for Will. "What's your name and are you a good shot?"

He said, "My name is Will and yes, I am a good shot." Timothy's mother tried to distract him by asking him to look out the window at the scenery.

"Why are you wearing a patch over your eye?" asked Timothy.

"I was shot and lost one of my eyes."

Julia had boldly looked at Will and said, "Our mama is struggling to take care of us all by herself. Our papa died in the war and mama needs to get married. Are you married? Do you like children?" Elizabeth was beyond embarrassed and tried to stop Julia, but her questions came out as fast as bullets out of a gun.

He said, "That is too bad about your papa. I am sure he was a brave soldier. No Julia, I am not married, and I do like children." Julia finally looked over at her mother and saw the stern look in her eyes and kept quiet. Elizabeth was thankful that Julia had eventually gone to sleep for awhile. Will seemed to take her comments about needing a papa good-naturedly, but she was embarrassed. It was true that they needed a man who would love them and watch over them, but Elizabeth didn't want to rush into anything. Some of the ache in her heart had diminished, but not all of it. She and her husband had a good strong marriage. *'Would it be possible for that to happen to me for a second time?'* Her mind, or was it her heart, went back to Johnny. There was something about him that right away drew her attention. She was sure that it was mistrust; someone had obviously hurt him deeply. Why was it that men seemed to group women all together? If one woman hurt them, then they'd better watch out, for women were all alike. That was so untrue, but she certainly couldn't bring up that subject to him. When she was around him, something inside her wanted to comfort him. Sometimes physical actions spoke more than actual words. Elizabeth missed being held so much and having someone to share her thoughts with.

One evening when Johnny was a patient, she had actually felt him lower his guard some. The way he had looked at her that night was as if he were trying to tell her that he wanted to trust her. He had asked her about her husband and she remembered telling him of their plans after the war was over. They had wanted to buy some land near a small town where the children could run free outside and have a nice school to attend. She had asked Johnny about his plans and she saw a strange look on his face, which he'd tried to hide. She felt at that moment that he had looked like a lost little boy and her heart had gone out to him. Elizabeth's heart was going to get her into trouble if she wasn't careful. A few days later when she had heard him talking to Samuel, she knew that she had to leave with the children as soon as possible. Now they were close to reaching Willow Bend.

Rafe Miller and his brother Jeffrey were very close, since their father had deserted them when they were both not even five years old. They had always been there for each other. Signing up to fight in the Civil War was only because they had nothing better to do and they were too lazy to work. Their hopes were high that they would end up somewhere that looked like they could start over. Just before the war was over, they had become friends with Josh Slater. The unit they were assigned to had lost so many men, that they were seldom sent to the front lines any more.

One day in late April of 1865, Josh said he needed to talk to Rafe and Jeffrey. The war had just ended and none of them had any special place to return home to. Josh had found out about a stage coming through their area and it was supposed to be loaded with gold. Jeffrey was only 17 and had never been too smart and was always indecisive. It was decided that Jeffrey would not take part in this robbery but was promised a cut. All he had to do was to keep his mouth shut and wait for the two of them to return. He was told where to wait but didn't like the idea of being left behind. The robbery was scheduled for the week after next and lots of excitement was in the air. Now all three of them wouldn't have to work for a living. It sounded almost too good to be true.

The stagecoach passengers rode for several days without incident, but it wasn't a very comfortable ride. They were bounced back and forth constantly from the rough roads. Will's long legs took up a majority of the space, but he did his best not to crowd the ladies. Timothy never ran out of questions, but Will was very patient with him. He also paid attention to Julia, which might have been a mistake. Her questions to him had nothing to do with guns or horses or anything like that.

Her questions were very personal and Will had to be careful about how he responded.

Elizabeth apologized for her daughter's behavior and he told her that she wasn't to be concerned about it. For a few hours, Julia dozed off and everyone could relax but then she woke up and you could feel the tension in the air immediately. Sarah hoped to distract her so she said, "I am a schoolteacher. What grade are you going to be in?" Julia had just started to answer her when shots rang out.

Rafe and Josh had been waiting behind some thick trees, watching the stage approach. Dust was flying everywhere, and the driver was cracking his whip and hollering commands to the four horses. Another man was sitting beside him, so he must be the guard. They pulled up their masks and rode straight at the stagecoach, with their guns out. "Stop this stage right now or get shot. It's your choice." The stage slowed down but then all of a sudden, the guard pulled out his rifle and aimed it at Josh, but Rafe was faster. He shot him in the shoulder and he fell to the side but managed not to fall, thanks to Worley grabbing him by the shirt. Worley was inching his left hand down towards his rifle, but he never got a chance to pick it up. Josh shot him in the wrist and he let out a yell. They didn't want anyone killed; just wounded, if they were putting up a fight. Their main objective was to steal the gold without getting shot.

Immediately, Will had his gun out of his holster. They heard Worley, the driver, cry out that he and Gus had been shot. The horses were running faster because of the gunshots. Will had no idea how many men were trying to rob the stage. Suddenly the horses slowed down and they could hear a man's voice telling them "whoa".

Will looked directly at Elizabeth and said tersely, "Get down on the floor right now with the children.

Quickly!" Elizabeth obeyed, putting the children under her.

Sarah quietly said to Will, "If you have another pistol, give it to me. I'm a good shot." This surprised him, but he didn't hesitate. He pulled another pistol out of a case he was carrying with him.

As Sarah started to check to see if it was loaded, Will said, "The gun is loaded! Wait until the gunmen approach the stage doors." Pretty soon they heard a crash as the strong box was thrown down to the ground. One of the bandits came over to Sarah's window and said in a gruff voice, "Alright lady, hand over your jewelry and cash and you won't get hurt." Sarah calmly pulled the trigger and shot him in the shoulder. He had a stunned look on his face as he fell to the ground. Now a second man came to Will's door and yanked it open. Will fired at him and down he went.

They still didn't know how many men were left when they heard Worley's voice cry out, "There is only two of them." That was all Will needed to hear. He told Sarah to stay with Elizabeth and her children and she obeyed.

Rafe and Josh had gone over this holdup over and over again, thinking of every detail. Nothing had gone right! Much to Josh's surprise, a woman aimed a pistol at him and pulled the trigger and shot him in the shoulder. Rafe was on the opposite side of the coach, receiving the same welcome as Josh. A male passenger, with a patch over one eye, had pulled out his pistol and shot the gun out of Rafe's hand, with the bullet going through his hand. The stage door was already open, so Will jumped out and held his gun on both of the robbers. Using some rope that Worley threw down to him, he tied them to a tree and then noticed that one of the horses had been shot in the cross fire and another one was limping. He probably had gotten hurt when they were running.

Now they were in trouble because Worley and Gus were both wounded and they were now short two horses. Will asked Worley how far they were from the next town and Worley said, "Willow Bend village is only five miles down this road."

Someone had to go for help but Will didn't want to leave the women and children alone. Sarah spoke up and said, "If you'll help me unharness one of the horses, I'll ride into town and get some help. I ride bareback all the time back home." By this time, Will didn't doubt what she was saying and he helped her unharness one of the horses.

Worley told her "It is a straight shot down this road, but you need to keep the pistol with you, just in case."

Will helped Sarah up onto the horse but he had a feeling she could have done it herself somehow. She didn't look the least bit afraid; she almost looked excited. Sarah put the pistol in a satchel and tied it around her wrist and spoke to the horse and off she went. This was one unusual woman, that's for sure.

4

JUNE 1865

What Are You Doing Here?

Sarah to the rescue

The horse from the stage line was easy to ride since Sarah was so comfortable as a rider. An hour or so later she could see the river and willow trees, just like Worley had told her. He had given her instructions as to where the stage office was and the doctor's office. She decided to find the doctor first. Right then Doc and Pastor were walking out of the café and they couldn't believe what they were looking at. A young woman was flying into town on a horse that looked like one that was usually pulling a stagecoach. Her hair was flying in every direction and her dress was billowing out on both sides and she was riding bareback. She reined in the horse right in front of Doc and Pastor and jumped off, all in one motion. Sarah had to catch her breath for a minute but then she was able to explain. They both looked down at her satchel and saw part of a gun protruding out.

Sarah looked down at what they were staring at and casually said, "Oh, this is the pistol that Will loaned me. Worley said that I should take it for protection. I was one of the passengers on the stagecoach and two men attempted to rob us. The driver and guard are both wounded, along with the two robbers. One of the passengers had a gun, thank goodness. He didn't want to leave a mother and her two children and myself all alone, while he went to get help, so I volunteered. Worley said to tell you that two of the horses are hurt and they'll need two replacements."

Doc ran inside to get his bag and pastor just stood there speechless. This was a man who always had a comforting or encouraging word for every situation, but his mind was empty. If someone had told him what he had just witnessed, he would have thought they were telling a tall tale. What kind of woman was she? On top of everything else, she looked unafraid and exhilarated. Doc came running out of his office and had someone bring his carriage around to the front.

"Pastor, run over to the livery stable and get the men to bring two horses right away, so they can bring the stagecoach and passengers into town before dark."

The town didn't have a sheriff at the present time, so Pete, who owned the saloon, offered to go and deliver the gang members to their jail. He managed to find two other men to accompany him. Pastor took off at a run for the stable, still puzzled about what he had just witnessed.

Elizabeth hoped to get to know Sarah better, once they got settled in Willow Bend. She had a feeling the men would flock around her because she was so attractive. Then again, because of her strong personality, most men couldn't handle a woman that secure with herself. Sarah had gone for help and the doctor and men from the stagecoach line should be here soon. Elizabeth had done her best to patch up Worley and Gus and the two outlaws with what little medical supplies the stagecoach had in the boot.

Rafe was furious and in a lot of pain. Hours later, a doctor arrived after that crazy woman had ridden a stagecoach horse bareback for help. He had also brought along two extra horses and two men who were going to escort them to the nearest jail. All he could think about was Jeffrey. He would have no idea what happened to both of them. He might even think that they had taken off with all of the gold and left him behind. This upset Rafe so much that his stomach was churning, but there was nothing he could do. He felt so guilty leaving his brother behind and not having any way to get word to him. There had to be a way somehow, but he was in so much pain at the moment, he just couldn't come up with an answer. The doctor took care of their wounds, and they were taken to a village called Willow Bend, to await an escort to a town with a larger jail.

Sarah had no problem finding the hotel, as it stood up taller than any other building. When she walked into the hotel, there was her dear friend Maude behind the front desk, looking like she owned the place. When Maude looked up, she let out a gasp of surprise and hurried around the front desk. Maude pushed Sarah back a little to get a better look at her. She had a puzzled look on her face and then Sarah realized what she must have looked like after that wild ride into town. "Maude, it's so good to see you again. I must look a fright, but I can explain. I rode one of the stagecoach horses into town for help. Two men tried to rob the gold. Please show me where I can go to freshen up. I'm afraid all of my clothes are still on the stage though."

Maude was amazed to hear how Sarah had reached Willow Bend. She said, "Sarah, you are a sight for sore eyes; dirt and all. I'll show you to our room if you will just give me a minute." Maude excused herself and then brought back someone to relieve her. She took Sarah by the arm and took her to the room they would be sharing. Maude had ordered tea and Charlie's stew to be brought to their room, and Sarah was very thankful. She had also asked for a hot bath to be prepared in their room. When Sarah had finished her tea and sandwiches, she sank into the hot, soapy tub and sighed. Maude had already laid out clean clothes for her to wear afterwards. Tomorrow Sarah would have her own clothes, but for now she was content. They talked for an hour or so, but Sarah was having trouble keeping her eyes open. Maude showed her the bed she would be using and suggested that they meet for breakfast in the morning.

When the men arrived with the doctor and the extra horses, everyone was relieved. They swiftly harnessed the horses while Doc took care of Worley and Gus and the two wounded outlaws. He complimented Elizabeth on what a fine job she had done with such limited supplies. He offered to let her and the children ride back into town in his carriage.

Elizabeth's children were exhausted and fell asleep right away in the carriage. Doc pulled up to the front entrance to the hotel and got down and helped Elizabeth. She woke up the children and he led them all inside the hotel. Maude was waiting at the front desk, since she was expecting them. Maude told Elizabeth that her room was ready for them. She took the key in one hand and put the other around Elizabeth's waist to help her. The children sleepily trailed behind. When Maude opened the door to their room, Elizabeth was amazed. The room was beautiful and a lot larger than she had pictured in her mind. There was a loveseat, coffee table, two overstuffed chairs, and a small table and chairs. In the adjoining room was a double bed for Elizabeth and two smaller beds for the children. There was also a nice size wardrobe and an end table with a pitcher of water and towels.

Doc had carried in their bags and set them down inside the first room. Maude had already ordered hot tea and a good meal, which would be on its way to their room soon. She asked Elizabeth if she would like a hot bath and Elizabeth said that it sounded heavenly. Doc told her, "I don't expect you to be at the office tomorrow. You just rest up and walk around the village and get acquainted. I'll check on you and the children tomorrow. I forgot to mention that all of your meals are included with the room, so you should order whatever you like."

Elizabeth was having a difficult time sorting all of this out in her head. Everything had happened so quickly. Hopefully after a meal and a hot bath and a good night's sleep, she would be able to think more clearly. The next thing she knew, it was morning and the children were already awake.

Johnny had offered to accompany Samuel back to his small village in Michigan, called Willow Bend. Their friendship had grown over the past few weeks and he had no destination in mind for himself. He had lost his parents during the war from cholera. His father's attorney had been able to contact Johnny, but he didn't have his other brother's units. Johnny provided what information he had been given, but he wasn't sure if they were still in the same area. He hadn't heard a word from Rusty and no one seemed to know what had happened to him once the war had begun. David had managed to write to him a few times but then the letters stopped. His father had left his estate to all three sons and he was amazed at the amount of money they had inherited. He had always known that his father was intelligent and wise with money, but he was not prepared when he found out the amount in his estate.

Once they started on their journey, they would travel slowly, so that Samuel would not be over exerted. From the sounds of it, he had a loving wife and son waiting for him to return home. Just thinking about it made Johnny feel very much alone. Was he making a mistake by avoiding marriage? There were plenty of women who had shown an interest in him over the years and once he had fallen for a woman who ended up not wanting to keep their child. His thoughts turned to Elizabeth, which was happening more and more often lately. It wasn't her looks that drew him to seek her out in a room. Her eyes were full of kindness and she was a loving mother to her children. He had heard her correct her children and knew that she could be very firm. One day he was telling a funny story to her children and she burst out laughing, which pleased him a lot. She probably didn't have a lot to laugh about most of the time, but he was pleasantly surprised to see her smile. Now he found himself trying to think of something to do or say to bring that smile back again.

He hadn't seen Elizabeth or the children for two days, which was very unusual. He finally caught the doctor without a patient to take care of, and he inquired about them. The doctor said, "A friend of mine back in Michigan is in need of a nurse and Elizabeth asked if I would send a wire, recommending her. I received an immediate response from him and she bought three tickets for the stagecoach. She left yesterday morning and sure seemed in a big hurry all of a sudden."

Johnny was having a hard time understanding this. He decided to ask Samuel what he thought. Samuel said, "I saw Elizabeth a few minutes after you and I were talking about marriage and kids. She must have been close by. She was crying and I feel sure that she had feelings for you Johnny. She was also obviously protecting her and the children from heartbreak." Johnny felt about as low as a man could feel. It never occurred to him that she would overhear that conversation. Now she and the children were gone and he couldn't explain why he had said what he had. She didn't deserve to be hurt like this after what she had already gone through.

'*Maybe after I get Samuel safely home, I can try and find her and the children. What if I'm able to find them? I could hurt her all over again by just showing up and then telling her why I don't plan on getting married.*' There didn't seem to be an easy answer, but he didn't feel right letting her go on hurting from his words without some kind of explanation. He also missed those children. Somehow Julia had managed to wrap herself around his heart and he didn't even know how she did it. Timothy had a look of hero worship on his face every time he looked at Johnny and that sure didn't hurt his ego any. What exactly was he afraid of? Elizabeth hadn't shown any signs of being deceitful like some women in his past. Now he was finding himself in a hurry to get Samuel home safely so that he could start looking for Elizabeth and her children. His brothers would both be laughing with glee if they knew he was even slightly interested in a widowed woman with two young children. He would have no peace if they were around but thankfully they weren't. Johnny decided that tomorrow he and Samuel would start the journey home to Willow Bend. The next morning they ate some biscuits and drank coffee and started their trip home. They had packed up the night before, to save time.

During the final months of the war, Johnny had seen his best friend shot and the rest of his infantry was running off, not realizing he was wounded. Johnny had been up a tree using his sharpshooter skills. When it was safe to come down, he managed to get to his friend Brett. He carefully put him over his shoulder and walked back to the area where the medical team was set up. His friend had pulled through, thanks to Johnny's fast action. A couple of weeks later, his friend's father, General Brett Collins, came to their camp to see his son and he looked up Johnny. He had said, "Son, if you ever need anything as long as you live, all you have to do is ask. I feel this war is coming to a close and wherever you end up, just send me a wire if you need me. I am a judge in a small town in Indiana and I'll help you any way that I can, for saving my son's life. I've written down how you can contact me. I am very serious about your asking me for help, son."

Johnny had contacted General Collins and asked for help in purchasing two sturdy horses to finish their journey to Willow Bend. The General had wired the livery stable and requested their two best horses and he gave them to Johnny as a gift. Johnny was given a handsome black stallion named 'Midnight' and Samuel was given a sturdy chestnut gelding named Jimbo. He had been pleased to hear from Johnny and it made him feel good to be able to repay him in some small way. He reminded Johnny again of his offer of any kind of help he might ever need in the future.

Johnny walked Samuel's horse over to a stump so that it would be easier for him to mount. It felt good to ride in the cool morning air but they both knew that it wouldn't last long. They were going to try and make 20 miles a day if that didn't wear out Samuel. Johnny was going to watch him carefully to see if there were any signs of fatigue or pain on his face. They started out riding side by side while the roads were wide. Even though the war was officially over, they knew that there was still danger out there from more than one direction. Guerilla bands were still causing problems in the area and some of them didn't seem to care who they hurt.

Samuel said "Rebecca and I have always had a dream of buying a ranch outside of Willow Bend. We attempted to purchase one but it got bought out from under us." Samuel knew that his son would be taking good care of Rebecca. It hurt him to know that she was probably worried by now. Johnny was pleased to find out that Samuel had a real gift with animals, especially horses. A thought quickly crossed Johnny's mind just then. He was wondering if there was any land for sale right now around Willow Bend. From what he understood from listening to Samuel, he and Rebecca would need several years to save up enough money to buy a ranch with a decent amount of land. What if Johnny bought a large enough spread that he could live on it, but also share some of the land with Samuel and his family? He could get some men together to help them build a house before winter set in.

Johnny wouldn't say anything to Samuel yet, but the more he thought about it, the better he liked the idea. He and Samuel were turning out to be good friends and his son sounded like a fine young man. He started thinking about settling down and becoming part of this small village that Samuel was talking about. He had always lived a simple life but he also enjoyed helping out others who were less fortunate. His parents had never attended church, so Johnny and his brothers were never raised to know anything about God. His friend Brett talked to Johnny sometimes about how reassuring it was to know how much God loved each individual person and that comment had gotten Johnny to wondering. '*Does God really know that I and my brothers exist? I think I will ask Samuel if he attended church back in Willow Bend. Maybe that has been a part of my feeling so empty inside all of my life.*'

His thoughts shifted back to Elizabeth and her children. Even though he had told Samuel that he liked his life the way it was, he was just kidding himself. Every year he seemed to get lonelier. Now that he had heard about Samuel's wife and son, he envied him, which came as a surprise. They were getting ready to stop for their first night on the way to Willow Bend. So far, Samuel seemed to be keeping up, but Johnny had a strong feeling that Samuel wouldn't be willing to let any discomfort show. He judged that they had made 25 miles, give or take a mile or two. They didn't want to push the horses and would always try to stop to let them graze for awhile and rest. Johnny noticed a good place to stop for the night, off the path of the road they had been following. He didn't want any surprises during the night. That is one reason that he slept close to his horse Midnight. He would alert Johnny the second he sensed danger of any kind. Johnny offered to unsaddle both horses and asked Samuel if he could fix them up some kind of overhang in case it decided to rain. He knew Samuel would figure out that Johnny was trying to take on any physical duties to help him save his strength. Each day they traveled, brought Samuel one day closer to his family.

As they got settled in for the night on the ground, Johnny decided to bring up the subject of a church in Willow Bend. "Samuel, I was just curious to know if you attended church in your village?" During the short time that they had known each other, Samuel had a strong feeling that Johnny didn't know the Lord. He had been hoping that the subject would come up without him having to ask Johnny outright.

"Yes, I attend a fine church and the pastor should be back now from the war. You will like him Johnny. He is a simple man who wears very casual clothes, except on Sundays. The ladies have their tongues a flappin' about that subject, but pastor just smiles and goes on his merry way. He is the reason that I have a daily conversation with the Good Lord. My faith kept me from worrying too much about my family back home during the war."

Johnny was quite certain that if a kind man like Samuel said that he attended church and had a daily conversation with God, then Johnny felt more comfortable about checking this out for himself. He had heard some pastors in his hometown who were always screaming at the top of their lungs about hell fire, and he wanted no part of that kind of religion. If he didn't have such a high opinion of Samuel, he never would have brought that subject up.

The next morning Sarah woke up bright and early and was eager to explore the village. When she walked up to the front desk, Maude offered to join her for breakfast and give her some ideas of what to see. Sarah wanted to check on Worley and Gus to see how they were doing. Maude had already anticipated that question. Doc had told her they were both doing well, and he expected a fairly quick recovery. While they were eating breakfast, Will came into the dining room and stopped at their table. He tipped his hat at the ladies and Sarah introduced him to Maude. They invited him to join them, which he promptly did. Sarah's trunk was brought to her late last night and so today she was wearing a pale blue everyday dress with white trim around the collar. With her hair back up in place, in one long braid wound around the top of her head, she hoped that she gave a better impression to Will then when he had last seen her.

She saw the front door of the hotel open and in came the pastor that she had hurriedly met yesterday. Sarah knew that she had probably looked like a wild woman, riding bareback on the stage horse. She had to hold back a giggle because she could still remember the shocked look on the pastor's face when he saw her riding into town at a gallop yesterday. The pastor noticed them, but as he drew closer to their table, he seemed to hesitate. Sarah waved him over so now he had no choice but to speak to them. Sarah introduced him to Will and he was offered a seat. Pastor didn't really want to sit down with them but he wasn't sure how to politely get out of it. "I have some errands to run and can only stay a minute or so." Will decided to fill Maude and the pastor in on the details of the robbery. After hearing the story about Sarah's shooting a hold-up man, the pastor just stared at him completely stunned. *'What kind of woman was this lady anyhow?'* He used the word 'lady' generously.

"Please excuse me, I have an appointment at the bank" said Will. "Sarah, I'd like a word with you later today. May I come back at two o'clock?" Sarah looked puzzled but agreed to meet him by the front desk. For some reason that pastor couldn't explain, he didn't like the idea of Sarah meeting with Will. Why should he care who she spoke to or was seen with? Something about Sarah was very unsettling and pastor had no idea why. "Sarah is applying for the position of the village schoolteacher. Isn't that exciting, Pastor?" Pastor couldn't believe it. This strange woman did not fit the image of a schoolteacher by any means.

Pastor tried to remain calm when he replied, "Are you sure you wouldn't rather work in the general store or become a nurse? Women are always needed for those occupations."

Sarah immediately took offense, even if those comments came from a pastor. "I've been a schoolteacher for the past three years, Pastor, and I'm a good one too. I just felt that there was so much going on outside of my little town and I wanted to expand what I knew, so that I could be a better teacher." Maude was ready to defend her friend, but she obviously didn't need anyone's help. Maude seemed to think highly of her and he had always liked Maude. This whole situation got more puzzling all the time. Maybe Doc could shed some light on the subject of Sarah. Not that it was any of his business! Pastor excused himself quickly before he said anything else wrong. *'Goodness, what a bold woman Sarah was.'*

Pastor was in the general store, when he saw Jonas walk in. "Hi Jonas, what's new?"

"It's funny that you asked that question Pastor. I was driving my wagon home last week, and I gave a young soldier and his dog a ride to the village. I ended up offering him a job and he is sleeping in my barn with his dog. His name is Danny and he has a left hand that's pretty useless, but that won't hold him back none."

"Is this young man Danny Washington by any chance? Doc and I helped him when he got hurt and then I saw him again on the train when the war ended. He was headed home to see his girl, Mandie."

"Well, that didn't work out too well, I reckon, so he just started walking. He found a dog that was caught in a trap and now they are the best of friends. I can tell that he is a nice young man and I feel like the Lord put me in his path for a reason. Please come out to see him anytime that you'd like to."

Worley had woken up that morning with his wrist aching, but he was sure thankful to be alive. He swung by the café for coffee and breakfast with Gus and then decided what he really needed was a beer. As they were leaving the café, they ran into Pastor James. "I was looking for both of you to see how you were doing. Are you in a lot of pain? I'm so glad to see you both walking around."

"I am not in too much pain Pastor, but don't let on to Daisy. I was on my way over to see her."

Pastor chuckled at that comment and said, "I promise not to let on that you aren't really at death's door. How are you feeling Gus?"

Gus was pleased that Pastor called him by name and he perked up and said, "It was mighty nice of you to check up on us. My shoulder is going to be painful for awhile but I was plumb lucky. Worley done caught me right as I was about to fall off the stagecoach. I wish that I had someone like Daisy to fuss over me."

"I'm workin' on that Gus. It won't be long now and I'll find you some fine gal" said Worley.

"I'll let you be on your way then. Please let me know if I can do anything for either of you."

As they were walking over to the saloon, Worley was practicing looking like he was in terrible pain, but at the same time he wanted to look like a hero. *'How can I look like both at the same time? I really need some special attention from Daisy.'* He wasn't disappointed in her reaction. When he walked through the swinging doors, he spotted Daisy wiping down the bar. When she looked up and saw Worley with his arm in a sling, she gasped and ran around the bar as fast as she could move.

"Worley, what happened to you? Are you in pain? Can I do something? Here, sit down right here and I'll bring you both a beer. My goodness Gus, you look like you are in pain too. I'm so sorry." Worley could handle this kind of attention any day. It was almost worth getting shot. As he sat down, he knew Daisy was watching him closely, so he winced and closed his eyes for a second. Daisy immediately yelled at Pete to bring Worley and Gus a beer and Pete's reaction was comical. He was not used to anyone yelling at him to do anything, especially when he owned the saloon, but he let it pass. He brought over the beers and inquired about Worley and Gus's injuries. Worley spoke up right away, "Oh, I was shot yesterday while two men tried to rob the stage. Gus got shot too but we'll both be alright, eventually."

"Daisy looked so upset and said, "Worley, when I get off work this afternoon, I'll bring you some hot soup to your room and I'll see if you need anything. I feel terrible that you are in such pain."

Pete caught on quickly that Worley was going to take advantage of his injury so Pete said, "Daisy, why don't you take the afternoon off and I'll pay you for the time. I think our friend here probably won't be able to take care of himself for awhile. I'll swing by and check on you later tonight Worley. Gus, you might need a second beer. I'll come by tonight with something for you to eat." Worley drank his beer and drank up all of the attention at the same time. When he was finished, Daisy helped him out of his chair and took his uninjured arm and walked him slowly out of the door. *'Oh yes, I am going to be able to get Daisy's attention now. I just have to figure out a way to keep it when I get this shoulder healed. In the meantime, I'm going to enjoy every second of this.'*

Will showed up at the hotel that afternoon, promptly at two o'clock, and Sarah was waiting. He asked her if she would mind taking a short walk so they could speak in private and Sarah said that was fine with her. He walked her to the edge of town and then stopped under a big oak tree with a wooden bench underneath. He sat down beside her and started to explain why they needed privacy. "Sarah, I worked partly for the bank but also for the stage line. When I turned in my report on the attempted robbery, the bank and stage company both decided to give us a generous reward. The strong box had been holding a lot more money than usual, which is why I was riding on the stage that trip. I wanted you to know that if you would open an account at the bank, this reward would be deposited into your account immediately." Sarah had never had a lot of money nor did she ever feel the need to.

She replied, "I don't want anyone to know of my receiving this reward. I would like to find some ways to help people in need without them knowing where the money came from." His admiration for her grew even more after hearing this. He said that no one would reveal her name nor the amount of the reward, which was $5,000. They walked over to the bank together and he helped her to open up an account and made sure that the money was deposited into her new account.

He registered for a room and then went into the dining room for supper. As he looked around the room, he noticed a woman who kept staring at him and he knew he'd never seen her before. She looked like trouble to him so he glanced in the other direction. Again, he felt someone staring at him and when he turned, the same woman was batting her eyelashes at him. That actually amused him so he let out a chuckle and turned away.

Norma Rolands was not used to being ignored by any man, and she felt her face flushing with anger. She had seen this same man being very friendly to a new woman who had just come into town, and Norma knew that she was far more attractive. Maybe he just had something on his mind at the moment. She was sure that she would see him again in the hotel dining room so she would make a special point of looking her best.

Perhaps a new dress would be in order. Yes, that was a wonderful idea. She would go over to the general store to see if they had something that would do. Their dresses were not up to the standard that she was accustomed to but she needed something quickly. She stood up and slowly walked past his table and tried to act as if she didn't even notice him. While looking for a dress, her best friend Ada came in the store and walked up to her.

"I wish I could shop for pretty dresses as often as you do Norma. I have to try and watch my money carefully. You always look so fancy, especially when you order dresses from back east."

"I have to always look my best. You never know when a special gentleman might come into our village. I might have a couple of dresses that I don't like anymore that I could give you Ada. Come by my house after you get off work and I'll give them to you."

"Oh Norma, that would be wonderful. Thank you for being so generous."

"I'm more than happy to pass them on to you. Just don't expect them to look as good on you as they do on me."

"Oh, of course not. No one can outdo you. Thanks again and I'll see you later."

Rebecca Jenkins was beside herself with worry. She had tried to be strong for her son, Jacob, but she was failing miserably. Her husband Samuel should have returned from the Civil War by now. His regiment was discharged in Pennsylvania two months ago, according to a short letter from an old friend of her husbands. At that time, he was alive and planned to head home on a train and then on foot or ~~on~~ horseback. Their friend warned her that Samuel had lost a lot of weight and was quite weak, but determined to make it back home. She knew if he weren't alive, she would feel a deep pain in her heart.

Their grown son, Jacob, was 23. Thank the good Lord he had returned home safely from the war. He had lost an arm, but he was alive. She had gladly altered her son's shirts and jacket; so thankful that he was back home and alive. If she didn't have such a close walk with the good Lord, she would have panicked by now. Rebecca had dark circles under her eyes. Her son was pretty sure that she hadn't slept much or at all recently. She had been a brave woman for four years, but was struggling now to keep up her faith. Jacob knew that his parents were very close and had a deep love for each other. He wanted to find a woman much like his mother, but so far he hadn't found the right one. He was a patient man and would wait. In the meantime, he would put as much money away as possible towards their future. Jacob especially took after his father as far as being very responsible.

Johnny and Samuel had now been traveling for several days. Some days because of the heat, they hadn't made as much time, but that was no problem. Getting Samuel home in good shape was Johnny's main priority. After a restful night, Johnny and Samuel started off again in the early morning. Johnny  was hoping to find some game today but he didn't want to shoot an animal. The noise could spell trouble if the wrong person or persons were nearby. He knew how to set up a snare for rabbits or maybe they could get lucky and find a place to fish. Part of their route today was a gradual climb and then it leveled off again. Johnny decided the next time they hit a high spot, he would pull out his binoculars and see if he could spot anything, man or animal. He felt a strong responsibility to make sure Samuel arrived home safely and as healthy as possible. They needed some vegetables and meat to give him more strength, but that could be a problem.

A few miles up the road, they reached the rise and Johnny pulled off the road and dismounted. He climbed the tallest, sturdiest tree he could find, with his binoculars hanging from his neck. At first he didn't see anything, but then he noticed a small trickle of smoke coming from a cabin up the road, about a half-mile away. He searched all around the cabin for any men and found none. He noticed a lean-to off to one side of the cabin and found two horses. He climbed down and told Samuel, "I will approach very slowly, and will knock on the front door while you go to the rear and wait for a signal from me." He said "Hello" as loudly as he could so the person or persons inside would not be alarmed. Pretty soon the door slowly opened, and a shotgun was pointed right at his midsection. Johnny was startled to see that it was a young boy of about eight years old. He explained, "I am taking my friend home from the war and we need food and would be happy to pay for it." The boy listened quietly and then backed up a step and motioned him into the cabin. Johnny heard a groan and when he turned toward the sound, he saw a young woman in labor on the bed, with no one else in the cabin.

Johnny told the boy "I have a friend with me and I need to tell him to come inside so that we can help you." The boy figured that he didn't have much of a choice since he sure didn't know what to do. His mother had been trying to have a baby since the early morning hours and was obviously in a lot of pain. The boy nodded his head and Johnny went outside to signal Samuel and explain what was going on. It turned out that Samuel had helped his wife birth their son. "What is your name son?"

"My name is Wesley and that is my mother."

"Heat up some water and bring me any blankets or towels that you can find." Johnny spoke up and said, "Samuel, what can I do to help?" He wasn't too eager to find out the answer. Samuel told him to find a strong stick for the woman to bite down on and he raced out the door with relief. Now this he could handle! When he returned, Wesley had laid the rifle aside and was doing everything that Samuel was telling him to do.

Samuel said "The mother's name is Maggie. They were expecting her husband home any day now. Wesley said that his papa had been fighting close by several months ago and was allowed to come home for one night. He had told Wesley that if anything happened and they had to leave, to put a note in a jar and showed him where to bury it." Now the baby was starting to appear, and Samuel was very calm and helping the mother by reminding her when it was time to push. Soon a little girl was wrapped up in Samuel's arms, crying a very healthy cry. He cleaned the baby up and laid her at Maggie's breast. Maggie was exhausted but happy and took one hand and grabbed Samuels and thanked him.

Now they had a problem! Johnny was happy that the mother and baby were alright but they couldn't be left here alone with only young Wesley to protect and care for them. Johnny and Samuel had agreed that they had to take this young family with them. They made a pallet on the floor and spent the night. In the morning, they gathered up all the food and water they could carry, and Wesley left a note for his papa and buried it. Now they had to find a way to bring Maggie and the baby with them, without jostling them around. They went out into the woods and built a travois like the Indians used. Wesley said, I have heard of Willow

Bend and it is about a two days' ride from our cabin." Wesley was a good hunter and had cooked several rabbits over the fire. There was also fish that he had caught and smoked before they left. Maggie had taught him how to find greens that were healthy, so they cooked those up over the fire and Johnny made Samuel and Maggie eat all of it and drink the juice. After giving Maggie and the baby one more day to rest up, at early morning they were ready. Mother and baby, Dinah, were settled with blankets underneath and over them so that they would be warm and comfortable. This trip to Willow Bend had turned complicated, but Maggie was so relieved that Johnny and Samuel had come by.

If all went well, in two days they would arrive in Willow Bend and Samuel could rejoin his family. Johnny had no idea where Maggie and the baby and Wesley could live but one thing at a time. The weather had held up, with no rain in sight. Maggie and the baby were asleep within a few minutes. Johnny rode up ahead as a scout and had Samuel guarding the rear, keeping Wesley and his mom and baby in between them. They stopped at noon and ate a quick meal and rested the horses. Samuel was looking stronger today. His eagerness was showing on his face, knowing how close to home he was getting.

A few days after the attempted robbery, Josh and Rafe were taken out of the jail in Willow Bend and escorted to a town with a larger jail. Rafe hadn't slept much at all the past few nights because he was worried sick about his brother, Jeffrey. *'What must he be thinking right now? He's always looked up to me and now he probably feels like I deserted him.'* He was still in a lot of pain from being shot and this didn't add to his bad mood. Josh was furious because of the botched robbery, being shot and put in jail. All of their glorious plans were ruined. Rafe had no idea what Jeffrey would do because he always did whatever Rafe told him to do. He wouldn't have the first idea of where to start looking for Rafe. How could this have turned out any worse?

At the end of the second day, Samuel started pointing out places that he recognized. Willow Bend was now only about a mile away. Johnny offered to let Samuel go on ahead to let his family know that he was safe but Samuel wouldn't have it. He knew that his friend had gone to a lot of trouble to bring him home safely and he wanted him by his side to meet his family. When they reached the outskirts of Willow Bend, a man driving a carriage came up to them, asking if they needed help. Samuel recognized the doctor the same time the doctor recognized him. He introduced everyone and explained about Maggie and Wesley and the baby. Doc said to follow him to his office and then he would show them where Rebecca was staying. As they drove around the bend, Johnny's eyes were drawn to a beautiful, peaceful river with willow trees bending over, touching the water. Up ahead on the right was a welcoming sight to Johnny. Two boys were fishing with their cane poles. A blonde-haired boy was laying on his stomach and a dark-haired boy was sitting on the bank with his feet dangling in the water. Johnny was reminded of some of the happiest days of his childhood. He and his brothers would spend the afternoon fishing as soon as their chores were done. He could easily picture himself sitting on the riverbank for hours, with his cane pole. If he decided to stick around, this was the first place he planned to visit when he got a few things taken care of that he felt responsible for.

When they pulled up to the Doc's office, Johnny went over to Maggie and reached for the baby with one hand and helped her down with the other. She was still a little weak and shaky so he kept his arm around her to steady her. Doc ran ahead and opened his office door and motioned them in. As Johnny stepped through the door with Maggie and the baby, he thought he was seeing things. There stood Elizabeth with her mouth wide open and shock and anger all over her face.

5

JULY 1865

Trail's End Has a New Owner

Pastor James always looked forward to his walks in the morning and his conversations with the Lord, but today he felt an urgency in his heart. As hard as he tried to be there for his congregation, he always ended up believing he was falling short. That feeling made him feel discouraged and he had to pull himself out of this somehow. Only one person understood his pain and that alone was a source of comfort. *Lord, here I am again, and you already know exactly how I feel. You've put so many hurting people in my life and I'm just one simple pastor. I want to always have the right answers for everyone, but sometimes all I can do is pat someone on the back. How can I ever learn to say and do the right thing when I see someone hurting? I pray so hard and so often about this same subject and I don't honestly see any change in me. I know you hear me,*

so why are you not able to get through to me? What am I doing wrong? Please find a way to get through to me. I'm trying to be sensitive to what you want to teach me. Would you please do something to bring me some encouragement soon? Thank you, Lord.'

As he was entering the village from one of the backroads, he noticed a woman slumped over in a field, sobbing so hard, he could hear her even across the field. He couldn't tell who it was from this distance. Pastor ran as fast as he could and when he got close, the woman heard him and turned towards him. Her eyes were swollen from crying and her face was all red. *'For heavens sake; it is Daisy, Worley's special friend who works in the saloon.'*

"Daisy, what is wrong? Are you hurt?" He reached down to help her up and she was shaking all over.

"Pastor, I am so embarrassed that you found me out here. I thought I was far enough off the road where no one could hear me. No, I didn't get hurt but I am so scared and I didn't know who to talk to."

"Please tell me what has gotten you so upset. I will not share anything that you tell me, I promise you that Daisy. I don't know if listening will help you, but you take your time and settle down a little. I see a log behind us, up against the fence. Let's go over there and sit down." She walked beside him and even put her arm inside the crook of his elbow. She seemed like she was calming down, which was a big relief to see. They sat down on the log and pastor handed her his clean handkerchief, which she took gratefully.

"I don't know if this will make any sense to you but I'm desperate for someone to talk to. I've never been to church in my whole life and I don't think God thinks too highly of a woman who works in a saloon. As you probably already know, Worley and I are sweethearts, with no hope of ever being able to be married."

"Yes, I know that you and Worley are sweethearts and he is a very hard-working man, who I consider my friend. I don't understand why you feel there is no hope of ever getting married. Please tell me why you feel that way."

"Even though we don't attend church, I would be afraid of him marrying a woman like me who works in a saloon. You make promises when you get married and I don't want God to be angry with Worley because of me." At this comment, she started crying again and he knew she was hurting unnecessarily. He needed guidance for a way to comfort her.

"Daisy, don't you know that God loves you, regardless of where you work? Pete has told me more than once what a hard worker you are and that you make sure that the saloon is kept as clean as possible. From what I hear, all of the men treat you with respect and Worley and Pete think the world of you. God loves everyone equally, regardless of our past or what we do for a living. He would never be angry with Worley because of you. I know that it is difficult to understand about God when no one has ever taught you about His love, but I'd like to help you. Would you be comfortable with Sarah talking to you about her experience with God?"

"Oh yes, Pastor. She is always so kind to me whenever we pass on the boardwalk or when she rides by on her horse. She waves to me and calls me by my name too. I would like to talk to her if she is willing. Can you teach me how to pray so that I can be like Sarah?"

"Daisy, I'd like to lead you in a prayer so that you can turn your heart over to God. He doesn't want you to try and be like anyone else; he wants you to just be like Daisy. Are you ready to give your heart to God?"

"Yes, I'm ready, right this minute. Do I close my eyes?"

"Most people like to bow their head and close their eyes out of respect towards God. I'll say the words slowly and you just repeat them after me."

'Dear God, please forgive me for my sins and help me to learn how to walk with you. I want a relationship with you and I thank you for loving me just like I am. Please let me feel a peace like I've never known before. Amen!'

When Daisy opened her eyes, and looked up at Pastor, her eyes were radiant and she was smiling. "Pastor, there is one thing that I don't understand. There just isn't any way that you could have heard me crying from that far away."

Pastor just smiled and said, "Daisy, God can do things that seem impossible to us. Just be happy that He loves you so much that He sent me along that road and increased my hearing, so that I could help you. I'll talk to Sarah today and I know that she will be happy to spend time with you. I would love to see you start attending our church service. I'll be honest with you, Daisy, there will be some people complaining because of where you work, but there will be more people who will be so happy to see you attending church. Don't let other people's mean attitudes steal your happiness." Daisy walked back to the village feeling a happiness that she had never known before.

Elizabeth looked upset and hurt and something else, but she didn't have time to explain. Doc asked her to take the baby and the mother into the room at the end of the hall and she silently obeyed. Doc was mystified at Elizabeth's attitude. He hadn't known her very long but she was always warm and loving to everyone, with a cheerful attitude. Something had greatly upset her and he had no idea what it was. He went back outside for a minute to tell Samuel where Rebecca was. Doc said that she was staying at the hotel and told him her room number. She also would often help out in the dining room. Samuel told Johnny that they could walk to the hotel, so off they went. Now Samuel seemed to have a lot more energy and Johnny was so relieved.

When they walked into the hotel, Maude was amazed to see Samuel standing in front of her with a man that she didn't know. Samuel made the introductions and then asked where he could find Rebecca. Maude led him down the hall and knocked on the door. "Who is it? Just a minute!"

Maude said, "It is Maude. You have a visitor Rebecca!" In a few seconds, the door opened, and Rebecca stood there stunned; as if she couldn't believe what she was seeing. Samuel was standing there with the biggest grin on his face and he held his arms out to her. She fell into his arms, sobbing and laughing at the same time.

Rebecca was relieved and thankful to see her loving husband Samuel, back home safe and sound. She could tell that he was exhausted and weak, but she would take excellent care of him. Samuel quickly introduced Johnny to his wife.

Johnny smiled and tipped his hat and said, "It's good to meet you, Rebecca. I've heard all about you. If you'll excuse me, I have some business to take care of. I'd like to buy you both dinner tonight, after Samuel gets some rest. Please be sure to invite your son also. I am looking forward to meeting him."

He needed to eat and get cleaned up and then go back to help Elizabeth understand that Maggie was not his wife and the baby was not his. Once she understood the facts, surely she would be relieved and they could talk about it. *'Why did women have to make everything so complicated?'* Simply answering

Samuel's question that she had overheard, was done in innocence on his part. Today helping Maggie and the baby into the doctor's office was nothing more than good manners.

All Samuel had asked for was a glass of water and a chance to rest in Rebecca's rocker for about an hour. She brought him the water and unfastened his boots and pulled them off. While putting a light blanket over his body, she kissed him on the forehead and then tiptoed out of the room. She had no intention of waking him up in an hour. He could rest as long as his body needed. Rebecca headed over to the restaurant to find Johnny, but he wasn't there. Her next stop would be the doctor's office. Halfway there, she heard a horse approaching, and when she turned, she saw Johnny. He dismounted and stood right in front of her. She gave him a big hug and thanked him over and over for returning her husband safely.

"I'd like to sit down and talk to you privately, to learn more about what Samuel went through and other details. Just in case something woke Samuel up while I am gone, I left him a note where he could easily find it."

"Why don't I rent a carriage so we can ride a little ways out of town. If you can be ready in 30 minutes, I'll swing by the front of the hotel to pick you up."

"I'll be ready, and I'll wait outside the hotel."

He rode his horse over to the livery, told the owner to take good care of Midnight and rented a carriage. Pretty soon he pulled up to the hotel and Rebecca was anxiously waiting. He put the brake on and jumped down and helped her up. She must have been in her 40's but today she looked like a young girl.

Rebecca was pointing out the beautiful landscape and giving him some background on the village before the war started. She made it sound like it was a great place to live, with the majority of the village helping each other whenever a need arose. In the short time he'd known Samuel, he was sure that this relationship with Rebecca was built on love and trust. It was the kind of marriage that he had never thought he could have himself. To trust a woman with his heart scared him more than anything he had to face during the war. *'What kind of a husband would he be anyway?'* He had tried it once and been made a fool of and was robbed

of his own child. Women needed a man to show affection and that was where he felt the fear creep in. In order for him to show a woman affection, it would mean letting the walls down around his heart. He wished that he could talk to Rebecca about Elizabeth but he didn't think it was right, so he kept silent.

He told Rebecca everything he knew about how Samuel got wounded and what had happened when Johnny first saw him being threatened by that man.

When he was finished telling her the story, she grabbed his arm and said, "I'll always be grateful to you and I don't want you to leave Willow Bend. There is plenty of land for sale if you want your own place and lots of men are needing work. The generous couple that owned the hotel, my son and I stay there while waiting for Samuel to return. We were given free room and board in exchange for my helping out in the hotel dining room. Jacob helped out in the stable, so it worked out well for everyone. Now with Samuel back, I'm not sure what is going to happen. I can't picture Samuel living in a hotel room for very long but there really isn't much choice."

As they were riding along, Johnny noticed a sign hanging out at the beginning of a long road, and it said, *"Trails End."*

Rebecca said, "That is the ranch that Samuel and I had dreamed of owning one day. Before we could come up with the down payment, someone else bought it. We are not upset about it; Samuel and I will find another place someday when we can get back on our feet. The important thing is that Samuel and Jacob are both home now. Perhaps we can rent a small cabin outside of the village."

He didn't mention anything to her about his thoughts of possibly buying a ranch himself. He didn't want to get her hopes up too soon and he also needed to discuss it with Samuel. Now that he had found where Elizabeth and the children were living, there was no reason to leave the village. In the short time he had known her, she stood out as a very special lady. He had only been in town for half a day, and he was already in trouble with her. That sure didn't take long. He was feeling more comfortable with thoughts of making his home here and purchasing a ranch. He wasn't a man to waste time.

Soon Rebecca was ready to return to the hotel to check on Samuel. When they reached the hotel, he helped her down from the carriage and received another hug. "I can't wait to find out more about you. I'll never forget what you did for us."

"I've already paid for a room in the hotel for a week. I'd like to meet you and Samuel and Jacob this evening for supper, which will be my treat. I just need a chance to clean up and change my clothes." Johnny took the carriage back to the livery and his mind was whirling with so many thoughts. He decided to let Midnight have a break and he took his saddlebags and slung them over his shoulder and walked back to the hotel. He ordered a hot bath and went up to his room.

After a bath and dressing in clean clothes, he felt like a new man.

Pastor told Doc about Danny living with Jonas so they both rode out in Doc's carriage to see him. Danny was walking across the yard with a dog limping right beside him. When he heard the carriage, he turned to see who was coming and then he was all smiles.

"Doc, Chaplain, it's so good to see you both. I just got settled in here recently and intended to look you up soon. Jonas must have told you about him taking Roscoe and I in." He looked down and patted his dog, whose tail was wagging like crazy.

"Yes, I saw him in the general store and was surprised to hear that you were in Willow Bend. I'm sorry that things didn't work out with you and Mandie", said Pastor.

"I'll admit it was painful but for the best. I don't want to marry a woman who would be ashamed of me or who thinks less of me because of my hand. Jonas is a kind man and has a loving family. That all made me feel welcome. His wife is an excellent cook, so that has added a few pounds to my frame. How are you both doing? It's so good to see you again."

"We won't keep you," said Doc. We know you must be busy, but we just wanted to tell you that we are happy to know you are close by. If you ever need anything, please let us know. It's good that you have a faithful friend. Would you mind if I looked at his paw? I made up a medicine for another dog that was caught in a trap and it seemed to take away some of the pain."

Doc examined Roscoe's paw and said, "I'll run out here tomorrow with the cream. If I don't see you, I'll leave it with Dora. I have to drive right by here to see a patient, so it won't be any trouble. It was sure Roscoe's lucky day when you found him."

As they drove off, Danny looked down at Roscoe and said, "Well fella, it looks like you might be on your way to feeling better soon. We sure ended up in the best place, didn't we?"

There were a couple of men who had recently come back from the war that Norma could use to cause some jealousy. She knew how to flirt and make men almost shove each other out of the way to do her bidding. Even as a very young girl, she learned how to lure a boy away from another girl who he was paying too much attention to. Most men were so gullible and would eagerly believe anything she told them. Norma didn't have many girlfriends because she had stolen their beaus away and now they avoided her. Norma didn't need their friendship; at least she tried to convince herself of that. There was one friend that she hadn't driven away and that was Ada. She wasn't very attractive, but she looked at Norma like she was someone she worshiped. Ada would do anything that she asked of her, so she could keep an eye out on any eligible men in the village.

She decided to stop by the restaurant and order some tea and one of their delicious cucumber sandwiches. As she walked into the hotel her eyes automatically were drawn to a man who looked nice looking, in a rugged sort of way, and very capable of taking care of himself. Norma chose a table directly in his line of sight and walked toward him as if she hadn't a care in the world. When the waitress came over to take her order, Norma was as sweet as could be and even complimented the girl on her hair. The waitress was well aware of Norma and her normally cold attitude and figured out what she was up to. She wrote down her order and went back to the kitchen. Soon she brought back a pot of tea and the sandwiches that

Norma had ordered. Without thinking, Norma started to complain that the water wasn't hot enough, but she stopped herself in mid-sentence and smiled at the waitress and said, "Everything looks just perfect."

Johnny was observing this conversation between this woman and the waitress. He could tell that the waitress was shocked when the woman complimented her hair. It looked like there were two sides to this woman's personality. He also caught how she had started to complain about something but then stopped herself. Now she was turning her attention to him. She sweetly smiled at him and said, "You are new in town, aren't you? My name is Norma."

"Yes, I am; I brought a friend home from the Civil War who had been wounded."

She never asked about the man, as if he wasn't the least bit important. Her next comment surprised him. "I am interested in looking at some property right outside of town but I'm afraid to go without an escort. Would you have the time to accompany me?" This woman didn't know a thing about him and yet she would risk riding out of town with him.

"I'm sorry but I don't have the time. I have plans to check on my friend." He got up immediately, tipped his hat and was out the door. *'Well, you could add this woman to the list of women he didn't trust. The list just seemed to be getting longer.'*

Norma wasn't happy at his refusal but she wasn't about to give up that easily. This man was worth being patient with. She hoped he didn't plan on leaving town too soon. She left the restaurant and went shopping for a new dress. Because she had the money, Norma often ordered dresses from back east. Today she was in a hurry and wanted something new for tomorrow, so she entered the dress shop at the back of the general store. There weren't too many dresses that were up to her high standards but luckily, she found one in pretty lavender with deep purple cuffs and collar. She asked Sadie to wrap it up carefully and then went on her way home.

Johnny was just relaxing with a cup of coffee, when the most beautiful woman came into the room with Maude. Maude led her right over to his table. "Johnny, I'd like to introduce you to a dear friend of mine who just arrived in the village; this is Sarah Waters. Sarah, this is Johnny Anderson."

He stood up and reached out his hand and said, "I am very pleased to meet you Sarah. I just arrived this morning. Would you ladies care to sit and have a cup of tea?" Both of them smiled and sat down and Johnny couldn't seem to take his eyes off of Sarah. *'She is nothing like that woman who was just in here flirting with me.'* Maude spoke up and started telling him about Sarah's adventure on the stagecoach.

When he heard about Sarah shooting one of the robbers, he said "I'll have to remember to call you 'Sharpshooter' from now on," and he grinned. Her reaction was a hilarious laugh that would have been unladylike with anyone else except Sarah.

He still had a couple of hours before meeting Samuel and Rebecca, so he took advantage of that and went to the land office and introduced himself to Michael Nelson. He explained that he wanted to see what ranches were available to buy in the area right outside of Willow Bend. He let him point out various ranches and after a few minutes, he asked about the ranch that Rebecca had shown him.

Mr. Nelson replied, "The ranch you are asking about was purchased four years ago; quite hurriedly, by Miss Norma. She has never lived there or worked the ranch. Nothing has changed in the past four years, when Samuel was interested in this ranch, the land was a lot cheaper. Once the war ended, word spread about good farming land and the price has shot up considerably."

Johnny looked up at him and said, "I would like you to contact the owner and tell her that you have just received an offer for the ranch. Be sure and tell her that this person is willing to pay $10,000 over what she paid for it. She must make the decision within one week or I will look at other ranches. This must be kept private between you and I." The man agreed and said he would take care of it that afternoon. This was the same woman who had been flirting with him in the hotel dining room. Well, his instincts about her were right on target.

Pastor walked over to Doc's office and waited patiently while he took care of some small children who had bad coughs. Now the office was quiet for awhile. He met the new nurse, Elizabeth. Doc said, "She has fit in just fine and is quickly becoming a big help to me."

"I am staying at the hotel with my two small children and slowly learning the names of the people in the village. What time does your church service start on Sunday, Pastor?"

"It begins at ten o'clock and I'm looking forward to meeting your children. I would sometimes welcome your company when it comes to visiting some of the ladies."

"I would enjoy that, if my schedule permits. That would help me to learn the names of the villagers faster." Elizabeth excused herself and went back into a room down the hall.

Doc said, "I'm sure it could be easily worked out to let her go with you, if we aren't too busy."

Before he could stop himself, the pastor blurted out, "Do you know what I found out about Sarah? She is going to apply for the position of the schoolteacher. What do you think of that?"

Doc looked back at the pastor and said, "Why does that have you so riled up? I admire her very much."

"Did she also happen to mention that she shot one of the robbers in the shoulder?"

Doc grinned and said, "Yes, I think she did tell me a little bit about that. She purposely wounded him, but she is a good enough shot that she could have killed him. Sarah is a very interesting lady, and I look forward to getting to know her better. Maude is so excited that she is here. Say, how about you join us tonight for supper at the hotel?" Pastor was quick to come up with a lame excuse for not joining them tonight. Doc knew his friend well and could tell that Sarah was rattling him in a way that no other woman ever had. *'This could turn out to be very interesting indeed.'*

The next morning Elizabeth was having breakfast with Maude when who should walk in but Johnny himself. He walked right up to their table and took off his hat and greeted them with a tentative smile. Maude was her friendly self, but she suddenly had something that needed to be done right away and she excused herself. Johnny asked if he might sit down, but Elizabeth was having none of that. She said, "I don't think we have anything to talk about except for one thing. How long will you and Maggie and the baby be staying in Willow Bend?"

He was trying to figure out how to get himself out of this mess. First Elizabeth had overheard him saying he didn't have a desire to have children and didn't want to get married and now this. He said, "I had no idea that this is where you and the children moved to. I've just brought Samuel back to be with his wife and son.

We stopped at a cabin to ask if they had any extra food and found a young boy with his mother about to have a baby. Her husband hadn't returned home from the war yet. Samuel helped her deliver the baby. We couldn't leave her alone with two small children and she was so weak. We waited two days, to let her get her strength back and here we are. I'm sorry that you misunderstood. I was only trying to help."

At that, he turned and walked out the door. Elizabeth hadn't felt this foolish in her whole life, since she fell in a mud puddle in her pretty church dress at the age of four. Not only had she jumped to conclusions about Johnny and Maggie but she had clearly shown that she was jealous. *'I don't know what to do now. I am so embarrassed. Maybe Maude can give me some good advice.'*

Franklin had waited until dark to put his food and blanket and other items onto the back of the saddle. He walked beside the horse for awhile, getting his eyes used to the darkness. He started walking down a road that went into the woods. Since he didn't have a destination in mind, his first goal was to get as far away from this camp as possible. After about two miles, he got up onto his horse. He had not been told her name, so he called her Beauty. There was no rush, and it was too dangerous to try and travel fast in the dark in unfamiliar territory. He hadn't taken the time to see what was in the bag that Chaplain had given him. One bag had food, and the other bag was pretty heavy, with oats for his horse. Directly behind him was a blanket with a waterproof tarp wrapped around it. After about four hours, he was starting to get tired and decided to pull off into the woods, out of sight. He found a good spot and tied up Beauty and gave her some oats and water out of his hat. There were plenty of leaves to cushion the ground, and he laid down close to his horse and fell immediately asleep. He woke up just as the sun was starting to come up. He went over to the larger bag to check it out. Chaplain seemed to have thought of everything and he must have some great connections or friends who were very generous.

That evening, Johnny went back to the hotel dining room and found Samuel and Rebecca, acting like a couple deeply in love, sitting with their son. When they saw him approach their table, they both gave him wonderful smiles. "Samuel, you are looking a lot better." His nap had turned into four hours and he needed every bit of it. He and Rebecca couldn't take their eyes off of each other and it made Johnny feel good inside.

"Johnny, we'd like you to meet our son, Jacob. I've told him all about how you saved my life."

Johnny shook Jacob's hand and said, "I'm sure he left out the part about saving my life in return." After dinner and dessert, Rebecca excused herself so that the men could talk. "Samuel, you are a very lucky man."

"Just being back home with Rebecca, no matter where we have to live in the meantime, is just fine with me." Johnny decided to wait a day or so to let him in on his plans.

A few days later, Johnny met with Samuel and his family again. "Samuel, all during the war, I couldn't stop dreaming about owning my own farm or ranch somewhere, but I had no idea where. When circumstances led me to Willow Bend, I had a good feeling about the village. I went to the Land Office, to get an idea of what ranches were for sale. Since I'm new to the area, I would like to rely on you to steer me to the best men to hire. One of the most important positions I need to fill immediately is the ranch foreman." Samuel started to mention someone's name when Johnny interrupted him and said, "You are the man that I want for that position, Samuel." Before he could come up with any objections, Johnny finished explaining more of his plan. He needed Samuel to oversee everything, but the physical labor was to be handled by several younger men. He was hoping that Samuel's son Jacob would be willing to hire on with him.

Jacob turned and looked at his father and back to Johnny. "I don't even have to think about it. This sounds like an answer to our prayers."

"I found a ranch that is exactly what I am looking for and I'm only waiting to see if the current owner accepts my offer. I requested a rush on the paperwork with the bank, if the owner agrees, and the bank would be happy to oblige. If I don't get the first ranch, I found another one that will do. I have a feeling that the owner won't be turning down my offer." Johnny didn't tell them which ranch he was attempting to purchase. He would provide a home for them, by moving them into the main house. Johnny said, "It may be one or two weeks before I actually have all the papers signed for the ranch I plan to buy, but I need you on my payroll starting tomorrow, if you are willing to start working that quickly for me. I would like you to go by the feed store and set up an account for me and also see if you can find at least four good solid horses for plowing. I also need an account set up at the general store. I have opened an account at the bank and they will vouch for my credit."

Johnny had a list of every position that he needed to be filled and the sooner the better. Samuel finally started to let Johnny's words sink in and he looked excited. "Johnny, I'll always do my best for you and I am ready to start tomorrow. You sure don't let any grass grow under your feet." Johnny showed him a piece of paper that outlined the salary that he would be paid each month and it was more than he had ever dreamed of making. On top of that, his son would be drawing a very good salary and if Rebecca was interested, they could use a cook. Johnny had already been wired enough money to put as a down payment on a ranch.

Samuel said, "I just have to tell Rebecca," and he rushed off to find her. A few minutes later, they both returned with flushed faces and happy smiles. This time Johnny received a big hug and a kiss on the cheek from Rebecca. She did want to take on the job of a cook, but Johnny let her know that she would have plenty of help and some days off. For several years he had dreamt of owning a large ranch and helping people that were having a rough time of it. It had seemed almost impossible until he had received his share of the inheritance that his father had left him.

"I've hesitated in telling anyone about this, but I trust that you will keep this to yourselves. I was married right before the war broke out, and when my wife found out that she was pregnant, she left me and went back to her father. I found a letter saying that she would find a good safe place for our baby. Soon after, I received divorce papers. I am going to hire a detective, who is a good friend of my brothers. Samuel, that is why I have trouble trusting women."

"Johnny, Samuel and I will keep this in our prayers daily. Thank you for trusting us with this information. The Lord is watching over your child right now, so please take comfort in that."

Johnny didn't want to hurt her feelings, so he just nodded and said, "Thank you Rebecca."

Johnny decided to write to his older brother, David, to let him know where he had decided to settle down.

Dear David,

I am hoping this letter finds you well. I am safe and now living in a small, friendly village called Willow Bend, in Michigan. How I ended up here is a long story, but I've decided to buy a ranch just a couple of miles from the village. Please send me a wire to let me know that you received this letter. David, I need your help. My wife, Carolyn, left me when she found out that she was pregnant with our child. I found her letter, telling me that her father wired her money to go back to her childhood home and that she would find a good home for the baby. I want my child back and I need your help. It doesn't matter if I have a son or a daughter, I would be happy with either. The child would be about five years old now. I know that you have a friend who is a detective and I will spare no cost to find this child. Will be anxious to hear from you. Have you any word about Rusty?

> *Your brother,*
> *Johnny*

He sent the letter in care of their family attorney. It would be wonderful to be able to hear from him again. Hopefully, all three of them had managed to survive the Civil War. He needed to know about their youngest brother, Rusty. Where was he now? He wrote a brief letter to Rusty, in care of the same attorney, just in case he had some knowledge of his whereabouts. It seemed like his life was changing rapidly all of a sudden. Here he was in a village that he never knew existed until last week and now he was buying a ranch and making big plans. More and more, he could see the ranch growing in his mind.

Rebecca's husband had returned home safely, but he was very weak from his injury and the long journey home. She was grateful to Johnny that he didn't expect any physical work from Samuel. Their son Jacob had returned a few weeks earlier, so Rebecca was overjoyed to have her family back together safely. Now she wanted to focus on someone else; her new friend Emily Sizeland, who was a widow. When Emily had shared the news about her pregnancy, Rebecca volunteered to send Jacob over with a cradle that she had been hanging onto for several years. Emily was so thankful to have Rebecca's friendship, as she had no family nearby.

Jacob was going to be coming by Emily's, later on. She had never met him before, but if he was anything like his mother, she knew he would be kind. The baby would need some blankets soon and she wanted the first one to be very special. Emily held her hand over her stomach and felt the slight kicking. The baby she was carrying seemed strong, despite the circumstances. Emily's husband had been in a battle during the final months of the war and had been wounded. He was sent home to recuperate and then went back to his regiment. Not long after, Emily received word that he had been killed. Her heart ached over the loss of her husband, but she was so thankful for the few months that she had been able to spend with him at the end. They had spent a lot of time talking about their future, and of wanting children soon. Now she had another reason to be thankful; Donald had left her with a baby to raise. This child would always remind her of the love they had for each other. He would have been a wonderful father. He had made her promise that if something should happen to him, that she would remarry. *'Who would want to marry a woman who was carrying another man's child? Lord, would it be possible for you to find a very special man for my baby and I?'*

Emily had a job sewing dresses for the general store. The owners, Wilbur and Dorothy Jones, had a special section in the back just for the ladies and they had a thriving business. Emily had first begun to sew when she was a little girl and now she had gotten very good at it. Before Donald's death, she had been putting the money aside that she earned, for some land they wanted to buy. Now she was living in a small room with Mrs. Benson. She had explained to her that she was now going to have a baby and was delighted to hear that there was a small room used for storage. It could easily be converted to a room for the baby. The good Lord was definitely looking after her and the baby. While at church one day, Maggie had happened to mention to Maude that she was an experienced seamstress and Maude came up with the idea of introducing her to Emily. Since Emily was also a seamstress and had more work than she could handle, they got together at the hotel dining room and worked out a plan. Mrs. Benson had a sewing machine that she no longer used and she told Maggie that she was more than welcome to use it and she offered to watch the baby anytime Maggie had a sewing project. It was working out well for everyone, but Maggie missed her husband so much. Emily would be happy with a boy or a girl except that without a husband, it would be easier for her to raise a girl. A boy needed a father to set an example of how he should behave. Someone to teach him about the outdoors and how to hunt and shoot a gun. Mrs. Benson had also offered to let Maggie and her son Wesley and the new baby move in to her large home. It was working out well for everyone. Emily and Maggie and her children had all been living in the hotel, so it was working out well.

There was a knock at the door and she opened it to find a very handsome man with kind eyes, smiling back at her. He had obviously lost his left arm but looked very strong. He introduced himself as Jacob and he was carrying a cradle full of toys. She stepped aside and invited him in. Jacob looked around this small room and noticed how neat and clean it was. Emily offered him a glass of water. She sat down on the love seat and motioned for him to sit in the chair close by. Since both of them were shy, the silence seemed to last a long time. Then both of them started talking at the same time and that made them laugh. "You first, Emily!"

She couldn't get over how good looking he was but even more than that, he seemed like such a gentle person. "It was so kind of your mother to share the cradle and toys with me."

Jacob replied, "Yes, I can remember playing with that little wooden horse. My mother likes the fact that she could find a good home for them. She wants grandchildren in the worst way but has almost given up on my ever getting married."

Emily couldn't believe the words that came tumbling out of her mouth without warning. "I am sure many pretty young girls have tried to get your attention, Jacob." Her eyes looked down and she kept fidgeting with her hands.

Jacob was pleased with her comment. He said, "Emily, I was sorry to hear about your husband. He must have been a fine man."

He could see that her eyes were tearing up a little when she said, "Yes, he was and he was looking forward to being a father. Once he heard the news, it was all that he wrote about. When I received the news about his death, it was a shock. The people in this village have been so kind to me."

As Jacob listened to Emily speak, he was amazed that there was no sign of bitterness or feeling sorry for herself. "If there is ever anything that I can do for you Emily, all you have to do is ask." He stood up to leave.

"Please thank your mother for the cradle and toys and tell her that I will drop by to see her soon."

As Jacob was walking back home, he knew something had really touched him when he met Emily. She definitely reminded him of his mother and that is what he had always known he was looking for in a wife. It didn't bother him that she was pregnant with another man's child. *'Well, this has sure been an interesting day. I look forward to getting to know her better.'*

Emily stood by the open door and watched Jacob walk away. He certainly made a great impression. *'Lord, is there any chance that you might have chosen Jacob and I to be man and wife?'*

6

JULY 1865

Willow Bend Now Has a Sheriff

As she approached the front door of her home, Norma saw the man from the Land Office trying to get her attention. *'Whatever would he want to see her about?'* She stood there impatiently, tapping her foot.

"What is it that you need Mr. Nelson? I'm very busy!"

"I think you will be happy to take the time to listen to what I have to say to you. I have a gentleman who has offered to buy your ranch at a handsome profit for you. He has offered to pay you $10,000 over the price that you paid for 'Trails End."

"Are you serious? He will pay me an extra $10,000?"

"Yes, I am very serious, but there is one stipulation. This deal is only being offered for one week and then it will be withdrawn. He has a second property that he is also interested in."

"Let me think this over and I will get back to you in a day or so." Norma had already made up her mind but didn't want to appear to be too eager. She would accomplish two things at once. It would give her an extra $ 10,000 that she hadn't counted on, plus it would get the ranch off of her hands. The only reason she had bought it was because she found out that Rebecca and Samuel wanted it so badly. *'Now, how am I going to spend that extra $10,000? A trip to Europe would be wonderful or maybe I might travel around the country in a fancy rail car. Goodness, I need to start deciding what to pack and I'll probably need some new dresses. How exciting this is going to be.'*

Sarah had been attending Pastor James' church for several weeks now with Maude, and she was making friends faster than she had expected to. Usually Sarah was withdrawn around people that she  barely knew, but most of the villagers were so open and friendly to her. The first time she attended a Sunday service, Pastor looked startled to see her and he stammered for a few seconds when he was beginning his sermon. Sarah tried not to look directly at him, hoping that he could relax faster and get a grip on his emotions. No matter how many times she thought about it, she couldn't figure out what she was doing that made him so nervous. It wasn't only when she came to church. He seemed to always be running into her. Maybe Maude could help her understand. She was making friends with several of the ladies, and children were always coming up to her to show her something or tell her a secret. Sarah's face just lit up when a child was close by.

Pastor had to admit that he could see now that she would be a wonderful teacher. Doc had been right all along but he didn't want to tell him that. *'What is it about this woman that keeps me so tense?'* This wasn't like him at all and he didn't like this feeling one bit.

Sarah had a list of her students and she was busy organizing their books and writing tablets. Each pupil would have their own tablet because she had brought more than enough when she packed her trunk. One of her students was a 10-year-old boy named Jadon Brown. His mother was a widow and he also had a sister named Charlotte, who was 8. She had gone to their house to visit and learned that Jadon would sometimes get bored in school because he was so far ahead in his studies. Sarah knew just how to handle that problem and was anxious for school to begin. She had offered a book to Jadon that she thought might interest him and he accepted it eagerly. *'He is so hungry to have more knowledge. He'll go far in this world with that kind of attitude.'* She would enjoy challenging him. His sister Charlotte was on the shy side and couldn't wait to attend school. Her main interest was in animals. She had shown Sarah her pet bunny, named 'Whiskers'. Sarah believed that every child was unique and all had a talent to do something special. She felt that it was her job to help the children to find their talent. Sometimes it was very obvious but other times it took a little digging and exploring.

Richard was up bright and early the morning after his meeting with Doc and Pastor. He wouldn't have taken the time for more than just a cup of coffee except his wife insisted on his having a decent breakfast first. He knew that Jennie was always looking out for him, but now he felt that he was going to be bringing in a good income for the first time in their marriage and he could hardly wait. Charlie brought him over a heaping plate of fried potatoes, eggs, sausage and fried bread, along with a refill on his coffee. "Please sit down for a minute Charlie. I'd like to get to know you better."

"I guess I could sit down for a minute or two. I hear that you like to make furniture, sir."

"Oh please, call me Richard. I'd like us to be friends. Are you and Martha happy with your room?"

"Happy? There ain't no words to say how we feel. Neither of us have ever had much and we are about as happy as it is possible to be. Everything seemed so hopeless to us, as far as getting married. I never heard that woman complain about anything, but now you can't wipe that smile off of her face. We'll be beholden to you till the day we die."

"I wish it was that easy to bring happiness into the lives of everyone. I've known a lot of folks over the years who had a lot of fancy things and were just down right miserable. You and Martha are wonderful examples of true happiness. This breakfast was about the best I've ever eaten Charlie, but I can't eat this much every morning. Can we settle on fixing me two eggs and some fried bread or a biscuit? My pants are feeling mighty snug from just this one meal but it was sure worth it. Thanks a lot Charlie. I've got to run down to the shop now and start cleaning it up. You won't be able to recognize it in a few days."

"I'll fix you anything you want, Richard. I'm mighty pleased that you like my cookin'. We are all sure happy with you and Jennie taking over this hotel. I gotta admit that some of us was plumb worried about maybe you letting us go. Martha and I love workin' here and now that we have our own room, we couldn't ask for anything more."

Russell Anderson, better known as 'Rusty', was the youngest son of three boys. There was only two years' difference between him and his older brother Johnny and many times they were mistaken as twins. Rusty had let his dark black hair grow long and it touched his shoulders. His coal black eyes had a way of making him look angry sometimes when he really wasn't. His beard and moustache made him look older, which he liked. The boots that he wore had a special heel that made him an extra inch taller. He had struggled all of his life to live up to his two older brothers, especially Johnny. It just seemed that no matter what he did, it wasn't good enough or he wasn't fast enough. Discouragement started to set in by the time he turned 16 and he started looking for other ways to feel important. He hung out with the wrong bunch and almost got arrested for stealing money from a ranch house. Luckily the kid who actually stole the money got caught.

His pa acted like he was ashamed of Rusty and that tore him up inside. Why couldn't he understand how hard it was to make people notice him without it being in a negative way? It wasn't like he never tried to do good things. When he turned 18, he left home and he was sure it was a relief to his pa and his brothers. Well, maybe not to Johnny. Rusty had to admit that he was always sticking up for him.

When the Civil War started, Rusty's two brothers signed up right away but he put it off as long as he could. When he was released from the Civil War, Rusty got involved with a small gang looking for easy money.

He was guilty just by association with a gang known for robbing banks. Rusty had just held their horses for them one day and that was enough. Somehow his name came up and he was on a wanted poster. Now he had no choice but to keep on the run. He wondered if his brothers would ever find out. That made Rusty hang his head in shame. Now that the war was over, he had no way to know if his brothers were safe. He couldn't write home because there was nowhere for anyone to answer him by sending a letter. Maybe someday he could go back. Somehow, during the war, his father's attorney had tracked him down to let him know of his parents passing away. He felt sad that he wouldn't see his mother again but he had to admit that not seeing his father was a relief.

Not too long after sending a letter to David, a wire came in from him. "Letter received." STOP "Glad you are safe." STOP "Would like to move near you." STOP "Purchased several horses to sell." STOP "Will contact my friend for you." STOP "Will write letter soon."

Johnny was so excited! He just had to tell someone the news and the first person he thought of was Elizabeth. He walked over to Doc's office in a rush and opened the door quickly.

His sudden appearance startled Elizabeth but when she saw the big smile on Johnny's face, she relaxed. "What brings you in here with such a big smile?"

"I just got a telegram from my brother. He wanted to let me know that he received my letter to let him know where I've moved. That's not all! He is going to be moving somewhere close by. I can hardly believe this. I'm about to burst so I had to tell someone and, ah, I decided to come and find you Elizabeth."

That remark put a pink blush on Elizabeth's cheeks, and she couldn't hide it. "I'm very happy for you Johnny and I look forward to meeting your brother." Now neither one knew what to say next. Thankfully a woman came in with her sick child and Elizabeth had to excuse herself to help her. Johnny nodded and turned around and left. *'It sure did feel good telling Elizabeth my good news; better than I had expected.'*

Doc and Pastor had lived in Willow Bend the longest and were highly regarded by the majority of the villagers. They realized that now that the Civil War was behind them, many strangers would be either passing through their village or possibly wanting to make a new start for themselves. They both agreed that the village needed a sheriff and they wanted to be prepared. It didn't make sense to wait until an emergency came up and then start looking around for a sheriff. Neither one of them felt they needed to look any further than to Johnny. He had served in the Civil War for four years as a sharpshooter and had risked his life to save Samuel.

Johnny was sitting down by the river with his cane pole and a can of worms, looking mighty contented when Doc and Pastor found him. "Would you mind some company Johnny?"

"Of course, I wouldn't mind. What are you two up to? You look mighty serious, to me."

Doc spoke first, "Johnny, we would like to offer you the job of sheriff of Willow Bend. You are our first choice and hopefully, our only choice. The job would start fairly quickly and comes with a nice monthly salary." Johnny didn't usually get caught off guard but this was something that had never crossed his mind.

Pastor decided to jump into the conversation. "Johnny, everyone has a high regard and respect for you. We need someone who not only is good with a gun but also has the kind of temperament that is cool and calm in an emergency."

Johnny could feel the wheels turning in his mind and he replied, "I would be honored to accept your offer, gentlemen. I can start early next week. I just want to tie up some loose ends before I start this job. I'd like to ride out each day and meet the families that live on the outskirts of town and learn my way around better." Pastor and Doc were so relieved that their offer had been accepted so quickly. They excused themselves so that Johnny could finish catching some fish.

Elizabeth felt her decision to move to Willow Bend was a wonderful decision if Johnny hadn't suddenly appeared in Doc's office with Maggie and a baby. The children were happy except for the fact that they wanted to live in the country where they could have pets. When she explained to them that it would be a few years off, they sadly said that would be fine. There wasn't anything that she could do to speed up the process unless God intervened somehow. In the meantime, she tried not to see too much of Johnny but that was almost impossible. He seemed to be everywhere that she went and of course her children talked nonstop about him. Now they were begging her to invite him to join them for dinner. She couldn't come up with any excuse that the children would understand so she grudgingly gave in and told them that they could invite him for tomorrow night. It wasn't an hour later that they burst into Doc's office to tell her that he had gladly accepted the invitation.

Elizabeth got off work the next day and decided to take a bath before dressing for dinner. When she was standing in front of the mirror with her robe on, she heard a knock on her door. It was Maude asking if she could come in for a minute. Maude stepped into the room and said, "I heard that Johnny will be joining you and the kids for dinner tonight. I have been knitting you an evening shawl and thought you might like to wear it tonight." She handed it to Elizabeth and it was a deep maroon and very soft and beautiful.

"Oh Maude, I adore it. Yes, I'll wear it tonight."

"I'm glad that you like it Elizabeth. It will make your pretty eyes stand out. I don't think that you spend much time buying things for yourself. Your children are just like my grandchildren and I love all of you dearly."

Elizabeth gave her a hug and kissed her on the cheek. "Maude, I don't know what we would do without you. We are so far away from any family. We have all adopted you into our family. Thank you for the thoughtful gift."

When she entered the dining room, Johnny was already sitting down with the children at the table and they were both talking to him at once. As soon as Johnny noticed Elizabeth, he stood up and held out a chair for her. "Elizabeth, I was very pleased to be invited to join you and the children tonight. Thank you for the invitation."

Elizabeth took her seat and said, "You are very welcome. According to the children, you are a very busy man. I was surprised to hear that you are now our sheriff."

Johnny said, "It was a big surprise to me, as well. After listening to Samuel talk about Willow Bend for several weeks, it helped me to fit right in." They ordered their dinner and then she gave the children a chance to ask Johnny more questions and tell them about their day. He sincerely looked interested and a couple of times they made him laugh out loud, which delighted them. When they had finished eating dinner, Maude suddenly appeared at the table. "Children, if it is alright with your mother, I have a surprise for you in the kitchen." Naturally they were both out of their seats instantly, but Elizabeth hadn't answered Maude yet. Elizabeth looked up at Maude who had the most innocent smile on her face, but Elizabeth wasn't deceived.

"You may go with Maude but behave yourselves."

"I'll take them back to their room and will read them some stories and get them ready for bed."

Now Johnny and Elizabeth were sitting there alone except for a few people at the other end of the long table. Elizabeth knew she didn't look very comfortable, but Johnny acted like nothing was wrong and he said, "You are doing a terrific job raising the children Elizabeth. I know it can't be easy doing it alone. They lift my spirits every time I'm around them."

His comment helped her to relax and she smiled and said, "I hope they aren't wearing you down with their constant questions. They obviously look up to you a great deal."

Johnny shook his head and smiled and replied, "Your children remind me of myself when I was young. I must have driven my older brother crazy back then. I followed him everywhere like a little shadow and asked so many questions, 'cause I was so eager to be like him. I've recently purchased a ranch a few miles outside of the village. Once I get settled, I'd be tickled to have you and the children out to see the ranch and check out all of the animals." This last comment caught Elizabeth off guard. *He is really serious about settling down here.* Somehow this evening hadn't turned out as bad as Elizabeth was expecting.

Johnny was walking down the street when he decided to check to see if he had any mail. Not many people knew where he was but he could always hope. He had written his brother to let him know more about the ranch he had purchased and some of his plans.

To his delight, there was a letter from David. He wrote "I am doing fine and can't wait to see you again. I am using part of my inheritance to start a horse ranch. I have no desire to stay here where we grew up, so if you have no objections, I would like to find a ranch in a village near you. I have hired my friend to track down your missing child. I was sorry to hear about this. He is the best there is and I have a lot of faith in him." The last part of the letter was hard to read. "Rusty is in trouble. He got mixed up with some rough men. Apparently, they decided to rob a bank and asked Rusty to watch their horses for them. Now his face is on a wanted poster, but no one knows where the gang is. Please let me know if you have heard anything." David didn't know that he was now the sheriff and would have access to the wanted posters. It hurt to know that their youngest brother was in with the wrong kind of people. He walked back to the jail and pulled out the pile of wanted posters and his heart sunk when he saw Rusty's face staring back at him. *'Oh Rusty, what have you gotten yourself into now?'*

Jeffrey Miller had been waiting for his brother to return for several weeks now and his anxiety was growing more each day. Rafe had promised to come back and get him after they had stolen the gold from the stagecoach back in July, but he had never returned. He was just sick with worry, having no way to know what had gone wrong. *'Has Rafe been killed or hurt;*

was he in jail somewhere or had he decided not to split the gold with Jeffrey?' He couldn't stay around here any longer; he would try to find someone who had information on the robbery. Jeffrey wished that he had paid closer attention to what his brother had told him. What was the name of the place where they were going to hold up the stage? His mind was totally blank. Surely his brother would not have abandoned him on purpose! He refused to believe that this was what happened. Rafe was the only family that he had left in this world.

Will was liking this village more and more every day. He had hoped in the beginning that either Sarah or Elizabeth might be the right woman for him. They had both quickly turned out to be good friends. It was amusing to watch Pastor whenever he was around Sarah. Will thought that Sarah needed a stronger man, but he was no expert in the romance department. Elizabeth seemed to be interested in Johnny, so that meant he could not pursue that relationship. He'd run across Norma a couple of times in the hotel dining room and she was always rude or uppity to every woman that crossed her path. *'I think if the right man put her across his lap and gave her bottom a good strong whack or two, she just might straighten up.'* That thought made him laugh to himself. He was enjoying his job at the bank, which gave him a good chance to meet more people. A couple of the young ladies had caught his eye, but he had decided to go slow before giving either of them any encouragement.

Franklin traveled four to six hours each night, except when there wasn't any moon shining. One morning when he was trying to decide which direction to head that evening, he decided to read an old newspaper that he had found caught up in some bushes. As he read through the paper, it was good to catch up on what was going on in the country, since the war had ended. All of a sudden, one name jumped out at him and it was Doc's. There was an article about Doc's practice in Willow Bend and how he had invented several different kinds of medicine from herbs that grew nearby. It mentioned some of the neighboring towns that used Doc because they didn't have their own doctor. From signs that he had recently seen on the road he was following, if he turned east, he would be about 100 miles from Willow Bend. Franklin had always felt that the good Lord was watching over him and leading him, so he considered this a sign to change direction. Now he had a destination and he felt hope welling up inside.

7
AUGUST 1865

Telling the Truth Is Sometimes Painful

It took Franklin a week to get close to Willow Bend because he wasn't traveling during the day. He had found a place to camp that had a stream nearby and he took a bath right as the sun was slowly coming up. He shaved and changed into the set of clean clothes that the chaplain had packed in his saddlebag. Even though he didn't intend to let anyone see him, he felt that as a matter of pride, he should look his best. Later tonight, he would reach Willow Bend and try to find a safe place to make camp. Once he got settled, he would have to find a way to exercise his horse in the evening, if even for a short while. Beauty had brought him this far and he wanted to be sure that she wasn't neglected. As he approached Willow Bend, the hotel was easy to spot because of its size. He led Beauty off the main road and in between the hotel and the store next to it. He slowly followed the fence line until he found an old gate that hadn't been used in a long time, from the looks of it. He got down off his horse and checked out the hinge and though it was stiff, he managed to get it open. He led Beauty through the opening and turned around and shut it. The next thing was to try and find some kind of path or trail. The moon was shining bright; otherwise he might have missed the path running directly behind the hotel. Just knowing that he was close to Doc and the chaplain made him feel a lot safer. It looked like someone had recently used this path, but the space wasn't very wide. No horse had been through here and probably not even an adult. Franklin was going to have to be very careful, making sure not to be discovered. If children were playing out here in these woods, he sure didn't want to scare them. He walked back as far as he dared and found a clearing big enough to tie up Beauty and set up his little tent. Somehow, he was going to have to find a way to get food and he wasn't about to steal from anyone. Doc had mentioned that there was a stream in these woods and he would start looking for it tomorrow. That would take care of the problem of water for his horse and himself and he could fish there. At least now he had made a decision of where to go and he knew that he had two good friends in this village.

Johnny was allowing himself a couple of hours to relax and naturally the first thing he thought about was fishing. He was having some good luck today and he could almost taste those fish coming out of his frying pan tonight. "Would you mind some company?"

He turned around and to his surprise, there stood Sarah with a cane pole and a can of worms. "Of course, I wouldn't mind. I've never known a woman who liked to go fishing before. You never cease to amaze me, Sharpshooter." In just seconds, she had plopped down in the grass and was reaching in the can for a worm.

He just stared at her as she managed to put the worm on the hook the first time she tried. She swung her line out into the river and looked so relaxed. *'Well, this is a first for me. I'm actually fishing with a woman.'*

Not only was she fishing and baiting her own hook, but she wasn't chattering away like most women. As the afternoon wore on, they had both caught a mess of fish. They had talked back and forth very little, which was perfect. As she got up to leave, she said, "Thank you for allowing me to join you. This was so relaxing and now I'll make Charlie a happy man. See you later."

He just chuckled as she walked away, swinging her bucket of fish and not caring at all that her hair was falling down in the back. *'She acts like she doesn't have a care in the world. Wonder what that feels like?'*

Bucky Sanders was so relieved to be released from fighting in the Civil War, but at least he had some friends back then. During the war he had been assigned to take care of all of the horses that were hurt or exhausted and he enjoyed his job. It hurt him to see any of them suffer, so he poured his heart into giving them the best treatment he was able to give. When he was discharged, there really wasn't any home to go back to. His mama had run off years ago on account of his papa's drinking. Bucky was only 14 then and now he was 20 and he still missed her. She used to sing church songs while she was working around their home and she had a habit of walking past him and running her hand along his back. That gentle touch had more affection in it then a lot of words that could be forgotten. Her name was Clara and he could still remember the love in her eyes when she looked at him. Because of the numerous beatings, she just couldn't take it anymore and Bucky was not strong enough to defend her. That made him so embarrassed when he thought about it. At first he wasn't aware of it, but somehow his anger had come to the surface and he realized that he blamed her for abandoning him. Living with his father was a miserable experience. If he wasn't drunk and cussing at him, he was passed out and rarely able to work. Bucky had tried to find odd jobs to buy some food. He had even resorted to stealing food a few times and he was ashamed of what he had done, but he was desperate.

When the war ended, somehow by stowing away on one train after another, he had ended up about 20 miles from Willow Bend. While walking down the road one night, someone had hit him over the head and stolen the only thing that meant anything to him; his grandpa's pocket watch. He had felt so proud, keeping that watch in his pocket. He was always careful not to pull it out of his pocket when someone else was close by. When he woke up with a lump on his head, he didn't know which way to start walking. Finally, he just started putting one foot in front of the other and a few days later, he came to Willow Bend. He noticed the livery stable and went over and asked if he could please sleep in the hay. The owner took one look at Bucky and felt like this was someone who needed a break. He led him to an empty stall, filled with clean hay. When Bucky had just got settled down, the owner came back with a cold cup of water and a rib full of meat. Bucky hadn't eaten in two days and it looked like a banquet. The owner had asked him if he would like a part-time job, keeping the stables clean and feeding the horses. Bucky jumped at the chance. He needed a job and he needed to eat.

Today, Bucky was walking one of the horses around for some exercise, when some of the school children came walking by and he sensed trouble. The oldest boy was taller than the rest and he never passed up the chance to cause trouble. He pointed at Bucky and said in a mocking voice, "Look at poor Bucky; his teeth are all crooked and he sleeps with the animals." Some of the kids started laughing and their laughter cut deep, but he didn't say a word. The same kid decided he needed some more laughs so he said, "Bucky's got no friends except for the animals."

This time he got a reaction but it was from one of the young girls. He knew her name was Julia because she was the only child who had ever smiled and talked to him. Julia said very boldly, "Stop that mean talk Bradley. He is my friend."

Bradley was shocked to see a young girl standing up to him but he wasn't about to back down in front of every one. "Bucky doesn't take a bath and he stinks 'cause he sleeps with the animals."

Jadon was one of the children in the group. He wanted so much to stand up for Bucky like Julia was doing, but he was afraid of Bradley. He really tried hard to find the courage, but it just wasn't there. This was too much for Julia to take. She ran across the dirt path with her head bent down like a billy goat and plowed right into Bradley's stomach. He let out a yell and down he went. Johnny just happened to be coming around the corner and he had heard Bradley's last comment and also Julia's. He was so proud of that girl his buttons could have popped, but he couldn't let her know it. He walked over and quickly helped the boy up, who was now very embarrassed and mad. "Did you see what Julia did to me, sheriff? She knocked me down with no cause."

Johnny said, "If I were you, I wouldn't be advertising that a little girl knocked me down. Besides, I heard the mean things you said about Bucky. I am also his friend and proud of it. You go on home and I'll be by to talk to your parents shortly." He turned his attention to Julia who was standing there, waiting for her punishment. He sent the other kids on their way home so he could talk to Julia privately. "Little bit, you've got to learn to hold your temper. You can't fight everyone who says things that are unkind."

Julia finally looked up and stared him in the face. "Go ahead and punish me but I'll never say I'm sorry that I did that. I couldn't have stopped myself; my heart hurt so badly." She walked over to Bucky and said, "Bradley doesn't understand how hurtful those words are Bucky. He doesn't have a happy home life; but that's no excuse for being cruel. I love you Bucky!" and she reached up and gave him a hug.

"You go back to the hotel and I'll be over later to talk to your mama." Julia waved goodbye to Bucky and headed off, her shoulders back and her head up high. Johnny was trying not to chuckle out loud. *'Man, she needs a father in the worst way.'*

"Bucky, I'm sorry for what just happened, but you sure have a wonderful friend in Julia. You couldn't ask for a better friend than that. I'll see you later."

Johnny had mentioned to Pastor James what Bucky had just been through, so he decided to go by and check on him. "Bucky, I've been thinking about taking a carriage ride out into the country, but I am not too comfortable around horses. I was wondering if you would be willing to show me how it's done, whenever you are not working. I feel pretty foolish that I haven't made the effort before this."

"I'd be happy to show you Pastor. I'll be finished with taking care of the horses in about an hour. How about I swing by the church with a carriage and pick you up then?"

"That would work out just fine. I'll pay for the rental of the carriage right now."

"No sir, you won't have to do that. I'm allowed to use them for free on my time off. I'll see you soon."

Bucky showed up right on time and he earnestly explained in total detail, all about how to be gentle with the horses and not to use the whip and how to set the brake. As they were riding down a pretty country road, Pastor said, "I know that Johnny thinks a lot of you Bucky. He's mentioned often how much you care about the horses and that they follow you around whenever you are feeding or brushing them."

"I know every horse by name and how they like to be brushed and if they have a sore spot that they don't like to have touched. Sometimes I talk to them when I am feelin' down."

"Bucky, I'd like you to know that I will always be ready to listen when you feel sad. If something good happens and you want to share it with someone who cares, that would be nice too. I really believe that you are going to have a good future here in our village. I appreciate your showing me how to drive a carriage. I might want you to show me one more time, if you wouldn't mind."

"I'd be happy to Pastor. I can go with you any day that you want, once my horses have been taken care of. I liked being with you. Johnny has always been good to me but I don't have many friends." They arrived back in the village and Bucky dropped Pastor off at the church. Pastor was feeling good about the time they had just spent together.

When Jadon got home, his mother offered him a snack and he shook his head. He went straight to his room and laid down on his bed. His mother came in to see if he had a fever, but there was no sign of one. "Jadon, is something bothering you? I've never seen you turn down a snack before."

Jadon was struggling to get the words out but finally he said, "I'm ashamed of myself mama. Today Bradley was making fun of Bucky and a lot of us kids were there. No one stood up for him except for Julia. I wanted to be brave like her but I didn't say a word. How do you ever learn to have courage? I was so scared of Bradley that I couldn't speak."

"There will be lots of times in your life when you'll need courage when you are afraid of something. I've learned that if you start out with something small that you are afraid of and you face that fear, the next time you face anything that scares you, you will remember how good it felt when you didn't back down. Somehow that makes it easier. Each time you have a victory in that area, your fear isn't as strong. I know that you have a kind heart Jadon and I'm so proud of you. I promise to pray about this and I feel sure that you will receive some encouragement soon. Now, how about some cookies and milk?" This time he jumped off the bed and raced into the kitchen.

Johnny had a stern talk with Bradley's parents and said that he wanted their son to come by the sheriff's office right after school the next day. His parents didn't look happy but they didn't stick up for their son either. Next stop was to talk to Elizabeth. *'How am I going to handle this? My relationship with her is never easy. Sometimes she looks at me with such tenderness and then before you knew it, she is furious with me about something.'* He knew her schedule at Doc's and timed his visit right when she was getting off for the day. "I need to talk to you about Julia." He could see her shoulders get tense. He led her down a side street that had a bench under a big oak tree and asked her to sit. He explained what he had witnessed today and he saw Elizabeth bite her lips, as if she was trying not to laugh. That was encouraging!

When she got herself under control, she said, "Johnny, I've got my hands full trying to raise her properly. She has a wonderful teacher and lives for school, and she is friends with just about everyone in this village. I want her to defend someone who is being picked on, like Bucky, but I need to have some sort of punishment for the way she knocked Bradley down. Do you have any suggestions? I'm willing to listen! She looks up to you so much; sometimes I think you know her better than I do."

It forced Elizabeth to talk to him and she wasn't upset with him. He ran a few ideas through his mind and then said, "I think I might have a couple of ideas. If she can go a month without losing her temper, I'll take her for a ride around my ranch and I'll also invite Timothy. I know he is crazy about horses. If she makes it for a month and gets her reward and then something happens afterwards that makes her lose her temper, I'll have to come up with something more serious." Elizabeth was so relieved that she didn't have to come up with something.

Elizabeth said, "She is going to have to go to Bradley's house tomorrow and apologize to him."

Johnny shook his head slightly, "Normally, I would agree with you, but if Julia apologized to him, it wouldn't be sincere. She wasn't the least bit sorry and even told me so."

Sarah was excited about the first day of her teaching school in Willow Bend. Since she had already brought her own supplies, there would be less for her to have to purchase. This village was small but there were about 12 children that were going to start school next week. Sarah was very organized and had already created a list of her students and made a special effort to introduce herself to all of her student's parents. She was especially impressed with Isaac and Melissa, who were going into the 11th grade. Isaac had told her that he had attended an Indian School back in Arizona but that didn't seem to be holding him back any. Sarah had several suggestions and he listened eagerly to everything she told him. He had already volunteered to write some of the lessons on the blackboard for Sarah, on the first day of school.

Isaac was running like the wind, on his way to his first day of school in this small village. He could hear thunder off in the distance and hopefully he could make it to school before a storm hit. No matter what Isaac was doing, his thoughts were constantly on horses. He wanted one of his own but right now that was out of the question. He had no idea where to even start in trying to earn some money, but he wasn't one to give up easily. Somehow, he had inherited a lot of determination and he intended to use it to own a horse.

His long lean legs felt like they were barely touching the dirt road and then off they went to eat up some more distance. Isaac was one quarter Apache and had learned a lot from his grandfather. There really wasn't any subject that he didn't like, but geography and history were some of his favorites. Isaac lived fairly close to the school, which was an easy jaunt for him. His parents had made friends with a man named Dwight Evans, who had offered Isaac a place to live while attending school in Willow Bend. They would miss him, but they wanted the best education for him.

Isaac was prepared to be teased when the other students found out that he was part American Indian, but he didn't worry. He was proud of his heritage and was always trying to learn more about his proud people, the Apaches. Being able to run so fast and not tire easily was probably passed on by his ancestors. Isaac often thought about his grandfather, because he was so close to him, and he already missed him greatly. He wondered if he would ever see him again. As he was running, trees went by in a blur and he was aware of some small animals nearby. All of a sudden, he heard a soft whinny off to his left and he stopped quickly to listen better. The sound was coming from behind a pile of rocks, among the oak trees. He carefully walked towards the sound, not making any noise. In case of danger, he was prepared to flee as fast as he could. As he drew closer, he saw a horse lying on its side, and its eyes were full of fear. Isaac spoke softly to the animal in his native tongue and he knelt down beside the horses' head. He reached out slowly with his hand and stroked its head, all the while keeping up his soft conversation. He gently ran his hand over the horses' body; looking for any injury and he found a deep gouge in its side and a sharp splinter. He must have run into a fence, but there wasn't a lot of blood. His main concern for this type of injury would be infection. He had to make a quick decision about what to do. He could not leave this horse all alone while he was in school. He searched through the nearby woods and found some leaves to make a poultice, like his grandfather had taught him. He spoke to the horse and told him that he had to leave, but that he would be back soon. Somehow, he felt as if the horse understood what he had told it. He ran back to Dwight's and found an old blanket and a tin can, which he filled with water. When he returned, the horse was still lying down, but didn't seem to be in as much pain. He gave it some water slowly and covered it with a blanket. He gently urged the horse to stand and then slowly walked him back to Dwight's farm. He found Dwight feeding the dogs and explained about the horse. Dwight promised to keep an eye on him while Isaac was in school.

Johnny had been driving some horses into a new corral when a barking dog startled one of the horses. He looked up when he heard pounding hoofs and saw a spotted Lakota horse take off down the road. He ran to his horse and jumped on bareback and tried to follow the horse. His horse was fast, but the runaway was so scared that it had gotten a good head start. He realized that the horse must have run into a nearby field or woods. He rode back and forth for over an hour without spotting it and finally gave up for the night. That horse was very unique and special, and he certainly didn't want to lose it. He would spread the word among the village people and go back out again tomorrow.

The next day he came into the village early, just as the schoolchildren were heading to the schoolhouse. He decided to ask Sarah if he could talk briefly to the children about his missing horse and she readily agreed. When all of the children were settled down in their seats, he was introduced to the class and he stood at the front beside the teacher. "I won't take up too much of your time this morning, but I'm spreading the word all over the village about a very special horse of mine that ran away yesterday. I purchased this spotted Lakota along with several other horses recently. I am hoping that he didn't run too far. There is a small reward for anyone who can give me any information that will help me find my horse. Thank you for your time."

Isaac sat in his seat with a knot in his stomach and his heart pounding. It was foolish of him to think that he could actually keep this horse. Now that he knew who the owner was, he had to tell the truth, but he felt sick inside.

He raised his hand and the teacher said, "Isaac, do you have something that you'd like to tell the sheriff?" Johnny looked over at a teenage boy who looked so sad and he knew inside that this boy had found his horse.

The boy replied, "Yesterday when I was on my way to school, I was running past the woods, and I found a horse lying on its side. When I got closer, I could see a piece of wood caught in its side. I removed the wood and then prepared a poultice. Then I ran home for a blanket and water. The horse hadn't moved so I doctored him up with some medicine and brought it some water. I managed to get the horse to its feet and slowly walked it to Dwight's farm. I can take you there now if the teacher will excuse me for awhile."

Johnny was so relieved to hear that his horse had been found and taken care of. He was also deeply touched that this boy had not only taken good care of the horse but was honest enough to admit that he had the horse at his home. The teacher said it would be fine for him to go with the sheriff so they both left and headed for the buckboard. Isaac was very quiet and was trying to hide his disappointment, but it was obvious that this was not easy for him to do.

While they rode to Dwight's in the buckboard, he was trying to prepare himself emotionally to say goodbye to the horse who didn't even have a name. He wanted the sheriff to see him as a young man who was able to handle life when it didn't turn out the way he wanted it to. As they rode into the lane that lead to Dwight's farm, Johnny saw a lean-to and his horse was standing with his ears alert. As they walked over to the horse, they were both amazed when the horse whinnied and reached his head over to nuzzle Isaac. There was no way to wipe the grin off of his face, no matter how hard he tried. Johnny said, "I think you have made a friend here." They tied the horse to the back of the buckboard and headed back to Johnny's ranch at a slow pace. Isaac kept turning to check on the horse and was always relieved when he was there, patiently walking behind them. Johnny dropped him off at the schoolhouse. "I want to thank you for taking such good care of my horse" and he reached in his vest for some money.

As he started to hand it to the boy, Isaac shook his head and said, "No sir, I don't want any reward. I have been raised better than that. I would like to ask you one thing though. Would it be alright for me to come out and visit the horse sometimes?"

Johnny was a good judge of character and he knew that this boy was very special. He looked at Isaac and said, "I would welcome your visits and so would my horse."

About a week later, Johnny saw Isaac as he was leaving school and he offered to take him out to his ranch. Johnny had just picked up one of his horses from the blacksmith's shop, so he told him to ride this horse. Isaac wasn't really expecting much in his mind as far as what the sheriff's ranch would look like. He assumed there would be some kind of a house and a barn and some corrals. Other than that, he hadn't pictured much else. When they turned into the long entrance to the ranch, he immediately sat up straight and was almost in shock at what he was looking at. There was a house alright, but there was also a second one set off down a dirt path, and there were two beautifully built barns and two storage sheds, along with several corrals full of horses of many varieties. He didn't know what to do first, so he jumped off the buckboard and asked Johnny where his wounded horse was. Johnny said, "Isaac, I think this horse deserves a name after what he has been through. How would you like to name him?"

Isaac had to turn his head a little so that the wetness in his eyes wouldn't show. He took a deep breath and said, "I think Thunder would be a perfect name for him. I think he will like that name sir."

Johnny wholeheartedly agreed and nodded his appreciation. As they walked to the barn, where Thunder was being kept, animals of every kind seemed to want to come close to the boy. He was so gentle with all of the animals and when he reached out to pet any of them, none of them shied away. Johnny decided to test one specific animal's reaction to Isaac and so he led Isaac over to a large black stallion who was pawing the ground and shaking its head up and down repeatedly. Johnny climbed over the fence and approached the stallion and it came up on its hind legs and was pawing the air. Johnny didn't back away but just held his ground and stood there silently. Before he realized what was happening, he saw Isaac coming up to the stallion softly, murmuring something that Johnny didn't understand. The horse immediately stopped pawing the air and came down only a few feet from him. That horse had been abused and Johnny had rescued it but hadn't had the time to work with him very much. The horse suddenly started walking toward Isaac, and put his nose in his hand. Isaac reached out slowly and stroked the horse's nose and continued to speak to it in a dialect Johnny had never heard. Isaac noticed the way Johnny was looking at him and he decided to share something about his past.

"I am part Apache sir and my grandfather taught me how to treat animals with respect and how to make medicine for their injuries. That is how I knew how to take care of Thunder. I feel this horse has been beaten, but he still has a heart to try and trust again."

Johnny immediately made up his mind; he would offer Isaac a job on his ranch. "Son, I am very impressed with the way that you have treated all of the animals and especially how you doctored up Thunder. I would like to offer you a job on my ranch after school and weekends with as many hours as you want to work." Isaac just stood there silently, drinking in the words spoken to him. Not only could he work on such a wonderful ranch surrounded by so many animals, but he would also be paid for it. He said, "It would be an honor to work for you sir."

"One more thing! I believe that you saved Thunder's life, so he should belong to you. I will write up the paperwork to prove that this is your horse. Will that be okay with you?"

"Thank you, sir!" He walked over to Thunder and wrapped his arms around him and stayed that way for a few minutes; letting tears run down his face in private.

Samuel was just coming out of the barn and Johnny walked Isaac over to introduce him. "Samuel, I'd like you to meet our new hired hand, Isaac. He has a definite gift with animals and I'd like you to be thinking about what ways you can use him around the ranch. He'll be working some after school and over the weekends too, if he wants to."

Samuel lifted his hand out to him and said, "Son, I can surely use some more help around here. I look forward to working with you."

Isaac had a big grin on his face. "It's nice to meet you sir. I'll encourage Johnny to buy all of the animals he can afford because I enjoy working with them. I'll do whatever you ask me to do."

Samuel & Rebecca couldn't have been any happier. Surviving the war, along with their son, was something that they would often thank the Good Lord for. Every time anyone came close to them, there was always a wonderful smile to greet them. Rebecca was constantly cooking and baking, and no one was complaining about that. She never took off her apron until she was ready to go to bed. She smelled like a mixture of all the good things she was creating in her kitchen. They had never had much in life but you would never hear either of them complain. They were both so pleased to see Jacob spending a lot of time with Emily.

Rebecca had to bite her tongue not to mention her strong desire to be a grandmother. Samuel wouldn't admit it out loud but she knew that he felt the same way about being a grandfather.

Not even a week later, Jacob was back at Emily's, holding some wildflowers in his hand. When she opened the door, she looked startled and then pleased when she noticed the flowers. Jacob looked a little uncomfortable, but he managed to say, "These are for you Emily. I hope you like them." She never expected any man to pay attention to her now that she was carrying a child. What would people in the village think? She had a feeling that it wasn't going to bother Jacob at all. She didn't invite him in this time because

the situation was different. He wasn't running an errand for his mother, like the first time he came by. Jacob said, "Miss Emily, would you care to take a walk with me? We won't be gone long."

They walked to the edge of town to the bench under the big oak tree. Jacob led her to the bench and then stood there beside her. They talked for a long time about their childhoods and how much they liked this village and how Jacob wanted to be a rancher. Soon it was time to go back and they were both becoming relaxed with each other. Now he had found out how to make Emily laugh and she even started teasing him sometimes. Their walks turned into a daily routine, unless it was raining.

One day Rebecca came to visit and she had brought tea and cookies. They had a wonderful time talking about the coming baby and Rebecca wanted to know how Emily was feeling. "I am feeling very healthy and I'm walking every day, thanks to Jacob. Her cheeks got a little pink when she said that. Emily said, "Do you mind that Jacob comes by to walk with me Rebecca? Is there talk in the village about us?"

Rebecca smiled and said, "I am all in favor of you and Jacob taking walks. As far as the villagers go, only a few comments have been made, but only from those who complain about every single subject they can think of. Emily, what are your plans after the baby comes? Will you have someone to watch the baby while you are sewing?"

"A few weeks ago, Mrs. Benson offered to let Maggie, and her children, and myself and my baby, move into her large home. She said that it will be a blessing to her because she is so lonely, plus we help out a lot with cooking and cleaning. She has been so good to us and we will take good care of her in return."

"I can't wait to get my hands on your baby, Emily. Since you don't have any family, I am hoping that you can look at me as a mother. I love babies and having you for a friend has made me very happy. I know that Jacob is sure smiling a lot more than usual after he has come back from spending time with you. Well, I need to go back and start cooking. Please let Jacob know when you'd like to come out to the ranch for a visit. I would welcome your company." They hugged each other and said their goodbyes.

Maggie's baby, Dinah, was growing so fast and her son Wesley just adored her. If her husband would just come home from the war, their life would be complete. She knew that her son was hurting, and she tried to comfort him as much as she could. Living with

Mrs. Benson was wonderful. It gave her someone to talk to and she enjoyed helping her around the house. Wesley was doing his best to be helpful by clearing the table after their meals and running errands for anyone who needed him.

Callie Brown, a young woman who worked at the post office, came up the walk at the Benson home. This was unusual because Maggie checked at the post office every day for mail. She came up to the steps and handed Maggie an envelope that was dirty and wrinkled but still readable. Callie turned around and started to leave when Maggie let out an agonizing cry. Callie quickly turned around and ran back. Maggie had dropped to the steps and was weeping and holding the letter, which was blowing back and forth in the breeze. Maggie managed to get out the words, "Please get Maude" and then she doubled over with grief.

8

AUGUST 1865

Very Interesting Guest Moves Into the Hotel

Callie ran as fast as she could to the hotel. Pastor was just leaving the dining room when he saw the look on Callie's face and ran up to her. "Callie, what is wrong?"

She looked up at Pastor and said, "I just delivered a letter to Maggie and it must be bad news. She let out a horrible cry and told me to get Maude." By then Maude had become aware that something had really upset Callie.

When she came across the lobby, Pastor told her quickly, "Maggie has asked for you. I am assuming it is about her husband. I'm going with you Maude."

It didn't take long to reach the Benson home and Maggie was still bent over, sobbing her heart out. Maude sat down beside her and held her in her arms and said, "Maggie, is it about your husband?" Maggie didn't say anything; she just handed Maude the letter. Maude rapidly read the letter and handed it to Pastor.

"Oh Maggie, I am so sorry for your loss. You are not alone. Can you tell me what we can do for you right now?"

Maggie's eyes were red and swollen and she just said, "Can someone tell Wesley? I don't think I can do it. I'll need someone to nurse the baby for a day or two."

Pastor said "I'll find Wesley and take him off by himself to explain."

"Pastor, please find Sarah and bring her back here, before you go to look for Wesley," said Maude.

Pastor was relieved that he would have a little extra time to prepare himself before talking to Wesley. He pulled his watch out of his pocket and realized that school had been let out a few minutes ago. Sarah usually stayed in the classroom for at least an hour afterwards, working on the children's paperwork. He reached the schoolhouse and Sarah heard his footsteps. One look at his face told her something was wrong.

"Is Maude ok? What's wrong?" Pastor told her about Maggie's news and that Maude was with her.

"Maude asked me to find you and bring you back to the Benson house."

"I'll leave as soon as I lock up the school, but I can go by myself. What about Wesley? Does he know yet? He went home with Julia and Timothy."

"I offered to tell him as soon as I found you. Maggie said she wasn't up to it. Sarah, I could use your prayers while I'm talking to him. He talks about his father coming home every time I see him. I hope I am up to this."

"Of course, I'll be praying for both of you and for Maggie and the baby. Thank you for coming for me, Pastor."

As Pastor walked to the hotel, he prayed the whole way. He asked God for strength and the right words. Wesley and the other kids were in the kitchen eating cookies and drinking milk and laughing. Pastor tried to keep his face calm as he walked up to them. "Hi kids; boy those cookies sure look good. Wesley, I'd like to talk to you outside for a minute." Wesley looked puzzled, but he followed Pastor out of the back door. Pastor took a deep breath and prayed one last time and then said, "Son, I'm so sorry to have to tell you this, but your father has passed away. Your mother received a wire today from your father's commander. I need to take you home right now."

Wesley just stared back at him like he was looking right through him. "That can't be true. There's been a mistake. We've been waiting for weeks for him to come home. He hasn't even seen the baby yet." Now the tears came out like a cloudburst and Pastor reached out and held him to his chest and he was crying too. He saw the kitchen door open and Charlie was standing there, looking concerned. Pastor just shook his head and Charlie went back inside.

When Pastor started to walk him home, Wesley jerked away and said, "Leave me alone. I don't need you; I don't need anybody. My father is coming home. He loves us and we need him."

Wesley took off at a dead run and Pastor just felt his heart crack in two. "Watch over them and protect them. Lord, please...I'm begging you."

A few days later, Hank was working at his blacksmith shop on a Saturday and suddenly he heard a crash and glass flew all over his shop. Luckily, he wasn't close enough to get hurt from the flying glass but it really startled him. Hank raced outside and saw a young boy running as fast as he could. Hank might be old compared to some young kid, but he could still run. He took off after him and was steadily catching up. Hank was so close and then he caught his foot on a root and almost fell headfirst. He must have let out a yell, because the boy stopped and turned around.

That was all that Hank needed to catch up with him. He grabbed him by the collar and turned him around. The boy's face was full of defiance, but also pain. Hank tried to catch his breath before speaking. Finally, he was able to say, "What on earth is wrong with you, young man? I've never done anything to you; I don't even know you. What is your name?"

The boy glared back at Hank and said, "My name is Wesley. My father just died and I'm so angry!" At that he started sobbing and dropped to the ground. Hank sat down on the ground next to him and patted his back over and over. He didn't say anything because there were no words to comfort a boy who had just lost his father.

A few minutes later, Hank stood and helped Wesley up. He said, "We are going to see the sheriff son. Do we need to see your mother first?"

"No", shouted Wesley. "She's already hurting enough. Please don't tell her." When they got to the sheriff's office, Hank kept a hold of the boy's arm, to make sure that he didn't try to run. Johnny's eyebrows went up when he saw Hank and the boy but he waited quietly for an explanation.

Hank nudged Wesley and said, "Tell the truth son."

To Wesley's credit, he looked straight at the sheriff and said, "I broke the window of his shop and I did it on purpose." Johnny looked over at Hank and he just nodded.

Johnny said, "Son, what reason did you have for doing such a mean thing?"

Wesley's head dropped, and he said, "I just found out that my father died. My mother received a letter a few days ago. We've been waiting weeks for him to come home to us."

Johnny knew how much this boy was hurting but he also believed that it wouldn't be good to let him off without some punishment. He said to Wesley, "Son, you are going to work in the blacksmith's shop for two months or until Hank says that you have earned enough to pay for a new window. You are also going to clean up that mess the first thing tomorrow. Now you go on home now. Thank you for being honest about what you did."

That afternoon, Hank walked Wesley home to talk to his mother. She was holding her new baby and looked like she had been crying. She waited quietly for her son to speak, knowing with her mother's instinct that he was in trouble. "Mother, I broke a window at Mr. Hawkins blacksmith's shop today 'cause I was so angry."

Maggie said softly, "I know that you are angry and hurt Wesley, but that gives you no right to take it out on an innocent person."

"The sheriff said I have to work at the blacksmith's shop until I pay for the window."

She looked at Wesley with so much affection in her eyes and she replied, "Yes Wesley, I think it is the right thing, to make up for the damage you caused. You must listen to everything Mr. Hawkins tells you and be very careful because there is danger being around that much heat. Now go inside and get washed up. Dinner will be ready soon, if you are hungry." Maggie turned to Hank and said, "I apologize that I didn't introduce myself. My name is Maggie and I am sorry for what my son did to your window."

Hank knew that she was going through a lot right now since she had recently lost her husband. "Ma'am, I understand what it's like to hurt when you lose someone you love. I lost my wife and son eight years ago to sickness and it still hurts. I am sorry for your loss. Wesley is a good boy and I'll try to help him any way that I can."

"Would you like to stay for dinner, Mr. Hawkins? We have plenty and it would be good to have some company."

"If there is somewhere for me to wash up, I'd be pleased to join you." When Wesley saw that he was joining them, he was happy but tried hard to hide it. Hank was thinking, *'I hope that I can make a difference in this boy's life.'* The meal was delicious and Hank thanked Maggie and said that he needed to go back and close up the shop. "I'll see you at eight o'clock in the morning." said Hank.

Wesley showed up the next morning, but he was dragging his feet. He picked up all of the mess and helped Hank put something over the window until the glass could be reinstalled. Hank gave him a break in the morning and gave him some cool water to drink. Wesley was curious about everything in the shop but didn't want it to be obvious. He looked over at Hank and said, "I'll be leavin' now."

"Not so fast son; there are other things you can do around here."

"I'm getting' tired!"

"You can go to bed early tonight. Those windows need washin.' I'll get the bucket and some rags."

Wesley was getting angry but he didn't want to get into any more trouble, so he shoved his anger inside. When he finished the windows, he said, "I'm finished now. See you tomorrow."

"Not before you dump the bucket of dirty water and rinse out the bucket and rags first. You should show some pride in your work, son, no matter how small the job is."

"Quit callin' me 'son'; I ain't your son. I'm glad I'm not your son." He stomped over and grabbed the bucket and took it outside and slung the dirty water out and then rinsed it and the rags out, obviously full of anger and pain. Hank watched him walk back into the shop and drop the bucket with a loud thud.

"You can go now Wesley and thank you for your work." As he watched Wesley walk down the road, a thought crossed his mind that shot pain unexpectedly into his heart. *'I wonder what my son would be like if he had lived? He would have been the same age as Wesley.'* The bitterness he felt against God started rising up and he didn't know what to do. He'd lived with this anger for so many years. Sometimes he wanted to get rid of it and other times it was almost comforting. If Pastor was praying for him like he'd said he would, it wasn't working. Nothing had changed, and he was wasting his time.

Will had been thinking about the idea of buying a house in the village. Nothing too big, but with a couple of extra bedrooms, just in case he ended up getting married one day. Since Sarah and Elizabeth had turned out to be great friends, he felt that he needed to be looking around more. Every time he saw Callie in the Post Office, she was always in a good mood and seemed happy to see him. He knew that she was raising a son and a daughter by herself and that couldn't be easy. He decided to ask her if she would like to join him for lunch at the café.

When he walked in the post office, she was busy sorting the day's mail. She looked up and said, "Hi Will, I'll be right with you."

"No rush. I just came by to ask you a question."

She finished her sorting and said, "How can I help you?"

"Well, I was wondering if you would like to join me for lunch at the café. You are allowed to eat, aren't you?" He laughed as he said this.

"I know that I probably look surprised, but I haven't had a man ask me to share a meal with him before. Yes, I would enjoy that very much. What day were you thinking about?"

"How about today? You just tell me the time and I'll come back for you."

"I'm ready right now. Just let me put a sign in the window to let folks know when I'll be back. Thank you for asking me Will."

At the café, they both found out that they had some things in common. Will had always been interested in older homes and so was Callie. They also both enjoyed riding horses. "Maybe someday I can borrow some horses from Johnny and we can take a ride out in the country."

"Oh, that sounds like fun. I don't get a chance to do much besides being a mother and my job. If you can just tell me a day ahead of time, I can schedule someone to fill in for me."

When Will took her back to the post office, he had a peace about him. Callie wasn't the kind of woman to get a man excited. What was important, is that she made him feel so comfortable, like he had known her for a long time. *'I think I'll enjoy getting to know her more and also her children.'*

Two weeks later Johnny had asked Maggie if she would please join him for dinner at the hotel. He said he had something to discuss with her that was important. Even though Maggie wasn't in the mood for going out in public, Johnny had become a wonderful friend, so she agreed. He hired a carriage and picked her up. He chose a place at the end of the long dining room table so that they could have more privacy. Johnny said, "Maggie, I've been wondering how you have been since you lost your husband?".

"I just manage to get through the day somehow with the Lord's strength. I go from feeling numb to such pain that I can hardly bear it. I worry a lot about

Wesley because his attitude is getting worse every day. He doesn't even try to hide his anger."

Johnny decided now was a good time to discuss something with her that would involve Wesley. "Maggie, I bought a large ranch recently and Samuel and his family have moved out there to help me run it. Samuel could use some help with feeding some of the animals and brushing the horses down. I was hoping for your permission to offer a part time job to Wesley. It won't interfere with his working at the blacksmith's shop. The pay won't be a lot, but he would be earning some spending money and being around animals seems to help people who are grieving."

Maggie stood up and walked around the end of the table and with tears streaming down her face, she reached up and put her hands on Johnny's face. Johnny stood up and put his arms around her shoulders lightly and patted her back. At that moment, Elizabeth walked into the room with Sarah and the look on her face was shock and anger. She turned around and left the hotel, with Sarah trying to catch up with her. Johnny saw her reaction and he was ready to have a heart-to-heart talk with Elizabeth, whether she wanted to or not. He walked Maggie out to the carriage and drove her home. At least he had managed to make one woman a little bit happier.

A wire came in for Johnny from his brother David saying: "Our friend making some progress." STOP. "I am also searching for your child." STOP. "Will keep you informed." STOP. After he read the wire, he had to force himself not to be discouraged. *'Why did this so called loving God allow this to happen? He would have taken good care of the child. There was no reason for their child to be put in an orphanage.'* The waiting was wearing him down, day by day. *'I need to talk to someone. I think I'll go find Pastor.'*

Johnny found Pastor walking down a path that followed the woods and he called out to him. "Pastor, can you spare a few minutes?"

"I have all the time in the world for you, my friend. Would you like to walk with me or find some place to sit down?"

"I don't think I am in the right mood to be sitting. I feel like pacing or stomping something or someone. Pastor, I've never told anyone besides Samuel, but I was married a few years ago. When my wife found out that she was going to have a baby, she wired her father for money and left me without any warning. I found a note saying that she would put the child in a loving orphanage. I wasn't even given a choice! I wanted children and she knew that.

"I can certainly understand why you are so upset about this, Johnny. So, you have no idea where your child is now?"

"My brother has a friend who is a detective and I have hired him to find my child. What I came over to ask you is, how could God allow her to take my child away from me and never even tell me where the child is living? I will give you fair warning! I don't want to hear how God is loving and kind; I want to hear the truth. Am I being punished for something?"

Pastor was praying silently and knew that he had to be careful about what words he used. "Johnny, you are definitely not being punished for anything. If God punished all of us for things we have done wrong, we would always be miserable. God gives us all free will. He won't ever force us to have a relationship with him or to turn our lives over to him. Your wife had a choice and she made it. Obviously, it caused pain for you and the child and I'm sure she'll live with regret for the rest of her life. I can tell you this; God will use this painful experience and you just might be amazed at what he does in your life because of this. The most important thing is to not feel bitterness towards your ex-wife; it won't do anything except make you sick inside. I understand your anger at God and so does He. He's big enough that he can take your anger and still love you regardless. Please keep me informed any time that you receive any information about your child."

Johnny was very quiet as he was trying to take in the Pastor's words. *'God can take your anger and still love you regardless.'* He wasn't so sure about that but he felt a tiny speck of hope inside. "Pastor, I don't know how to pray and even if I did, it wouldn't be sincere. I will let you know anytime that I hear anything from David. Thank you for listening."

Robbie Anderson was now five years old and he needed some answers. He went up to his teacher, Miss Owens, and asked her if they could talk privately. Of course, she agreed, wondering what serious subject he had on his mind. She could tell by his expression that it was important.

"Miss Owens, would you please tell me about the day I first came to the orphanage."

"Well, let's see, you were only a few weeks old and such a happy baby. Your hands were waving all over the place and you were full of energy."

"Who brought me here?"

"Your mother brought you, Robbie, and she was very sad. I could tell how hard it was to leave you here. She told me that she didn't think that she would make a very good mother. She hired someone to find the best orphanage for you; one where you would be safe and happy and receive good schooling."

"Where was my father?"

"She told me that she and your father were getting a divorce and that he wouldn't be able to take care of you alone, because he had a farm to take care of."

"I guess Jesus thought I would be happier here in the orphanage, don't you think so Miss Owens?"

"I think you are absolutely correct Robbie. We won't always understand why we have to go through some painful things in our life, but Jesus can always turn it around and make it something good. I can't imagine what it would be like without your smiling face to look at every day. You lift up everyone's spirits, especially Lucy's. Now, it's time to get back into the classroom. Do you feel better now, Robbie?"

"Yes ma'am, I do. I like talking to you because you don't treat me like a little boy."

As she watched Robbie walk away, she wondered how much longer he would be here. She had a strange feeling that she would be saying goodbye to him soon and that made her feel sad. No one had said anything to her, but she felt like she had to be prepared, so she began praying about it. Wherever he went, she hoped that no one would dim the light that was always shining when he was around. What she had told Robbie was true; his mother did love him. What she didn't mention was the fact that his mother wasn't too impressed at what the outside of their building looked like. The paint was flaking all over but the building was extremely sturdy and well built. When she was taken inside to see the rooms, she was amazed at how everything was so clean and neat and well cared for. The committee in charge of their finances had decided the money would be better spent on new materials for the classroom and the paint could wait for another year. When she heard that explanation, she felt that she had found the best place for her baby boy.

Rusty Anderson had been traveling with the same gang for several weeks now and he was feeling very uneasy at the way they looked at him, off and on. One night he had been asked to feed and water the horses, so he was away from the campfire. He got the feeling that something wasn't right, and he trusted his hunches. He carefully walked back towards the camp, but kept well hidden. When he found a tree that he could stay behind and listen, he knew his instincts were right. Murphy, the leader, was saying, "We've got to get rid of Rusty but make it look like an accident. We don't need any more trouble. Let me think about how to handle this and I'll let you know. It's got to be done soon." Rocky interrupted by saying, "Why would you want to hurt him? He hasn't done anything wrong."

Murphy raised his voice a little and said, "We offered him some of the money we stole and he didn't take even one dollar. If we ever got caught, he'd be singing like a canary. We can't risk that."

That was all Rusty had to hear. He backed up a few steps and rattled some bushes to let them know he was coming into camp. "The horses are fed and watered. I'm a little hungry. Is there any grub left?"

Rocky handed him a plate of beans and said, "Here you go; help yourself." Rusty nodded his thanks and cleaned the plate. Everyone started getting settled in for the night. The guys were passing around a bottle but Rusty didn't take any. Finally, they fell asleep but not him. He waited another hour to make sure they were sleeping deep and then he quietly slipped out of the camp, carrying his boots. When he got close to his horse, he put his boots on and walked his horse for about a quarter of a mile. When he got up on his horse, he headed for the woods, looking for a path where he could get out of sight quickly, if he was followed. He didn't really have a destination in mind yet. His main concern was to get as far away from the gang as possible. He knew Murphy wouldn't give up easily, trying to track him down. He felt so stupid when he thought about the dumb decisions that he had made, which led him to join up with that gang. Rusty started thinking about his two brothers; wondering if they had survived the war and where they were now.

Murphy and Rocky woke up to find out that Rusty was no longer in their camp. He must have snuck out during the night and they were furious. "Do you reckon he heard us talking about getting rid of him last night? I didn't know he was anywhere near us." said Rocky.

"I'll tell you one thing right now; we have to find him before he turns us all in. As soon as we have some coffee, we are leavin'." said Murphy. "It shouldn't' be too hard to catch up to him." Both men saddled up and took off in the direction of the prints from Rusty's horse. That led them within an hour to a stream and no telling where he went into the water or where he got out. They decided to spread out and signal with one gunshot if they found a trail. Another hour later no one had fired their gun and eventually they met back where they had started from. "Now where are we goin' to go?" asked Rocky.

"We'll just head south and keep our eyes and ears open." said Murphy.

Melissa Williams couldn't have been happier. She had recently been asked to take on the duties of the village librarian and would even get paid for doing it. Her teacher, Sarah, let her come to school one hour earlier than the other students so that she could leave ahead of them in the afternoon. Melissa was crazy about books and would probably have accepted the position even if she wasn't able to receive a salary. She had once thought she wanted to be a schoolteacher but then her love of books changed her mind. She had been keeping a diary ever since she was a young girl, and it was full of details about her life and those around her. Very little escaped her attention and she enjoyed writing about her family and friends and even people she knew only by name.

Melissa had a secret desire to write a book or maybe several. She would start out with the first one and see what the response would be. Her head was constantly filled up with words to put on paper. For Christmas she had asked for more journals and pencils and she went through them very quickly. She especially enjoyed writing about the stories that the older people often shared with her. Many people didn't want to take the time to stop in their busy day to listen to their stories. Melissa never stopped asking them for more stories. Some were so sad and yet there was always something positive that happened during their trials. Some of the women had lost children to sickness or husbands to accidents or old age. The courage that these early pioneer women showed, just fascinated Melissa. She often wondered if she could ever be that brave when faced with some of the difficulties they shared with her.

She was now 16 years old and was not in any special hurry to get married, unlike a lot of her girlfriends. It bothered Melissa to listen to some of her friends talk about how they were going to convince a certain young man to marry them. '*Who would want to marry someone that you had to convince? That was totally ridiculous!'* She did have a special relationship with a young man who was far away, and she had no idea if he was hurt or where he was. His name was Albert Brooks and he came from a very wonderful family. Melissa would always let his mother know if she had heard from him. His letters were quite infrequent as he was on the move a lot. The mail often didn't catch up with his regiment for several weeks. In one of his letters he had written that he had recently received three of her letters at the same time and it lifted his spirits very much. She wrote to him twice a week, regardless if she had heard from him that week or not. Melissa told him about what was going on in the village and the weather and what she was currently reading. Albert was the only person that she shared her dreams with, about someday being a writer. He never laughed at her and in fact he encouraged her in several ways. For Christmas he had sent her a beautiful journal and a fountain pen, which she would always treasure. She had sent him a picture of herself and a scarf and mittens that she had knit for him. Neither of them spoke of anything romantic, as far as their relationship. It was more of an unspoken understanding that they had between them.

Melissa didn't seem to realize how many young men tried to get her attention before the war started. She was always so busy helping her mother with household chores, catching up on her schoolwork and of course her writing. Melissa was never rude but she just had more important things on her mind than what boy was trying to drop a hint that he liked her. She always kept her hair clean and shiny and fixed her hair so it looked stylish but she didn't waste time if it didn't look perfect. Her pretty brown hair was almost to her waist when it was down. When she looked in the mirror as she was brushing her hair, she rarely saw a pretty face looking back at her. Instead she would pick out something about her face that she wished were different.

She really had missed Albert the years that he had been away and was anxious to see him again. There were a lot of things to share with him that she hadn't wanted to write in a letter. It was so nice to be able to be yourself with a young man who never made her feel foolish. She actually enjoyed talking to him more than with her girlfriends. Her mother had once told her that her future husband should first become a good friend and then the courting could begin. She further explained that marriage wasn't always easy and there were going to be times of disagreement between the husband and wife. Melissa was positive that she wanted to have several children; as many as the good Lord would bring to them.

Albert's mother, Louisa Brooks, came into the library, her face all red and flushed but she wasn't upset, just very excited. "Albert will be coming home on a train within the next week." Because the trains were so crowded and sometimes broke down, there was no such thing as a schedule. "I promise to let you know as soon as he arrives. I want to have a special coming-home dinner for him, but I'll wait until the following day of his arrival, to give him a chance to rest up. You will, of course, be invited." Mrs. Brooks ran off in a hurry to spread the good news and Melissa was left alone in the quiet library. She did some of her best thinking when she was in the library all by herself. Right now, she was wondering how much different Albert would look after three years. He left a young boy of 17 but now he would be a man of 20. She was sure that he had experienced many horrible things that he would never be able to discuss with her and she understood why.

There wasn't any way that she could relate to the horrors he must have seen. The newspapers were graphic enough. She had no desire to know more details. Melissa was wondering what she should wear when she visited his home for dinner. In the past, she had never thought much about it but this was such a special time. Her brown dress with the white collar set off her dark brown eyes, so that would probably be her best choice. She was tall for a young girl but had always liked her height. She wanted to give Albert a small gift but didn't know what to give him. She didn't have much money to spend and couldn't come up with something that he would like or need. All of a sudden, a big smile crossed her face. She would write him a coming home poem. What a great idea. She had better get started on it today. She pulled out a sheet of paper and a pencil and the words came swiftly, as usual. When she finished writing, she sat and reread it and was pleased, but she felt like there should be more. She would think about it later tonight when she was alone in her bedroom.

Four days later, Albert's brother, Ryan, came knocking on the door. He told her "Albert is home and he looks tired and hungry but mother had cooked some meals ahead of time. She has already started to fatten him up", he laughed. Melissa was so thankful that he had made it through the war safely and was now home. She knew so many soldiers were not coming home and that was a pain that she could not imagine having to feel. Before Ryan left, he said "Remember, you are to come to supper tomorrow night. Oh, I almost forgot to tell you. Albert brought a friend home with him that will be living here in Willow Bend. You'll meet him tomorrow night." Melissa stopped off at the general store on her way home to buy yarn for her mother. She was confined to a wheelchair because of a bad fall that had broken her hip. Doc had told them that she would always need that wheelchair, but it didn't seem to hold her back a lot. Her husband had passed away several years ago, when a farm accident had claimed his life. Their house had many bedrooms, so they rented two of them out for extra income. Taking care of her mother was something that Melissa looked forward to. When she arrived home, her mother had company so she walked over and gave her a hug, handed her the yarn and greeted the visitor for a minute. She excused herself and went back to her room to reread her poem for Albert. She would ask Richard tomorrow to make her a special frame.

Gerard Burns was getting stiff from his long ride in the stagecoach. He was a tall man, so it wasn't easy for him to get comfortable for such a long period of time. He had been traveling for a week and had not been able to get out and stretch his legs very often. Now that he was finally at his destination, it was a big relief. He was eager to start writing his new book about the earlier settlers to this area. Gerard spent many hours studying history and was always ready to learn something new. His traveling clothes were pretty well wrinkled but that could get fixed soon. He wasn't eager to meet too many people when he felt all rumpled and worn out. As hungry as he was, a hot bath was high on his list right now and then a change into clean clothes.

Maude was excited about their new guest at the hotel, who should be arriving sometime today. They had received a wire from a man named Gerard Burns, an author who had recently been discharged from his unit in the Civil War. His wire said that he planned to rent a room for a minimum of three months but might be extending his visit a month or so longer. She had assigned Ellie that room because she was the most meticulous and energetic maid in their hotel. Maude was fairly certain that Mr. Burns was used to staying in the finest hotels and she didn't want him to be disappointed in any way. Maude was standing outside the front door of the hotel because she had heard what sounded like Worley bringing in his team of horses, pulling the stagecoach. Worley was quite a character and she often teased him about his special girl, Daisy.

At first she saw a cloud of dust coming her way and then the stage burst into view and stopped right in front of the hotel. Maude put her hands up to protect herself from inhaling too much dust. Worley swung down very easily for a man of his age and opened the stagecoach door for the passengers. It wasn't difficult to spot Mr. Burns. My, he was a fine-looking man! He would definitely have many of the ladies in the village going out of their way to get his attention. He was at least six feet tall and very solidly built with black wavy hair that just touched his collar. At the moment he was helping an elderly lady exit the stagecoach and she seemed to be loving the attention. Two other men followed behind the woman and that seemed to be all for this trip.

Gerard turned and noticed Maude and she reached out her hand and said, "You must be our new guest, Mr. Burns. I am Maude and I hope your trip wasn't too rough."

"I've been looking forward to meeting you Maude, but please, you must call me Gerard. You have been very kind to respond to all of my letters and wires. I can't wait to get started on my new book."

She led him inside to sign in the ledger and Worley came in behind him with his trunk. As he stepped inside the hotel, he was impressed with the furnishings and how well kept up it was. "Your room will be upstairs, off to the left. Here is your key and if you need anything at all, please let me know." Gerard took the key and picked up the trunk, even though

Worley offered, and started up the stairs. He told her that he would be right back down for his valise and satchel, which held the beginnings of his new book.

When he found his room and unlocked the door, he was pleasantly surprised. The curtains were blowing in the breeze and he recognized the smell of lilacs, which was his mother's favorite flower. The fresh flowers were in a beautiful porcelain vase that were sitting on a nightstand by his bed. The sudden memory of his mother choked him up for a minute but then he relaxed and started investigating the room. He had asked if a small desk and chair could be brought up to his room, and they had obliged, and also added a lamp. With windows on two sides, the light would be wonderful. He noticed that one of the views was overlooking the front of the hotel and the window on the side of the hotel, looked out over a field of wildflowers. He walked over to the bed and sat down to test it out and found that it was rather comfortable. Gerard was a sound sleeper and not much kept him awake at night. A knock at the door brought him the hot bath that he had ordered. After he locked the door, he removed his dirty clothes and eased into the hot water. Oh, this was perfect! He ducked totally under, in order to rinse the dust and grime out of his hair and knew he was spilling water over the edge of the tub. He had been given several towels and some were already on the floor to catch the overflow. The water was looking pretty grimy but he could always take another bath tomorrow. This was good enough for now. He stepped out of the tepid water and dried himself off and got dressed. He ran his fingers through his thick black hair. There was a little bit of silver starting to show on the sides. His beard and moustache brought out the resemblance to his father. Gerard was a very masculine man without trying to be. When he smiled, a dimple popped out and softened his look a little bit.

Eliza Jane was the happiest maid you could ever imagine. She preferred to be called Ellie and she was always humming. Her light brown, naturally curly hair was always done up in braids and then pinned on top of her head. She hoped that it made her look a little taller. A few years ago, she had stopped growing and had always wished to be taller. Every day she hopped out of bed, full of energy and in good humor. Ellie knew that some people looked down on her because of her job but that never bothered her. She knew that it was hard for most people to understand how happy this job made her. Making beds, dusting and emptying chamber pots was never something that she disliked or dreaded. It made her feel so good to walk out of a room, knowing that it was now orderly and clean. She treated each guest in the hotel as if they were a guest in her imaginary home. Today Maude had explained that a very interesting guest would be arriving that afternoon, if the stage was on time. He would be given a special room that had a small desk and a nice view of the wildflowers beside the hotel. This guest was an author, and he would be writing a book. Ellie had walked around the room that would be assigned to him and she looked for anything that she could have missed. The windows were sparkling, fresh flowers were in a vase, and the entire room had been dusted. Ellie had even lugged the heavy carpet out to the back steps of the second floor and beat it for several minutes. Now she braced herself to lift it back up and drag it back to the room. Maude had given her a pad of writing paper and a pen and ink to place on the desk. Fresh towels were folded beside the wash basin and the bed was made very neatly and topped off with a quilt that looked perfect for a man. It had log cabins, animals and trees and might even inspire this man's writing.

Ellie was coming up the stairs, when she saw a man starting to come down. She had to catch her breath and force herself to try and act normal. This had to be the author because they weren't expecting anyone else today and she knew everyone currently staying in the hotel. As he drew closer, it was impossible to miss his broad shoulders, black wavy hair and eyes that seemed to miss nothing. He stopped her when they were just a few feet from each other and in a very friendly voice, said "Good afternoon, my name is Gerard, and I am your new guest. Are you the one who prepared my room?" Ellie nodded yes and seemed nervous. He reached inside his jacket and produced a coin and handed it to Ellie. "I couldn't be happier with this room and the view. You did a wonderful job. May I ask your name?"

"My name is Eliza Jane. If there is ever anything that you need, please let me know and I'll be happy to get it for you. Please excuse me; I have several more rooms to clean today." When she reached for the coin, Gerard could feel her small hand tremble a little. Ellie couldn't get away fast enough. "Oh, my goodness, if I have to see him every day, it is going to be hard on my heart. Maybe I can get one of the other maids to switch rooms with me."

Ellie went about her duties for the rest of the day but she kept thinking about Gerard and he was distracting her thoughts. Later that afternoon, she approached Maude and asked her if she would please assign one of the other maids to Mr. Burn's room. Maude looked puzzled and said, "Ellie, Mr. Burns is a very important guest and you are the best maid that we have. I'm sorry, but I can't switch you with someone else." Ellie didn't know what to say, so she just gave a small smile and nodded yes to Maude.

As a writer, Gerard was fairly disciplined. He wrote every day, whether he wanted to or not. At times, he was amazed at what came out of the day's work when he really hadn't been in the mood to write. People fascinated him and he was always watching people without directly staring at them and making them uncomfortable. Normally he was fairly good natured, but he was no fool. Reading people became second nature to him because of his line of work. He continued down to the front desk and smiled at Maude and walked into the dining room.

A waitress quickly came over and offered him a cup of coffee and a menu. Gerard looked over the menu carefully and chose a light meal of fish, vegetables and a salad. He had learned the hard way that eating too heavily would make him feel sleepy and it made it difficult to write. He asked the waitress to give his compliments to the cook and that made her blush. She shyly said that their cook was the very best and she would pass on the compliment to him. Gerard had a feeling that the cook was someone special to her and he decided that he would like to meet the cook in person some time. He left a generous tip for the waitress and was anxious to rent a carriage and look around. Now he needed to find someone who knew something of the history of this area. Driving in on the stage, he had noticed several elderly villagers, so that shouldn't be too difficult.

Melissa was so excited to see Albert again and she wondered how he had changed. She went to his mother's house and before she could knock, he was standing there with the door partially open. "Melissa, I've thought about this moment for years. I pictured it in my mind so many times. You look so pretty, but then you always have. Please come in and I'll introduce you to my friend, Joshua." She noticed immediately that Albert was leaning on a cane, but she didn't want to mention it.

"Albert, you don't look like a young boy any longer. I'm so happy that you made it back safely."

A young man walked over to them and Albert said, "Melissa, I'd like to present my best friend Joshua to you. We managed to spend the entire war in the same unit. "Joshua, this is the Melissa that you heard so much about."

"He is telling the truth about how often he mentioned you. I am delighted to meet you Melissa. I know you both have some catching up to do, so I'll leave you two alone for now."

His mother came into the room and greeted Melissa and led them into the parlor so they could talk for a few minutes before the meal would be served.

"Melissa, before we talk about anything else, I want you to hear something from me, before you hear it from anyone else. I was wounded two years ago and I almost didn't pull through. Your letters kept me going and I wanted you to know how important it was to me to be able to see you again. Joshua spent a lot of time taking care of me and I am so thankful for him. This cane will be with me for the rest of my life. The bullet that hit me did some damage to my leg. So many of my friends lost their leg or arm so I have nothing to complain about. I just wanted you to know that I will never be able to run again, and I'll always need this cane to walk."

"Albert, I feel so bad for what you went through but your needing a cane doesn't bother me at all. Thank you for telling me about what happened to you. Your friend Joshua is a true friend and I look forward to getting to know him better. We'd better go in and join the others now."

"I just wanted to tell you one more thing. Joshua received a telegram from a close friend of his who was wounded but is not expected to live much longer. I have agreed to accompany him so that he isn't traveling alone. It may be several weeks before we return. When I get back, I intend to spend a lot of time with you, catching up."

"I hate to see you leave so quickly but I do understand why you want to go. What about your leg? Won't it hurt you to travel?"

"As long as I'm on my horse, there is no pressure on that leg, so I'll be fine. I'll try to write you to let you know how we are doing."

They spent an enjoyable evening with his mother and Joshua offered to walk Melissa home to save Albert the effort. As he was walking back to Albert's house, he was thinking, *'How I wish I had a girl like Melissa in my life. She is definitely a special young lady. I envy my friend and wish that I could find someone soon who looks at me the way that Melissa looks at Albert.'*

Norma had signed all of the paperwork at the land office and at the bank and the money was deposited into her bank account. She was just giddy with excitement about how she was going to spend the money. When she was walking down the boardwalk in front of the hotel, she saw some men bringing a trunk out of the hotel and Rebecca was giving them directions where to deliver it. The directions were to the ranch that Norma had just sold. She thought there must be some mistake because she knew that Rebecca and her husband didn't have that kind of money. She walked over to Rebecca and tried to act as friendly as she could, even though she was furious inside. "Rebecca, are you moving somewhere? Are you tired of living in a hotel room?"

Rebecca had no clue about Norma's normal personality and she was all smiles when she said, "The sheriff just bought a ranch outside of town called 'Trails End'. He has asked Samuel and I and our son to move out there and run the ranch for him." Samuel had never told Rebecca who had bought the ranch out from under them a few years back. Norma's smile was frozen on her face, but Rebecca didn't notice. Norma stormed down the boardwalk and headed for her home so she could stop and think. First the sheriff totally ignored her in the hotel and then he went behind her back and bought the ranch to help Samuel and Rebecca.

When she reached her house, her housekeeper took one look at her face and was afraid that she had done something wrong. "Can I do anything for you Miss Norma?" she said in a shaky voice.

"No, except get out of my sight right this instant. I want to be alone. Go find some place to go and don't come back until tomorrow morning." The housekeeper didn't have to be told twice. She grabbed her satchel and fled the house. Norma paced back and forth like a caged animal and then poured herself a glass of sherry and then a second one. Her hand was trembling so much that she spilled some on the beautiful tablecloth, but she could care less. She had to find a way to get back at the sheriff, but she couldn't think straight at the moment. Norma went to her bedroom and laid down on top of the bed and knew she was about to have a painful headache, but she didn't want to move. She spent several hours hoping that she would fall asleep and wake up to find she had been dreaming. '*The sheriff must have checked to see who had purchased that ranch a few years ago, and that land agent told him my name. No law had been broken. I had every right to buy that ranch or any other piece of property that I wanted. I'm going to make sure that the sheriff is going to be very sorry that he bought that ranch.*'

Crystal Peaks Youth Ranch

"Crystal Peaks Youth Ranch exists to RESCUE the Equine, MENTOR the Child, provide HOPE for the family and EMPOWER new Ministries into existence. Founded in 1995, Crystal Peaks Youth Ranch is a nonprofit organization that rescues abused and neglected horses and pairs them free of charge with children in need. Together, all are introduced to the redeeming power of Jesus' healing love.

During the last 22 years, the Ranch has assisted in the rescue of more than 300 horses. Annually, the Ranch serves about 5000 visitors most of which are children free of charge. Crystal Peaks has also helped to establish more than 200 Similar Ministries throughout the United States, Canada and over a dozen in foreign nations. To read more about the loving mission behind the ministry.

Please visit our website at:
www.crystalpeaksyouthranch.org."

9

SEPTEMBER 1865

A Heart to Rescue Animals

Johnny had made up his mind about someone that he wanted to help. He just couldn't get that day out of his mind; when the kids had teased Bucky and only Julia had come to his defense. He had always had a soft heart for anyone being picked on. He walked over to where Bucky was out feeding the horses. "Hi Bucky, can you spare a few minutes to talk to me this morning?"

He really liked the sheriff because he always treated him with respect and went out of his way to speak to him. "Of course, I can sheriff, if you'll just give me a few minutes to finish feeding the horses." He could tell that the horses liked Bucky and he noticed that Bucky called them each by name and patted them one by one. When he was finished, he walked over to the sheriff. "What did you want to talk to me about, sheriff?"

"Well, as you probably already know, I bought a ranch a few weeks ago, a couple miles out of the village. I hired Samuel and his son to run the place but now my plans are expanding. I want to buy about two dozen horses to start with and I am very particular about who would be taking care of them. I'd like to offer you the job if you are willing. I have someone in mind who can take over this job at the stable if you accept my offer. Besides your pay, I'd like to give you a small house to live in, rent free. It will be yours as long as you work for me." Bucky had slept in the barn ever since he'd had this job and never had any thoughts of actually ever having his own place to live.

"Sheriff, I don't have to think twice about it; I'd enjoy working for you. Having my own place is great news." When he was told what his pay would be each month, Bucky's eyes popped out. "Are you serious? I've never earned that much money in my life and now I can feel respectable for once. When can I start sir?"

Johnny replied, "Tomorrow will be just fine. I am counting on you."

"Sheriff, I'm definitely ready to go out to your place tomorrow." Bucky looked like someone who had just been told he had inherited a gold mine. Johnny reached out to shake his hand and Bucky pumped his arm up and down so fast that it was like he was priming a pump. As Johnny was walking away, he heard "Dang! I got me a real job and a home." Johnny broke out in a big grin.

David had sent his brother a wire to be looking for him and a couple of men he had hired, any day now. They were bringing the two dozen horses that Johnny had purchased from David. He was going to buy more horses anyway and who better to buy from then his own brother? They had discussed prices and Johnny had transferred the money to David. He knew David was not asking top dollar for these horses, but he seemed so pleased that Johnny wanted to buy his horses for his new ranch, so he didn't argue. Now he already had Bucky working for him and Jacob and Isaac were helping to build new corrals and add on to the stable. Whenever he saw Bucky he was either smiling or whistling. What a change in that young man! He was sure glad that he had bought a ranch with a lot of room to expand. He couldn't wait to tell Isaac about the new horses that were on their way to his ranch.

The next morning Johnny was up early, and as he walked outside, he could hear the sound of several horses and he knew it must be his brother. It would be good to see him again. He had promised to stay for a couple of days and he hoped things would stay calm around the village, so he could spend some decent time with David. Bucky and the boys had heard the sound too and they already had the corral gate wide open. Here came David and his men and they looked tired but happy. They drove the horses into the corral and Bucky shut the gate. He had the water trough full and feed was sitting in buckets, just waiting for their arrival. Wow, what beautiful horses were looking back at him. He trusted David to sell him the best but he hadn't been exaggerating one bit. *'Wait a minute; there are 25 horses in that corral, not 24.'* David dismounted, and his men took their horses into the barn. David had a huge grin on his face when he walked up to Johnny. Johnny said, "I ordered two dozen horses David. Where did the extra one come from?"

David looked at him with pride in his eyes and said, "He is my gift to you; the solid black with white stockings. I've raised him from a colt. He'll give you a run for your money. He usually has one speed and that is all out."

Johnny didn't know what to say. "I was going to be looking for something to give Midnight a break, but I just haven't gotten around to it yet. He is a handsome horse and I much appreciate it David. Thank you for this generous gift." He walked up to him and pounded him on the back and introduced himself to the other men. "Come on inside; breakfast and coffee are ready. My men will take good care of your horses for you." When they entered the kitchen, Johnny introduced his brother to Samuel and Rebecca and the men sat down at the table. Samuel and Rebecca were happy that Johnny was able to see his brother after all these years. After they had finished eating, Johnny suggested that they rest for awhile but David didn't want to.

"I'd like to get a tour of your ranch and hear about your plans. It is easy to see that you have the right people working for you. Everything I've looked at is neat and well cared for" said David.

Johnny nodded and said, "I have Samuel and his son to thank for that; along with Bucky and Isaac. Samuel runs the ranch for me and I think he is probably thinking that he bit off more than he'd wanted to chew. I keep getting more ideas for expansion. I heard about some horses recently that have been abused. I want to set up a separate area for those weak and injured horses and rescue them as quickly as possible."

"That sounds just like something you would do. You were always rescuing someone or something when we were growing up. I think that is a great idea," said David. "Johnny, my friend and I are doing everything we can to find your child. I am going to hold off moving to a ranch nearby, so that I can concentrate on searching for orphanages on a list that we came up with. If it is ok with you, I'd like to stick around a few weeks and look for a ranch where I can raise horses. Even though I won't move here right away, I don't want to miss out on finding the right place." Johnny couldn't be happier to know that his brother would be living nearby. Now if only they could find out something about Rusty.

The day after David arrived, Johnny went in search of Sarah. She had told him to let her know when he had some horses for sale. He found her in the dining room, chatting with his deputy, Curtis. "Hello Curtis, is everything quiet today, I hope?"

"Yessir, no disturbance except for Charlie complaining that we are all eating him out of house and home. I told him that it's his own fault for being such a darn good cook."

Sarah was looking at him, as if she knew that he was coming to see her. "Sarah, my brother David brought in two dozen horses for me yesterday and I promised you the first pick. Do you have any time this afternoon?"

"I'll just run down to the stables and rent a horse and I'll meet you out front in ten minutes."

"That won't be necessary; I brought along an extra horse for you to ride to the ranch. I hope he's not too much horse for you." She knew that he was teasing her, so she just let out one of her laughs that lit up the room and followed him out. The horse standing next to his was a russet colored gelding. Sarah walked over to the horse and with no hesitation, she swung up onto the saddle. As soon as both horses were headed in the direction of his ranch, they took off at a gallop. Sarah had always had a beautiful smile, but today she was absolutely radiant. She didn't worry about her hair getting messed up or her dress billowing in the breeze. All that mattered was that she was riding all out and loving every minute of it.

When they reached his ranch, she stroked the horse's neck and turned to him and said, "Is this the horse that you chose for me? He is so full of spirit."

"You guessed right! This is the one that I picked out for you, but if you see another one that you like better, that is fine with me."

"I wouldn't even consider looking for another horse. I'm going to name him 'Spirit'. Just write me up a bill of sale and I'll have your cash to you by tomorrow."

"I've already written it up for you" and he reached in his pocket and pulled out a folded piece of paper. When she opened it and read it, her head jerked up and she said, "You are giving me Spirit? I have the money in my bank account."

"This is my gift for a dear friend. I know you will enjoy him and will take good care of him. I haven't had many friends in my life, but I count you as one of the best."

"I already knew that you were a generous man but this is incredible. Thank you so much. I'll never forget this day. Come on Spirit, it's time that we start getting to know each other."

'That woman ranks higher and higher every time I'm around her. Sometimes it actually hurts to be around her, because she is going to be married to Pastor one of these days. I guess that I'll just have to settle for having her for a special friend.'

Pastor James was feeling a little discouraged in his search for a wife. He decided to take his daily walk in a different direction and hopefully he would receive some comfort or direction from the Lord. "Lord, when I asked you to choose a wife for me, I guess I didn't mention that I was in kind of a hurry. The only new woman I've met since the war ended is Sarah, and I can't even talk clearly when she is nearby. Surely, she couldn't be your choice." After walking around for quite awhile, he ended up at Docs, but he was out checking on a patient.

Elizabeth greeted him warmly and said, "Is there anything that I can do for you Pastor? It may be some time before Doc returns."

"I just needed to talk to him about something that is bothering me. I guess it will have to wait until another day. Well, would it make you uncomfortable if I confided in you? Maybe getting a woman's point of view would help me understand my problem."

Elizabeth wasn't prepared to hear her pastor ask if he could confide in her but she didn't want to tell him no either. "I'm not sure how much help I can be, but I'll be happy to listen."

"Well, you see, I've been praying for a long time for the Lord to choose me a wife. As soon as I returned from the war, I was sure that my prayer would be answered soon. I thought when Sarah came to town, that maybe she was the Lord's answer to my request, but she has three times the courage that I do. I am so uncomfortable around her and it is pretty obvious. I have always pictured in my mind, once I was married, that my wife and I would both go around visiting the people in our church and the ladies would like to visit her at our home. It's not easy for me being an unmarried man. Several of the mothers have done everything except bribe me to court their daughters. I am under a lot of pressure because I don't want to hurt anyone's feelings, but I don't like someone trying to force themselves on me. Is any of this making any sense to you Elizabeth? You are a kind woman and I am hoping that you could give me some advice from a woman's point of view."

Elizabeth was silently praying for the Lord's help. "Pastor, Sarah has become a dear friend of mine. She was raised by her father and brothers. She's strong because she didn't have any other choice. She has a big heart and all the children love her. I believe that she would make a wonderful wife and mother. I will advise you to stand your ground in regard to the mothers trying to push their daughters on you. I feel that the Lord has one particular woman for you and you alone. She will enjoy supporting your work as a pastor's wife and will take some of the load off of your shoulders. You know that the Lord has perfect timing. Perhaps there is something that she must learn before He brings you together."

"Elizabeth, you've really helped me to understand Sarah better. I keep wondering what is wrong with me whenever I get so uneasy around her. I'll try to be more patient."

"I seem to have a problem similar to yours. My children are constantly trying to bring Johnny into our lives, but I am upset with him so much of the time. I'm starting to have doubts about him and the children and I becoming a family. I will not let my children force me into something that I don't have peace about. Don't be discouraged Pastor. Once you do meet this special woman, you'll forget all about these years of waiting. I hope I was some help to you."

"Elizabeth, I want to thank you for listening to me and for the encouragement you gave me. I certainly didn't intend to unburden myself on you. I hope I didn't offend you in any way. It sounds like you and I both are feeling pressure that we don't need. I'll keep you in my prayers, as always."

Jacob had been seeing Emily at least twice a week and he decided it was time to have a serious talk with his parents. "I have waited a long time, trying to find a girl who is the most like you Mother and I believe Emily is the one. She has a gentle spirit, a warm heart and I want to ask her to be my wife. I am hoping for your blessing, because without it, I wouldn't feel right."

"Oh Jacob" said Rebecca, "We couldn't be happier. Not only is she a delightful young lady, but we would be grandparents right away. Your father and I have talked about this a lot and you definitely have our blessings."

Samuel looked over at his son and said, "Jacob, I would be so happy to see you and Emily become man and wife and the thought of a little grandchild running around here would be wonderful." Jacob had already picked out a ring but he was waiting for the right moment to propose. He hoped that day would come soon.

Timothy and Julia often played in the woods together behind the hotel. Today Julia said she had other plans and his friend Jadon was sick, so he would have to play by himself. He went over the fence behind the hotel and decided to go to their hiding place. He had grabbed some apples from the kitchen and a couple of biscuits, just in case he got hungry. Maybe today he would try to find a new path that he could show his sister. He had gone into the woods around four o'clock and was always supposed to come back before dark. Timothy guessed that he'd been out here for about two hours so he had a little time left. He left their secret spot and started trying to find a new trail. This wasn't quite as easy as he thought it would be. There were bramble bushes everywhere, but he tried to find places where they weren't so thick. Before he realized what was happening, he felt himself falling and he couldn't get a grip on anything to break his fall. He landed on his feet but then fell to his side. When he looked up, he knew there was no way to get out of that deep hole by himself. Now would have been a perfect time to have a dog that he could send for help, but he didn't have one. He didn't think anything was broken but he was scraped up. Because he didn't know what else to do, he cried out for help, over and over.

Franklin had been picking berries for his dinner and heard the cry for help. The past few days he had watched a little boy and girl come into the woods to play but they had always ended up in the same place each time. He didn't move, hoping to hear the cry for help again. In a few minutes, he heard it again, although it was weaker. He yelled out, "Keep calling so that I can find you. I'm pretty close to you now."

Timothy was so startled to actually hear someone talking to him. "I'm over here. I fell down a big hole. Be careful!"

Franklin now knew what direction to turn to find this child. It was smart of the child to warn him about the hole or he might have fallen right on top of him. "Keep calling; I'm getting closer."

"I'm right here. My name is Timothy." Franklin could tell that he was just a few feet away. Now he could see the opening. He got down on his hands and knees and called down to the child.

"My name is Franklin and I've been camping in these woods. I need to go back and get my rope but it's not far from here. I promise to come right back. Are you hurt?"

"No sir, just pretty scared."

"I'll be back in about ten minutes so just sit down and wait."

When Franklin returned, he took the rope and tied it in a loop and dropped it gradually down to the boy. He told him to put it over his head and then under his arms and pull it tight. When Timothy said that he had done that, Franklin said, "Timothy, I feel that I need to warn you about something. My face is badly burned and it might scare you. Turn your head away when I pull you up."

Timothy immediately called back, "I'm sorry that you were hurt. I'd like to be your friend." Franklin had a big lump in his throat when he heard those words.

He started pulling Timothy up, little by little. When he saw the top of his head, he took in a big gulp of air and tried to prepare himself for Timothy's reaction to his face. Now he had pulled him completely out of the hole and Timothy had his back to him for a moment. "Son, if you'd like, I'll walk in front of you and lead you back to the place where I know you came into the woods. That way you won't have to look at me."

"Sir, I don't want to do that. I want to see the face of the man who saved me. I said I wanted us to be friends and I meant it." Timothy turned himself around and looked right at Franklin's face. "Does the burn hurt you a lot?"

"No son, it doesn't hurt anything like it did the day of the accident." Timothy reached into his pocket and found two apples; a little worse for wear but still good enough to eat. He reached out and gave one to Franklin and they both sat there and ate the delicious fruit.

Timothy said, "How are you getting food to eat?"

"I found some berry bushes and then I saw the place where the hotel throws out their scraps."

"You won't have to do that anymore. I'll bring you food and anything else that you need. My mother is a nurse and she works for a doctor. If you ever need medicine, I can help with that too."

"What is the doctor's name, Timothy?"

"His name is Doc Stone and he's a good man."

"He's the man who took such good care of me when I had my accident. He even gave me two jars of cream for my face, but I've used most of it up. It really works great. Timothy, can you bring me some paper and a pencil so that I can write a note to him?"

Timothy stood up and said, "I'll bring it to you in the morning. I have a secret place here in the woods. If I tell you where it is, can I meet you there?"

"I already know where your secret spot is and yes, I'll be there in the morning. Let's get you back home now." Timothy reached over and took Franklin's hand and they walked back to the place where Timothy always climbed over the fence.

"Good night Franklin. I'm glad that I have a new friend."

"So am I Timothy. I don't have any friends except you, Doc and Pastor."

The next morning Timothy came to the secret spot as soon as the sun was up. He had several pieces of paper, envelopes and a pencil. He also had a bag full of something that smelled wonderful. Timothy said, "I told my friend Charlie the cook that I knew of someone who didn't have enough to eat. He fixed me this bag and said if I'll keep bringing the bag back, he'll fill it up for you."

"Will you have time to bring a letter to the doctor today?" When Timothy nodded 'yes', he found something solid to write on and wrote a quick note to the doctor.

"Doc, you probably didn't expect to hear from me this soon but I am camped out in the woods directly behind the hotel. I would like to meet you in secret so that I can ask you for a favor. My new friend Timothy has agreed to bring this to you. The medicine works well and I could use another jar, if you have one to spare. I feel like I am exactly where the Lord wants me to be, but I'd like to talk to you if you can spare the time. Your friend, Franklin."

Timothy took the letter and said he would deliver it on his way to school. Franklin asked him to be sure that no one saw him give the letter to the doctor and he promised that he would be careful.

When he handed Doc the letter, Timothy waited to see if Doc wanted him to do anything else. Doc scanned the letter and looked surprised and pleased. He said, "Timothy, can you take me to Franklin tonight after supper? I'll tell your mother that you will be with me for awhile, so she won't worry." Timothy was happy that he wasn't hurt, plus he had made a new friend. The fact that he was going to be able to help Franklin made him feel important. He could hardly wait until tonight. Doc hurried over to tell Pastor James the exciting news about Franklin. They would both go to see him tonight.

Doc and Pastor came by the hotel to eat dinner and asked Elizabeth if they could take Timothy with them for company for a short time. She agreed, and they started to leave out the back door of the kitchen. Charlie saw them and handed Timothy a bag of food. Doc realized that Franklin had more friends than he realized. Doc gave Charlie a knowing smile and then they left. Doc opened the gate but Timothy sailed over the fence. He could tell that Timothy had done this many times before.

In a few minutes, they stopped and Timothy called out, "Franklin, I have Doc and Pastor James with me. Come on out." Franklin stepped out from behind a tree and Doc and Pastor went over and pumped his hand and Doc said, "You don't know how happy we were to read your note and to find out that you were right here in Willow Bend. How is your face doing?"

Franklin said, "The pain level has dropped a lot and I can tell that the salve is the reason. It feels like it is healing some, but I don't know what I look like. It's good to see you Doc and Chaplain, er, Pastor James.

Franklin decided to tell them about his plan and see what they thought about it. "I want to help some of the people in this village, but I don't know them or their needs. I was hoping that between you both, you might come up with some creative ways. I need to help people in secret, but am not quite sure how to go about doing that."

Doc asked Franklin "What would you think about chopping wood and we would sell it for you? You might also chop wood for some of the older people in town who couldn't do that for themselves."

When Franklin heard that, his face lit up. "That's a great idea Doc. If you can loan me the tools that I'll need, I can get started right away. Timothy would you mind being our official messenger?" When Timothy heard that, he had a big smile on his face.

Doc said, "I want you to make me a list of anything you might need for the coming winter. I'll bring you extra blankets and heavier clothing and a lantern. I have a good feeling that God will come up with several ways for you to help others."

Timothy said, "Doc, I fell in a deep hole the other night and Franklin rescued me. Can we maybe cover up that hole so no one else will get hurt?"

Doc was amazed when he heard about Timothy falling down the hole. "Does your mother know about this son? She didn't mention anything to me."

Timothy shook his head and said, "If I told her, she wouldn't let me come back into the woods and now I have to. Please Doc, don't say anything to her." Doc didn't like it but he agreed not to tell her. He told Franklin that he had to get Timothy back to the hotel but that he would be back tomorrow evening at the same time with the tools.

Millie Campbell had spent her last bit of money buying a ticket on the stage, not knowing how far it would take her. When the stage pulled into Willow Bend, she was told that it was the end of the line for

194

her. She was worn out from little sleep for several days and her stomach was growling, but she was penniless. The driver handed her the one bag she had brought with her and now she was on her own. No one would hire her to work in a store, she thought to herself. What did that leave her to do except hope that she could be hired to work in the one saloon she had noticed. As she started to walk away, a woman with a soft voice asked her, "Would you like to come in and have a bowl of soup with me?"

"That sounds wonderful, but I don't have any money. I hope to find a job soon."

"You don't need any money; our cook always goes overboard by making too much."

Millie looked into the kindest eyes and gave a half smile and walked up the steps to the hotel. The lady's name was Maude and she worked in the hotel. She led her to the dining room and she was not the least bit embarrassed to be seen with Millie. They sat down and a kind waitress came over to bring them some coffee. Maude requested soup for both of them and a basket of rolls. Millie added a lot of cream and sugar to her coffee and stirred it a long time. When she took her first sip, she closed her eyes and smiled. Maude was watching her closely and had figured out that this woman had been through a lot. The soup looked so good and was filled with meat and vegetables and the rolls smelled heavenly. A plate of butter was on the table and Millie couldn't wait to put some on the roll after she broke it apart.

Maude said, "Are you here visiting anyone? "

Millie shook her head and told the truth. "I bought a ticket on the stage with all the money I had and this is where my money ran out. I'll be walking over to the saloon in a few minutes to see if they will hire me. I noticed where the church was, when we entered the village. I intend to start going to church this very Sunday."

Maude really admired her honesty and that she was willing to work and not take handouts. While they were eating, Maude said something to Millie that made her stop with her spoon halfway to her mouth. "I would like to be your first friend in Willow Bend and if you ever need to talk or need something to eat or a place to lay your head, come right to me." Millie was fighting tears so she just looked at Maude and gave a little nod. She got up to leave and thanked Maude for everything. Maude wrapped up the remaining rolls in a napkin and handed them to Millie. "Please don't forget what I said Millie." Millie had to leave before she broke down, so she turned and walked away as quickly as she could.

When she reached the saloon, she tentatively pushed the swinging doors aside, took a deep breath and came inside. The room was dark and smelled of sawdust, beer and smoke, but it was basically clean. There was a big man behind the bar and Millie pulled her shoulders back and her chin up and marched up to him. She had to tilt her head way back to look into his eyes, but she wasn't afraid of him. She introduced herself by saying "Hello, my name is Millie and I need a job. I'm a hard worker but I have some rules."

He was so surprised to hear this little bit of a thing telling him that she had rules, but he forced himself not to laugh. "And what are your rules little lady?"

"I like to be called by my name. Next, no one lays a hand on me. I will be friendly and will talk to the men, but that is all. Am I making myself clear? Oh, and one last thing. I will not work on Sundays because I intend to be in church."

"Millie, my name is Pete and I own this saloon. You have found yourself a job starting tomorrow. I sleep upstairs but there is a room in the back for any ladies that work for me. Right now there is only one woman working here. I'll introduce you to Daisy tomorrow. I think you two will get along great. You'll have a bed and there are a few hooks for your clothes. No one will bother you back there; you have my word on that. I will also pay you one week's pay in advance. Tips are yours to keep! I'll need you here from four o'clock until midnight. You can sleep in as long as you want to. I always order something from the hotel kitchen for supper, so you will not have to buy your evening meal, except on Sundays. Most of the men will not give you any trouble and if they do, it will be taken care of quickly." He reached behind the bar and handed her some coins and led her to the room in the back. Millie felt safe around Pete and not only because of his size. Today was Friday, so she only had to work tomorrow and then she could attend church. Pete told her to stay in that room the rest of the afternoon and evening, so no one would know she was back there.

'Well, I've found myself a job and I'll work hard at it, but I can't say that I'm proud of where I'll be working. No matter; God will take care of me. I don't always understand what He is doing in my life but I've never stopped trusting Him and that's a fact.'

Sunday morning Millie woke up quite early because she was eager to get dressed and walk to the church. Her first night of work wasn't too bad. Naturally the men were excited to see another woman working in there but word was passed around very quickly that Pete was watching her closely. A couple of times one of the men had too much to drink and tried to grab her as she walked by, but somehow Pete was close by and stopped the arm in midair. He added a little twist as he directed the arm away from her and then everyone was back to talking and playing cards and drinking. She liked Daisy, the other girl who worked with her. She was the biggest flirt but very kind hearted. She didn't waste any time telling Millie that Worley was her sweetheart. Millie couldn't have imagined a more unusual couple, but they seemed to be crazy about each other. Even though Millie didn't have any one special in her life, she was genuinely happy for them.

Once she was dressed, she started walking towards the church and the hotel was on her way. Maude must have been waiting for her and she asked Millie if she would care to come in for coffee first. Millie would enjoy some more of that delicious coffee so she said yes. The waitress brought over some sweet rolls along with the coffee so Millie had breakfast after all. Soon it was time to leave and both of them were eager to attend the church service. Maude told her about Pastor James and how friendly he was, along with having a great sense of humor. During the service, Millie listened intently to every word and sang along with the hymns, which she knew by heart. After the service, Pastor stood outside to greet everyone and when he saw Millie, he gave her the friendliest smile. "Pastor James, I would like you to meet Millie. She just arrived in our village two days ago."

Maude didn't mention where she worked, but Millie told him herself and she showed no shame. "Good morning Pastor. I could hardly wait for Sunday morning to come. I am now working at the saloon and I told Pete that I can never work on Sundays."

Pastor didn't act shocked and he shook her hand and said, "Millie, I am so pleased to meet you. I'm glad that you wanted to attend our church so soon. You are very welcome, and I look forward to seeing more of you."

Sarah walked over to them and Pastor immediately felt uneasy. Sarah ignored this and offered Millie her hand and introduced herself. "Millie,

I am a friend of Maude's and it's a pleasure to meet you. I'd like you to join Maude and I for lunch as my guest." Sarah was very different than most women; there was something about the way she carried herself and the way she had of looking at you. She would make a wonderful friend, Millie thought. The three women walked together to the hotel and had a wonderful meal and lots of laughter.

Millie explained "The man that I thought I was going to marry turned out to be a crook. He tried to involve me in a scheme, so I left town the next day. I don't know if he will try to find me, but I hope not. You wouldn't want to see his type in your village."

As soon as Millie, Maude and Sarah walked away, Norma had strutted up to the pastor and he knew by her face what was coming. "Pastor, I can't believe that you would allow a saloon girl to come into our church. You must do something about this right away. I could hardly concentrate on what you were saying, I was so appalled."

Pastor had started silently praying as soon as he saw her walking over to him. In as calm a voice as he could muster, he said, "Norma, do you not realize that Jesus loves Millie as much as he loves you. He looks at her heart and that is what matters the most to Him. We have to be very careful about judging others. The Bible says that we are not to do that." This was obviously not what she wanted to hear so with a swish of her skirts, she left without even saying a word. *"Lord, please do something to melt her heart towards you and toward others. She must have been hurt a lot in the past to turn out so bitter and mean. Also, please give me patience when I encounter her and I do mean a lot of patience. Amen!"*

Pastor was at the hotel having breakfast a few days later, and he noticed Pete walking in the room.

"Pete, please join me. Have you eaten yet?" Pete shook his head 'no' and a waitress was headed his way to bring him some coffee.

Pete was pleased to be invited over and he sat down across from Pastor. "I've been hoping to get to know you better Pete. I've had the pleasure of meeting Millie and she is delightful. She has not even been in the village for a week and already made sure that she was in church. She told me how kind you were to give her a job."

"I wish you could have heard her the day she came into my saloon, looking for work. She said, 'I won't be working on Sundays because I plan to be in church that day.' There is definitely something special about her and I aim to watch out for her. Most of the customers have been very friendly to her, but I'm more concerned about some that come in from out of town."

"I'm glad to hear that, Pete. I've been concerned about all of our soldiers that have returned home. I understand that you were shot during the war. Are you having any problems because of that?"

"Sometimes at night my shoulder aches but I sure can't complain after what I've seen a lot of our soldiers go through. I didn't enjoy having to shoot at the soldiers on the other side. Some of those boys were too young to shave, let alone be in a war. I tried to shoot to wound and not kill. I just couldn't make myself kill another man. Pastor, how did the war affect you?"

"You are the first person to ask me that question. Even though I wasn't in danger of being shot at, I saw hundreds of boys on both sides, dying or close to death, or those who lost limbs or their eyesight. I find myself crying a lot when I'm off by myself. I think I am carrying a lot of pain inside of me that needs to come out. Sometimes I wish I had a temper so I could let loose some of my feelings, but that isn't me. God will find a way to help me. He always knows what is best for all of us. It pleases me that I don't have to explain anything to Him. Do you have a relationship with God, Pete?"

"I have to admit that I don't yet, but I sure thought about it a lot during the war. I just don't want to be the kind of person who only thinks about God when they are in danger or in trouble. Maybe I could come by the church sometime and talk to you about that. I need to understand what God expects out of me."

"I'll be happy to meet with you any time that you want to come by. I will tell you one thing right now to set your mind at ease. God loves you just like you are. He doesn't expect you to change your personality overnight, if you give your heart over to Him. He has so much love and patience, it is incredible. He'll help you make small changes as you can handle them. If you try to change and then stumble back to your old ways, He'll just pick you up and help you to try again. He always wants what's best for us, even though we won't always understand what we need." Pete and Pastor enjoyed their breakfast together and agreed to meet again soon.

As the weeks passed swiftly, Gerard was having a lot of success finding interesting information for his book. The old timers were more than happy to talk to him and show him family pictures and trinkets. The small farming community of Willow Bend was originally discovered in 1832. Many weeping willows were found growing alongside the river, thus the name of the town came to be. Back then there were several friendly Indians living nearby and they had not caused any trouble. Erecting a log cabin had been backbreaking work. The first settlers found the land mostly forest with some small openings. Eventually houses, barns, and fences were built and wood was cut to heat the home and for cooking food. Clearing the land was no easy task. Stumps were burned, chopped and left to rot. A horse-pulled wench was used to pull some of the smaller stumps. One year a huge windstorm toppled a large number of trees, so this made it easier to remove the stumps.

Word had spread back to families living in New York, Vermont and other states back east. Little time was wasted when the men heard of an opportunity to better themselves. They were coming by covered wagon over very rough trails to settle in this area. Now that the Civil War had come to a close, word was passed among the troops that there was land to be had, if you were willing to put your back into the hard labor required in the beginning. Some families brought three generations for the journey, not wanting their families to be separated. Babies were born on the wagon trip to Willow Bend but sadly some of them did not survive. Unless a doctor was traveling with a wagon train, there was normally not a doctor available out in the middle of a forest. Soon the original plat of the village was laid out.

One of the first buildings to be erected was their three-story hotel. More and more families were coming into Willow Bend and would need a place to stay until their own log cabin home was built. For those without the funds to stay in a hotel, setting up camp on the land they had purchased was their only option. When winter came, it was often freezing at night and some of the ranchers would wake up to find dead animals or their water buckets frozen. Many wives made the decision to stay back home until a suitable log cabin was ready for them. It wasn't difficult to picture this little village back in the early 1800's; mostly forests and some friendly Indians.

Even though the book was going well, Gerard had his mind on something else; rather, someone else.

Every time he ran into Eliza Jane, something happened inside of him that he'd never felt before. Before the war, other women had caught his attention and he had taken several ladies out for a meal or to the opera, but this was different. One day he heard someone call "Ellie" and it was Eliza Jane who responded. She glanced over at him and blushed and said, "That's what my friends call me." Gerard asked permission to call her Ellie and she got flustered and said, "I guess you may call me that." And then off she went.

When Gerard came into the dining room the next day, he asked Maude if she would join him for breakfast and she said that she would be happy to. After they had been served their coffee and given their order, Gerard tried to figure out how to start the conversation. "Maude, I need some advice and you seemed like the right person to talk to. I'd like to know more about Eliza Jane; I mean, Ellie. She is always friendly to me but then she runs off like a young fawn. What is there about me that is making her so uncomfortable?"

Maude smiled at Gerard and decided to be honest with him. "I've noticed that you are attracted to Ellie, but you need to understand something about her. Ellie looks at someone like you as so far above her socially that she wouldn't dare give you any encouragement. I think that she is puzzled when you show her so much attention. Please, Gerard, don't hurt Ellie. She is so precious to all of us and has the biggest heart. She cleans every room in this hotel like it was her palace. Ellie is like everyone's daughter. If we thought you were about to hurt her, we would have to ask you to leave."

Gerard was shocked to think that anyone would think he was capable of hurting Ellie. "Maude, I have no intention of hurting Ellie. I just want her to give me the opportunity to get to know her better. So far, we speak a few friendly words and she dashes off. I would like to take her out for dinner but not in this hotel. Maybe just the café down the street or take her for a ride in a carriage and explore the area around Willow Bend. Will you please help me Maude?"

Maude was thinking about her own life with a man who she believed cared for her as much as she cared for him, and how nothing was happening. She looked up at Gerard and said, "I'll be happy to put in a good word for you, but I can't promise anything. Ellie is a proud young lady and at some point, she is going to find out about what a successful man you are. Before that happens, you are going to have to have some kind of a break through. I know her very well and once she finds out the truth about you, she'll run for the hills. She would never encourage you when she finds out about your wealth. At Gerard's startled look, she said, "Yes, I know Gerard! I have friends all over this country who are familiar with you. I'll do my best when I talk to Ellie but don't get your hopes up too high."

10
SEPTEMBER 1865

The Orphan Train Comes Through Michigan

Austin Templeton was bracing himself for whatever family he ended up with; that is, if any family chose him. His parents, living in New York City, were too poor to properly take care of him and when they heard about 'The Orphan Train', Austin's name was given to the Children's Aid Society. Thousands of children were put on these trains as early as 1854 and were accompanied by two people from the Children's Aid Society. Hopefully a kind family would choose a child to become a part of their family. Unfortunately, many farmers wanted what was actually slave labor and didn't treat the children well.

At that time, he was 15 years old and a very sturdy young man. At one stop in Michigan, a farmer pushed his way through the crowd and said, "I want this one." Austin was a very sensitive boy and he had noticed this man earlier. He had been yelling at a child and then back handed another one.

When Austin heard this man's comment, while pointing at him, he knew he would do anything to get out of this situation. He pretended that he was throwing up, doubled over, put his hand to his mouth, and ran back into the train and hid. He nervously waited in a dark corner, hoping that they wouldn't come looking for him. Eventually he felt the train moving and he breathed a sigh of relief. That was too close. He would have to be alert every time the train stopped to show the children to the people in each village.

As the train kept moving through small villages in Michigan, the train stopped in Albion. Austin cautiously went onto the train platform. He wished he wasn't so tall and stocky. He was sure that there would be other farmers looking for someone to do heavy labor. Working wasn't the problem; it was being treated badly that he wanted to avoid. His eyes scanned the crowd, looking for a friendly face and he found one. He made eye contact with a farmer who gave him a nod and a slight smile. He turned to his wife and pointed at Austin and her face lit up in a big smile. They were trying to work their way through the crowd to him, so he moved towards them, to shorten the time. 'Please God, don't let someone else say that they want me. I want to go home with this family.' His prayers were answered, because a few seconds later, the man and his wife approached Austin and said, "Son, my name is Jonas Whitestone, and this is my wife Dora. We have a farm a few miles away and we have three almost grown children, who all live with us. We'd like to open our home up to you, if you would feel comfortable with that."

His wife said, "You would be treated well and I'd like to add that I'm a good cook. Our children are well mannered and are in favor of us coming out here today. Our village is small but very friendly. We are hoping that you will agree."

For the first time, Austin spoke up, "I'd like that very much. I mean, to go home with you. I'm not afraid of hard work but I prayed that I wouldn't end up with a family who was mean. I do have a healthy appetite and that's a fact." They both smiled at that and the wife reached out and gave him a brief hug. They walked over to the person keeping a list of all of the children and gave them their information. Before long, they were on their way to a village called Willow Bend. Austin had been tense ever since he'd left New York but now he felt like he could actually relax. He wasn't sure how much he would be asked about his background and he decided to wait and see what they might want to know.

His parents worked their fingers to the bone but they just couldn't earn enough money to feed all six of their children. Since Austin was the oldest, it was decided to send him on the Orphan Train. The day he had to say goodbye to his family wasn't easy, but he felt like they didn't have any choice and he didn't blame his parents for their decision. His mother had taught him a lot about Jesus and he often prayed out loud when he was off by himself. He merely asked for the strength to leave his family and go out into the unknown world. His mother told him that Jesus loved every single person the same and that was difficult to comprehend. There were some very hateful people in this world but Austin chose to believe that this was true, regardless. A few hours later, they turned into a long entrance to a farm and he saw animals in every direction. Some were in the fields with fences and some were running loose. He wondered what kind of work he would be doing and hoped that at least some of it had to do with animals. The wife had packed a nice hearty lunch, which they ate while driving the wagon home, but he was already hungry again. He hoped that his stomach wouldn't start growling.

The wagon was stopped by the front door of the house and Jonas got out to help his wife down. She said, "Austin, right now let's get you settled. I'll show you to your room and then you can have some milk and cookies to hold you over until supper."

He turned to Jonas and said, "Sir, would you need my help this afternoon? I'm not sure what you had in mind for me to do for you, but I'm willing to learn anything."

"Son, I had no plans to give you any work today. After my wife has stuffed you with her cookies, I thought I might give you a tour of the farm. Would you like to do that in about an hour?"

"Yessir, that sounds just fine. I'll be ready."

Austin followed Mrs. Whitestone into the house and down the hallway to a bedroom that was clean and neat and very comforting. She had laid out some towels and a clean pair of overalls and a shirt and some work boots, socks and underwear.

"How could you possibly know my size? They look like they are perfect for me."

"These are some of Billy's hand-me-downs, but they are clean. You can wash up and change clothes and I'll be waiting out in the kitchen."

Getting clean again felt wonderful and he rushed to change into his new clothes. He folded his traveling clothes neatly and put them on the end of the bed and walked back to the kitchen. He sat down at the long table and drank half of the glass of milk and reached for a handful of cookies. *'Maybe I should have taken one at a time.'*

Mrs. Whitestone laughed and said, "It would be a good idea for you to always take a handful of cookies whenever you have the chance, because our son will always be reaching for them whenever he pops in the house. I hope you like baked chicken because that is what we are having for supper tonight."

Later, as he was riding in the wagon with Jonas, he found himself wondering how long he would be able to stay with this family. He had been told some rough stories about what had happened to some of the children from the Orphan Train. He would do his best to work hard, be friendly and keep his room neat. He was curious about their children and how they would react to meeting him. A man was coming out of the barn, with a dog trotting right at his heels. "Danny, come over and meet Austin. Austin, this young man is Danny and he is our newest worker."

"Austin, I'm very pleased to meet you. You couldn't have asked for a better place to live. This is my dog Roscoe and he is as friendly as all of the dogs on this farm. If you need any help with anything, just let me know and I'll do my best to give you advice. I'm sure you'll be happy here."

As Danny walked off towards a field, Austin noticed his hand. "What happened to his hand, Mr. Whitestone?"

"He was hit with a minie ball and it tore it up inside. I admire him because he works as hard as any man with two good hands and doesn't feel sorry for himself. If you ever see him struggling with something, just walk over and help him, real natural like. You don't have to ask if he needs help. We told him ahead of time that we were looking for a young man, so he would be aware of us bringing someone home with us. We have quite a variety of animals, as you can see. All of our children are crazy about animals and we have taken in several over the years. We found a baby deer one year who had apparently lost his mother. Our daughter Sadie hand fed it for several months. Even though she has been set free, we will still find her at the outskirts of the woods some evenings."

When they returned back to the house, supper was ready and Austin was too. He hadn't eaten a regular meal very often with the exceptions of a kind neighbor inviting him over. Jonas introduced his children to Austin and each one had a welcoming smile for him. "This is our eldest, Billy, who returned from the war. He has taken over as the manager of my farm and I couldn't run this place without him. This is Sadie and she works at the General Store in the village and also helps a lot with cooking and baking. Now this is Nellie and she cooks at the café and also helps her mother with housekeeping and cooking. You can count on gaining some weight, now that you'll be a part of our family."

Billy looked over at Austin shyly and said, "You'll find out soon enough that I'm the quiet one, but my sisters more than make up for it with their constant chatter. If you ever need help with anything and need someone to explain something that you don't understand, just let me know and I'll be happy to help you."

Austin was a good judge of character for someone only 15 years old and he liked Billy right away. He wanted to learn as much as he could so that he would be useful. Sadie took her brother's teasing good naturedly, as did Nellie. "Our brother will have an attitude change when he meets the right young lady. Isn't that right, Billy?" At that comment, Billy turned red in the face but he wasn't upset. "I'd like to show Austin around, Pa. While I do my chores, he can get an idea of how things are done around here."

"That was a fine meal, Mrs. Whitestone. I come from good parents, but we didn't have much. A meal like this would have lasted us for a couple of days. I'm ready Billy. I'd like to see what chores you have. Will I be able to take care of any of the animals?"

"You can definitely help us with several kinds of animals. I think you will fit in around here just fine. We'll be back later."

Billy led Austin out to the barn and he noticed that it was as neat and clean as the house. They fed the horses and made sure they had water, and then they gave the pigs some slop and the babies were so cute. The three dogs followed them everywhere and he noticed ducks waddling by, across the lawn, headed for a pond. *'What a peaceful farm this was. I wonder how many children from the train I was on, ended up somewhere like this? Not many, I'm afraid.'*

That evening, as he was laying in his comfortable bed, a few tears trickled down his face. 'I know I can be happy here as long as I'm allowed to stay. Lord, please help me to adjust and make friends. Watch over all of my family back in New York. I'd like to see them all again, but I can't do that without your help. Thank you for choosing this kind family for me to live with. I want to laugh again. It's been a long time since I did that.' A few minutes later he was sound asleep and didn't hear or feel the dog jumping onto his bed, to lay at his feet. Molly was a very sensitive dog and she always sensed when someone needed comforting. When Austin woke up in the morning and saw her on his bed, his face broke out in a wonderful smile. "Hey girl, how did you get up here?" Her tail starting wagging and she looked like she was trying to smile. Someone was knocking on the door, which was partially open. It was Mrs. Whitestone and she said, "Molly, I might have known I'd find you in here. Good morning Austin. I hope you are hungry. We always have a big breakfast to start everyone off each day."

"Yes, ma'am, I sure could eat. Is Molly in trouble for coming up on my bed? I didn't hear her during the night. She sure is pretty."

"No, she's not in any trouble. You couldn't ask for a sweeter dog. I doubt if she'll be far away from you from now on. You've just made yourself a devoted friend. I'll leave so you can get dressed."

Austin reached over and petted Molly and said, "Thank you for coming to stay with me last night. I was feeling pretty lonely, but I don't think I'll feel that way again, if you'll stay with me."

Melissa managed to keep busy while Albert & Joshua were away, but still she found herself wondering where they were, were they safe and when would she see them again? She had been separated from Albert for three years, during the war, but now a few weeks seemed very hard. More than once, her thoughts ended up, surprisingly, thinking about Joshua. He was a good friend of Alberts and she was grateful that they had each other's support during the war. The fact that he had taken such good care of Albert when he was wounded, made their friendship extremely special. Both men were alike in some ways but very different in others. *Why am I thinking about Joshua, anyway? I'm sure he will soon find a wonderful girl to fall in love with. If he ends up making Willow Bend his home, we will be spending a lot of time together. Albert hasn't spoken of marriage to me, so maybe I'm jumping to conclusions. If I am, it wouldn't be the first time. I'm too young to be thinking about marriage, any way.'* She had only received two short letters from Albert and it was mainly to let her know that they reached Joshua's friend in time and it seemed to lift his friend's spirits considerably.

A few days later, Albert and Joshua walked into the library and Melissa was so relieved and happy to see them. "I'm sorry that we were gone longer than we expected to be, but it was worth it to see Joshua's friend before he passed away."

"Joshua, I am so sorry that you lost your friend but it was so thoughtful of you to want to make that journey to see him. Albert, how has your leg held up during the trip? I imagine it was more painful than you expected it to be."

"I'll be honest and will admit that it is aching quite a bit right now but a good soak in the tub should bring me some relief. Doc gave me some pills to take with me but I used them sparingly because they made me so sleepy. Now that we are back in Willow Bend again, I have no intention of leaving you again. May I take you to the hotel for dinner tomorrow night, after I have rested up?"

"I would love to have dinner with you, and Joshua you are also welcome. You must both be exhausted so why don't you go on back to your house and I'll see you tomorrow evening."

When Gerard had been at the hotel for about a month, Maude stopped Ellie one morning to talk to her. "Ellie, I know how hard you are saving your money and I was wondering if you would be interested in some extra work? We could use some help in the dining room since one of the waitresses is leaving the village. You can keep any tips plus we will pay you each week." Ellie was excited to hear about being able to make some additional income, so she quickly agreed. Maude asked her to start the next day during the breakfast hour.

The next morning, she walked back into the kitchen and asked Martha if she had time to explain her new job. Martha was happy to find out that Ellie would be helping her and she showed her where everything was kept and handed her an apron and a pad of paper and a pencil to take orders. Martha said, "You can follow me for a little while and after that, when you feel comfortable, you can take orders by yourself." Ellie followed her out to the dining room and there sat Gerard looking so handsome and friendly. Martha had been waiting on him every day so she already knew what he liked. She told him that Ellie would be helping her in the mornings and evenings from now on. That news seemed to really interest Gerard and Ellie could hardly look him in the eye. Martha led Ellie back to where they kept the coffee and she asked her to bring Gerard his coffee. Ellie tried to keep her hands from shaking but it was impossible. When she finally managed to get the cup on the table, a little bit had sloshed over the top. Ellie apologized and offered to get a fresh cup. Gerard said, "Ellie, there isn't any reason to bring me another cup. This one will do just fine."

At the moment, there weren't any new customers, so she ran back into the kitchen and out the back door. She just stood there, drawing in big deep breaths of fresh air and it helped her to settle down. *How was she going to wait on him every day without spilling something on him or the tablecloth?* She could avoid him when she was cleaning his room. She had found out quickly when he was going downstairs for breakfast and as soon as he was seated in the dining room, she had raced up to his room and worked at top speed. There was no way to avoid him in the dining room and Ellie didn't think her nerves could take it.

Listening to Maude really scared Gerard. He just couldn't lose Ellie because he was a successful man. Lose Ellie? He hadn't even spent five minutes alone with her. What could he do to help her understand what kind of a man he was? He was tired of her looking at him as just someone whose room she kept clean. He had to wait to see if Maude would make some progress; even a little would be wonderful. The next day Maude asked Ellie if she would keep her company while she drove around the country and Ellie said she would be happy to. Maude said that she would provide a picnic basket and would meet her out in front of the hotel at noon. Ellie showed up right on time and hopped up into the carriage. Maude kept the horse at a leisurely pace as they left town and headed out in the direction of Johnny's ranch. Ellie said she had never been outside of Willow Bend and was excited to see what was out there.

Every time they drove past any animal or a field of wild flowers, Ellie chattered away about how wonderful this ride was. Maude decided to start the conversation slowly so she said, "I had a nice conversation with Gerard about his book. He has interviewed several of the oldest villagers and they have been very helpful." She noticed that at Gerard's name, Ellie tensed up.

Ellie said, "I'm happy that his book is coming along so well. When do you think he will be leaving?"

"I don't think he is in any rush Ellie; he feels right at home here in Willow Bend. The villagers are often saying that he fits right in."

"He can't stay here much longer. What I mean is, he must miss the kind of life that he is used to. He dresses so fine and he has such a look about him. It's as if he has seen the world and we're just a little village."

Maude was trying not to laugh out loud. "Ellie, Gerard wants to get to know you better, but he keeps getting the feeling that you are uncomfortable around him. I've gotten to know him pretty well since he moved into the hotel. I think highly of him and I wish you would give him a chance. Just spend one afternoon with him and see if I am right. He'd like to take you for a ride in the country. He only has the best intentions."

Ellie was so scared inside because she still didn't understand why a good-looking man like Gerard would want to spend time with her. She trusted Maude, so she decided to face her fear and say yes to him. When they returned to town, Ellie started work right away in one of the empty rooms of the hotel. Maude made a point of finding Gerard and telling him the good news. His face lit up when he listened to her. Maude said, "Ellie is very nervous about spending time with you and she doesn't understand what you see in a girl who is nothing but a maid. Please be gentle and patient with her." He promised that he would.

The next morning, he went down to the dining room and Ellie timidly walked over to his table. She said, "Maude told me that you would like to take me for a drive in the country. I think that will be alright."

Gerard responded, "Miss Ellie, it would be an honor to take you for a ride. Would tomorrow morning be convenient for you?"

"As soon as I get my work done. I can be ready by eleven o'clock." Gerard said that would be just fine.

For a man who normally could fall asleep within minutes, Gerard tossed and turned that night; he was so excited. He finally managed to fall asleep after midnight but woke up at dawn. After he got dressed, he tried to write but he couldn't concentrate, so he finally had to give up. When he was eating breakfast, he wasn't sure what he was tasting. He actually felt like he was going to be sick. Gerard had escorted many women in his life and he'd never felt this nervous. Finally, it was time to get the carriage and he drove up in front of the hotel and tied the horse to the railing. He walked through the front door and there was Ellie, standing there with Maude. She was trying to smile but it was a little one. Maude gave her a quick hug, handed Gerard a picnic basket and told them to have a good time. Gerard offered Ellie his arm and she slowly put her hand in the crook of his arm. He helped her gently into the carriage and went around and untied the horse and stepped up beside Ellie.

They drove in a different direction from the way she had traveled with Maude yesterday. Gerard had already traveled this road and he knew the scenery was beautiful and interesting. He pointed out where the first pioneers had built log cabins and where Indians had once lived. Ellie seemed sincerely interested in whatever Gerard was telling her. A little further up the road, a young colt was standing by the fence with its mother. Ellie let out a soft cry and asked Gerard to stop. As soon as the carriage came to a halt, Ellie was already jumping out. Gerard was delighted at her interest and he got down and stood beside her. She reached her hand through the fence and let the colt nuzzle her. Soon the mother came over and Ellie stroked her neck. She looked so happy and more relaxed that he had ever seen her. This was working out better than he had planned. Gerard didn't speak; he just watched Ellie. She turned around and looked up at him with the most radiant smile. "Thank you for taking me out here for a ride. I have never seen a baby colt up close. I've only lived in a small house in a city and then in the hotel. I had no idea what the country would be like. I wonder what it would feel like to live out here with all the beautiful trees, flowers and animals, and to have so much room to walk or ride?"

They had such a wonderful day, stopping to eat at the side of a small creek, picking wild flowers and talking. "Ellie have you ever had a dream; maybe what your life would be like in ten years?"

She shyly said, "Someday I would like to own my own hotel. I have no idea how that could ever come to be, but that would make me so happy. I love getting the rooms ready for our guests and getting to know them."

"I definitely feel that is a dream worthy of your hard work and how much you care about taking care of people."

She was so relieved that he didn't laugh or try to talk her out of it. As they were driving back to the village, Gerard felt as though he had made a little bit of progress, thanks to Maude and her close relationship with Ellie.

Johnny had been talking to Pete recently and he said that he had a suspicion that someone was stealing from his customers in the saloon. He had a good idea of who it was, but he needed to catch him in the act. Since Curtis was a new deputy, Johnny had asked him if he would go down there for a beer every so often, but not wear his badge and see if he could spot anything unusual. He had been in there three times so far, but no leads. Today Curtis walked through the doors and nodded to Pete and walked up to the bar and ordered a beer. Pete was to mention the weather if the man he suspected was in the saloon. "How do you like this cooler weather? I've been waiting for it all summer long."

"I prefer this kind of weather myself." He casually turned to his side and slowly scanned the room. It didn't take long for his eyes to spot a shifty character, sitting at a table by himself. He was paying attention to a man who looked like he was just traveling through. Possibly a salesman who was carrying a case of samples of some kind. Curtis walked over to this man and introduced himself. "Howdy, my name is Curtis and I kind of picked you out as a salesman. Am I right? I've been looking for something special for my girl."

The man smiled and shook his hand. "Nice to meet you. My name is Joseph Collins. You must be a very observant fellow. I am indeed a salesman. I'm sorry that I don't happen to sell things for the ladies. I cater to bankers and congressmen that like the high dollar watches."

"Whew, that would be out of my price range. Are you pretty successful in your travels?"

"Not so much in this small village, but the one that I just left a few days ago, I more than doubled my sales. They have a lot of bankers in that town. I'll be leaving in the morning. I found a nice room at the hotel here."

"Well, it was nice meeting you and be alert when you are traveling. There are some men who don't like workin' for a living; they'd just rather steal someone like you blind." He made sure that his voice carried over to the man that he suspected was the robber. He walked back to the bar and softly told Pete who he had his eyes on. He also told him about his conversation with the salesman. Curtis decided to follow the salesman when he left the saloon. It would be dark soon and he felt like tonight would be a perfect night for the salesman to be robbed.

Curtis left the saloon right at dusk and he hid his horse and stepped into a dark alley. It wasn't long before he saw the salesman leave, headed for the hotel. Not a minute later, the suspicious man was slowly walking behind him and now he was picking up his pace. He called out to the salesman, "Hey mister, I might be interested in one of your fancy watches. I won me some money at a saloon last week and wanted to get me somethin' special for my father. Can you let me see what you have left to sell?"

The salesman had stopped walking, but it was obvious that he was uneasy. "I can meet you in the hotel lobby and I'll be happy to show you what I have."

The robber pulled out a gun and said, "Why don't you step back into this here alley and we'll look at it right here." Curtis quietly came up behind the man and put his gun in his back and said, "Drop that gun mister. You are under arrest." The salesman took off running and didn't stop to look back. Curtis took his gun, handcuffed him and led him down to the jail. When he walked in, Johnny was just about to leave. He explained who this man was and Johnny said, "Good work, Curtis. While I put him in the cell, why don't you go get his horse and we can take a good look inside his saddle bags."

"You don't have no right to look in my saddlebags. I ain't done nuthin' wrong. You're takin' his word against mine."

Not long after, Bucky walked into the jail, wanting to ask Johnny a question about one of their new horses. Curtis came inside, and dumped the contents of both saddlebags onto the desk. There were watches, rings, necklaces and some big bills.

One thing caught Bucky's eye right away. "That's my grandpa's pocket watch that was stolen from me the day I was on my way to this village. I can tell you what is engraved inside. It says, *'For 20 years of service above and beyond the call of duty.'* He was a sheriff, Johnny."

Johnny opened it up and read the engraving. He handed over the pocket watch to Bucky and said, "Your timing couldn't have been better. I'm glad that this has been returned to you. It must be extra special. What was it you came in here to ask me?"

"I can't even remember right now. I'm so excited. I guess I'll have to ask you tomorrow."

Dwight was not exactly handsome, but he had a very kind and distinguished looking face. You never saw any anger in his face unless he saw an animal hurt or abused. At that point, you would see a different side of him. A hurt animal brought out his deep compassion. An abused animal made him boil up inside with rage. Thankfully that didn't happen often. He was always taking in another dog and everyone knew that he was a soft touch. Sometimes if the right person came along, he would give one of his dogs to someone who really cared about animals. He was very careful when it came to making that kind of decision.

When he woke up in the morning, Dwight always took the time to talk to the Lord and pray for his friends and neighbors. Several of them were sick or came home from the war injured. One thing that he had started last year was a large garden that was open to the entire village. It was sectioned off in plots and when a name was assigned to a plot, he painted that name on a stake. So far several families had gladly come out to his farm to work on their own garden. All Dwight asked from each individual or family was to keep their area weeded and to put surplus vegetables in bins that he supplied. This would partly go to the hotel kitchen, because they never turned away anyone who was hungry. The other part of the excess was given to the families who lived too far away from his farm to take care of a garden. Most of these were elderly folks and he gladly hitched up his team once a week and made a wide circle to visit each family.

This morning he was trying to comb back his thick, silver, unruly hair. There was always one piece that refused to lay down like the others. Dwight put some water on it and did his best to make it flat against his head. He was now close to 55 years of age and yet he looked at least 10 years younger. He always had a nice tan from being outside constantly. Before putting on his favorite green cap, he decided he needed to eat something before tackling his chores for the morning. Over the years he had turned into a half decent cook. Scrambled eggs and toast was easy enough. Dwight drank his first cup of coffee of the day facing the big window that looked out over the barn and stables. This was his favorite place to sit in the entire house.

Dwight had several farm hands working for him and he treated them all like family. The only one in question was the newest young man he had hired, Jimmy Duncan. In the short time he had known him, it was obvious that Jimmy hadn't been raised to appreciate hard work. He had a streak of laziness in him that Dwight was determined to cure. The other workers were polite to Jimmy, but they didn't reach out to try and be friends, because they didn't respect him. It had gotten to the point that some of the men had come to Dwight and told him that it would be a wise move to find him somewhere else to sleep. After looking over the barn, he found a small room that had been used for storage. He cleaned it out himself and put in a cot and a bale of hay to sit on. He really needed to spend more time with Jimmy, but he hadn't had the time yet. It was obvious that Jimmy hadn't had any good male role model as he was growing up. Dwight saw potential in him if someone would just take the time with him.

Dwight hitched up his team to the carriage and loaded up all of the vegetables in the baskets. He had also fixed a couple of sandwiches and threw in a couple of apples and a jug of water. He hadn't packed anything fancy; just something to keep him from getting too hungry. At the last minute, he called Jimmy over and asked him to go with him. Jimmy's attitude was hard to read but he certainly wasn't eager to ride along in a wagon full of vegetables. Dwight tried to be patient with this young man so he said, "I could use some company this afternoon and it will give you a chance to meet more people. Hop in!" Jimmy climbed up beside Dwight and off they went. For awhile, no one said a word and then Dwight said, "Jimmy, I've noticed that the other workers aren't exactly friendly with you. Do you know why?"

He could see that Jimmy stiffened up immediately but he just shrugged and said, "I have no idea. I haven't done anything to them." Dwight was praying silently for the right words to say in response.

"Most of my workers have been with me a long time Jimmy and they work hard to put in a full day's work. Since you've been here, I believe that they don't understand a man like you. You are young and strong and intelligent, but you are lazy. I can't defend you to them in a way that they would understand, so I've decided to try and help you change your attitude."

Jimmy was hanging his head and Dwight saw no anger in him, which was a relief. "I've never been around men who worked hard, sir. My Pa was a drunk and he even got my Ma into drinking. My two brothers ran off after so many years of half starving and being beaten. For some reason, I didn't get beaten but I was never around any decent men. You are the first person to ever give me a chance. I don't know if it is too late or not, but I will try harder. You've got my word on that."

Dwight was pleased with his comments and he replied, "Son, you have a lot of potential. Every time you have a decision to make in this life, it can improve your life or it can help to ruin it, but it's always your choice. Just remember that."

Jimmy had been hired a few months ago to work on Dwight's ranch. All of the other people working on the ranch stayed far away from him and he hadn't made even one friend. Although Dwight was friendly and treated him with respect, Jimmy had a feeling that he had his doubts about him. His father had run off when he was only ten years old. All he could remember was his mother crying her heart out every night for months and his little sister, Tara, was just starting to walk when he left them. There was never a man around their house after that and Jimmy seemed to feel an over-whelming sadness one day and deep anger the next. He had no one to set an example for him of how to take pride in doing any type of job. Jimmy struggled in school and the other kids always teased him about his rundown clothes and his poor grades. Even the teacher didn't take the time to try to help him and sometimes joined in the children to make cruel comments about him. When he turned 15, he had taken all of the pain he could handle. He told his mother that he was sorry, but he was leaving. The look on her face was pitiful. She had already given up on life. His sister Tara had grown up to be a pretty girl but not good in school. He hugged them both goodbye and never looked back. He had walked for days, hitching a ride on a wagon whenever he had the chance. One day it was Dwight himself who offered him a ride and then a job and a place to sleep and eat.

Jimmy should have worked hard for the chance Dwight was giving him but he just couldn't figure out how to apply himself. He did the least amount of work that he could get away with and often hid behind a building and took a nap. Finally, the other workers had had enough and complained to Dwight about him. They said that they didn't want him sleeping in the same building with them, so Dwight fixed up a small room in the barn for him. There was just a cot and a bale of hay and a lantern on a nail, but it was his.

One day Dwight sent Jimmy into town to pick up some supplies and he noticed a beautiful young girl walking down the boardwalk. He slowed down the horse and wagon to keep pace with her. She turned to see who was driving beside her and gave him a scornful look and keep on walking. He swallowed his pride and drove beside her once more and said, "Good afternoon, my name is Jimmy. What's yours?" The girl didn't even respond; she just turned and walked into a store and left Jimmy feeling ashamed.

Norma had spent a lot of time trying to come up with a way to get back at the sheriff for buying her ranch behind her back. Now she remembered some young man who had tried to be friendly to her but she hadn't given him the time of day. He had a job at Dwight's ranch and just worked in the fields and got his hands dirty. To be seen in public with him would have made her a laughing stock. *What was his name, anyway?* She had heard Dwight mention his name one day when he was sitting near her in the hotel. He was complaining about how slow and lazy his new worker was. *'Jimmy! That was his name.'* She was going to have to find a way to talk to him without anyone else being aware of it. Where was it that she had seen him when he was in town recently? She thought maybe it was the feed store. Norma felt sure that she could use Jimmy to get revenge on the sheriff and no one would know she was behind it.

Jimmy was back in town a few weeks after seeing that pretty girl, running errands for Dwight. Today he ran into the same girl who had ignored him, but today she looked directly at him. She asked Dwight if she could hire him to do a job for her. She had of course forgotten his name and never told him hers. Jimmy jumped at the chance to do something for her, especially when she said she would pay him well. She told him to drive the wagon behind the feed store and to meet her behind the building. When she explained what she wanted him to do, he initially said he couldn't do it. "What are you afraid of? It will only take you about ten minutes and it will be dark. No one will see you and I am paying you well. Maybe I should find another man who is braver than you are." That was more than Jimmy could stand so he agreed to what she wanted. He told her that he would wait two more nights when there was a moon to help him see where he was going.

Most of the village was abuzz with talk of a village dance coming up in the fall. It had been the inspiration of Maude and Jennie. They were talking about an idea to help bring the community together. Ever since Jennie had taken over the hotel, she was anxious to do something with the third floor but had no idea what. Maude suggested using it part of the time for a seasonal dance and Jennie was thrilled with the idea. Soon they were writing down ideas and lists of supplies and furniture needed and the names of other people who could be asked to participate. As soon as Jennie wrote down one thing, Maude already had several names or ideas to add.

Jennie suggested that a donation box be set up at the front desk of the hotel because they did not want to charge any admittance fee. No one was to be turned away because of lack of income. Refreshments had its own separate list and was being kept remarkably simple but elegant. They were going to ask Betsy, who lived in the hotel, if she would be kind enough to organize the decorations. She had plenty of experience in that area, since her social life had previously been extremely busy.

Some of the ladies would not have a dress to wear and this challenge was to be given to Emily, if she accepted. She was a gifted seamstress and would be given payment for any dress that she could sew in the time given to her. Maude already knew the names of several people who would be happy to donate funds to cover the cost of materials and to pay Emily. Hopefully this would bring in much needed income to her, as long as she didn't over work. Her baby was due in December but as of right now, she was feeling very healthy. They would also ask one of the younger girls in town to be an assistant to Emily. Maude also had on her list a number of women who could easily donate a dress or two for the evening. The only problem that she could see would be not making the women feel like a charity case, but she had already come up with an idea. Both women were getting more excited by the minute.

That afternoon Maude and Jennie went up to the third floor to see what shape the ballroom was in and they were pleasantly surprised. Maude brought her lists of chores with her. One side would have the refreshments set up and a special section for those not able to dance, but who would enjoy watching everyone. The musicians were added to the list and since Maude knew all of the villagers, she knew every instrument that could be played. The musicians would be set up on the stage area. There would be no alcohol at this dance and some men that could be trusted would be overseeing it at all times. The drapes were added to the list, to be shaken out and beaten and pressed or mended where needed. They were giving themselves three weeks to put this all together and were confident that it could be done on time.

Maude started adding men who were strong enough to carry furniture up these stairs and noted who had wagons to carry the furniture to the hotel. Next on the list was advertising and the first name that popped into Maude's head was Jennie's husband, Richard. He was such a likable man and spoke to everyone in the village, regardless of their position. He saw everyone as a human being that he would like to know and everyone was treated with respect. She would ask Sadie Whitestone to design some flyers to be posted or passed around the village. Maude and Jennie wanted no one left out if they had anything to say about it. Even people just traveling through for the night were more than welcome.

Maude excused herself for a minute and went back out into the hallway and noticed another door to the left of the main door to the ballroom. As she always kept the keys on a chain with her, she pulled out the key ring and tried a few with no results. Finally, a smaller key did the trick. She opened the door and walked in and found a nice sized room with only a love seat and two small end tables. She went back to the ballroom and asked Jennie to do something strange. She asked her to sing any song quite loudly but to give her a minute to get back into the room next door. Jennie seemed puzzled, but she did as she was asked and started singing a hymn that they had recently sung in church. Maude could hear her very clearly. Jennie asked what was on Maude's mind and she was told, "I don't really know for sure yet, but I will. There is a special reason that I found that room next door. I'm going to pray about it and see if I can figure it out."

The weeks were flying by and very few people turned them down when asked to help. Maude seemed to know what everyone was gifted at or willing to do. When Jennie approached Norma about donating a dress, she was made to feel like a complete fool for even thinking of Norma letting another woman wear one of her precious and expensive gowns. Jennie was hoping that she would at least offer to donate some money, but no offer was made.

Many of the families volunteered their children to scrub and dust and wax floors. The window washing was left to the grownups who took pride in their windows being spotless. Several pieces of furniture were donated, and the room was filling up nicely. Maude had been very clear that any furniture given to the hotel was not to be on loan but a permanent donation. If this dance went off as well as they thought it was going to, there would be many more galas to look forward to.

Not one of the musicians had turned them down; in fact, they were excited to be asked. When you walked around the village in the evening, you could often hear the musicians practicing and that just added to the excitement. Posters were hanging in the General Store, the hotel, the restaurant, the library and there was even one at the train station. Elizabeth came by and asked for one for the doctor's office. This solved the problem of Maude having to ask Doc if they could. If they ran into each other in the village, he would nod and say something pleasant but would keep walking. Maude wanted to stick her foot out and trip him the last time he did this to her. That would give her a great deal of satisfaction except she was afraid that she would be the one to fall down.

Sarah had a surprise for Maude. One day as they were eating lunch in the hotel kitchen, Sarah said she wanted to do more than to donate money for a gown. Maude ran over her lists to see if that would give Sarah any ideas and it didn't seem to help at first. All of a sudden Sarah spoke up with excitement in her voice. "Maude, I could sing some songs to give the musicians a break." Maude didn't want to hurt her dear friend's feelings, but she had to know that she could really sing before she accepted her offer. Sarah grabbed Maude's hand and started walking up the stairs to the ballroom. They went inside and closed the door. Sarah asked Maude to sit down and to tell her the absolute truth about her singing and Maude agreed to do that. A few seconds later, Sarah opened her mouth and the sound coming out of her was breathtaking. She was singing a very popular tune but in a way that Maude had never heard before. It brought tears to her eyes. When Sarah finished that song, she immediately started up with another song, equally touching. Her final song was more uplifting and had Maude tapping her feet. This was the first time that Sarah had sung in front of anyone since she was a young girl. She needed no practice, no warming up; she would just relax and let the words flow out. Maude was clapping her hands with delight and Sarah looked pleased. *'This was going to get one Pastor's attention and I can hardly wait to see his reaction. I love Sarah like a daughter and I want to shake Pastor James sometimes for not trying harder to understand my dear friend and recognize her good qualities. Perhaps the sheriff might also be surprised at her friend's lovely voice. He thought that no one noticed how he sometimes looked at Sarah, but Maude didn't miss much.'*

That night Jimmy rode his horse over to the sheriff's ranch and tied his horse up in the woods. He walked quickly across the field and then stopped when he had made his way through the barb wired fence.

Looking in every direction, he didn't see anyone outside. He went behind the tool shed and lit a match to some kerosene he had brought in a can. The fire took off immediately, so Jimmy turned to go back towards the fence. All of a sudden someone yelled FIRE! and he took off running.

Johnny was sitting at the long kitchen table, making another list of supplies to order and a separate list of extra chores. Samuel was out checking on the animals one last time and the sliver of a moon had hid him well. As he came out of the barn, something caught his eye that was out of the ordinary. Flames were shooting up out of the shed where they kept their tools. It was close to the barn but it hadn't spread enough. Samuel gave a loud shout of, "Fire" and his voice was loud enough to get Johnny's attention quickly, along with Jacob. Johnny saw a dark figure running off towards the barb wired fence. By the way this person was moving, it was a slightly built young man. The person was pulling the barbed wires apart, trying to get through them. Johnny heard a rip and then the man made it through. Now he was running all out and Johnny knew he couldn't catch him. He went up to the fence and found a jagged piece of a flannel shirt, which would be useful evidence.

Jimmy heard someone shout for him to stop but there was no way that he was going to. He thought he would make a clean getaway when he got to the fence. In his haste to get through the barbed wire quickly, he heard his shirt tear. Finally, he was clear and he took off running like a deer. The man who was chasing him gave up and turned back toward the fire. This had not turned out the way he had hoped but he was safe and had some good money to show for it. No one would be able to recognize him in the dark, and the only one who knew what he was up to was the girl who had paid him. He had nothing to worry about. He had done what he was paid to do and no one was hurt. That was some easy money, that's for sure!

Johnny went back to the shed and found that Samuel and his son had the fire out and were pouring water everywhere there could have been sparks still alive. "I can't thank you all enough for alerting me and putting out the fire. Samuel, your timing couldn't have been any better." By now Rebecca was waiting on the porch for news about what had just happened. She had coffee waiting for all of them and some of her cookies. They all sat down at the big table and tried to relax. Johnny thought it was time to explain what he had found out at the land office. He told them, "Norma was the one who had suddenly bought the exact ranch that you had been saving up for. She had no use for it nor did she ever want to live there. It was just out of meanness that she had purchased the ranch. Somehow she must have found out that I was the one who had given her a deal she couldn't turn down."

"Oh Johnny," sighed Rebecca, "the day I was moving out of the hotel, she came up to me and asked me if I was tired of living in the hotel. I was so excited that I blurted out where we were going to be moving. I am so sorry that I caused this trouble for you." Johnny immediately spoke up and said "Rebecca, don't worry yourself at all. She would have found out anyway in a village this small."

He had noticed the other day in the hotel dining room; she had looked at him with anger in her eyes and then turned away. He was mentally going through the list of young men in this village who would start a fire and the list was very short. When the fire had started out at his new ranch a few weeks ago, he had a nagging suspicion that Norma was somehow behind it.

"No, she wouldn't have gotten her little hands dirty, starting the fire. She was well able to convince someone to do her work for her. Since I became sheriff two months ago, everything has stayed so peaceful, with the exception of having to put a few drunks in the jail overnight. Now my main job is to find out who set fire to my shed. It shouldn't be too much longer and somehow I'll figure it out."

11

OCTOBER 1865

An Old Sweetheart Comes Back From the Past

Julia Randolph was quite happy living in the village hotel, except she wanted a pet and she wasn't allowed to have one in the hotel. She decided to pray about it and see what God had to say about the situation. Julia knew that God loved children, so she prayed about wanting a pet. She tried hard to be patient, waiting for an answer.

Each day she helped her mama by picking up around their hotel room and especially making sure that there was nothing on the floor to trip over. Timothy was always leaving one of his toys around and more than once, she had heard her mama scold him for not listening to her rules. Today Julia had the room looking neat and her mama was pleased with the results. She asked permission to go and visit Mrs. Moses, who was the elderly lady who lived down the hall. Her mama said that would be a good idea and she gave Julia some special tea bags to give to her.

Julia skipped down the hall, her braids bouncing off her shoulders. Mrs. Moses was always happy for her company. She knocked on the door and waited. Pretty soon she heard Mrs. Moses telling her to come in. When Julia opened the door, she was greeted with a smile and then she went over for a hug. She put the teabags into her hands and reached over and gave her a kiss on the cheek. Mrs. Moses always smelled like the pretty powder that she wore every day. Julia asked if there was anything she could do for her and there was. Her shawl had fallen off the back of the rocker and Mrs. Moses couldn't reach it. Julia went behind the rocker and picked it up and put it around her shoulders. Julia asked if she could continue reading a story to her. Mrs. Moses always looked forward to hearing Julia read and she looked forward to these visits so much. The new schoolteacher, Miss Sarah, had been impressed with Julia's hunger for reading and had loaned her books for children older than eight years old.

A few days later, Julia went out the kitchen's back door to shake out a rug. She heard a pitiful cry and looked behind a bush and found a tiny kitten. She immediately dropped the rug and ran over to the kitten and picked it up. The kitten snuggled up close to her neck and was purring. Forgetting about the rug, she went back into the kitchen and asked Charlie, the cook, for some milk for the kitten. He was such a kind-hearted man and he quickly found a small tin and poured some milk in it. He told Julia that he would carry it outside so it wouldn't spill. Julia plopped down on the ground and put the kitten close to the milk. The kitten started lapping it up and soon there wasn't much left. Julia asked him, "How can we take care of this kitten Mr. Charlie? I'm not allowed to have a pet in the hotel. We can't just leave her out here all alone at night."

Charlie told her "I have a solution. I found a box in the store room and put some rags inside and then I'll put the kitten on the rags." She immediately curled up and was fast asleep in no time. He asked Julia if she had a name for the kitten and she said, "Pitty Pat". Charlie said "It is true that pets aren't allowed in the hotel but I happen to know that there was a mouse or two roaming around at night and this kitten would grow up to be a good mouser." That made Julia happy and she gave him a big hug.

"You are so smart Charlie. Thank you for helping me and Pitty Pat." That night when she was lying in bed, Julia was going over the day again in her mind. She suddenly realized that God had answered her prayer about a pet in a way that only He could do. She fell asleep with a big smile on her face.

"May I Escort You to the Dance?"

Gerard had just been told by Maude that she was helping to organize a big dance at the hotel. His heart got so excited, just thinking about taking Ellie to the dance. *'Whoa, there, you haven't even asked her yet! I can just imagine her reaction.'* He needed to rely on Maude again. Thank goodness she trusted him and seemed to like him. *'What if someone else asked Ellie before he did?'* There was no time to waste. Ellie was so pretty and friendly that at least a couple of the young men in the village would be delighted to escort her to the dance. He decided to find Maude right now so that she could put in a good word for him.

Gerard found Maude talking to Sarah, so he tried to wait patiently until they were finished. Sarah noticed him first and she said, "Hi Gerard, are you waiting to speak to Maude? We can talk another time. I'll see you later."

Maude looked up at him and her eyes were dancing. "Hmm, let me guess! You'd like me to speak to Ellie about you escorting her to the dance. Am I correct?"

Gerard could feel his neck getting flushed and he actually looked insecure; which was not like him at all. "You are correct Maude! I want to ask her before some other young man does. If she turns me down, it's going to be hard to take. Can you say something like, "Gerard doesn't know anyone in the village that well and he'd like to take you to the dance?"

Maude shook her head slightly and said, "That makes it sound like she's not very special. How about, 'Gerard wants to escort you to the dance but he is nervous, thinking you might turn him down?'

His eyes got big after hearing that comment but Maude said, "Well, that is the honest truth; is it not?"

"I don't want her to know that I am nervous. How about, 'Gerard was wondering if you would accept his invitation to the dance, but he wasn't sure that you liked to dance?' "Maude", Gerard said out of desperation, "please tell her that if she doesn't want to dance with me, I'd be happy to just be her escort." Maude agreed to talk to Ellie that very day and would let Gerard know what her response was. Gerard needed a man to talk to and he decided to try and find the pastor.

Pastor James was painting a wall in the church but was happy to take a break. He offered Gerard some cold water and he gladly accepted. They sat outside on a wooden bench and Pastor said, "I'm so pleased that you came by today. I have a feeling that you have something particular on your mind. I'm willing to listen to anything you would like to share with me."

Gerard took a deep breath and a big swallow of water and burst out with, "Pastor, do you think that you understand women?" Pastor had been in the process of trying to swallow some of his water, but he spit it out instead and started to roar with laughter. "Son, if you looked all over the village, you couldn't find a man who understands women any less than I do. I might suggest that you talk to Will. He seems to really make an impression on the ladies in our village. Maybe he could be more helpful. I could use some advice myself, if you want to know the truth."

"Well, Pastor, I could still use someone to talk to and I think I would be more comfortable with you. You see, since I've been living in the hotel, writing my book, I've come to be very interested in one of the maids named Ellie. Whenever I try to spend some time with her, she acts like she is afraid of me. I have asked Maude to intervene for me and that has helped somewhat. I have never before had any woman resist my attempts to get to know them better. This experience is all new to me."

Pastor had to hold back a chuckle because Gerard had a problem just the opposite of his. "Gerard, I am glad that you feel comfortable enough with me to share your concerns. I wish that I could be more help to you. You see, I've been praying for over a year for God to bring me the woman he has chosen for me. I think I might have found her but she makes me so nervous that I can't put two thoughts together. Sometimes my stomach gets upset just knowing that she'll be coming into the church in a few minutes. Her personality couldn't be more different than what I have been picturing in my mind. I've never felt so insecure in my life."

Gerard looked puzzled for a moment and then said, "Pastor, I have a feeling that you are talking about Sarah. I've never known a woman like her before and I think that I can see why you would be nervous around her."

Pastor jumped up off of the bench and said, "How on earth did you know I was talking about Sarah? I mean...I didn't mention her name."

Gerard said, "I am a people watcher and I've picked up on little things whenever I've seen you two near each other. Don't worry, I would never mention this to anyone. I think I'll go back to the hotel now and try to write some more in my book. Thank you for taking the time to listen to me." Pastor was so shaken up that he hardly noticed when Gerard walked away.

Danny had now been working and living with Jonas and his family for several weeks. Many times he found himself looking at their oldest daughter Sadie. She was so pretty but didn't act like she had any idea that she was. A couple of times she had brought him a pitcher of water and a cup and that pleased him more than he could say. He had not once seen her stare at his injured hand. One day he was struggling to pick something up and she came up to his side and gently said, "Here, let me help you." To his amazement, he was not embarrassed, and it felt so natural. He thanked her, and she left to help her mother hang up clothes. Danny couldn't stop thinking about what had just happened. He would have normally been angry if someone had acted like he wasn't able to do something by himself but there was no anger in him. Was it possible that he could become someone special to Sadie? He was almost afraid to hope, so he would not rush into anything.

Sadie decided that if she had any hopes of attending the dance with Danny, she was going to have to swallow her pride and ask him herself. She was pretty sure that he was insecure because of his hand. It wasn't hard to find him, since she knew which field he would be in; clearing away brush. She had brought him a slice of apple pie and some water. He wiped his forehead with his handkerchief and thanked her. Instead of leaving him with his pie, she stayed. Sadie said, "Danny, I was hoping that you would accompany me to the village dance that is coming up soon."

Danny didn't know quite what to say but he knew he had to respond soon. He said, "I would be honored to take you to the dance Sadie. I'm not the greatest dancer, but all this marching business has taught me to keep step quite well." They both laughed at his comment. He handed her back the plate and cup and thanked her again. As she turned to leave, he saw her sweet smile and he felt wonderful. Not every girl was going to be like Mandie and that was a relief. He still couldn't believe that she had asked him to escort her to the dance.

Gerard was up in his room, pacing back and forth constantly, until he realized what he was doing. This was the day that he was going to find the courage to ask Ellie to the dance. He couldn't put it off any longer because some other man might jump in and ask her and that would be the end of him. *What on earth is wrong with me? I've faced down an enemy who outnumbered us and not been this nervous. Well, here goes! What on earth am I going to do if she turns me down?* He walked out into the hall and who was standing right in front of him but Ellie herself.

Ellie looked startled to see him and he knew his face was flushed. "Um, good morning Ellie. What are you doing? I mean, how are you doing? It's a lovely day, isn't it; not that I've been outside yet or anything."

Ellie looked like she wanted to walk away but she couldn't be rude. "I'm doing fine Gerard. I have a lot of work to do now that I'm working two jobs. Can I do anything for you?"

"Um, I was wondering if; I mean if you'd care to, um, what I mean is, would you allow me to escort you to the dance?"

Ellie's eyes got big and she gulped in some air and tried to calm her stomach down. "You want to attend the dance with me?"

"Well, yes I would be honored if you would agree to, ah, let me escort you. I'm not the best dancer but I'd be willing to give it a try. This would be my first social gathering since I've arrived in Willow Bend and I'm looking forward to meeting more of the people of the village. That doesn't mean that I'm not looking forward to escorting you Ellie." *'You sound like a bumbling idiot Gerard; get a grip on yourself.'*

"I guess I could go with you Gerard. I wasn't planning on attending, to be honest. I don't know if I can find a pretty dress or not but maybe Maude can help me. If you are sure that you want to attend the dance with me, I'll be willing to go. Thank you for inviting me. I've never been to a dance before so I hope I don't trip."

"I wouldn't let you fall Ellie; I promise. Thank you for saying yes. I'll be very proud to walk in the door with you on my arm." He ducked back into his room before he looked any more foolish and threw himself across the bed. *'If any of my friends could have heard that conversation tonight, they would be laughing with glee for hours. Thank goodness no one else heard me besides sweet Ellie.'*

Ellie practically tripped over her own feet, trying to get to the stairs to go and find Maude. She was shaking all over and her face felt hot. *'Goodness, where is Maude?'* When she spotted her, she almost ran across the room. 'Maude, Gerard asked me to attend the dance with him and I don't have a pretty dress or shoes. What will I do?"

Maude was so happy to hear that Ellie had accepted Gerard's invitation. "We'll get Maggie over here tomorrow to start figuring out what kind of dress you would like her to make you and I would like to do this as a special gift for you Ellie. You are like a daughter to me."

"Oh Maude, you are the most generous woman I've ever known and I'm so relieved that I won't have to worry about what I'm wearing. Now I've just got to find me some pretty shoes. I've never owned any before so I'll need someone to help me."

Right then Elizabeth walked into the hotel and Maude asked her if she could possibly help Ellie find some shoes for the dance. Elizabeth said, "Ellie, your feet look about the same size as mine and I have an extra pair that you can borrow, if you would like to." Ellie couldn't believe how everything was falling into place.

"Maude, what about my hair? I don't know any other way to fix it except up on my head, out of the way when I'm working." Maude just smiled and said they would start practicing right away that evening.

Worley and Gus stood outside at the back of saloon, out of sight of everyone, trying to build up their courage. Worley just had to ask Daisy to the dance, but he felt like he could swallow his tongue trying to get the words out. Gus wasn't going to attend because he didn't have a special girl but Worley suggested that he ask Millie.

Gus' eyes got huge and he said, "She's too purty to go to a shindig with the likes of me. All the fellas in the saloon would laugh their heads off if I got the gumption to ask her. I couldn't stand to be laughed at."

Worley assured him that he would find a way for both men to talk to the girls in private. They walked around to the front of the saloon and just stood there for a moment or two, trying to calm down the butterflies in their stomach. Worley was the bravest so he pushed the swinging doors open and plunged ahead; Gus trailing behind him. It didn't take long for Daisy to spot him and she sashayed right on over to greet him. "Hi Worley; hey Gus! Are you two fellas thirsty?" Now she realized that something was up because she'd never seen Worley this uncomfortable. "What's wrong Worley? You don't look so good."

"Could I have a word with you in private? It won't take long." She grabbed his arm and led him over to a table off in the corner.

"Just a minute; let me get you and Gus a beer first. You both look like you could use one right away." When she had handed Gus his beer at the bar, she came over to Worley's table. "Tell Daisy what's wrong Sugar." Worley's ears turned red as a beet but he loved it when she said those words.

Worley took a big slug of his beer and then blurted out, "You wouldn't wanna go to the dance with me, would ya?"

Daisy's eyes started to sparkle and she replied, "I sure wouldn't want to go with anyone else." Now that Worley had faced that question, it didn't seem too hard to bring up Gus and Millie.

"Do you think that Millie would be willing to go with Gus to the dance? He's afraid to ask her for fear of being laughed at."

"Oh Sugar, you fellas are so sweet. I'll go ask her and I'll be right back. Don't you go anywhere." Worley felt like he could melt in a puddle. He was going to take Daisy to the big shindig and he felt like that had been pretty brave of him to ask her. *'Of course she said yes. Who else would she want to go with? I was worried over nuthin.'*

Daisy and Millie both came walking across the room, headed right for Gus. It looked to Worley like he was going to make tracks for the door and leave but somehow he managed to stand his ground. Millie took one of Gus' hands and said, "I would like to attend the dance with you Gus. Thank you for asking me." Gus just stood there in a trance.

Worley sidled up to him and gave him a nudge. "That's wonderful that you are going to the dance Millie. Perhaps we can all walk over together."

Finally, Gus came out of his stupor and said, "That's just what I was about to say 'cept Worley beat me to it." Worley took his friend by the arm and walked him outside before he blurted out something wrong.

"Whew, Worley, I'm gonna go to a shindig with Miss Millie and I'll be the envy of everyone there. That wasn't as hard as I thought it would be."

"Everyone will be envying you, except me", said Worley.

Johnny kept hearing about the dance, no matter where he went, so he supposed he should mention it to Elizabeth. He had such a hard time trying to figure her out. She went to being friendly to furious with him in a blink of an eye. *'Why couldn't she be more like Sarah?' he thought.* He walked over to the hotel and found her talking to Maude at the front desk. "Good morning ladies. I was wondering if I might have a word with you Elizabeth?" Maude quickly excused herself and Elizabeth stood there looking at him but not saying a word. This made Johnny uncomfortable, but he decided to speak to her about the dance anyway and take his chances. "Elizabeth, I was wondering if you would do me the honor of letting me escort you to the dance?"

"Yes, I would like that very much. Thank you for asking me Johnny. My children ask me every day if I'll be attending the dance and I can't seem to make them stop. I believe that a good part of the village plans to attend."

"Out at the ranch I've overheard several comments about who everyone wants to go with. There are a lot of insecure fellas trying to get up their nerve to ask someone."

"I hope that Pastor will be asking Sarah soon. He always seems to be so uncomfortable around her and yet I've never seen anyone else act that way. We are really becoming good friends and I enjoy being with her."

"I don't understand it either. She is so easy to talk to and I enjoy her sense of humor. I call her 'Sharpshooter' after the way she shot that stage robber, and she isn't offended at all. Well, I need to be on my way, but I'll be talking to you soon," he said.

Maude had been hoping that Doc would bring up the subject of the dance, but so far he always had some other subject to talk about. He knew how hard she had been working on this event. It would have been nice for him to say something; to act like he had even noticed her hard work. If he didn't say something to her soon, she actually thought about asking someone herself and it wouldn't be Doc. As soon as she thought of a man, she would quickly find out that he already had plans to take another lady. At her age, she didn't have too many choices. Today they were expecting a new guest from Indiana, who planned to stay for a month, doing research on Civil War Veterans in the area. She would have to be sure to introduce him to Gerard. She wasn't sure of his name because he just signed his initials, H.D. He had sent several wires to her, asking questions about the village and surrounding area. Even in the short wires, she could tell that he was a likable man and had a sense of humor. *How refreshing that would be for a change!*

Isaac had been attending school for a couple of months and had become friends with Melissa; one of the few students who was his age. She was not only pretty, but also really intelligent and interesting to talk to. She never talked down to him and they both loved school. Melissa had plans for the next ten years, in her mind, and Isaac was just dealing with one day at a time. In that way, they were total opposites. Often the subject of animals would come up and Isaac would talk so seriously about how much he had learned, working at Johnny's ranch. Melissa wanted to be a nurse, but she was also interested in animals, so it was always easy to find something to talk about. Today they were walking home from school and Melissa had a question for Isaac.

"Isaac, are you going to the dance?"

"No, I hadn't intended to. I don't really know any girl that I could escort to the dance. There just aren't that many girls near my age."

"Well, one of my best friends is Nellie and I know that so far she doesn't have anyone to escort her. She's a little on the quiet side but she is very interesting."

"Now that you mention it, I just might ask Nellie. My mind always seems to be thinking of what I'll be doing when I get out to Johnny's ranch instead of the people around me. Someday I'd like to have a ranch of my own but that seems like such a crazy dream sometimes."

"I don't think any dream is crazy as long as it's not hurting anyone. I need to get to the general store right now. I hope you will ask Nellie soon because I don't want her thinking that she won't be attending the dance. I'll see you tomorrow Isaac."

Isaac knew that Nellie worked in the café, so he stopped by after leaving Melissa. "Hi Nellie, I'd like a piece of pie and a glass of milk please."

When Nellie had brought his pie and milk to him, she didn't look too busy so he plunged ahead and asked, "Nellie, I was wondering if I might escort you to the dance." Nellie looked so surprised and then pleased.

"I would like that very much. We don't often have a dance in our village and I wouldn't want to miss it. Thank you for asking me. I have to admit that I am not too experienced at dancing but I'd be happy to just watch everyone else."

"I'm no expert myself but I believe in just relaxing and having a good time. Maybe we can invent some new steps." They both had a good laugh out of that comment.

"Well, I'm off to the ranch. I look forward to being your escort Nellie."

"Isaac, would it be alright for me to come out to Johnny's ranch sometime and watch what you do out there? I've heard a lot of comments about how you have a real gift with horses."

Isaac tried not to show how pleased he was that she wanted to come out and watch him. "Of course, that would be just fine. Let me know when you'd like to do that and I can ask Johnny to borrow a carriage to pick you up in. I think you'll be amazed at how much there is to see out there."

"I'll let you know soon when I can schedule some time away from the café. I'm really looking forward to coming out there. I'd better wait on the customer that just came in."

Albert dropped by the library to have a quick visit with Melissa. As usual, she had her nose buried in a book and finally got the feeling that someone was staring at her. She was startled and then embarrassed but Albert just smiled back at her. He knew how much time she spent with her books. "Hello Melissa, can you take a few minutes to talk to me?"

"Of course I can, Albert."

"I wanted to be sure that I could be your escort to the dance. I didn't want to take that for granted. I was afraid someone else might have asked you before I got the chance."

"I would like to go with you Albert. I was hoping that you would be the one to ask me. I just finished sewing my new gown this morning. Are you a good dancer?"

"I wouldn't say that I was good at it but I think I can keep from making a fool of myself. I love music, so maybe that will help. When I returned from the war in August, I was planning on spending more time with you. When Joshua received a telegram that a good friend of his was not doing well, I felt it was my duty to go with him. I never intended to be gone so long, but I'm glad that I decided to travel with him. We ran into some rough characters twice and he would have been out numbered. He was there long enough to spend several days with his friend and the day he passed away, Joshua took it very hard. Now that he is back in Willow Bend, I was hoping that you could find someone for him to attend the dance with."

"As a matter of fact, I was just talking to Maude and Ada hasn't been paired up with anyone yet. I just want you to be aware that her best friend is Norma, who tends to cause problems quite often. You'll need to tell Joshua this ahead of time so that he isn't caught off guard. Ada is very sweet and Norma takes advantage of that every chance that she can."

"I appreciate your advice and I will speak with Joshua tonight. It will only be for one evening, so I think it should work out nicely. The four of us can attend together. I need to go find him now. You can get back to your book now." He was grinning as he said that. No sooner had the door closed when Melissa looked down at her open book and was lost in another world.

Albert found Joshua later that day and brought up the idea of him escorting Ada to the dance. "I'll be happy to be her escort if she is agreeable. When will I be able to meet her? Soon, I hope."

"I'll ask Melissa to bring her into the hotel for tea tomorrow. I believe Melissa mentioned that she is released from her job at the general store at 3:30. I'll set it up for that time tomorrow. You'd better be on your best behavior."

"You needn't worry about me, my friend."

"The next afternoon Albert and Joshua were waiting in the hotel dining room, when Melissa walked in with a shy but pretty girl, who must be Ada. Both men stood up to greet them. "Ada, I'd like to present Albert and his friend Joshua. This is my friend Ada that I was telling you about." When Joshua looked at Ada and saw the fear in her eyes, he knew she was afraid that he wouldn't like her. She seemed like a frightened doe, but as soon as he smiled back at her, he could see her face relax. He saw Melissa reach over and pat her hands, to help her relax.

"Ladies, please sit down and we'll order some tea for you. Would you like something to eat, also?" said Albert.

Both girls looked at each other and shook their heads no. Ada especially was too nervous to eat. Joshua was a fine-looking man and such a gentleman. *'Why would he want to attend a dance with me? He could ask any girl and she would be anxious to accept.'*

Joshua looked across the table at Ada and said, "I would be pleased if I could escort you to the dance. Would that be agreeable with you?" He was thinking to himself, *'This girl could turn out to be a real lady if someone would give her a chance.'* Girls who were too bold made him uncomfortable.

Ada had to clear her throat before she could respond back to him. "Yes, I would like that very much, Joshua."

Ada turned her head slightly and looked uncomfortable all of a sudden. Norma had just walked into the dining room and when she spotted Ada sitting at the same table as two attractive men, she immediately was scowling. She quickly pasted a fake smile on her face and boldly came over to their table.

Both men rose to greet her and before Ada had a chance to introduce her, Norma said, "My, my Ada, what are you doing, sitting here with two good looking men and not even telling me about them? Hello, I'm Norma, Ada's best friend. How long have you been in Willow Bend?"

"Norma, this is Albert, Melissa's friend and this is Joshua, a good friend of Alberts. Joshua has just asked if he could escort me to the dance. Isn't that exciting?"

Norma couldn't hide her anger for a split second but then she managed to get ahold of her emotions and as sweet as sugar she replied, "I'm so happy for you Ada, that you finally found someone to escort you to the dance. I was afraid you were going to miss all the fun. Would you like to come over and borrow one of my dresses, like you usually do?"

Melissa was totally being ignored and she was biting her tongue, trying not to say what was really on her mind. She and Norma had never gotten along but she didn't want to embarrass Ada. After that cruel comment, she had heard enough. "That won't be necessary Norma. Ada is going to wear a brand-new dress that I finished making for her just this morning. I can't wait until you see how pretty she'll look at the dance. It was nice of you to come by, but we must be leaving now. I'm going to help Ada pick out something to wear in her hair that matches her gown. Please excuse us."

It was almost comical to look at all three faces react to Melissa's mention of a brand-new dress for Ada. Albert was the only one who knew that this dress was intended for Melissa herself to wear to the dance. Joshua had a pretty good idea what Melissa had just done and he couldn't have admired her more. Ada looked shocked and then extremely excited.

Norma knew that if she stood there another minute she would explode, so she turned around and left the room in a rush. Ada looked over at Melissa and said, "That gown was meant for you, wasn't it?"

"I'll admit that it started out that way, but I'll enjoy it a lot more when I see it on you. It is my gift to you; not a loan. Now if you gentlemen will excuse us please, we have some shopping to do."

Joshua was troubled because Albert was his best friend and he felt guilty having thoughts about Melissa. *'It seems like whenever I am around her, she does something else that draws her to me. It amazes me that she really doesn't seem to have any idea of how attractive she is, inside and out. How am I going to live in this village and be around her so often and keep my feelings hid? I don't know if it is even possible. She is everything I've ever wanted in a wife and yet she is my best friend's girl. I don't know what to do, but I'd better do something fast before Albert realizes my feelings for her.'*

Michael Nelson had been thinking about the dance and there was only one woman that he would even consider asking and that was Cynthia. She seemed completely unaware of the fact that he often watched her. No matter who she spoke to, it was always in a gentle, caring voice. Because he had studied her face so often, he realized recently that something was troubling her and he wished that he could come right out and ask her. He thought better of it but he did want to talk to her about the dance. He knew that she often went to the hotel dining room for tea in the afternoons and that was where he found her today. As he was walking towards her, she looked up and gave him a friendly smile.

"Would you mind if I joined you, Cynthia?"

"Of course not Michael. I would enjoy the company. I usually just have a nice cup of tea, but today I couldn't pass up Charlie's pumpkin pie. Have you tried it yet?"

"You talked me right into it." He gave his order to Martha and Cynthia was surprised to hear him ordering a cup of tea. "I have something on my mind that I hope you can help me with."

"Are you interested in any of my quilts?"

"No, not today at least. I would like to offer to escort you to the dance or are you already spoken for?"

"I would enjoy attending the dance with you Michael. It's been years since I've danced but I think I can remember a few steps. This is a nice surprise, to be asked by you. How is your land office business coming along?"

"I'm pleased that you accepted my offer, Cynthia. As for my business, I've been busy recently with several people interested in farms right outside Willow Bend. I hope this village doesn't grow too large. I like it small and friendly."

"I couldn't agree with you more. I used to live in a big city and I don't miss the hustle and bustle and all of the noise. I'm afraid I need to leave right now so that I won't be late to meet with Maude and Jenny. I've offered to help them with the dance. I look forward to seeing you then Michael."

He stood up as soon as she did and watched her walk away. She was such a graceful woman and very kind. *I'm so glad that she said yes. I want to get to know her better. Maybe after the dance we will feel more comfortable around each other.'*

Their new guest would be checking into the hotel today. Maude heard the stage pull up and Worley's booming voice yelling, "Willow Bend". She stayed behind the desk because she wanted to make sure that everything looked ship shape. She had asked Ellie to do some extra dusting and to put fresh flowers on the desk. When she heard the front door open, she couldn't believe her eyes. The man walking in the door was someone that she hadn't seen in years; Harrison Daniels. Maude had given him her heart over 20 years ago but then he had left town suddenly with just a little explanation and took her heart with him. Only two short letters had followed for the next year and then nothing. It had hurt her deeply and it took her several years to get over it. Now he was standing right in front of her, in her hotel, and would be a guest for at least a month. She had tried to forget about how handsome he was with his wavy brown hair and deep blue eyes. Age hadn't hurt him one bit. *I wonder what he thinks, looking at me after all these years?'* She had no idea how to react but she had to say something.

"Harrison, I had no idea that it was you sending me the wires about staying here in our hotel. Why didn't you tell me, instead of just using your initials?"

"Because I was afraid if you knew it was me, you would refuse to let me stay here and I had to see you. You deserve an explanation, even after all these years. I want to apologize properly, but not like this. Would you be willing to dine with me this evening, so that I can talk to you? I know that you must not be thrilled to see me, but I am hoping that my explanation can at least clear some things up."

"I must admit that I am shocked to see you, after all these years. The years have been kind to you. Yes, I'll be willing to dine with you tonight. We have an excellent cook here at the hotel. Now, let me get you checked in and settled in your room. Maybe this evening I can introduce you to a good friend of mine who is also a guest and an author."

"Thank you for being so gracious Maude. You still look so much like the young girl that I last saw almost 20 years ago. I look forward to having you catch me up on your life."

Maude signaled for Worley to help Harrison with his suitcase and then she ran outside to find Sarah. She was so rattled, that she hadn't even asked someone to cover the front desk. *'Oh well, I can't help it. I've got to talk to Sarah right away.'*

When she reached the schoolhouse, Sarah was saying goodbye to the students and she looked so perfect, as if she couldn't have been anything except a schoolteacher. Maude waited until the last child had left and then she said, "Oh Sarah, I need you to help me. I am so upset right now and I don't know what to do."

"Maude, are you ill? Did you receive some bad news?" "Sarah, a man from Indiana has been sending me wires, asking me to book him into our hotel for at least a month. He is doing research on Civil War Veterans. Well, today he arrived and he is an old beau of mine; Harrison Daniels. He broke my heart in two about 20 years ago and now he is staying in our hotel for at least a month. I agreed to eat dinner with him tonight so that he can explain why he left me so suddenly without warning." Sarah wrapped her arms around Maude and gave her a gentle hug and led her to a chair.

"Oh Maude; what a shock that must have been, to see him again after all these years. There must be a reason for God to bring him back into your life. Maybe after he talks to you, it will give you the peace you've been missing all these years. I promise that I will lift you both up in prayer. Please come to my room tonight after you have met with him and let me know how you are doing."

Maude was so thankful for her dear friend Sarah and she gave her a quick hug and left. On her way back to the hotel, none other than Doc was crossing the street. "Hi Maude, I was just coming over to talk to you. He followed her into the hotel and she went back behind the desk, which somehow gave her comfort. "What did you want to talk to me about Doc?"

"I know you've been spending a lot of time on this village dance, but I was hoping that I could ask you a favor. Could you possibly convince an elderly patient of mine to come to the dance? She is very lonely since her husband passed away last year and I've been trying to convince her that she needs to get out more." Maude couldn't believe that this same man who obviously cared very much about his patients, couldn't see how much she needed to hear something encouraging from him. Before she could stop herself, she said, "Are you planning on attending the dance, Doc?"

"Well, I guess it would look bad if I didn't show up, being the village doctor and all." *That did it, as far as she was concerned!*

"I have a wonderful idea Doc. Why don't you escort your sweet patient to the dance. I'm sure it will just make her day. Excuse me, I have a new guest who is expecting me to have dinner with him tonight. I need to change clothes first and I don't want to keep him waiting."

Doc watched Maude stalk off, with her back as straight as a ramrod. *'What guest was she talking about, anyway? She said it was a 'him'. Why was she acting so unfriendly to me? I need to go talk to Pastor about this. He seems to understand women better than I do.'*

Harrison was sitting at one of the smaller tables in the dining room, and he was watching Maude as she walked into the room. He immediately stood up and held her chair out for her. "You look even lovelier in that color then when I first saw you today. Lavender was always your best color, if I remember correctly. Your hotel is very charming and friendly. I'm looking forward to my stay here, but only if it doesn't distress you."

"Why would it distress me, Harrison? You are an old friend who has come into town for a short visit. By the way, we are holding a village dance on the third floor of this hotel next week. I was wondering if you would like to be my escort, since you don't know anyone else in the village." Harrison looked like she had caught him off guard, but he recovered nicely and said, "My goodness, I would enjoy that ever so much. Thank you for asking me."

Just then Gerard came into the dining room and Maude signaled for him to come over to their table. "Gerard, I would like you to meet an old friend of mine who has something in common with you. This is Harrison Daniels, and this is my friend Gerard Burns, who is writing a book on the early pioneers. Harrison is writing a book on Civil War soldiers."

"Gerard gave Harrison a friendly smile and said, "I am pleased to meet you Harrison and I would enjoy getting together with you to discuss your book. There are several veterans here in this village and I am one of them. I'm sure you two have a lot to discuss, so I'll talk to you soon, hopefully."

Harrison said, "Maude has really sung your praises and I am looking forward to reading your book. This is a perfect setting to write about the early pioneers. Enjoy your evening; good night Gerard."

After they ate their delicious meal, they both decided they would like dessert and coffee. The waitress cleared off the table and brought over a scrumptious bread pudding and coffee. Harrison cleared his throat and said, "Maude, I don't want to waste another moment before helping you to understand why I left town so suddenly and then stopped writing to you. You see, your father came to me one evening and told me that he didn't feel that I was good enough for you. He felt that if I left town, you would find someone else who was more successful and could make a better life for you. He gave me $1,000, with the stipulation that I leave town and never come back. Maude, you've got to believe me; I loved you so much that he convinced me that I was doing the right thing for you; an unselfish thing even though it broke my heart. I just couldn't face you to say a proper goodbye. Please forgive me for the pain I've caused you. Through all of these years, I've never met another woman who has interested me in the least. I compared everyone to you and I've never married."

She reached in her pocket for her hankie and was dabbing at her eyes while saying, "Harrison, my father told me that you wanted to leave our town so that you could make more money and that someday you might come back to me. I waited three years, praying every night that you'd either return or contact me. After receiving a few short letters, and waiting for so long, I just couldn't stay in that town any longer and I accepted a position in this village to work at the hotel. I've never married either, but I have wonderful friends and I enjoy my position here. Everyone feels like my family. My father passed away several years ago and he never told me the truth."

"Maude, I've never been bitter about what he did. I'm sure he thought that he was protecting you, because goodness knows, I wasn't much of a success back then. I have since found a career that makes me happy and I've been able to travel all over. One day last month I met someone who had stayed at this hotel and he was talking about how friendly you were to everyone. When he called you by your first name and described you, I thought that it must be you but I wasn't certain. I just had to come to see for myself. Would you like to take a carriage ride tomorrow and show me around your friendly village?"

"Yes, Harrison, I would enjoy that very much and I'll ask Charlie, our cook, to pack a lovely picnic basket for us. If you'll excuse me, I'd like to go back to my room and just sit awhile and try to absorb all of this. Just come down to the front desk and let me know what time you'd like to leave for our carriage ride."

Maude hadn't even noticed but about 20 minutes earlier, Pastor and Doc had been seated at the long dining room table and they couldn't take their eyes off of Maude and this stranger. "Doc, you have asked Maude if you can escort her to the dance, haven't you?"

"Well, no, I haven't gotten around to it yet. I'm sure that she assumes that I'll be her escort. In fact, she asked me just today if I planned on attending the dance. I told her that I thought it would look funny if I didn't, since I'm the village doctor and all."

Pastor put his head in his hands and just groaned and shook his head. "Doc, you are absolutely unbelievable! She was obviously dropping a not too subtle hint to see if you would ask her to attend the dance with her. How can you be so blind? She's done everything she can to show how much she cares for you and you give that poor woman no hope. She's getting up right now and that man is staying at the table. Hurry up and catch up with her when she leaves the dining room and for heaven's sake, speak up and stop being so timid."

Doc did as he was told and followed Maude out of the dining room and then called out to her. "Maude, do you have a moment please?' She turned around and suddenly had a gleam in her eye and a smile on her face. "What is it Doc? I'm tired and I'm on my way to my room. Please hurry!"

"Well, I was a, I mean, are you going to the dance? I guess you are, since you went to all that trouble getting it organized. What time should I come by to escort you?"

'I'm so sorry Doc, but I already have someone who will be escorting me. He's a dear old friend that I knew years ago, and he'll be staying here as our guest for at least a month. I'll have to introduce you to him the next time I see you. Thanks for the offer though. Good night!'

Pastor saw the look on Doc's face a few minutes later and it was obvious that something was terribly wrong. He looked like he was in shock and in pain. Doc said, "She actually turned me down James. She's already made plans to attend the dance with that man she was sitting with tonight. The way she looked at me tonight, I felt like I didn't even know her anymore. I think she enjoyed turning me down. I'm going home and I'll talk to you tomorrow."

When Doc arrived home, he looked in the back of his kitchen cabinet and pulled out a bottle of whiskey that had never been touched. He poured himself half a glass and put the cap back on. He went into his small living room and sat in the dark, sipping his drink, with tears rolling down his face. The pain in his heart was so strong that it took his breath away. *I've tossed Maude's affection away, year after year. Heaven knows how much pain I've caused that dear woman. Oh Lord, what have I done?'*

Pastor looked around the dining room and spotted Sarah talking to Ellie. He waited until they were finished with their conversation and approached her. "Good evening Sarah. I know I should have asked you sooner but I'm not too comfortable about social gatherings. I was hoping that you might allow me to escort you to the dance."

"Why yes James, I'd be happy to. I've asked Maude to teach me some of the easier steps so that I won't embarrass myself. This dance is what everyone is talking about. Maude is doing her best to make sure no one is left out if she can help it."

"I understand that we have a new guest in the hotel."

"Yes, Maude was so surprised when he checked in today. She knew him a long time ago and he seems very attracted to her. His timing was perfect to be able to escort her to the dance. I kept hoping that Doc would ask her but he never did."

"I don't understand that man and he is my very best friend. I'm afraid that he is going to deeply regret not making a commitment to such a sweet woman. Have a good evening Sarah. I need to finish working on my sermon."

Pete had seen the silly look on Worley and Gus' faces since they finally asked Daisy and Millie to attend the dance with them. After thinking about it quite awhile, he decided to go over to the hotel and ask

Madelyn if she would like to go with him. He walked over to the hotel and sat down at the long dining room table. He sat at the far end where no one could over hear his conversation. Madelyn had waited on him several times and she was shy but very sweet. "Good afternoon Madelyn, I was hoping that you would be the one to wait on me today. I would like to escort you to the dance; that is, if you have not already made other plans."

Madelyn hadn't even considered going to the dance because she thought that no one would ask her. At first she didn't know what to say, but finally she said, "I didn't really expect to go to the dance Pete, but I would be pleased to have you as my escort. I'd better hurry up and find a dress to wear. I don't attend many social gatherings. You have pleased me very much and I'm looking forward to it."

The next morning, Maude decided to go into the pantry to check on what supplies needed to be ordered. She was surprised when she found Ruthie in tears, trying to stay out of sight. "Oh sweetie, what is the matter?' and Maude turned her around and held her and rubbed her back. "Oh Maude, I listen to all the other girls talking about the dance and how excited they are that someone asked them, and no one has asked me. I know it is because my teeth are crooked but I can't help that. It hurts so much Maude."

"You are a beautiful young lady, Ruthie, and don't you forget it. Your smile just lights up the room. I know a young man who isn't planning on going to the dance because of his teeth being crooked. I'm going to ask him if he would like to meet you, if that is agreeable to you."

"Oh yes, Maude, that would be wonderful. Is he nice?"

"Our sheriff, Johnny, thinks very highly of him so that is a powerful recommendation. You dry your tears and I won't be gone long. Just remember, if he turns me down, it's not because of you; it will be because of how he feels about himself.' Maude kissed her on the cheek and gave her one last hug and ran out the back door.

Maude went to the sheriff's office and Johnny was inside, talking to a young cowboy. "Maude, how can I help you? I've just finished with my business with this young man. Come on in and have a seat."

Maude sat and then said, "I'll come right to the point Johnny. I just found Ruthie crying in the kitchen pantry and I found out that she has no one to take her to the dance. She said she knows it is because her teeth are crooked and I immediately thought of Bucky. Would you be willing to talk to him to see how he would feel about being Ruthie's escort? She is such a sweet person and I hate to see her miss out on the dance."

"I was just on my way out to the ranch to check with Samuel, so I can talk to Bucky right away. I have a feeling that he'll jump at the chance, but I'll need to ask him first. I should be back in a couple of hours. I think that is a great idea Maude and I appreciate how tender hearted you are to everyone who crosses your path. I can hardly wait to hear what his response is."

Johnny rode out to his ranch and it gave him a thrill every time he saw it. He went to look for Bucky right away and found him grooming one of the horses that Johnny had recently brought to the ranch. Bucky was talking softly to the horse and it was already looking a lot healthier than when he had found it. "Hey Bucky, can I interrupt you for a minute? I am very pleased with how gentle you are with all of the animals, especially the ones who have been abused."

Bucky stopped his grooming but kept one hand on the side of the horse and was stroking him back and forth. "What can I do for you Johnny?" "Well, this has nothing to do with my ranch or animals. I was just talking to Maude and one of the maids named Ruthie, doesn't plan on attending the dance because she has no escort. Bucky, her teeth are crooked, and no one has asked her to go to the dance. Maude said that she is a very sweet young girl and she hates to see her so sad. We were wondering if you would be interested in being introduced to her this afternoon. If you agree, I'll take you into town and we can eat in the hotel, my treat."

"Johnny, I know all about the pain of being made fun of because of my teeth. Even during the war, the guys enjoyed picking on me. I tried not to let it get me down too much but it was difficult, especially when they would talk about their sweethearts back home. Yes, I would definitely like to meet Ruthie today and I'll be happy to be her escort."

"I just need a few minutes to talk to Samuel and then I'll swing back by to pick you up. It means a lot to me that you have such a good attitude about this."

Johnny and Bucky walked into the front door of the hotel and Maude was behind the front desk, as usual. As they walked up to her, Maude came around the desk and gave Bucky a hug and said, "Young man, you are about to meet one of the sweetest young ladies that I've ever known. Go into the dining room and sit at one of the smaller tables and I will bring Ruthie over to meet you." Bucky was definitely not used to receiving hugs and he was in heaven. It felt so good; almost like his mother used to hug him.

After Johnny and Bucky were seated, Maude came over with a timid but sweet looking girl, who had to be Ruthie. She had pretty dark brown hair put up in braids on top of her head, and soft brown eyes with long lashes. Johnny glanced quickly over at Bucky and he acted like he was looking at the most beautiful girl in the world. Johnny stood up and then Bucky followed suit and Maude made the introductions. Bucky was just sitting there staring at Ruthie, so someone had to start the conversation. Maude spoke up and said, "Bucky, I was telling Ruthie that Johnny speaks very highly of you, especially how you are so good with animals." Johnny lightly kicked Bucky under the table and he jerked slightly and then said, "Yes Ma'am, I enjoy all kind of animals. Johnny has recently started taking in abused animals and that is what I like the most."

Listening to him speak about the animals, Ruthie suddenly spoke up and said, "Could I ever come out to your ranch sheriff and see your animals? I used to live on a farm and it was my job to feed and care for several. We had all kinds of animals."

Bucky blurted out, "I can take you out to the ranch; that is, if I can borrow one of your wagons Johnny."

"Of course, you can, son. How about tomorrow after Ruthie gets off of her job?" Bucky and Ruthie were talking back and forth about animals and had totally forgotten that Johnny and Maude were at the same table. After they had finished their meal, Johnny said, "Wasn't there something you wanted to talk to Ruthie about?"

"Oh yes, Miss Ruthie, would you like me to take you to the dance? I know a few dancin' steps that my mother taught me a long time ago."

"I would be very pleased to go with you, Bucky. I am also excited about coming out to the ranch with you tomorrow. I really miss having my own horse, like I did back home. I used to ride everyday as part of my job and also for fun."

Johnny had an idea that Ruthie would have her own horse sooner than she could have ever expected. After Johnny and Bucky had left and Ruthie went to her room, Maude started making a mental list of everyone else who wasn't paired up for the dance. Bertha was one of the other maids that came to mind and maybe that shy boy who worked for Dwight would work out. She expected Dwight would come in tomorrow during the noon hour as usual, so she would mention that to him.

The next day, Dwight came in, right on schedule and he liked Maude's idea. He promised to bring Jimmy in the next day. When he mentioned it to Jimmy, he seemed to perk up and said he was interested. The following day Maude introduced Bertha to Dwight and Jimmy. Even though they were both on the quiet side, they finally got them to talking about the dance and soon made arrangements, so that was one more couple taken care of.

While Dwight was in the hotel, he ran into Betsy in the front of the hotel. They had often had long conversations about where they had traveled and places that they would still like to see. He enjoyed talking to her so he decided to ask if she would like to attend the dance with him. Betsy said she would be delighted to go and agreed to meet him by the front desk at six o'clock the evening of the dance. Since they were both widowed, they also had that in common. Betsy's husband's insurance policy had left her with all the money that she would ever need, but she lived very frugally except she still enjoyed traveling once or twice a year.

Curtis Wells was a widower with a young daughter. He didn't need the income, but wanted to work with Johnny, as his deputy, as soon as he'd met him. When the dance came up, Johnny had tried to think of some nice lady for Curtis to go to the dance with and Maude came up with Mamie, one of the waitresses. Maude arranged for them to meet each other and they both acted like they were interested in pursuing this friendship. When this seemed to work out so well, Johnny chuckled and told Maude that she was a professional match maker. She took that good naturedly and laughed.

Curtis was raising a young daughter by himself named Riley. His wife had passed away right before the war started and an elderly aunt had taken care of her while Curtis was fighting. Now they were getting reacquainted and Riley had grown to be quite independent. He wasn't sure if that was going to be something positive or negative; he'd just have to wait and see. When he told her to do something and she wasn't happy about it, she usually told him exactly why she didn't want to do it. He tried very hard to calmly listen to what she had to say, but he didn't always agree. Sometimes he would honor her request to not do whatever he had asked her but he was no pushover. He was trying to find a balance of allowing her to stand up for herself but to also respect his wishes.

Right now, at only the age of 12, she was positive that she wanted to be a nurse. There were times when he came home, expecting her to be there waiting for him, but the house was empty. He'd find a note on the kitchen table that she was "assisting Doc" and would be home soon. Elizabeth had told him that Riley was very helpful. She would often comfort a crying child or hand Doc some of the items that he needed. One of the patients had been bleeding from a head wound and Riley didn't even look away. 'Where has she gotten this determination and strength? I surely can't take any credit for it.'

Riley had long dark brown hair and was naturally curly. According to her teacher, Sarah, she had a little tomboy in her, which delighted Sarah. In school she was always prepared and eager to learn. One day she stayed after school and walked up to Sarah's desk.

"Riley, is there something you would like to discuss with me?"

"Yes ma'am, there is. I'd like to know why none of the subjects you are teaching us have anything to do with medicine or being a nurse. How am I going to be a nurse if no one is teaching me what I need to know?"

"I think it is wonderful that you have such a strong desire to take care of people who are sick or hurt. You need to learn how to spell so that you can read the descriptions on the bottles of medicine or the medical books. You have to know how to add and subtract in order to decide how much medicine to give someone, especially a child that can't take a full dose. I think it would be a good idea for you to sit down and talk to Ms. Elizabeth. She can answer questions that I don't know."

"Thank you for answering me with things that make sense to me. I don't like answers like, 'That's just the way things are 'or "Because I said so.' I'm going to marry a doctor and I'll be his nurse. He won't have to hire anyone else."

Sarah smothered down a laugh and kept her face straight as she said, "Riley, it will be exciting to watch you learn more about nursing. It is not an easy job and sometimes you will lose your patients. I just don't want you to be thinking that it will always be easy going. I'd like to know what you learn from Ms. Elizabeth." Riley turned around and headed for the door, anxious to get to Doc's office. Today he was going to check a child's chest to see if her breathing was better, after taking the medicine that Doc had given to her mother. Riley wanted to spend time with Doc whenever he needed her, and even when he didn't. She watched him like a hawk and didn't miss much. She intended to be the best nurse that she could possibly be and nothing was going to stop her.

The day before the dance, Austin and Billy were taking turns plowing up a field and decided to take a break. They both sat down under an apple tree and munched on their sandwiches. "Billy, are you going to that dance I keep hearing about?"

"No sir; not me. I've got two left feet and besides, I don't have a girl."

Austin spoke up and said, "I've never danced in my life but I'd sure like to go and watch. I've never had a special girl and I wouldn't know what to say to a girl anyway. They are always talking and giggling about something and they never seem to run out of things to say."

They heard a horse approaching fast and they weren't surprised to find that it was Sarah. She had obviously been looking for them. Austin was doing great in school so he knew that couldn't be the reason she was here.

"Hi, boys! I need a favor from both of you. We have a family staying at the hotel for a week or so, while they look around to buy a farm nearby. They have two daughters who have heard about the dance and are all excited. The only problem is, they don't know anyone. It is my understanding that neither of you have found anyone to attend the dance with, so I've solved that problem for you. Would you come by the hotel after supper so that I can introduce you?"

Both Billy and Austin look stunned. Neither one of them wanted to disappoint Sarah but they also were scared to be matched up with girls that they'd never laid eyes on. Austin slowly turned his head to see how

Billy was reacting and he had to force himself not to laugh out loud. Billy look petrified! *'I guess I'd better go so that he has some support'* thought Austin. *' It's only for one evening and it can't be that bad. At least, I hope it can't.'*

Austin decided to speak up and said, "We'd be pleased to help you out, Ms. Sarah. We'll come by tonight after supper to meet them. Thank you for asking." This entire time Billy hadn't said one word but he was looking at Austin as if he couldn't believe what he had just heard. *'No matter how the evening turns out, at least it will be a new experience for us and we can probably laugh about it afterwards.'*

Will had been in the village for a couple of months now and Sarah and Elizabeth had both ended up being friends with him, but nothing romantic. That left Will with having to find someone to bring to the dance and he thought of Callie Brown. Whenever he went to the post office, she was always friendly and they even had a few interesting conversations about various subjects. Today he would ask her if she had plans to attend the dance.

When he walked into the post office, she was friendly as usual. Will said, "Callie, I was hoping that you didn't already have plans to attend the dance with someone." "As a matter of fact, I don't have plans. Because I have a child, it seems to make some of the men uncomfortable."

"Well, I would be pleased to be your escort Callie. This was a great idea of Maude's and Jennie's. I know it must be hard raising the children alone but it looks like you are doing a terrific job. If I can ever help you with anything around your house, please don't hesitate to ask me. I'm pretty handy with tools, thanks to watching my father every chance I got. He was very patient with me and always made me feel like I was a big help to him. Now that I look back on those days,

I'm sure I was more in the way than anything, but he had a way of making me feel like I was never in the way. I need to get back to the bank now but I'd like to stop by in a day or two and see if you can think of anything around your house that needs fixing up."

Callie was very impressed with Will. "I'll definitely start making a list. You may be sorry that you asked me to do that." She gave him a big smile and watched him walk out the door. *'He's the first man I've known who didn't run in the opposite direction because I am raising two children. Even if he ends up just being my friend, that would be a blessing indeed.'*

Johnny's brother, David, decided to try out the hotel for dinner. As soon as he had given his order, he noticed a very attractive young lady sitting nearby. She wasn't the least bit shy about trying to get his attention. David smiled back at her and then started looking around the room at the other guests. Most of the people at the long dining room table where he was sitting, were starting to leave. David looked back at the young lady and she perked up right away. He stood up and walked over to her table to introduce himself. "Hello, my name is David and I was hoping to find out your name."

"Oh goodness, my name is Norma. Are you new in town?"

"Yes, I've only been here for a couple of weeks. I'm looking to buy a ranch where I can raise horses. Would you care to take a walk after you have finished your meal?"

"Oh, that would be wonderful. May I join you?" Without waiting for his answer, she picked up her tea cup and saucer and walked over to sit across from his place. *"Well, this is no shy young lady, that is for sure."* This was the first time that he had ever met a woman that was this bold, but it sure wasn't bad for his ego.

It was a perfect evening for a stroll. The weather was not too chilly and the leaves had turned colors, which brightened up Main Street. David walked with Norma for about half an hour and then escorted her home. He knew right away from the size of her house that she had money and was used to nice things. *"Oh well, I am just making a new friend. This will never be anything serious. I'll just enjoy it while I am in the village."* When they had reached her door, Norma didn't hesitate to say what was on her mind. "David, we are having a village dance in a few weeks and I would be thrilled if you could be my escort."

"I would consider it an honor, Ms. Norma. I've heard a lot of talk about it but wasn't sure if I'd be attending it. I'm pleased that you asked me to accompany you. Have a good evening and I'll see you soon."

Norma hadn't been inside for 30 seconds before she twirled herself around in a circle and laughed with glee. *'Just wait until the other ladies see who I have for my escort. The most handsome man in the entire village and single at that. And I'm going to be wearing the prettiest and fanciest dress in the entire ballroom. I'll make those women sorry that they snub me all the time.'*

12

October 1865

The Special Room on the Third Floor

VILLAGE DANCE ON SATURDAY NIGHT

Austin was feeling at home on Jonas's farm and he threw himself into everything he was asked to do. Billy and his father had a lot of patience so Austin felt comfortable asking questions. He chopped wood, helped to weed the garden, fed the lambs, cleaned out the corral and was learning to ride a horse named Rascal. The horse certainly earned that name but since Austin was so gentle with him and kept him brushed well, he rarely did anything bad. He did have the habit of sneaking up behind him and nudging him. Billy told him to carry carrots in his pocket. Rascal could smell them and would trot over to Austin as soon as he picked up the scent. He made him laugh and it felt good. He and Billy had gone to the hotel to meet the two girls who needed an escort to the dance. Bertha was 15 and tall for a girl, so Austin felt like he should volunteer to be her escort. She was nervous and giggled a lot, but otherwise, she was friendly enough. She was crazy about animals, so that encouraged Austin to talk about all of the animals on Jonas' farm.

Billy ended up with Geraldine who was 17 and on the shy side. She and Billy were so much alike, that neither of them said a word, so Austin felt like he should get the conversation started. "Billy fought in the war and now he runs his father's farm." Billy's ears were turning red and it was making everyone uncomfortable but then somehow he managed to say, "I never want to do anything else with my life besides living on the farm." His voice came out a little crackly but at least he was trying. Billy seemed to find some courage deep inside because he suddenly blurted out, "I've never been to a dance before and I've probably got two left feet."

Bertha said, "We don't need to dance much. It will be fun to just watch everyone else and see all of the pretty dresses." Geraldine still hadn't said a single word, so Austin was wondering what kind of an evening they were in for.

Austin spoke up and said, "Well, we need to get back and finish up our chores", so they left in a hurry, promising to see the girls the night of the dance. On the way back to the farm, Austin didn't say much because he was thinking that he'd never gone anywhere with a girl before. This was all new to him. He had heard that there would be food to eat, so that gave him something to look forward to.

The day of the village dance was finally here. Of all the people anticipating this evening, Gerard was the most nervous. He was so afraid of saying or doing something that Ellie wouldn't understand. He wasn't a cocky person by any means, but he did feel like he was normally very confident. He hardly recognized himself today. Part of him couldn't wait to see Ellie and the other part of him couldn't wait for the evening to be over. He hadn't been this nervous during any part of the Civil War.

Maude watched Jacob sitting in the dining room beside Emily, holding her hand. Both of them were tapping their feet lightly to the music drifting down from upstairs. Because of her pregnancy, Emily could not attend the dance and it was making her sad. She went up to Emily and gave her a hug and said to her, "Honey, I would like you and Jacob to follow me." They both stood up and followed Maude out the back door and up the back stairs and watched her pull a key out of her pocket. Soon she had opened a door next to the ballroom and motioned them to come in.

Jacob said, "I don't understand; why are we in this room?" Emily was looking around the room and had a feeling that she understood. There was a loveseat and a small table with beautiful flowers in a vase. They could hear the music perfectly.

Maude said, "This is your private room for the remainder of the evening. You can dance without anyone watching and you can talk privately. Enjoy yourselves and I'll come back later when everyone else has gone. I've left you some refreshments."

Jacob took Emily in his arms and started dancing. Emily might have been pregnant, but she was light on her feet. When they finished that dance, Jacob led her over to the loveseat and asked her to sit down. He got down on his knee and held her hand. Jacob hadn't planned the night that he would propose to her. He only knew that it would be soon and he had been carrying a pretty ring around in his pocket for the last two weeks. Now he reached into his pocket and pulled it out and put the ring box in Emily's hand. He opened it, lifted up the ring, and Emily gasped with delight. "Oh Jacob, it is beautiful. I will never forget tonight."

"Emily, will you please marry me? I have fallen in love with you and you make me so happy."

"Of course I will marry you Jacob. You have had my heart for quite awhile now. I do so love you too."

The music drew everyone up into the ballroom and there were several astonished gasps at how lovely the room looked. Beautiful ribbons were tied in bows, hanging on the drapes and gorgeous arrangements on the tables, made out of items found in the woods behind the hotel. Cynthia had organized some of the women to go into the woods with baskets and they found several bushes with beautiful red berries and she taught them how to make arrangements. Maude and Jennie had outdone themselves and even though they were exhausted, it would be worth every sore muscle and loss of sleep. Maude and Harrison were the first ones to arrive and he looked so proud of her. Her maroon gown showed off her beautiful eyes and she was wearing her hair in a fancier hairdo than normal. Jennie and Richard came into the ballroom, hand in hand. Maude had never seen him dressed up before and he surprised her. His hair was slicked down and his attire was neat and trim and he looked comfortable all dressed up. Richard was a very down to earth man with no pretense, but to please his wife, he had gone all out.

Charlie and Martha looked extremely hesitant at the door but when Maude drew Harrison over to greet them, they relaxed quickly. Charlie didn't own any clothes that were fitting to wear to a dance, but someone had loaned him an outfit that made him look like a new man. Martha was wearing one of Emily's new creations and she had never worn anything fancier than a plain second-hand dress before, except her wedding dress. She kept touching the material as if to convince herself that this was real. Charlie had always been protective of Martha and he kept his arm around her waist. Danny and Sadie were the next ones to make their way into the ballroom. Danny didn't look anything like the farmer he had become. Tonight, he was wearing one of Jonas's jackets and pants and they fit perfectly. Jonas and Dora came in right behind them. They were another happily married couple and Maude knew that they thought the world of Danny. Sadie wore one of her nicest dresses that she had made herself, with the help of her mother.

Within 15 minutes the room was starting to fill up and there was much laughter and light conversation. Maude was a little nervous about how Ellie would handle all of this attention tonight. Right at that moment, Gerard walked into the room, looking so proud and handsome. Ellie looked pretty but not very comfortable. Gerard walked her right over to Maude, as if he needed someone to help him show Ellie how to relax. Maude realized what he needed her to say. "Ellie, I've never seen you look prettier than you do tonight. Bertha and Ruthie will be here shortly, along with their escorts. I think they are both nervous, so I am hoping that you can help make them feel welcome. I want you all to enjoy yourselves."

Ellie said, "I'll do my best Maude." Gerard smiled down at Maude and let out a deep breath.

Johnny and Elizabeth walked in at the same time as Sarah and Pastor. Both couples seemed to be struggling with their relationships but Maude was praying that in time, everything would work out. They each had their individual struggles to work through. Sarah felt just like a daughter to Maude and she wanted her to find the right man. She wasn't sure that Pastor James was exactly that man though. Maude greeted Worley as he came in with Daisy on his arm. Following close behind were Bucky and Ruthie. and Jimmy and Bertha. Now Gus came in, all smiles and chest puffed out because he was escorting Millie. Millie was such a special young lady. She wasn't the least embarrassed to let anyone know that she worked at the saloon. Pastor just loved the fact that she came to church every Sunday and fit right in. All four couples stuck together like glue, so apparently, this was a new experience for all of them. They looked so cute together and Maude hoped that soon they would find people to talk to and would start dancing.

Samuel came in with Rebecca on his arm, and they looked like such a happy couple. What a wonderful ending for them, with Samuel returned home safely. Will had shown up with Callie, who worked at the Post Office. He could probably have his pick of most of the single girls in Willow Bend, so hopefully Callie felt special tonight. Michael Nelson, from the land office was escorting Cynthia, who created gorgeous quilts in her home. They were both shy, but friendly, and seemed happy to be attending the dance. Just as she was wondering who Dwight would be accompanying, here he stood in the doorway with Betsy Morris. They had both been widowed and were close in age, so maybe something could come of this relationship. Next, she saw Austin and Billy walking into the room, looking very nervous and uncomfortable, with two young ladies that Maude had never met. They must be here in the village visiting with friends or relatives. She had heard good things about Austin from Sarah. He had been through a terrifying experience but thankfully he ended up with Jonas and Dora.

She couldn't stop thinking about the little room next door and hoping that Emily and Jacob were enjoying themselves. She assumed that Emily would share some of the evening's details tomorrow. Jacob was a perfect choice for Emily and he would be a great father to her baby, if they did indeed get married. Maude was pleased to see that Harrison wasn't feeling at all uncomfortable. If she was busy greeting someone, he would introduce himself and chat briefly with everyone that he met. This helped her to relax and enjoy herself. When she had looked in the mirror tonight, she had caught a quick glimpse of the girl that she used to be, back when Harrison had first met her.

Pete was now walking towards Maude with Madelyn by his side and Curtis came in with Mamie. Because the two girls both worked in the hotel, they had decided to come to the dance at the same time so they would feel more comfortable. "You girls look lovely tonight. I'm so glad to see you both here with your handsome escorts. There are refreshments over on the tables, so help yourselves." Maude was mentally going over in her mind to see who was missing and right then Isaac showed up with Nellie. He looked so happy and excited and he had given Nellie has arm, which was so sweet. "Good evening Nellie. I'm happy to see you here tonight. For once you can relax and not have to wait on anyone. I like the color of your dress. It really shows off your pretty eyes. Isaac, you look like you could dance all night. I'm glad that you decided to attend our dance. Enjoy yourselves!"

Maude and Harrison danced together tonight for the first time ever. "Maude, I feel like the past 20 years have been wiped away. So many times I've dreamt of holding you in my arms and dancing with you, just like this."

"I feel the same way. We never got the opportunity to attend a dance years ago. Tonight is very special to me and I'm so glad that you are here." They decided to take a short break and sat down with Jennie and Richard. "Jennie, all of our hard work was worth it. This evening has turned out even better then I'd imagined."

"We do both seem to work together well, don't we Maude? Without your lists and your knowing everyone, we couldn't have accomplished this. I enjoyed working with you."

The families that lived the furthest from the village were delighted to see some of their old friends. Suddenly the room got quiet and when Maude turned to see the reason, she said something under her breath and didn't look very pleased. Norma had just strolled into the room, escorted by Johnny's brother, David. Maude knew that Johnny was not happy about this but he couldn't convince his brother to stay far away from Norma. You could feel the tension in the air, as no one came forward to greet Norma. Maude felt that she had to be the one so she walked over with a smile and said, "Norma, is that a new dress? It is just beautiful."

"Why, yes, it is Maude. I ordered it from back east from one of my favorite shops. There was nothing in Willow Bend that could compare to what they have to offer. Your dress looks nice Maude." David looked as though he was seeing Norma for the first time and he glanced over at Johnny. Johnny nodded hello but didn't move from where he was standing. He didn't trust himself to keep quiet if he got into a conversation with Norma. Right then Melissa came up to Maude with Albert by her side and she was so happy for her that Albert had returned safely from the war. Maude didn't miss much and she realized that Melissa was wearing a dress that Maude had seen on her before. It was a lovely dress but she had told Maude that she had almost finished sewing a new dress for the dance. Suddenly she realized where that new dress had ended up. Ada came in on the arm of a young man that Maude hadn't met before. Melissa spoke up and said, "Maude, I would like you to meet Joshua, a good friend of Albert's. Joshua, this is my dear friend Maude."

Maude saw out of the corner of her eye, that Norma had noticed Ada standing there in a beautiful gown of dark blue satin and lace across the bodice. She had never seen Ada look so attractive and part of it was because someone had fixed her hair up in the latest fashion. She looked like a totally different girl and the affect was stunning. "Ada, you are positively one of the prettiest girls here tonight. Your hair looks so becoming like that. Joshua, I am so pleased to meet you. I hope to see all of you out there dancing tonight."

Norma came up to Ada and said, "I'm sorry that you didn't take me up on my offer to borrow one of my gowns like you usually do. I had several that would have looked better on you than your gown that you are wearing tonight." Norma didn't even try to keep her voice down, so several people turned towards them.

Everyone in the village knew Norma's reputation for being cruel and Ada was always so soft spoken and shy. Tonight a new Ada spoke up, to everyone's astonishment. "Norma, I'm sorry that you don't care for my gown but I have never felt prettier in my entire life. You were kind to loan me some of your gowns in the past but from now on, I'll be sewing my own with Melissa and Emily's help. I hope that you have a wonderful time this evening. You look beautiful, as usual."

For once, Norma didn't know what to say. She was looking at and hearing someone she'd never known before. '*What has happened to the Ada that I could ridicule and make her do anything to please me? I don't like this new Ada one bit. I've got to find a way to get her back to the way she used to be.*'

The musicians had just started the first dance and the floor was filling up. Norma wasn't dancing but she was looking around the room, picking out a target. She spotted Ellie dancing with Gerard and her eyes shot out daggers at Ellie. As she was walking over to the couple, Sarah could see what was about to happen and she was trying to get over to head Norma off. Norma had grabbed David's arm and was leading him towards Gerard and Ellie. David looked very uncomfortable and he avoided talking to Johnny. He looked like he had resigned himself to get through the evening, one way or the other. As the music ended, Norma said to Ellie, "I'm surprised to see you here this evening. Shouldn't you be dusting or making beds or something?" Ellie was shocked and wasn't sure what to say. She looked up at Gerard and he was just about to say something in Ellie's defense when Sarah walked up and faced Norma. "Hello Norma. You are looking attractive tonight. I see you found a dress in our general store after all." Sarah turned to her left and looked at Ellie and said, "Ellie, you are definitely the prettiest young lady in the ballroom tonight. That dress makes you look like a princess. I think Gerard has been about to pop his buttons, since he is the lucky man to be your escort tonight. I hope everyone is enjoying themselves."

Gerard looked down at Ellie and said, "I'm sorry for what Norma said to you. She is the most bitter person I've ever met."

"She is bitter Gerard, but she is also lonely and sad. I try to be nice to her but she won't let me speak more than a few words and she walks away. I feel sorry for her." Gerard could hardly believe that Ellie could be so kind to a woman who had just insulted her.

"May I have this dance with the prettiest girl in the room?"

Ellie blushed but she looked pleased and said, "I don't have a lot of experience with dancing, so I might stumble sometimes."

"You don't have to worry about anything Ellie; I won't let you fall. Thank you for accepting my invitation to escort you tonight. If you had turned me down, I would be sitting in my room tonight, feeling very unhappy."

Ellie smiled up at him and said, "I just hope you won't end up regretting your decision. Well, let's get out on the floor and see if I can pretend to know what I'm doing." As Gerard held her in his arms, his heart was beating so fast that he was afraid that Ellie would notice. It took her a minute to figure out the steps but she managed to catch on quickly and he could feel her relaxing, which was what he had hoped for. Gerard thought to himself, *'Tonight will be a wonderful beginning to our relationship. It is finally starting to go somewhere.'*

The musicians started to take a break and everyone was working their way over to the refreshments. Very few people noticed Sarah walk up onto the stage, except Pastor. With just one person playing the violin to accompany her; she opened her mouth and sang the most beautiful song. The sound coming out of her voice was like imagining an angel singing. He could almost envision a halo around her hair. He just stood there mesmerized. Everyone had stopped talking completely. When she finished, the applause was incredible. Sarah started singing the second song and still Pastor hadn't moved an inch. When she sang the third and final song, there were several people with tears in their eyes. Doc walked over to him and put his arm across his shoulder and said, "I think that lady now has your attention." Across the room, Johnny had the funniest sensation in his stomach when he heard her beautiful voice. He hoped that no one noticed the look on his face when she first started singing. He casually looked around the room to see if anyone was staring at him but he didn't see any strange looks. As he turned to his left, he noticed Maude looking at him and he realized that she had picked up on his expression. *'I might have known that nothing would get past her. I can trust her not to tell anyone else.'*

Later on, in the evening, Johnny summoned up the courage to ask Sarah for a dance. Pastor would be agreeable, but he wasn't so sure about Elizabeth. "Sarah, your singing was magnificent tonight. You certainly are full of surprises. With your permission James, I would like the honor of a dance with Sarah so that I can let her know I was stunned by her voice."

Pastor smiled and said, "Of course you can Johnny; I think I've stepped on her toes quite often and she could use a break. Elizabeth, may I get you a glass of punch?"

Elizabeth smiled and nodded but it wasn't a sincere smile. *Why does Johnny always seem so relaxed around Sarah but never around me? Do I come across as so cold and unfeeling? I guess if you compare me to Sarah, I probably do, to be honest about it.'*

Doc couldn't seem to take his eyes off of Maude and her friend, Harrison. *I haven't seen Maude smile like that in years. Tonight, when someone told a joke, her laughter just bubbled out of her. She even looked prettier than ever and he noticed that she was almost giddy at times. Is this the same Maude that I've known for several years? How can someone change almost overnight? I've got to talk to James later tonight. Maybe he can set me straight.'* He walked off into a dark corner and pulled out a small flask and took a big gulp and put it back. *There, maybe now I won't feel so miserable. I've got to get out of here soon before someone notices that I'm not having a good time.'*

Johnny was keeping an eye on this new man, Harrison. Maude was special to everyone, but he had especially gotten close to her recently and he didn't want her to get hurt. Doc seemed to cause her a lot of pain and he didn't even seem to realize it. This Harrison fellow could sure put a big smile on Maude's face. Tonight when he had held Sarah in his arms, something happened to his heart and it had really shaken him up. It felt so natural to hold her in his arms and she looked at him sometimes like she could see through him; straight into his heart. *'Pastor is going to be a lucky man if things work out between him and Sarah.'*

This evening Maude truly felt like a young girl again. It was almost like the past 20 years had disappeared completely. When she had looked in her mirror tonight, before leaving her room, her cheeks were rosy and her eyes were sparkling and it amazed her. *'The last time I noticed my face in the mirror, I was frowning.'* Harrison had gone to get her a glass of punch and she watched him as he walked back over to her. He wasn't acting possessive of her and yet he seemed very proud to be with her. He had noticed that she had styled her hair differently and had complimented her dress. She had to be careful with her heart because she wasn't going to allow him to break it again.

"Maude, would you like to sit down for a spell? You've been on your feet the entire evening. I don't want to wear you out so you won't feel up to our carriage ride tomorrow."

"Yes, I think I'd enjoy sitting and watching everyone else. I'm so pleased that this dance turned out so well. Our village is really growing and several people either haven't met each other or they live a few miles away and don't get into the village often. Jennie was a perfect person to work with me on this evening. She is definitely a go-getter."

"I've spoken to several people tonight and they all have sincere compliments about not only how hard you worked on this evening, but you seem to take care of everyone. They don't know what they would do without you."

"I can't imagine living anywhere else, Harrison. There is so much love in this village and it is also full of hurting people who just need someone to listen to them. Working in the hotel puts me right in the middle of all of the action in this village. I couldn't be happier if I had a pile of money and didn't have to work. Look Harrison, several of the men have asked Mrs. Benson and Mrs. Moses to dance. That is so thoughtful of them. I have a feeling that Gerard was behind that. I think tonight they feel like they are at least 50 years younger. I'm so happy for them."

Gerard felt as though he were floating on air this evening, especially when he was holding Ellie in his arms. Can everyone see how much I care for this sweet girl? Of course, Maude knows but I hope that it can be my secret for as long as possible. "Ellie, am I wearing you out?"

"Oh no, Gerard, I have plenty of energy. You can't clean all of the rooms in this hotel if you aren't an energetic person. Dancing is so much fun; I'm not tired at all. You have been very patient with me tonight; teaching me all of these new steps. I can tell that you've had a lot of experience at dancing."

"I can honestly say that I've never enjoyed dancing more than I have tonight with you Ellie. You have picked up these new steps very quickly and you have a natural feeling for the music. Let's walk over and say hello to Maude and her new friend for a few minutes."

It would be hard to tell who was smiling more right now; Maude or Ellie. "Oh Maude, you gave me some wonderful lessons on these dance steps and I've had so much fun. Thank you for encouraging me to attend the dance tonight." All you had to do was take one look at Maude's face to tell that she was enjoying her old friend's company.

Maude looked across the room and found Doc slipping something back into the inside of his jacket pocket. She hoped that wasn't what she thought it was. She'd never seen Doc take a drop of liquor in all the years that she'd known him. Maybe Pastor or Johnny could check up on him later tonight. She'd never meant to hurt him but she was totally out of patience with him. When she stopped to compare Doc and Harrison and the way that they treated her, Doc came out looking pretty bad.

Bucky and Ruthie were enjoying themselves so much and neither one of them cared that they didn't know all the correct steps. In between dances, they talked about their love of animals and country life and he had already invited her for a ride on one of Johnny's horses for tomorrow. He wanted to give her a tour of the ranch and show her all of the animals that he took care of. Ruthie looked at him like he was someone that she wanted to know better and he for sure wanted to see more of her. He could see that he would be making more trips into town in the near future. *'Offering to run errands for Johnny would be helping him out, wouldn't it?'* He wished this night would never end.

Worley and Daisy were having a lot of fun. He'd never held Daisy in his arms before and nothing could have prepared him for what it did to his heart. He could hear it pounding like a drum, and he felt like a young man again. He knew that Daisy flirted with the customers at the saloon but that was part of her job. She had told him one evening that whenever he was in the saloon, she didn't look at another man and that gave him a big head. *'How can our relationship go any further when I have absolutely nothing to offer her? Well, tonight I'm not going to worry about that. I want to enjoy every second of this dance. I just hope another man doesn't come along to steal her away from me.'*

David was absolutely miserable and embarrassed after he'd witnessed Norma's rudeness to Ada and Ellie. He couldn't wait for this evening to end. He'd danced with her a couple of times and brought her some refreshments, but the rest of the time she was flirting with every single man and even with some of the married ones. Facing Johnny was going to be very tough but he had it coming. Johnny had tried to warn him away from her. Well, here comes the social butterfly now. "David, are you having a good time? This has been such a wonderful evening. I hope we are the last ones to leave. Oh, I see someone that I need to speak with. I'll be back soon!"

Jimmy wasn't having a very good time tonight; mostly because being anywhere around Norma made him feel uneasy. She had paid him the money for starting the fire and never said another word to him afterwards. Whenever he was around the sheriff, he could feel guilt all over and he couldn't ever look him in the eyes. He was so glad that the fire was put out quickly and that no people or animals were hurt. As he looked around the room, it seemed like everyone had friends except for him. Bertha was nice enough but she didn't have a special fella from what he had heard and she didn't know how to keep up a conversation. Pretty soon he was going to make up an excuse for having to leave.

Johnny walked over to Pastor and asked if he could have a word with him. They walked away from everyone else and then Johnny said, "I'm getting concerned about Doc. He is not acting like himself and tonight I think I saw him putting a flask back into his jacket. I'm sure it has something to do with Maude and Harrison. Have you had a chance to talk to Doc?"

"I've hinted for weeks that he needed to show Maude how much he cares about her and lately I've stopped the hinting and just came out and told him that he is going to lose her if he doesn't speak up soon. Last night I told him that he was running out of time with Maude's new friend in town. He finally asked her to accompany him to the dance and she told him that she already had an escort. He told me that he has never seen her so happy, and I'm sure that he feels like he's already lost her. I've never known him to take even a drop of liquor. I'll go over and check on him the first thing tomorrow morning. Thank you for speaking to me about this Johnny. He'll be needing all the friends he can get to bring him through this."

Maggie knew that she couldn't attend the dance since she was a recent widow, but it made her sad to miss out on seeing everyone all dressed up and having a good time. She had put her baby to bed and Wesley was in his room doing some homework. Someone was knocking on the front door. She opened it and was surprised to see Hank standing there with a fiddle in his hands. "I know you weren't expecting company tonight Maggie, but I was just sitting at home alone and I thought maybe you'd like to hear some music."

"Well, my goodness Hank, please come on in. I didn't know that you could play the fiddle. Let me tell Wesley that you are here." He walked into the parlor and sat down and laid the fiddle beside him. He'd surprised himself, coming over here like this but it seemed like a good idea. When Maggie came back into the room with Wesley, he jumped up from his seat and Maggie asked him if he would like something to eat or drink. She went into the kitchen and came back with some cold cider and homemade donuts.

Hank played one song after another and even Maggie was tapping her feet to the music. Wesley said, "Hank, do you think you could teach me how to play the fiddle? I mean, if it wouldn't be too much trouble."

"I've never taught anyone before Wesley, but I'll do my best. I'd be happy to show you as much as I know. I learnt by listening and watching my daddy. Maggie, if it is alright with you, may I come by one evening this week?"

"Why don't you come by for dinner Wednesday evening and you could give Wesley a lesson afterwards?"

"I sure won't turn down a chance to eat some of your cooking Maggie. Wednesday sounds good to me. I'd best be goin' now but I've enjoyed your company. Good night Maggie. You too Wesley."

"What a thoughtful thing for him to do, Wesley. I'm sure he was hurting tonight, being widowed and all and knowing most of the village would be at the dance. I think more highly of that man all the time. Please do your best at learning the fiddle son. It's time for you to get some sleep. I'll see you in the morning."

Maggie had just settled down with some knitting when Emily came in the front door, and she looked like she could have floated across the room. "Maggie, look what Jacob gave me tonight. He asked me to marry him and I said yes. I knew I was falling in love with him but I was afraid to believe that he loved me too." Maggie gave her a big hug, and was so happy for her dear friend.

When the evening was winding down, Harrison asked permission to walk Maude to her room and she said yes. At her door, he hesitated and finally said, "Maude, I didn't expect you to be so kind to me but it shouldn't have surprised me. I enjoyed this evening more than words can say. I wish you a good night and I'll come by with a carriage at noon tomorrow."

"Harrison, I couldn't have been more surprised, watching you walk into my hotel yesterday. Tonight, brought back many special memories for me and I thank you for being such a gentleman. I am looking forward to our drive in the country tomorrow. Sleep well my friend."

As Albert was escorting Melissa home, he was smiling to himself. "Just before I left for the dance, my sister, Emily Paige, was having a fit because she wanted to go to the dance. I explained that it was only for grownups but that didn't stop her from coming up with a reason that she should be allowed. 'I don't care if I can't dance; I just want to watch Melissa and see what gown she is wearing.' I had to ask my mother to intervene and finally we promised her that you would come by and let her see your gown. I hope you don't mind. She wants to look just like you when she grows up, even though there is absolutely no resemblance. There is no talking her out of something when she has her mind made up."

"I think that is so sweet. Of course I'll be happy to come over tomorrow to let her see my gown. Maybe with your mother's permission, I can fix her hair a special way to make her look older for a few minutes. I remember feeling just like that when I was her age. How is your brother Ryan acting, since you are home safe? I know he was acting up for awhile, when he was afraid you would never come home. He is such a sensitive boy."

"He is happy that I'm home safe but he acts uneasy whenever I leave the house. I've explained several times that the war is over but somehow he doesn't seem to understand. I'll try and come up with some ways to help him to understand that better."

The day after the dance, Elizabeth asked Johnny if she could talk to him about something. She sat across from him and said, "Johnny, I'm getting concerned about Timothy and I need someone to find out what he is up to. Almost every night I see him putting food into his pockets and going out the back door and over the fence. At first I thought he was feeding a dog because he's always asking for one. Now I just want to know that he is not putting himself into any kind of danger. I don't want him to know that I'm worried about him. He has such a big heart, and I'm sure he is doing something good, but I'd just feel better if I knew what he was doing."

Johnny agreed to go out that next evening to see what Timothy was up to. He went out the front door but circled around and waited towards the back of the hotel. Pretty soon, he saw Timothy running across the lot and then climbing over the fence. He was moving pretty fast so he knew that he must know the path. He waited until Timothy got a little ahead of him and then he moved quietly to catch up to him. In just a few minutes, he saw Timothy stop and then a young man came up to him. Johnny was able to get up close enough to hear their conversation, but they were not aware of his presence. "Hi Franklin, I've got some good food for you tonight. Charlie gave me a big slice of ham and some fried potatoes and vegetables. He also put a big slice of apple pie on top."

The young man walked over to Timothy and took the bag from him and smiled. "You and Charlie are sure fattening me up. I was about skin and bones when I first got here. Since my accident, most people can't look me in the face like you do."

"Doc says that he'll be by tomorrow to bring you some things on your list and to pick up the wood that you've cut. He said to tell you that he gave some of your wages to an older widow lady who has been having a hard time, like you asked him to do. She doesn't know who gave her the money, but she was sure happy."

Johnny stood there and thought to himself that he was so glad that they didn't know he was standing here. Timothy was sure a wonderful example of a giving person. Johnny couldn't see Franklin's face in the dark but apparently it was pretty rough. He was so proud of Timothy. That boy was going to grow up to be a fine young man. If he could find his missing child, he would hope the child would be something like Timothy or Julia. He could tell that the boy was about to leave so he stayed where he was for awhile. With his long stride, he caught up with Timothy just as he was about to go over the fence. In a soft voice, he said, "Well, hello Timothy. What have you been up to?" Timothy almost fell off of the fence and you could tell that he was thinking fast about how to answer. He knew it had been drilled into him to be honest.

Timothy said, "I was just helping a friend." Johnny decided to be up front with him. He asked him to sit on the back steps.

Johnny said, "Your mother has been concerned about you slipping off with food every night and going into the woods. She thought you were feeding an animal and she asked me to follow you to be sure you weren't in any danger."

Timothy's eyes got very big and he said, "Sheriff, did you follow me tonight?" Johnny nodded yes and waited to see what else Timothy would say. "My friend Franklin is a good man Sheriff. He was working on a cannon in the war and it blew up and burned his face really bad. Our doc here in town was the one who took care of him. Doc gave him some special salve for the burns and Pastor gave him a horse and supplies to help him get to wherever he was going. Franklin said no one would look him in the face except for Doc and Pastor."

"But you have been able to Timothy and I am very proud of you. You are acting like a man more than a lot of grown men that I've known in my lifetime. Timothy, I can't keep this from your mother. She has gotten upset with me several times and we have finally become friends. I want you to tell her the truth tonight and I will be right there beside you. I'll do my best to make sure that she doesn't try to stop you from going into the woods to help Franklin."

He knew that the Sheriff was treating him like a grown up so he said, "I'll go find her now Sheriff. Thank you for not being upset with me. I hope my mother doesn't get mad at me."

He and Timothy walked in the back door of the hotel, into the kitchen. Elizabeth was sitting at a small table, looking anxious. She stood up immediately when she saw them. Timothy walked right over to her and said, "Mother, I've been going into the woods every evening to bring a man some food. His face was burned during the war and no one wants to look at him except Doc and Pastor. They took care of him after it happened. They gave him the name of our village in case he needed anything. Mother, one more thing I need to tell you is how I met Franklin in the first place. A few weeks ago, Julia was too busy to go into the woods with me so I went by myself. I thought it would be a neat surprise if I could find a new path in the woods. When I was pushing some bramble bushes out of my way, I fell into a deep hole. I wasn't hurt because the dirt was soft but there was no way for me to get out by myself. I didn't know what else to do so I cried out for help several times. A couple of minutes later, I heard a man's voice say, "I'm going to go get some rope and I'll get you out of there."

"When he pulled me up out of the hole, I ended up with my back to him. He said it would be a good idea if he walked in front of me, while we were headed back to the hotel. That way I wouldn't have to look at his face. Mama, I told him that I wanted to see his face and he had tears in his eyes. I told him that I wanted to be his friend. He saved me so now he's my friend."

Elizabeth had tears running down her face and she reached out and held Timothy with all her strength. She said, "Timothy, thank you for having such a loving heart and for telling us the truth. I would like to meet your friend if he will let me. I want to be his friend too. Maybe I can sew him some warm clothes. Will you ask him please? I'm not upset with you son but please always be careful. You can't trust everyone who comes into your life and I don't want anything to ever happen to you."

"I'll be careful mama. I always ask God to protect me and he did when I fell in the hole. I'm tired mama. Goodnight Sheriff and thank you for understanding about Franklin."

Elizabeth just sat there looking at Johnny, her face still wet with tears.

"Johnny, thank you for following him tonight and for making sure he told me the truth. He thinks the world of you and I hope maybe you can teach him something about how to judge people, especially men. I need to go check on the kids. Oh, I saved you a big piece of apple pie."

"Elizabeth, I would like to accompany you when you meet Franklin. I have an idea of how I can help him."

Johnny sat there thinking that every time he turned around, either Julia or Timothy was tugging on his heart but he just didn't feel comfortable with his relationship with Elizabeth. He didn't know if it was something wrong with him that made things always seem uncomfortable when they were together. Johnny had changed his attitude so much since arriving in Willow Bend. He wanted what Samuel and Rebecca had but was it even possible for someone like him who struggled to trust women? Sarah was the only woman in his life that he always felt comfortable around and knew he could truly trust. She was a wonderful friend.

The next evening when Timothy met with Franklin and brought his food, he had a question for him. "Franklin, my mother was getting worried about me coming out here at night with food. She thought that I was feeding an animal and she asked the sheriff to follow me to see if I was in danger. He followed me and he knows about you and he's a good man. He insisted that I tell my mother the truth. Franklin, she was so happy to find out that you saved me when I fell into the hole. She wants to meet you and she'd like to make you some warm clothes. The Sheriff will be coming along with my mother. Would that be alright with you?"

Franklin was stunned that God seemed to be adding people to the list quite often who wanted to meet him and help him. He remembered telling Doc and Pastor that God must have a plan for his life, so he had surrendered his life to God. "Yes, Timothy, I would like to meet your mother and the sheriff. Please bring them with you tomorrow night. I hope your mother really can prepare herself for when she sees my face." Timothy was so happy and could hardly wait to tell his mother and bring her back here tomorrow night.

Elizabeth had stayed up half the night, making a warm shirt for Franklin, out of one of the shirts that her late husband had once worn. She had asked Johnny to give her an idea of what size shirt he would wear and it wouldn't need too many alterations. As she sat there sewing, she was talking to God. "Lord, first of all I want to thank you for giving me such loving children and for saving Timothy's life when he fell into the hole. Thank you for allowing me to meet Franklin tomorrow night. I pray that you would bless and protect him. Amen!"

When Elizabeth met Timothy at the back door of the kitchen, she was holding the warm shirt and couldn't wait to meet her son's friend. Timothy took her hand and led her through the gate and made sure it was closed securely. Johnny followed behind them and was anxious to meet this young man. The moon was shining so it made it easy to see the path. After walking for a few minutes, Timothy stopped and said, "Franklin, I've brought my mother and the sheriff to meet you." Slowly Franklin stepped out from behind a large bush and she could see some of the scars on his face, even in the darkness.

"I'm so thankful that you allowed me to meet you Franklin. My name is Elizabeth! I can't thank you enough for saving my son when he was in trouble. I've brought you a woolen shirt that I hope will help to keep you warm." She looked him right in the eyes and didn't flinch. As a mother, her heart broke when she thought about the pain he had been through; the physical and emotional.

"I am pleased to meet you mam'm. You sure have a fine son. He has a big heart."

"I would like to bake you some cookies, if you would like that. I want to be your friend also. I'm sorry for your suffering but I believe that the Lord has a perfect plan for your life. I can walk back by myself son. Don't be too long. I hope to see you again soon, Franklin."

Johnny walked closer and looked directly at Franklin and said, "Son, I'm mighty pleased to meet you. Timothy is very special to me and I heard how you saved him when he fell into that hole. I would like to offer you an alternative to living out here in the woods. It's going to start turning a lot colder at night, and snow can come at any time in these parts. I own a big ranch just a couple of miles outside of the village. I'm offering you a small house of your own, plus there are plenty of places for you to cut firewood. What would you say to that?"

"Sir, I'm speechless! Yes, I would like to accept your generous offer. I never considered the idea of having a real home. I'd like to chop firewood for anyone that needs it at your ranch. I've heard about the many things you have done to help the people in this village."

"I would really like it if you would call me 'Johnny.' It will take the men another month to finish the inside of the house and the pasture fences. They have the frame up already and the roof and have started on the rooms inside. How about my coming by to pick you up tomorrow evening when it first gets dark and I'll see if Timothy might like to keep you company to show you your new home.

Timothy didn't have to say a word; his lit up face said it all. Franklin said, "I'll be more than ready sir; I mean, Johnny."

The next evening, Johnny pulled into the back of the hotel in one of his wagons and Timothy was seated proudly beside him. He hopped off to go find Franklin but he didn't have far to go. He was waiting at the edge of the path. As they rode out of the village, Timothy was constantly pointing something out to Franklin, while they both sat in the back of the wagon. As they turned up the long road that led to the ranch, his hand was in motion back and forth, to make sure that he didn't miss letting Franklin know about every building and all of the animals. Johnny was getting so tickled, just listening to him.

As they pulled up in front of the house that Johnny felt would be perfect for Franklin, all of a sudden it got very quiet in the back of the wagon. This house was built about ¼ of a mile past Jacob and Emily's house, on a road set off on a dead-end path, where there would be a lot of privacy.

"This is your home Franklin. Right now there is a small corral and a lean to, to protect your horse in bad weather. I have plans to add on to this fairly soon, but we can talk about that later."

Johnny opened the front door and then stepped aside so that Franklin could enter first. The living room had a stone fireplace along one wall and a small bookshelf. Franklin entered the room and then he went into the kitchen. By now he was fighting tears. His eyes took in an iron cook stove, a sink with a pump and a window that over-looked the trees in the back. As he left the kitchen, he found his bedroom and next to that was a second room that could be used for anything.

Johnny walked into the room and asked Franklin to go back out to the kitchen for a minute. "I'd like you to check out the inside of your cupboards to see if I missed anything. I asked the men to be sure and get the cupboards up as soon as they finished the frame."

Franklin opened one of the cupboards and saw that it was full of plates, cups, pans and utensils. Another one was full of flour, salt, beans, canned peaches, and sugar.

Johnny said, "You are always welcome to eat with us at Samuel's house up the road but if you are not comfortable with that, someone will bring you a plate and leave it on your front porch. We are also going to bring you some eggs two or three times a week. If you can tell me what else you will need, I'll be happy to get it for you."

There was no stopping the tears this time; Franklin was so overwhelmed with this kindness and he knew that the Good Lord was pouring out more blessings than he could ever have imagined. "I don't hardly know what to say sir. If you can ever think of anything that I can do for you, just say the word and I'll try my darndest to do it."

Franklin wiped his eyes with his bandana and then started smiling as he saw Timothy scampering up a ladder, which led to a loft. "Look, there is a small bed up here."

Johnny chuckled and said, "I thought maybe once in awhile you might be invited to spend the night."

Murphy and Rocky had been traveling for over two months, desperately looking for Rusty. Twice they thought they were on his trail, but it turned out to be false leads. They hadn't spent too much money so far, because they didn't want to draw attention to themselves. By next month they would have to find somewhere to hole up during the winter. There were often abandoned cabins up in the hills if they were lucky enough to find one. "We've got to buy us some clothes for the winter or we will freeze. I ain't got nothing except this rain slicker" said Rocky.

"The next mid-size town we hit, we'll find us the general store and get some warm clothes and some grub. Do not go flashing around your money. You never know who could be watchin' and listenin' to our conversations," Murphy growled to Rocky. He was not in a good mood because he wanted to find Rusty once and for all and to stop wondering if he was talkin' to a sheriff or if he was in jail somewhere. Not knowing was tearing up his gut. "Alright, lets bed down for the night and tomorrow we should be close enough to a town to get the supplies that we need. "Rocky, did Rusty ever mention to you where he was from or where he had kinfolk?" asked Murphy.

"He didn't say much at all to me about his past or any family. He just seemed kind of lonely, so I don't think he had anybody back home."

"Maybe someone in this village has seen him travelin' through. Keep your eyes and ears open and be careful what you say. We don't want people lookin' at us too closely."

"Are you sure that he'll tell someone about us? Maybe he'll keep quiet and not want to get himself in trouble."

"That fella has a conscience and it will come back to bite us. Why do you think he wouldn't take his share of the loot? I know of a place nearby where outlaws hide out. We're gonna check with them to see if they've seen Rusty or heard somethin' about him."

The next day they woke up shivering because the temperature had dropped. "Dang, I can't wait to get some decent clothes on my body. I hate bein cold, said Rocky."

"Oh, quit yur bellyaching and get saddled up. We ain't got far to go and then we can get our supplies. Remember what I tole you; no showin' off how much loot you got. Just buy the things I tole you to buy. When we reach the next town, we can buy more. Ya gotta be smart about these things."

After buying their supplies, they stopped off at the saloon and had themselves a beer and then got back on their horses. They rode for about two hours and then they heard someone yell, "Stop right there and put yer hands in the air. What are ya doin way out here?"

"Murphy whispered to Rocky to keep his mouth shut and let him do the talkin. "I'm Murphy Allen and this here is Rocky Simmons. We are here to talk to Big John about someone we're trackin. We mean ya no harm." From behind a huge boulder, a giant of a man stepped forward and said, "Wul, I'll be darned. Ifin it ain't Murphy. Put your arms down and get off yer horses and folla me. I seen yer faces on a wanted poster a few months back. Where's the other fella?"

"That's what we came to talk ta you about, Big John."

"Sit yourselves down and have some beans and saltpork. What's that big jug you're totin?"

"This here is some mighty fine whiskey that I brung along just fer you. I'm hopin' you might know someone who has some idea of where Rusty Anderson ended up. He stole some of our gold and took off in the middle of the night. We're afraid that he might have the idea of turning himself in and tellin' them about us. We've gotta stop him, if we aren't already too late."

"I gotta idea! Why don't you two hole up here for a couple a weeks and get rested up. I can send one of my men into town fer some warm clothes fer ya. I have a man here who is really good at trackin' people down. He will want some money fer his trouble but he is good. He has a lot of friends, spread out all over the place. I would be very surprised if he couldn't come up with yer former gang member or at least give you a clue where to look."

Murphy and Rocky looked at each other and knew that they both agreed to stay and let someone else do the tracking for a change. Now Murphy felt like he could relax for awhile. "That Rusty is gonna be sorry that he ran off like that. I can't wait to see his face whenever he finds out we have caught up with him."

13

OCTOBER 1865

An Unwanted Suitor

Annie Reynolds was a waitress in the village café, but she had a dream to one day be the owner. It was a big dream, but she had a lot of faith and determination to make it come true. As she waited on her customers each day, her first thought was making sure they were well taken care of. Knowing each person by name was important, but even more, she wanted to learn little things about each customer. Like, Doc always wanted two lumps of sugar in his coffee or Pastor James was usually going to ask her if anyone was ill that she had heard about. Annie tried hard not to show favoritism to any customer, but it was so hard when it came to Worley. He was always wearing a bright pink scarf around his neck, which caused a lot of teasing. He told everyone that someone special had given it to him and he liked it. She looked forward to hearing his stories about being the driver for the stagecoach and she figured that some of them were a little exaggerated but she always laughed anyway. He had finally admitted that he was sweet on a girl named Daisy who worked in the village saloon. His face would get a little pink when he mentioned her name and he looked like he was getting serious about her. Annie asked him to bring Daisy to the café but he said that she would be too embarrassed. That comment really bothered her because she wanted everyone to feel welcome in her café.

Some of the young mothers came in with their children so Annie kept a box of toys in a corner to entertain them. Many of the older gentlemen from the village came into the café on a regular basis so she kept issues of magazines on ranching and farming on a corner table. She had fresh flowers in little vases on each table and kept the floors spotless. This may seem like a small café to some people but to her it was such a special place. All of her customers were her guests and she wanted each one to feel welcome. If one of her regulars didn't show up, Annie always made a point of checking up on them. She found out that Mrs. Moses, an elderly widow, had fallen and wasn't able to leave the hotel. Annie brought her over a bowl of her special soup and some homemade rolls and then stayed and talked with her for awhile.

This morning was a beautiful day and Annie was humming as she was washing the front windows before the café opened. Her dark brown hair was always coming undone from the quick way she fixed it each morning. Annie's eyes were a dark brown and full of warmth. She had a tiny gap between her front teeth but that never kept her from smiling as each new guest came into the café. The ranchers and farmers liked to tease her about finding her a fella but she just laughed it off. She wasn't losing any sleep over finding a man to make her life complete. All she wanted was to find a way to become the owner of this café. She saved every penny of her tips and a good part of her wages. Since her best friend Melissa had offered to let her rent her spare bedroom at a decent monthly amount, her savings were growing quickly. The current owner of this café was an elderly man who had told her that he wanted to sell the café within a year. That wasn't a lot of time to come up with the money she needed but Annie wasn't discouraged. She just knew that she was meant to be the proud owner and she could hardly wait.

It was time to open up for the day, so she pulled up the shades and turned the open sign around and unlocked the front door. Nellie Whitestone did a lot of the cooking but Annie pitched in too. Today Nellie would come in at eleven o'clock but Annie could handle it until then. She walked outside to check the front windows for any spot that she might have missed, when she heard a soft "meow". She looked up and saw a frightened kitten on the roof. Annie was always independent, not waiting around for help when she knew she could handle something, and rescuing that frightened kitten was no different. She ran inside and back to the storeroom.

She grabbed the heavy old ladder and drug it along the floor until she finally managed to get it through the front door. By then she was panting and out of breath. The rickety ladder wasn't stable, but she was in a hurry and didn't worry about that. Somehow she managed to get it propped up against the building and up she went. In her haste, she hadn't stopped to hold her dress up and she looked down to see that she was stepping on her dress. She jerked her foot too quickly and the ladder started sliding to the right. Annie felt helpless when she realized she was falling. All of a sudden she felt strong arms around her waist. The ladder fell on the boardwalk with a crash but Annie was safe.

She tried to squirm out of this man's hold but he was definitely strong and he wasn't in any hurry to let her go. Annie turned to look at him and was about to ask him to please put her down. When she looked into his eyes, her stomach started to flutter and she couldn't stop staring.

Her rescuer said, "Well, good morning to you miss. I don't believe we've met before. My name is Pete and I own the saloon. Pleased to meet you. Say, I didn't see you at the dance." He was still holding her in his arms and by now people were starting to walk by and laugh.

Annie said, "Please put me down immediately. I don't like to dance; that's why you didn't see me there. I do thank you for helping me but I am fine. I was just trying to rescue a kitten."

He laughed and said, "It looks like you needed rescuing more than that kitten." He set her down slowly and then picked up the ladder and set it back up against the roof. He didn't need to climb up very far because he was so tall. He reached out and lifted up the scared kitten and put it on his shoulder and climbed back down.

They both turned as they heard Julia running down the boardwalk saying, "Pitty Pat, you bad girl. I'm sorry that she got away from me."

Annie smiled at her and said, "She looked so scared when she was up on the roof but she is alright now."

Pete looked at the ladder and shook his head. "This needs to be fixed. It is not safe for anyone to be climbing on. I'll take it to my place and will fix it for you. I'll bring it back tomorrow morning, if that is all right with you. I still don't know the name of the lady that I just rescued."

Annie's face was getting red and she said, "My name is Annie and I work in this café. Thank you for your assistance. Yes, tomorrow will be fine to return the ladder. I will be happy to pay you for repairing it."

He lifted the heavy ladder as if it didn't weigh anything and went walking away with a big grin on his face. This could be his lucky day. He had been in this village for several months but had not met any lady that interested him; that is, until today. *'I may have to start having some meals in the café instead of ordering from the hotel kitchen.'*

Annie could hear people laughing behind her and she tried hard to shrug it off. Her stomach was in knots but she couldn't let anyone know it. *'Where had Pete come from all of a sudden?'* She'd never seen him before and he sure would be hard to miss. His arms felt like big tree limbs and yet he was gentle with her and the kitten. What a contrast that was. Oh well, she had a café to run, so back to work.

As usual, Julia always had a habit of saying what was on her mind. "I think that fella kinda likes you, Miss Annie."

Sarah was just leaving the general store when she ran into Pastor James outside. He said, "Good afternoon Sarah. I, uh, what were you doing in the general store?" he stammered. She bit back a smile and said, "I was just shopping for some things I'd forgotten the other day. How are you doing Pastor?" Before he could think of an intelligent response, they both heard the sound of a horse running towards them rapidly. Pastor immediately moved back onto the boardwalk, closer to the door to the store. Sarah, on the other hand, dropped her bag and ran out into the street. As Pastor stood there watching her and not being able to move or speak, Sarah stood in the middle of the street with her hands held up high and was trying to stop the runaway horse. When the horse got within a few feet of her and was about to run her down, it came to a stop right in front of her. She reached up and with one hand she patted the horse and with her other hand, she got ahold of the reins.

Now they heard someone running down the street and it was Bucky. "Miss Sarah, you are a wonder. That horse just decided that I wasn't going to get a saddle on him and he just took off. Did he hurt you? He's normally a good horse but somehow he got it in his head that he wasn't going to be ridden."

Sarah was still petting the horse and they were acting like old friends. She handed the reins over to Bucky and said, "I've been around horses all of my life Bucky. I wasn't in any danger." When Sarah turned to go back onto the boardwalk to pick up the bag that she had dropped, she saw the shocked look on Pastor's face. He ran into the store without speaking to her.

Johnny walked up and said, "Sarah, I am proud of you. Not many people would have the nerve to do that."

She looked up at Johnny and he could tell that she was very upset. "But Pastor James looked at me like I'd done something that embarrassed him. Johnny, I just don't understand that man. It seems like I'm always doing something to make him uncomfortable. He didn't even speak to me after I gave Bucky back the horse."

Johnny was a tough man in most ways but he also had a sensitive side that he didn't let many see. He thought that maybe he could help Sarah understand something. He asked her to walk into the hotel with him to get a cup of coffee and she was happy to do so. When they were seated, Johnny tried to be sure that the right words would come out of his mouth. "Sarah, I hope I'm not speaking out of turn here, but I believe that Pastor James thinks highly of you. The problem, as I see it, is that he has never been around a woman as brave as you are and I think it makes him feel like he is less of a man. The first time he ever set eyes on you, you were riding bareback on a horse belonging to the stage line and then he finds out that you shot one of the men trying to rob the stage. Today you stopped a runaway horse as if it wasn't any more dangerous than a puppy. He just doesn't know how to handle this. I think in time, he will start seeing other parts of your personality and that will help to balance what he sees in you now. Sarah, don't ever feel bad about the brave things you have done. You are like a bright ray of sunshine in this village. I would like to count you as a good friend, if that is what you would like too."

Sarah's eyes were wet but she wasn't going to let the tears flow. "Oh Johnny, what you just said makes me feel better and it does help me to understand Pastor. I just wished that he could understand that the things that he has seen me do are not planned. I see something that needs to be done and I know I can do it. I'll try to be more patient with him because I do care about him. Maybe you can put in a good word for me with him once in awhile." To Johnny, Sarah was not complicated and she was one woman whom he felt that he could trust. That was a refreshing feeling.

As she stood up to leave, Sarah said, "I would like to count you as a good friend also, Johnny. If I can ever help you in any way, I would do my best to try."

As Johnny watched her walk away, he thought to himself, *'This is the first woman that I've ever known where I know without a doubt that she can be trusted. Wouldn't you know that she is interested in another man.'*

Jacob woke up before daylight, so excited to tell his parents the news about last night. He had promised to pick up Emily bright and early and take her out to Johnny's ranch. He made himself wait another two hours but that was as long as he could hold off. They would tell his parents the news together. When he pulled up in front of the home where Emily was living, he leaped out of the carriage and took the steps two at a time. He knocked softly so that he wouldn't wake up Maggie and her family. Emily opened the door immediately and it was obvious that she was just as excited as he was. He helped her into the carriage and gently put a blanket over her lap. Even though he wanted to race out of there as fast as possible, he made sure the ride didn't jar her. When they pulled up in front of his parent's home, they both looked over at each other and had big grins on their faces. He jumped down and ran around to help Emily down. Before they could even make it up the steps, the front door opened and Rebecca said, "Is everything all right? Emily, are you feeling well?" Now it started to register to her that neither one of them looked like anything was wrong and that everything was more than fine.

"Come on in and have breakfast with us. We haven't started yet. Your father will be in any minute now. Emily, would you like a glass of milk?" Without waiting for an answer, she poured a glass and set it down in front of her and brought her son a cup of coffee, just the way he liked it. Right then, Samuel and Johnny walked into the kitchen and now came the moment they had been waiting for.

Jacob reached over and took Emily's left hand, which she had been hiding in her lap. They both looked at each other briefly and Jacob said, "Last night I proposed to Emily and she has agreed to be my wife."

Rebecca started crying and came around to hug Emily, saying "Oh, I couldn't be happier with our son's choice. We have already thought of you as part of our family. Now we will become grandparents soon. Jacob, you have waited a long time for the right woman and now the long wait is over."

Samuel came over and pounded Jacob on his back and said, "Son, you've always said that you wanted to wait until you found someone like your own mother and that you've done. Emily, we want to welcome you into our family."

Johnny also had something to say to the new couple. "I've been watching the two of you recently and had a feeling that this was going to happen. I hope you don't mind but I've already had some men building a small home for you, just down the lane. I wanted it ready by the end of this month, before the winter weather comes in. Would you like to see it?"

Now Emily was in tears and she had to pull out her hankie and was happy to have her future mother-in-law sitting beside her, holding her in her arms. "As soon as we've all had breakfast, we can go down to inspect your new home" said Samuel.

Jacob and Emily were both so overwhelmed that they hardly knew what to say. "Johnny, you have been such a blessing to our family. I had no idea where we were going to live except maybe ask my parents if we could move in with them. Thank you doesn't seem like enough, but I think you can tell how we feel."

After breakfast, Samuel brought over the largest wagon and they all drove down the lane to see their new home. When they pulled up in front, everyone was speechless. This was not your normal small house that most people started off living in. This was a house with a wrap-around porch, and beautiful windows that gave a wonderful view of the meadow across the lane.

Rebecca spoke up and said, "I can help you with the curtains, Emily. I enjoy sewing. As a matter of fact, I've been sewing up some things for the new baby; our new grandchild."

They all walked into the new home, letting Jacob and Emily enter first. The open living room ran into the dining room. In the back was the kitchen, with windows on three walls. Off of the living room were three bedrooms. Jacob and Emily were going from room to room, as excited as little kids.

"Oh Johnny, this seems like a dream" said Emily. We didn't expect to have our own place for quite some time. I'm going to start sewing right away and with Rebecca's help, we can have all of the windows covered and lots of other things. I agree with Jacob that to say 'thank you' doesn't seem to convey our feelings very well, but just look at our faces and that says it all."

Jacob walked up to Johnny, just beaming, and said, "Johnny, you have gone out of your way to help our family and we won't forget it. When we get married and settled in here, we'll have you over for dinner."

A week later, after the kitten and ladder incident, Annie had her back to the door while she was pouring coffee for her customers. The chatter had suddenly stopped and now there was only silence. Curious, Annie turned around and nearly burned herself with the hot coffee. There stood Pete like a proud oak tree, looking straight at her. If that wasn't bad enough, he was holding a single flower in his big hands. "Good morning Miss Annie, this is for you." He reached out his long arm and put the flower within an inch of her hand.

Annie managed to get out the words "Thank you" and took the flower from him. It was hard to find anyone in the café who wasn't waiting for her reaction. Annie smiled and said, "That was very thoughtful of you Pete. Are you hungry? We have wonderful pancakes this morning."

Pete chose a chair at a table where he could see her no matter what she was doing. When his meal was ready, she brought it over to him and started to walk away but he stopped her saying, "Can we be friends?"

Annie was never rude to anyone but she didn't want to encourage Pete either. She said, "Yes, no one can ever have too many friends. Excuse me Pete." She dashed off to do something, anything, besides standing there, looking silly. Nellie had taken the single bloom and put it in a small vase with water, which Annie should have thought of doing. *'He just can't make a habit of coming to this café. How could I discourage him without hurting his feelings? Maybe there is a single girl in the village that I can introduce him to. Yes, that's it! But who? Think, Annie, think!'*

Jadon Brown was walking near the school one afternoon, when he heard someone crying. He turned to see where the sound was coming from. Bradley had cornered one of the younger boys and was tormenting him. He remembered the conversation that he had with his mother, when he hadn't stood up for Bucky. "Bradley, you sure enjoy picking on anyone smaller than you, don't you?"

When Bradley turned around with an angry look on his face, he said, "What did you just say to me Jadon?" As soon as Bradley turned to face Jadon, the little boy ran away as fast as he could.

Thank goodness he had startled Bradley enough that he had let go of the little boy. Well, even if he got hit by Bradley, he wasn't going to back down. "I'm smaller than you, so why don't you pick on me? You may be surprised at how hard I can hit. Come on over here."

Bradley wasn't moving because he couldn't believe that Jadon had the nerve to stand up to him. Jadon sounded serious about being able to hit hard. "I don't feel like picking on you right now. I've got better things to do."

Jadon said, "Bradley, wouldn't it be nice if you had some friends, instead of everyone being afraid of you? I'd like to be your friend. We could do things together like go camping or play in the woods or go out to the sheriff's ranch. What do you say?"

No one had ever wanted to be Bradley's friend before. "Yeah, I'd like us to be friends. I've never been camping before. Going out to the ranch sounds like fun too. Can you meet me after school tomorrow on the playground? We can decide what we are going to do."

Jadon walked home, feeling like he was floating. Not only had he faced his fear, but he had made a new friend. It felt good to know that he was going to help Bradley see what it felt like to not be a bully. He couldn't wait to tell his mother.

Doc woke up with a pounding headache and an upset stomach and for a few seconds he couldn't figure out why. Then the pain in his heart came rushing back, along with the memory of the past two days. To make matters worse, someone was knocking on his door. Before he could get up out of his chair, the door opened and Pastor walked in. "Doc, I was worried about you and wanted to check to see if there was anything I can do for you."

Doc glared back at him and said, "There is nothing that anyone can do for me. I've messed up so bad, it can never be undone. Please leave me alone James. I know you mean well, but I want to be left alone."

Pastor had no intentions of leaving. He went out to the kitchen and started a pot of strong coffee and went back into the living room and said, "I know you are hurting my friend, but nothing you can say or do can push me away, so you are just wasting your time. Go wash up and change your clothes and I'll have your coffee ready." Doc knew better than to argue so he did as he was told. By the time the coffee was ready, there was also some toast on his plate. "You don't have to eat much but at least put something in your stomach. I won't do this without your permission, but I am offering to talk to Maude and see if I can help to straighten things out between you."

"No, absolutely not! I feel like such a fool and I don't know how I can ever face her again. I am so ashamed of how many times I've hurt her and pushed her away and taken her affection for granted. You have tried to tell me, over and over again, but I was too stubborn to listen. Now I've got to pay the price for my stupidity. Don't think that I don't appreciate your coming over here this morning. This is something that I've got to do on my own. You are a good man, James; a lot bigger man than I'll ever be. You should be spending time courting Sarah instead of wasting your time on me. Now, I would like to be left alone for a bit before I have to go to my office." Pastor James stood up and patted him on the back and walked back out the front door.

Bucky went looking for Johnny and when he found him he said, "Sir, I'd like permission to let Ruthie ride one of your horses, so that I could show her around your ranch. I mean, when all of my chores are done for the day."

His response was to tell Bucky, "I think that I have a better idea. I asked Ruthie last night what time she gets off and she told me she will be finished at noon. I'm going to give you the afternoon off so that you can bring her back here to look over the ranch. What horse would you suggest she ride, since she has experience with riding horses?"

"I think Goldie would be perfect for her sir. She loves to run but she is also very obedient if you want to go slower. I can't thank you enough Johnny. I want to show her all of the animals that I take care of and give her a tour of the whole ranch." Bucky was almost out of breath.

Johnny said, "When you bring her back out here, would you find me right away so that I can say hello to her?"

"Of course; I'll do that first thing. Well, I'd better get a move on. I've got a lot to do before I leave to meet her." Bucky took off like something was chasing him and Johnny couldn't stop laughing out loud and smiling at what he planned to do. Bucky raced around the horse barn like his pants were on fire. He told every single horse all about Ruthie coming out that afternoon.

When he was almost finished, Rebecca came into the barn with something in her hands. "Hi Bucky, I wanted to give this to you since I finished it this morning. I thought you might like a new shirt since you seemed to have such a good time at the dance. Just in case, you might want to impress some young lady."

Bucky hadn't owned a new shirt since his mother had sewn one for him years ago. "Rebecca, I will cherish this shirt and will only wear it when I've washed up good and proper. Thank you for going to all this trouble for me. I'll wear it proudly."

She walked over to him and gave him a little peck on his cheek. "I'm sure you will look handsome in that shirt and you are most welcome."

Austin and Billy had become fast friends, which was just what Austin needed. He missed his siblings back home, but especially Amanda, who was 13. She had learned at a young age to be a good cook, but she rarely had much of a variety of food to work with. They often talked about their dreams to find jobs where they could help out their parents. He kept hoping that he was the only one in his family that would end up on the Orphan Train. Today he and Billy had rounded up some runaway sheep and they came back hot and sweaty. Billy's mother met them with a glass of cold milk and some cookies. Austin noticed that he was actually getting some muscles in his arms, from all of the work he did around the farm. A few minutes later they heard a carriage pull up and it was Pastor James, Elizabeth and her children, Julia and Timothy. Julia was clutching her kitten, Pitty Pat, who was afraid of the barking dogs. Elizabeth called out to her to be careful of the mud puddles and Julia was only half listening. She had her eyes on some of the animals that she wanted to pet.

Pastor had helped Elizabeth down and had just turned around to speak to Austin and Billy, when he heard Julia yell loudly, "Pastor, please catch Pitty-Pat; she might get in the mud puddle." Johnny was in the barn, visiting with Jonas and he knew it was Julia screaming. His heart was in his throat when he rushed out of the barn with Jonas close behind. It only took Johnny a few seconds to make sense of what was going on. Julia's kitten was running fast and had just flown by Pastor. When he heard Julia screaming for him to catch that darn kitten, he reacted faster than he thought was possible. Before he could stop himself, he took a dive for the kitten but totally misjudged, and now he was sliding head first into a large mud puddle.

Someone was laughing hysterically and to everyone's amazement, it was Elizabeth. In fact, she was laughing so hard that she had to sit down and she couldn't see because of the tears in her eyes. When Pastor came to a sudden stop, he looked over at her through one small slit in his mud-spattered face. Johnny had rarely seen Elizabeth laugh and it made him feel good to know that she did have a sense of humor. Johnny and Jonas went over and helped Pastor up, and Dora ran into the house to get him some dry clothes. He was led over to a water tank and Jonas dipped a bucket in and poured it over Pastor's head, to get the mud off. Julia was now holding her kitten, who was as clean as could be. Julia was confused because she expected a strong scolding from her mother and yet she was laughing and trying to dry her eyes. Julia timidly walked over to Pastor and looked him in the eye and said, "Pastor James, I am so sorry for what happened to you. It was all my fault."

Pastor walked over to her and said, "I bet that was a pretty funny sight, wasn't it? I wish I could have seen what I looked like as I was sliding into that mud puddle. At least we found a way to make your mother laugh, so that was worth it. I am not upset with you, Julia. You didn't do anything wrong."

Dora helped Elizabeth to stand up and now she felt foolish but it had released something inside of her that felt wonderful. *'Sometimes I've thought that I would never laugh again, but I was wrong.'* She was so touched that Pastor wasn't upset with Julia. She walked up to him and said, "I want to apologize for laughing at you, Pastor. It wasn't very kind of me to do."

"Elizabeth, it did my heart good to hear your laughter so don't worry about it. I'm going to go in now and get some dry clothes on. Go ahead and visit with Dora." Dora handed him the clothes and told him where he could change.

Johnny was watching Pastor and Elizabeth and a thought crossed his mind. *'He would make a perfect husband for Elizabeth; much better than I would.'*

Danny was out in the fields, looking for any fences that were broken or damaged, when Sadie walked out. This time she wasn't bringing him a drink or something to eat, which was unusual. He was happy to see her anyway, especially after the evening of the dance he had just spent with her. "Danny, I know you are busy but I wanted to take the time to thank you for such a wonderful time. It wasn't easy for me to ask you to accompany me but I'm glad that I did. I wasn't sure if you would turn me down or not."

"I'm glad that you did ask me Sadie. I'm not sure that I could have found the courage to ask you. You see, when I got shot towards the end of the war, I had a girl back home named Mandie. I told her about my injury and that I would never be able to use my left arm again. She wrote back that it didn't matter to her, as long as I was safe. Well, the day I walked up to her house, she'd been sitting on the porch. When she saw me up close, she had tears in her eyes and she turned her back on me. Since we lived in the same town, I just couldn't stay. I'd heard about Willow Bend from a friend and just started walking. The day your father picked me up was one of the brightest days of my life. Your whole family has treated me like a whole person and I feel welcome and cared about. Sadie, you've never stared at my wrist or treated me any different. You can't imagine how good that makes me feel. I hope you can understand that I just couldn't risk asking you to the dance, although I sure had wanted to."

"Danny, thank you for telling me about some of your past. I'm sorry for the pain that you've been through. You have truly found the place to live where you are accepted by everyone. I'm just thankful that you survived the war and the Good Lord sent you to us. I need to get back to the kitchen. I baked some cookies and I'll bring you some in a little while." As he watched her walk away, Danny felt that his heart was melting. The wall of protection that he had placed around his heart was starting to crumble.

Sadie's mother had noticed a difference in her daughter recently. She was often caught day dreaming and would be startled when someone called her name. Her face would turn red and then she would look away quickly. Dora wondered if anyone else had noticed. The other day Sadie had made biscuits and had forgotten an ingredient that she normally used on a daily basis. Another day she had let the biscuits burn but she had caught them in time to still be eaten. Dora wasn't the kind of mother to pry so she kept her thoughts to herself; not even telling Jonas, which was unusual. In her good time, Sadie would come to her for a private conversation.

Maude was eager to leave for her carriage ride with Harrison, but she still had about 30 minutes before she would be relieved at the front desk. She looked at the front door and saw a beaming Emily walking towards her. As soon as she got up close, she thrust out her hand to show Maude the beautiful ring on her finger. "Oh, my goodness; it is beautiful. Did this happen last night?"

"Yes, it did. In the special room that you provided for us. Oh, it was so romantic. We danced and talked and then Jacob asked me to marry him. He said he'd been carrying the ring around for a couple of weeks, trying to find the right moment. Well, you provided the perfect setting and I'm ever so grateful. We drove out to Johnny's ranch to tell his parents and Johnny the news and guess what? Johnny has already had a house built for us, right down the lane from Samuel and Rebecca."

"Honey, I couldn't be happier for you both. When I saw that room weeks ago, I had a feeling that God had a special reason for my finding it. Your baby is going to be blessed with such loving parents and grandparents. Look how God is taking care of you. I've been knitting baby clothes for you but you can't see them just yet. I'm going on a carriage ride with my old friend Harrison but can we have lunch later this week?" Emily said yes and hugged Maude.

Harrison was patiently waiting and immediately climbed down to help Maude up. He was wearing more casual clothes today, as was Maude. He took the picnic basket and blanket from her, and placed them behind their seats. As he was helping her up, she happened to look down the street and saw Doc staring at her. He didn't look angry; just defeated. At some point she was going to have to have a talk with him, but not today. "Tell me where you would like me to drive us and then you can explain what we are seeing along the way."

"Just go straight ahead for awhile and I'll be happy to tell you all about the scenery. The leaves are so beautiful; all shades of yellow, gold and red. I wish I knew how to paint, but I've never taken the time to learn."

"It's funny that you mentioned painting because that is something that I just started playing around with, a few years ago. I've only painted a few landscapes and nothing too difficult but I must say, it is very relaxing. What do you do to relax, Maude?"

"I have tea with lady friends, and I am always knitting something for someone. Sometimes I will hear about a good book, so if I can find a copy, I'll do some reading during bad weather, when I can't get out much. A good part of my life, I've had the urge to travel and see places that others have told me about, but I never seem to find the time."

"There are some very exciting and interesting places out there, in every direction. I have managed to travel a great deal and I always enjoy seeing something that I've never seen before. "Where would you like to travel to, Maude?"

"I've read some travel articles through the years and the places that get my attention have been Colorado, Wyoming and Oregon. They all seem so far away and out of reach. A single woman will rarely travel alone and most of my women friends have children that couldn't be left behind. It never hurts to dream though, does it Harrison?"

"You are quite correct, my dear. It's true that I've traveled quite a bit but it has never been as exciting as I had hoped, because I was always traveling alone. It is a lot safer for a man to travel by himself, but not as enjoyable."

They spent the afternoon going down every side road that they came across and then they were on the long entrance to Johnny's ranch. When they pulled up in front of the main house, Rebecca popped out right away, with a delighted look on her face. "Oh, I do love to have unexpected company. Please come right on in. I just baked some cookies and put on a pot of tea."

Harrison helped Maude down and greeted Rebecca and then said, "If you ladies wouldn't mind, I'd like to roam around a little and see some of this ranch I've heard so much about. I won't be gone too long, and I doubt if you will even notice that I'm not around." He chuckled as the ladies were already walking into the kitchen. Hearing hoofbeats, he turned around and saw the young couple that he'd met at the dance last night. *'What were their names again? Bucky and Ruthie; that's it.'*

Right then Johnny came walking out of the horse barn. "Hello, Harrison! Is Maude in the house with Rebecca?" Harrison nodded yes to this question.

"Hello, Miss Ruthie. How did you like the horse that Bucky picked out for you to ride?"

"She is so beautiful and can really run fast. I felt like I was back home on my father's farm. Thank you for allowing me to ride her this afternoon. Bucky made a great choice."

At that comment, Bucky threw his shoulders back and raised his chin and looked so proud. Johnny walked over to Ruthie and patted the horse she was on and said, "I asked Bucky to pick out the best horse for you, because I trust his judgment. The horses perk right up whenever he is around. Miss Ruthie, I'm giving you Goldie as a gift. As of today, she is your horse and please feel free to come out to the ranch as often as you'd like to ride her."

Ruthie looked over at Bucky and he looked as stunned as she was. "Do you really mean that she'll be my very own horse Johnny? I'll take such good care of her. I know all about grooming a horse and how to feed and water them. This is the most exciting thing that's ever happened to me." She dismounted on her own and came over to give Johnny a big hug. "How can I ever thank you enough?"

"Just by taking good care of her is all the thanks that I need. Now if you'll excuse me, I'd like to spend some time with Harrison."

He walked over to the carriage that Harrison had rented and said, "If you don't mind, we can ride around the ranch some in this carriage. I'm sure the ladies won't be missing us for quite a while." Harrison handed the reins over to Johnny. They went down the lane and he showed them Jacob's new home and then Bucky's home and further on down the lane, Johnny said, "I plan to build a larger home out here in the spring time. It is so peaceful out here. I've seen deer back here and all kinds of little critters. I enjoy being the village sheriff but I want a place to get away, off by myself sometimes."

Harrison had a good feeling about Johnny and decided to be open and frank with him, regarding Maude. "Johnny, I know that I caught Maude off guard by arriving in Willow Bend without warning her, but she seems happy to see me. I'm not blind to the fact that Doc has not been happy about my arrival. I didn't come here to cause problems and if I think that I'm hurting Maude, I'll leave immediately. I know that she thinks the world of you and I don't want you to be worried about my intentions."

"I appreciate your being up front and honest with me, Harrison. This entire village thinks the world of her. It's true that Doc is hurting right now, but I do know that he has had years to declare himself and he hasn't done that. I don't know where you could ever find a finer woman than Maude, and I think that now he is beginning to open his eyes. I want only the best for Maude, regardless of who she chooses to be with. I'm going to check on Doc this afternoon. Please just go slow and think long and hard about how you handle your relationship with her. I need to get back into the village, but maybe some evening we can have dinner together and get to know each other better."

Doc went through the motions of going to his office and taking care of his patients, but he couldn't have told you the names of anyone that he took care of today. His brain was in a fog and his heart hurt so badly that he thought he surely might die. *'If I died today, would anyone really care? Stop thinking like that; this is nonsense.'* The only person he cared about right now was Maude. Was this Harrison fellow the man she had prayed for all these years? Doc had never thought of himself as a cruel man but what he had done to her all of these years was not only cruel; it was so foolish. She had gone through years of pain and he just nonchalantly went through life as if he didn't have a care in the world.' Elizabeth kept looking at him like she wanted to say something but didn't know quite what to say. She loved Maude and he wished that he could talk to her, but it was so embarrassing, he just couldn't do it. Finally, he told her to go home for the day and that he was going for a ride in the country. She looked surprised but did as he asked and left. Right as he was leaving, across the street, Maude was in a carriage with Harrison and she caught his eye for just a moment. He didn't see anger in her face but definitely sadness and maybe even sympathy, which was the last thing he needed.

Doc drove his carriage aimlessly, not caring where he ended up. He was so thankful that he hadn't run into any one, and that was a miracle in itself. Talking to people was not something that he could handle today. He found an old dirt path that was wide enough for his carriage and he led his horse down it. When he reached an old fallen log, he stopped the horse and got out. He was shaking and felt sick to his stomach. Where is my coat? I must have left it in the office. It doesn't really matter anyway. Before he could stop it, he started sobbing and although it was painful, it also felt good. He just couldn't hold it in any longer. He rolled off the log and laid in the leaves and continued crying. Without realizing it, he found himself yelling in a rage at his deceased father. *"How do you like what you drove me to, old man? You were so cruel to me when I was growing up. I hated you, but I was trapped. Your cruelty pushed me to find a way to get away from you. I became a doctor who cared about his patients but I must have gotten that from mother, because it certainly didn't come from you. I've had so much pain bottled up inside me all of my life, and it has kept me from marrying the only woman I've ever loved. I've lost her and I not only blame myself, but I blame you. I hope you are happy now."* He was now laying on his back, looking up through the trees and he felt like he could just close his eyes and hopefully end up in heaven. He took a big gulp of the whiskey in his flask and felt it burning his insides.

Someone was calling his name; was he dreaming? "Doc, where are you?" It was Johnny's voice. He tried to answer but nothing came out. "Here you are. What happened to you? Is it your heart?"

"Yes, it's my heart but it's not a heart attack. It's just broken, that's all."

He felt Johnny's strong arms, lifting him up to a sitting position. Once Johnny saw the tears in his eyes, he knew it wasn't a heart attack. "Doc, I'm taking you to my ranch and Rebecca will help me take care of you. This is not a suggestion and it's not up for discussion. Here, I'll help you up and into the carriage and I'll drive." Johnny drove slowly but luckily, they weren't far from his ranch.

When he reached Samuel and Rebecca's house, Samuel was just coming across the yard. He rushed over when he saw Doc. "What's wrong Johnny?"

"Doc isn't feeling well and I told him that he was coming home with me. I'm going to ask Rebecca if she will help me take care of him."

"We will both take care of him; follow me."

Samuel helped Doc down from the carriage and he supported him with his arm and led him up the steps. By now Rebecca had heard voices outside and she had opened the kitchen door. "What is going on? Who is sick?"

"Doc isn't feeling well Rebecca" said Samuel "and I told him that you and I would take care of him until he is feeling better." Samuel led him down the hall to an extra bedroom and Johnny was right behind him. Together they got him undressed and in bed. Rebecca knocked softly on the door and said she had some hot soup for Doc. They managed to get a little bit down his throat and he fell asleep.

"That's exactly what he needs at the moment. I'm sorry to bring him here but I didn't know what else to do. He is hurting right now, emotionally. He probably won't want to talk about it, but that is all right."

"He is welcome here as long as he needs a place to stay. I'll be happy to take care of him. The poor man! He takes care of everyone but himself," said Rebecca.

"I'll swing by his house and pick up some clean clothes and anything else that I think he'll need and I'll be back this evening. Thank you for doing this for Doc."

Johnny rode back into the village to find Pastor. He was walking home and smiled when he saw Johnny, but then he looked puzzled at the look on Johnny's face. "What's wrong?"

"It's Doc. I found him almost passed out in the woods and he was crying and yelling. I took him to Samuel and Rebecca's house and they'll take good care of him. He's in bad shape. I asked him if it was his heart when I first found him and he said *'Yes, it is my heart. It is broken.'* I also had a good talk with Harrison earlier today and he is a decent fellow. I think highly of him and he is trying to not put pressure on Maude. He really does love her and he is not afraid to show it. I don't know what we can do for Doc."

Pastor hurt for his dear friend, but he had said enough lately. Now it was up to Doc. *'Lord, I lift up my friends to you; both Doc and Maude. You know what is best for both of them, even if they don't. Keep them on the path that you have set before them. Please help Doc with his drinking problem.'*

Elizabeth had so much on her mind lately and it was starting to get her down. She knew that Maude was always willing to listen but right now Maude had her own problems between Doc and Harrison, so Elizabeth didn't want to add anything more for her to worry about. Because she worked for Doc so often, she knew how much he was hurting. He had let her know one day recently that it was something that he had to work out by himself. She went to find Sarah and since school was out for the day, she was available. "Sarah, can we go to your room and talk in private?"

"Of course we can. Something must be really bothering you. I'm always willing to listen but I can't promise that I can give out good advice." She followed Sarah to her room and right away she started talking.

"Sarah, I am so mixed up. All of a sudden, I felt unhappy and I couldn't figure out why. This morning I think I figured it out, but I don't know what to do about it. When I first took care of Johnny and Samuel, there was a definite attraction to Johnny. One day I overheard him talking to Samuel and he said he didn't have any plans to get married because women couldn't be trusted. That's when the doctor that I was working for, told me about an opening here with Doc. I bought those tickets for the stage that same day and left without even saying goodbye. You should have seen my face when Johnny walked in the doctor's office with Maggie and a baby. I understand now that he was just trying to help her. Sarah, I get upset with him so often and I know it makes him uncomfortable. Whenever I see him around you, it is just the opposite. He is always relaxed and smiling when he is talking to you. What is wrong with me? I want to change but I don't have any idea how to start."

"Oh Elizabeth, thank you for sharing this with me. I've seen a difference in you lately but I didn't want to pry. Now I understand but I'm not sure that I can be of much help. I am totally relaxed around Johnny so he picks up on that and it means he doesn't feel any pressure. We are just two good friends who enjoy talking to each other and teasing. I even went fishing with him one day, uninvited. I just plopped down on the grass beside him, baited my hook and caught some fish. We hardly said much of anything between us and yet it was so relaxing. I'm not trying to impress him, so there is never any tension. Does that make any sense to you?"

"Yes, it makes perfect sense when you put it that way. The only problem is that I can't make myself be relaxed. As soon as I see him, even across the street or across the room, my whole body gets tense. I feel like someone I don't even like any more. I used to be a lot more carefree but since I've been a widow, I feel such responsibility to my children. Another thing that's bothering me is that I'm getting tired by the end of the day at Docs. His business is growing so fast. I want to have fun with my children and with my friends, but I'm so exhausted. When I listen to myself, I sound like someone's very old grandmother. Riley is such a help to Doc and I. I'm not sure if she realizes how much she takes off of our shoulders. I swear that she would try operating on someone if we told her she could. She'll make a wonderful nurse when she gets older. I wish she was older right now, so that I could work less hours."

"Don't try to make any drastic changes Elizabeth. You have such a wonderful personality and I don't want that to change. Just make little changes now and then and that should encourage you. I'll try to put in a good word for you sometimes. Men are quick to pick up on tension, so we need to teach you how to relax more. Maybe when you first see him, start humming a tune to get yourself to relax. Let me know if you start feeling better. I'm so happy that we are good friends. I need to correct some papers from school but let me know whenever you need to talk again." They gave each other a quick hug and Elizabeth left Sarah's room. *'What she said about being relaxed around Johnny, makes me so envious that she can do this so easily. Well, I've got to at least make an effort to change.'*

The next afternoon, Johnny decided to go fishing for awhile to help him relax. Seeing Doc in such a state, made him feel so bad for him. He could see both sides of the situation between Doc and Maude, along with

Harrison's side too. He told his deputy where he was going and as he left the jail, he almost bumped into Elizabeth. "I'm sorry Elizabeth, I nearly knocked you over. My apologies."

She looked up at him and her mind went numb but she did notice that he had a fishing pole in his hands. "I see you are going fishing. I've always wanted to learn. Would you mind some company? Maybe you can teach me a little bit about it."

Johnny didn't know what to say. He didn't want to hurt her feelings but he wanted to be alone. Finally, he decided that it would be rude to not invite her to come along.

"Of course, you can come along. You might want to get your cape in case it gets cooler. I'll wait right here for you."

Elizabeth ran to the hotel, breathlessly went up to Maude and said, "Can you watch out for the children for a little while? I'm going fishing with Johnny."

"You know I'll be happy to but aren't you a little overdressed for fishing?"

Elizabeth looked down at her pretty pink dress with little blue flowers, which was one of her newest dresses. "I don't have time to change; he is waiting for me at the jail. I just need my cape. Thanks Maude."

By the time she got back to the jail, she was breathless and her cheeks were rosy. "You didn't have to rush Elizabeth. I would have waited."

"Oh, I wasn't rushing; I was just excited about the chance to learn how to fish. Thank you for allowing me to come along." Luckily it was just a short walk to the river because she was chattering the entire way. *'I hope the fish are hard of hearing today"* thought Johnny.

When they reached the edge of the river, Johnny sat right down and Elizabeth hesitated, trying to find a spot that wasn't too dirty. Johnny was busy pulling a long worm out of a tin can, and it was squirming. She finally found a spot to sit down beside him and she couldn't believe what he was about to do. He was going to run that sharp hook through the poor worm. She turned her head and felt sick to her stomach. "Here you go, I'll let you use my pole first. Take this and fling it out into the river. When you feel a tug, let me know and I'll help you pull it in." She tentatively took ahold of the pole and swung the pole behind her and snapped her wrist. Before she knew it, she had caught Johnny's hat and flung it into the river. "Oh my goodness; I'm so sorry. I didn't mean to do that. I didn't realize how strong I was."

Johnny was still staring at his hat, floating in the river. He had to pull off his boots and socks, roll up his pants legs and wade into the cold water. *'Well, I wanted to get my mind off of Doc for awhile so this ought to do it.'* He tried not to react too much when he first stepped into the water but he couldn't help it. "Dang, it's like ice water." He finally reached his hat and turned to walk back to the bank. When he got back on land, he had nothing to dry off with and the thought of sitting there with his feet soaked didn't make him very happy. He gritted his teeth and pulled on his socks and then pulled his pants back down. His boots were next but he felt miserable when he got them on.

"Johnny, I don't know what to say. I feel so bad. Are you cold?"

'I'm not just cold; I'm miserable.'

"No, I'm fine. Don't worry about it. Well, I guess you're ready to go back to the hotel now, aren't you?"

"Oh no, I'm having so much fun. I'd like to try it again. I don't give up that easily." She picked up the pole and said, "What happened to that poor worm?"

"He must have slipped off the hook. Just get another one out of the pail. If you have trouble putting it on the hook, I'll help you."

Elizabeth's face looked pale and she said, "Could you please do that for me?"

"If you are serious about wanting to learn how to fish, you need to learn to do it yourself. Just put your hand in the can and pull out the biggest worm in there."

She just couldn't look in that can so she slowly put her fingers in until she felt something wiggling and squeamish and she let out a scream and pulled her hand out. "Oh, it feels terrible."

Johnny was determined not to give in to her so he just shook his head slightly and said, "You can do this; now try again."

This time she gritted her teeth and slowly reached in and pulled out a worm. They all felt huge to her so she didn't care which one she had in her hand. She pulled it all the way out of the can and tried to hand it to Johnny. "Just put one end right through the hook and make sure you run it through the hook twice securely."

Elizabeth sincerely was trying to do what he was telling her to do, but when she looked at that poor helpless worm, she just couldn't do it. She dropped the worm and ran over behind a tree and threw up and never said a word. She just walked as fast as her legs would carry her. Johnny wasn't about to tell her that she had a big grass stain on the back of her dress. She needed to get far away from Johnny and she wanted to wash her hands and mouth about a dozen times. *'Well, I can scratch one thing off my list to try and make Johnny feel relaxed around me.'*

Johnny, on the other hand, had lost all interest in trying to have a relaxing afternoon fishing. He stalked off to the jail and was not in a very good mood. *'How can two women be so totally opposite of each other? When Sarah was fishing, I was so relaxed and pleased to have her nearby. Today was a terrible experience and one that I would like to quickly forget.'*

Later that evening Samuel said, "What has you in such a sour mood Johnny?" When he related the event of trying to teach Elizabeth how to fish, Samuel was just doubled over from laughing and even had tears in his eyes.

Rebecca scolded him right away. "That is not funny Samuel. You should be ashamed of yourself. Poor Elizabeth must have been so embarrassed. I feel really bad for her. Johnny, you need to say something to her to make her feel better. I'm sure she's going to dread seeing you anytime soon."

Between Samuel's laughing and Rebecca's scolding, his mood hadn't improved one bit. "I'm going to check on the horses. Good night!"

Rusty had been riding all day and he was starting to get cold. *I've just got to find a place where I can do some work and maybe sleep in the barn. I wish I knew how to contact Johnny but I haven't a clue where he might be.'* Just before dusk, he found an abandoned barn, which gave him and his horse some protection from the cold. There was some old bales of hay, which gave him food for his horse and something comfortable to lay on. When he went outside to walk around, he found a good-sized puddle of water from a recent rain, so he went back and led his horse for a good drink. Once back inside, he had his horse lay down and he made a place to sleep, with him laying back to back to his horse for warmth. *I wonder what my future looks like? I have never felt so helpless in my entire life. I have two brothers that I can't find, a price on my head and probably two men trying to track me down. I'm hoping that it is time for me to have a break.'*

The next day he had ridden for several miles and came to a small village called Albion. He had to take a chance of talking to someone who could lead him to a place to work for his meals and a place to sleep. He hoped no one had seen his face on a wanted poster. He had grown a heavy beard to help disguise his face and he kept his hat pulled down quite a bit in front, so you couldn't see as much of his face. He walked into the general store and bought some canned peaches and some jerky. The man behind the counter seemed to be taking a real good look at him and Rusty tried not to show how nervous he felt.

"Do ya need anything else?"

"That's all I need today but you could possibly help me. I'm trying to find a place that could use some help in exchange for some meals and a place to sleep in their barn. Do you happen to know of any place like that? By the way, what village is this?"

"I reckon I don't know of anyone needin' help right now. This here is the village called Albion. Where did you come from?"

"After the war, I decided to try and find my brothers but I don't know where to start looking. Right now I need to find a way to get out of this weather. Much obliged for your help."

Rusty walked away with an uneasy feeling in his stomach. *That man was making the hair stand up on the back of my neck. I've got to get out of this village and just keep looking.'*

Gerard was feeling pretty confident that he was making some progress with his relationship with Ellie. Today was their third carriage ride, driving around the countryside, piled up with thick, warm blankets. Ellie was bundled up in a cape and hood that Sarah had loaned her, along with some warm gloves from Maude. On their first carriage ride, he had asked her if she had a dream and she was very honest about telling him that someday she wanted to have her own hotel. He had quickly encouraged her dream. Today Ellie surprised him when she said, "Gerard, I've been wondering if you have ever had a dream."

"Yes, Ellie, I have had a dream for a long time to get married and have children."

Ellie was stunned! She wasn't expecting an answer like that. "I'm not feeling well; please take me back to the hotel right away."

He was so upset with himself for what he had said. It was a stupid thing to say so soon. He reluctantly headed back to the village. Ellie's face was white as a sheet and her hands were balled up in knots. The entire light-hearted mood had vanished and a great sadness ran through Gerard's heart. How could he ever undo the damage he had just caused? Ellie didn't say a word all the way back to the village, nor would she look at him. As soon as the carriage stopped in front of the hotel, she jumped out without a backward glance.

Maude saw the look on Ellie's face and knew that something had gone wrong but she didn't ask her. Ellie ran upstairs as fast as she could and Maude let her go. Soon after, Gerard walked into the hotel, looking like a defeated man. When he looked at Maude, she saw such sadness and misery in his eyes. She reached out her hand to his shoulder and said "Gerard, do you feel like talking about it?"

He nodded and asked if she could take a walk with him. He told her, "We were having the most wonderful time Maude. Ellie always gets excited over a baby colt and its mother and we had stopped so she could pet them. She had previously told me about her dream to one day own her own hotel and I encouraged her. Then today she asked me if I'd ever had a dream and I said, 'Yes, I've dreamed of getting married and having children.' That is when she totally froze and asked me to take her back to the hotel immediately. I feel like such a fool Maude. She asked me the question that she wasn't ready to hear the answer to and now I don't know what to do. I am falling in love with Ellie and it's tearing me apart that she is so afraid of a relationship with me."

Now Maude understood what was going on between them. She patted Gerard's arm and said, "Gerard, with your permission, I would like to have a talk with Ellie about why she is so afraid of a relationship with you. I know she thinks that you are so far above her in society but I want her to understand that it is not how you think of her. I believe that you would be good for Ellie, but you definitely need some help here. I'll give her time to calm down and will talk to her tonight. You'll know soon enough if I've had any success. I know that she trusts me and looks to me as a mother figure, so that is in my favor. Try not to be so hard on yourself, Gerard. All relationships have their ups and downs and I'm in your corner."

He didn't know what he would do without Maude. As they walked back to the hotel, he felt a little better but not much. He had always believed that he had wisdom about how to treat others, but he couldn't have messed this up any worse if he had tried. It would take a miracle to get Ellie to trust him again.

Doc had spent three days and nights with Samuel and Rebecca and he couldn't have asked for any greater care. Rebecca brought him delicious soup every day and was often found just sitting in his room, knitting. She was a very wise woman, and seemed to understand that he needed some company but not much conversation.

"Rebecca, I don't know how to thank you and Samuel for taking me in like this. It is pretty embarrassing to think about how Johnny found me. I think I was at a breaking point, but hopefully there is nowhere to go now but up. I've never had anyone take care of me like this; not even my own parents."

"You've been a good patient, Doc, and a pleasure to take care of. Elizabeth sent word that everyone misses you but things are running fairly smoothly. She said not to rush back to your office too soon."

"I can't ever remember being this relaxed before. I think I'll take a little nap. If Johnny can send word back, please let them know that I'll be back by tomorrow afternoon."

Rebecca silently prayed for Doc and was so thankful that she and Samuel were able to let him stay with them. *'I pray that he finds the peace and love that have been missing for so long in his life.'*

Ellie had gone to her little room and thrown herself across the bed and cried her eyes out. Luckily, none of the other maids were in the room but she was hurting so much, that she couldn't have held back the tears if they had been in here. She had never felt pain like this before and it scared her. *'I don't know what to do and I just can't face Gerard again. I wish that I knew somewhere that I could go to get away from this village but I don't have anyone to visit.'*

There was a soft tapping at the door and then she saw the doorknob turning. It was Maude! She didn't say a word at first; she just sat beside Ellie and pulled her into her arms. Now the sobs came tumbling out and Ellie couldn't even get a word out at first. Maude just kept holding her and rocking back and forth, rubbing Ellie's shoulders and back. Eventually the sobs ended and Maude handed her a clean hankie. Ellie blew her nose several times and dabbed at her eyes. When she looked up at Maude, her eyes were swollen and there was a deep sadness there.

"Maude, I asked Gerard if he'd ever had a dream, and he said...and he said, that his dream is to be married and have children. Those words just terrified me, Maude. I've tried so hard not to be attracted to him but it is almost impossible. There's nothing about him not to like. I have no right to be interested in a relationship with him. I feel just sick inside because I don't know what to do. I can't run away because I have nowhere to go and no money to help me get there. I just want to get far away from him but there is nothing that I can do. Please help me Maude; I'm so scared. Tell me what to do. Please!"

"Ellie, I'm sorry that you are hurting like this and I hate to see you so full of fear. Gerard is a kind man. If he was anything else, I would never have asked you to go on a carriage ride in the first place. I knew about him before he came to our hotel and he has an excellent reputation. You couldn't ask for a finer man. Ellie, what you are afraid of is not being good enough for him and that is ridiculous. You are attractive, and a hard worker and everyone likes you and you have this wonderful dream to have your own hotel. Gerard doesn't look at you like you are nothing but the maid that cleans his room. You need to find a way to have more confidence in yourself. You are making yourself miserable for no reason. Now go splash some water on your face and I'll ask Martha to bring you up something to eat. You just stay here in your room for the rest of the afternoon and evening."

As soon as Maude came down the stairs, Gerard came over to her, acting like he was expecting to hear the worse possible news from her. "Maude, is she going to be all right? How is she feeling? Do you think she'll talk to me? I've got to apologize to her for scaring her like that. When can I see her?"

"Gerard, settle down. Let's go for a walk and get away from the hotel. I'll go get my cape and I'll be right back. Please stay right here and I won't be long."

It seemed like a long time to wait for her to return but it was actually only a few short minutes. She went outside and started walking towards the back of the hotel. There was a path that followed the fence line, that she enjoyed following. Gerard was trying to be patient but he couldn't hold it in any longer.

"Maude, I'm worried sick about what I said to Ellie. You've got to tell me how she is feeling."

"Gerard, you already know that she is upset. I gave her about an hour to try and calm down and I went up to her room. I just held her in my arms and comforted her and let her cry it out. At first I couldn't understand what she was saying, but when she settled down, I was able to. I told her that I knew you were a good man with an excellent reputation and I'm sure she had no trouble believing that. The problem is how she sees herself. Before you arrived, she was so happy and excited about wanting her own hotel someday. She's never had a special beau and she had no idea what men and women feel when they are attracted to each other. I know that she cares about you and that is what scares her. Taking an innocent carriage ride with you was one thing, but hearing you say that your dream is to be married and have children, made her feel terrified. I want you to understand something Gerard. You did nothing wrong and you have nothing to feel guilty about. This is Ellie's problem. She has got to find a way to have more confidence in herself, regardless of what happens between the two of you. I think the wisest thing you can do is to try your best to act like you aren't feeling guilty. Just talk to her sometimes about your book and how excited you are. Ask her to read some pages and give her opinion. I know this isn't going to be easy but you have to give her time to work this out herself."

"I like the idea of asking her to read parts of my book and I would value her opinion. This is going to be so difficult for me, but I understand what you are saying and I'll try my best to do what you suggested. If I lose her over this, I honestly don't know what I would do. Thank you for being such a good friend to both of us, Maude. I'm going to go out to Johnny's ranch and see if getting away from here for awhile will help me some." He gave her a quick hug and walked down the street to rent a carriage.

Gerard felt himself calming down a little, as he rode out of the village. It would be snowing sometime next month and he could tell how beautiful the trees would look, all covered with snow. He found himself trying to think of the perfect present for Ellie for Christmas. It couldn't be expensive but he wanted it to be personal. This was not going to be easy. When he reached Johnny's ranch, he saw several horses in a corral and they looked underfed and weak. These must be some of the abused horses that Johnny was taking in to restore their health and strength. He admired him for being so generous and good hearted; not only with people but also with animals. Gerard pulled up near the barn and tied the reins to a fence post. He was wandering around, enjoying all of the animals, when from behind him, he heard a terrible sound and thundering hoofs. Someone was yelling at him to get in the barn, but there was no time. A huge horse was rearing up on his hind legs and was pawing the air. The sound coming out of its mouth was terrifying. Before he could move, the horse came down on all fours and knocked Gerard over on his back and stomped on one of his legs. The last thing that he remembered was seeing Isaac calming the horse down and leading it away, and then he passed out from the pain.

14

NOVEMBER 1865

Two People Are Given Two Choices

Isaac had gotten the angry horse under control and had yelled to Bucky to find Doc. Isaac was the only one on the ranch who could control this horse and wasn't afraid of him. With all of the noise going on, it got Samuel and Jacob's attention, who had been in the barn. Bucky didn't bother to saddle a horse; he just jumped up on his horse bareback and took off like a shot. Samuel and Jacob ran over to Gerard, who was still unconscious. Samuel asked Jacob to get some blankets and sheets from Rebecca and some whiskey and he asked one of the hired hands to find him a sturdy tree branch. During the war, Samuel had seen several men with broken bones and he knew that this was pretty bad. Jacob came running out of the house with his mother close behind. Gerard was starting to come to and Samuel knew that the pain would be intense. He held the whiskey up to Gerard's mouth and he took several swallows of it. He knew what was about to happen and he tried to mentally brace himself. Samuel showed Jacob how to hold Gerard's other leg in place and another hired hand held his hands on Gerard's chest. Samuel gave Gerard a sturdy stick to bite down on. He cut his pant leg wide open and the sight was tough to look at. When Samuel quickly brought the pieces of bone back together, Gerard passed out, which was good. Samuel taped up his leg with the material that Rebecca always kept on hand. They managed to get a blanket under Gerard and gently lifted him up and carried him into the house.

Bucky had come flying into town and stopped quickly in front of Doc's office. He ran inside yelling for Doc and Elizabeth told him that Doc was at the hotel dining room. He barely took time to tell her what had happened and he added, "Go find Johnny, quickly."

Bucky ran into the hotel and Maude knew something bad had happened. He raced over to Doc and when he could catch his breath, he told Doc what had happened to Gerard. Maude had overheard and she was having trouble trying to comprehend what he must be going through. Suddenly Ellie came up behind her and said, "Maude, what is wrong? What has happened?"

"Ellie, Gerard has been hurt. He was out at Johnny's ranch and a huge horse knocked him down and stomped on his leg. Doc is on his way to help him. Bucky said that Samuel was a medic in the war and he was already starting to take care of him."

"Maude, I've got to get out there now. I can't stand the thought of him being in pain like this. I can take care of him. Will someone please take me out there, right away?"

"Pastor just came in and we'll ask him to take us. Get your cape and I'll meet you by the front door. Now hurry, Ellie."

Ellie took the stairs two at a time and grabbed her cape and didn't even put it on. She came down the stairs so fast that Maude was afraid she would fall and hurt herself, but she made it all the way safely. Pastor drove them out to the ranch and Ellie was shaking all over and not from the cold. She had been through so much today and now everything was completely turned around. First she had been afraid to get more involved with Gerard and now she couldn't get to him fast enough. Poor Ellie was so wound up inside and there wasn't much Maude could do now except be there to support her. When they reached the ranch house at Johnny's, Ellie was out of the carriage before Pastor had even stopped the horse. She didn't bother to knock; she just opened the door and came in like a small tornado. Rebecca saw her first and she held her arms out to Ellie. Ellie said in a loud voice, "Where is he? Where is Gerard? Is he hurt bad? I've got to see him right now."

Rebecca tried to calm her down with her soft voice. "Ellie, he is in our spare bedroom and Doc gave him some medicine to put him to sleep and to help with the pain. The break was pretty bad but Samuel bandaged him up as good as Doc could have. We have to let him sleep as long as possible. When he wakes up, he is going to be in a lot of pain. There is nothing that you can do for him right now. Go back to the hotel and get some rest and come back out tomorrow."

"No, I'm not going anywhere. I don't care if he is asleep and doesn't know that I'm here. I'll sleep on the floor by his bed. I just have to be there when he wakes up. You can't make me leave. Maude, tell her, I've got to stay."

Rebecca thought quickly and replied, "Ellie, I'll let you sleep in the chair in his room on one condition. You will take a pill that Doc has that will calm you down. Gerard does not need to see you all upset like this. He has enough to deal with. Will you agree to take the pill?"

"Yes, I will take a pill. I'm sorry for what I said to you but I'm just so upset. Please show me where he is. Tears were pouring down her face as she followed Rebecca down the hall, with Maude and Pastor right behind them. When Ellie saw Gerard laying there on the bed with his leg all wrapped up, she almost ran over to hold him. His face was deathly white and she felt so helpless. Rebecca had quietly explained to Doc that she wanted a sedative for Ellie and he got one out of his bag. Ellie took some water and the pill and pulled the chair as close to the bed as she could and then sat down, never taking her eyes off of Gerard. After a few minutes, Ellie was starting to look sleepy. Maude came over and put her cape around her shoulders and a blanket across her lap. Before long, Ellie was sound asleep, with her hand touching Gerard's shoulder. Maude looked down at her and thought, *'This is going to change everything; hopefully for the better. It's a shame that this had to happen to Gerard to force Ellie to be honest about her feelings.'*

After a week of staying with Samuel and Rebecca, Gerard was moved back to the hotel, but he was given a room on the ground floor. Ellie worked herself into a frenzy, trying to keep up her normal job as a maid and constantly checking on Gerard. He was enjoying her attention, but he didn't like what it was doing to her. She looked totally exhausted and had dark circles under her eyes. She refused to take any more of Doc's pills and Maude was getting very concerned about her. Maude offered to give some of Ellie's duties to two of the other girls but Ellie would have nothing to do with that. She looked on it as her responsibility and she continued to push herself.

After a few more days of this, Gerard decided to do something about it himself. "Ellie, I would really like to have some more privacy please. If you can just bring my breakfast and do your cleaning quick like, I'd like to be by myself for the rest of the day. Charlie has offered to bring me my meals at noon and the evening. I hope you can understand that I have a lot to think about and I need to be alone as much as possible."

Ellie looked hurt and confused and it made Gerard feel like a heel for doing this but it couldn't think of anything else to do. She finally nodded 'yes' and finished her cleaning and left, with one last look at him over her shoulder. She looked so rejected and obviously didn't understand what was going on. *'I wish she knew how hard this was for me to turn her away like this. Normally I'd be kicking up my heels to have this kind of attention from her. Maybe Maude can lift her spirits. I'll have to talk to her tomorrow.'*

Pete now showed up at the café every day at the same time for lunch. Annie arranged for some of her young, single girlfriends to drop in when she knew Pete would be in the café. Not once had he even looked twice at any of her friends. Two of them were very pretty but that didn't seem to matter to Pete. He just kept grinning at Annie and she was becoming a wreck. Today she had asked Melissa to stop in because she was so pretty and a very sweet girl. Melissa was a little on the shy side but several young men in town were attracted to her. Surely she would be the one that could divert Pete's interest. Annie introduced Pete to her good friend and he smiled and said, "Tell me everything you know about Annie so that I can get to know her better." This comment caught Melissa off guard and

Annie was trying to signal her not to say anything. Finally, Melissa said, "Well, she likes to collect unusual rocks that she finds out in the country side and she doesn't like to go anywhere without her sketch pad and pencils. Does that help?"

Pete gave her one of his most sincere smiles and said, "That is perfect. You've been a great help Melissa. By the way, I have a good friend that I would like to introduce you to. He doesn't have a special girl and I think you two would get along very well."

He got up to leave and when he was out the door, Annie said, "I don't believe that man. You are the prettiest girl in this village and he is going to introduce you to his friend? Now do you see how exasperating that man is, Melissa?"

Melissa looked confused and said, "Annie, he is perfect for you and he is so sweet. I think you are making a mistake, trying to discourage him. Most of the girls in this village would do anything to get his attention."

Annie just sighed and shook her head. "I am not going to give up. There has to be something that I haven't thought of yet."

Pastor and Doc were sitting down for coffee in the hotel and a few minutes later Will and Gerard came over to join them. Gerard was getting pretty good at moving around slowly on his crutches but he was getting tired of having to use them. Martha came over with her coffee pot, all smiles as usual. "Would you gentlemen like anything to eat? My Charlie has just made some of his special bread pudding." All four of them ordered some because they knew how delicious it was.

Pastor spoke up about something that had just occurred to him. "I just realized something that has never occurred to me before. Charlie and Martha don't own a thing besides the wedding gifts they received a few months ago. They don't have fancy clothes, no horse and carriage, no land or home, but have you ever known a happier couple in your life? That just proves a point that all the things that we think we have to have are meaningless. There should be more happiness in this world, like they have. I need to preach a sermon about that subject. I think I'll start making notes even today."

All three men agreed but each had a different thought. Gerard was thinking, *'All of my money and success mean nothing to me, unless I can find a way to convince Ellie how much I care for her. I could almost envy Charlie and Martha. Here I am feeling so empty inside and I have the income to buy anything that I want or need. If Ellie could only read my mind.'*

Doc sat there thinking about his own life. *'I could have had what Martha and Charlie have, but I threw it all away. Why? Because of a stupid fear of what it would mean to surrender my heart to someone who really cared for me. How many years have I wasted and I can say the same for Maude? I've got to find a way to change.'*

Will was happy for Charlie and Martha and hoped that someday he might find a woman who would love him for who he was; not for what he could buy her. That thought immediately made him think about Norma. She obviously had a lot of money, as her fancy house could attest to. Whenever he saw her, she looked miserable and was always looking for someone to hurt. Wealth hadn't brought her any happiness. *'I've become friends with Sarah and Elizabeth and now Callie, but the key word is "friends". Why do my thoughts so often go to Norma, when it is obvious the kind of woman that she is? There must be something wrong with me.'*

Willow Bend had just received their first snow of the season and everything looked beautiful. The big spruce trees were so majestic looking, with their long branches full of snow. As Johnny was headed back to his ranch, he was thinking about the mail he had received today. There was a long letter from David, letting him know that a lead turned out to be false. When Johnny had first met his ex-wife, she had been very secretive about her past and where she was raised. Whenever he would ask about her family, she would quickly change the subject. Because of this, there was very little for them to go on. The detective had tracked down a woman with the same name as Johnny's ex-wife, but it was obviously not the right person.

'Please don't give up hope Johnny. This may take more time than you would like, but my friend doesn't give up easily. He is already figuring out a different way of trying to find where your child is. He has a long list of children in various orphanages and he is slowly eliminating the names, but there are so many children placed in private homes or orphanages; it just breaks my heart. I have placed ads in several papers and have received some responses. If nothing else, it helps my friend to scratch more names off of his list faster.'

He was trying to be strong, but this news hit him hard. *'If God is real, then He must know where my child is. Why isn't He helping me?'* He decided to take a walk and found himself in front of Franklin's house. He knocked on the door and raised his voice so Franklin would know who was outside. The door opened and he was welcomed with a friendly smile. "Johnny, it is so good to see you. Please come in and have a seat. I just made a pot of coffee."

"I'm sorry about just showing up like this. I got some disturbing news and decided to take a walk and ended up on your doorstep."

"You are always welcome here, whether I have advance notice or not. If I don't answer the door, that will usually mean that I'm either taking care of my horse or chopping wood. I'm never far away."

"Well, since I'm here, I'd like to run something by you. I've always wanted to take in abused animals, but I had no idea how fast they would start coming in. Just today a man dropped off two half-starved horses that he found abandoned in a field; just tied to a fence. The house was empty, so some heartless person just left them with no food or water. Anyway, I was wondering if you would be interested in giving me a hand with some of them? I can get my men to build a sturdy pen behind your house and I'd like to add a second area where you might need to separate some of them until they get used to being around other animals. They will also build you a small barn so that you can bring them in during bad weather, and we can store their feed in there. You will receive a good salary, plus my deep appreciation."

"I would jump at the chance to help these poor animals; the sooner the better. Once your men get me set up, you can bring over however many you need help with. I wouldn't feel right about taking any money for this after you provided me with a house."

"How does this sound then? I appreciate your good heart and not wanting to take money for this but think of this. You can help some of the villagers when you have this extra income coming in. I'll have my men out here first thing tomorrow morning and they won't be bothering you. Just stay in your house until they are finished. I feel much better, knowing that the horses will be in the hands of someone who will take good care of them."

"I will accept your offer to be paid for this, but only because of your mentioning how I can help some of the villagers. You are a sly one, Johnny."

Johnny was determined to find out who had set that fire out at his ranch. He had to have absolute proof; not just a gut feeling. From the way the person was running away that night, it must have been someone young. After speaking with several of the villagers, he could eliminate several people on his list. Now Johnny remembered Dwight had mentioned a young man working on his ranch who was very lazy and unpopular with the other workers. What was the name Dwight had mentioned? Jimmy; that was it! He wasn't going to mention to anyone about the material caught in the fence. Now was the time for some night work; staking out Dwight's ranch first, hoping to follow Jimmy. If he could ever catch him even talking with Norma, that would cinch it for him. Mr. Nelson from the land office had told Johnny that Norma was furious when she found out who had bought her ranch, especially finding out that Samuel and Rebecca were living out there. Norma would normally look down her nose at someone like Jimmy and wouldn't give him the time of day. He wouldn't put it past her to take someone gullible like this young man, who would do anything to get a pretty girls approval.

He went out at night for three nights in a row with no luck. He decided that he had to have Dwight's help. He told Dwight what he suspected and asked him to send Jimmy off on an errand so Johnny could check the small room where he slept. No one wanted him in the bunkhouse, so Dwight had fixed up a place near a storage area. Dwight was sorry to hear about Johnny's suspicions, but he really couldn't come up with any defense for Jimmy. They both suspected that Norma had offered him money that he just couldn't turn down.

That afternoon Johnny was told that Jimmy would be gone for at least a couple of hours, so he went directly to his sleeping quarters. There wasn't much to go through; just a cot with a slim mattress and the sheets and an old blanket and a pillow. Johnny looked around for any hiding place and finally spotted an old crate with empty bottles in it. Upon a closer examination, he saw a bright piece of cloth sticking out between some of the bottles. He had carried the torn scrap in his pocket and it was a perfect match.

Johnny found Dwight and showed him the shirt that he had removed from the crate of bottles and then the torn scrap. Dwight felt so bad that one of his workers was the cause of the fire. If Samuel hadn't been out there that late, the barn could have burned down, along with all of the animals. Both men heard a horse riding up and they each moved to one side of the door. It wasn't long before the door opened and Jimmy came into the small room and quickly got a startled look on his face. Johnny said, "Jimmy, you are under arrest for starting the fire on my ranch. I have all the proof that I need" and he showed him the shirt and the torn piece. Jimmy's face went white as a sheet and he started stammering, "It wasn't my idea. Please, I needed the money and she knew it. I don't want to go to jail. Please, listen to me."

Johnny pulled out his handcuffs and cuffed Jimmy's wrists. He told Dwight that he would like him to be a witness and he agreed. By now Jimmy was crying and shaking. "I can't go to jail. I'll tell you everything but please don't lock me up. I've still got most of the money and you can have that." Johnny asked him how much money he had been given and was told it was $100. Then Johnny wanted the name of the person who had paid him and out came the words that he knew he would hear. "That snippy lady named Norma was the one. She said no one would ever find out and I believed her. The coins are still in the bag that she gave me and it's underneath my saddle." Walking outside to Jimmy's horse, Johnny lifted the saddle up and there was the bag and it looked very familiar. He had seen Norma with it one day at the bank. Johnny told Jimmy, "I'm going to make you an offer and it will be your choice. You can go to jail for starting the fire on my ranch or you can work for me for a year and your wages will help to replace what burned down. I don't think you are a bad person; just misguided. What will it be?" Jimmy didn't take even a few seconds to think about it. "I'll work for you on your ranch and I'll work hard. You'll see that I can change sheriff." Johnny unhooked the handcuffs and told him to gather up his belongings and to meet him at the ranch later that night. Jimmy looked over at Dwight and said, "I owe you an apology for letting you down sir. I believe I have learned my lesson and I hope you won't hold this against me."

Dwight was surprised by the apology and he replied, "Jimmy, you do a good job at the sheriff's ranch and I'll be very pleased. Don't do anything to mess up this chance."

Johnny wasn't looking forward to his conversation with Norma but he couldn't put it off any longer. He rode over to her house and knocked on the door. It took a few minutes but she finally answered the door. She didn't look surprised to see him nor did she look very happy. "What can I do for you, sheriff?"

Johnny stood there quietly for a few seconds and then he said, "I came to talk to you about the fire that was set on my ranch a few weeks back." He could see her body tense up and try to find the right thing to say.

"I heard about that fire and that it was put out quickly. That must have been quite a relief to you." Johnny decided to stop with the small talk and get right to the point.

"Norma, I arrested Jimmy for starting the fire. He confessed when I confronted him. He said that you paid him $100 to start that fire."

Norma's face went white and she was having trouble looking at Johnny. "He is lying sheriff. I would never do such a thing. I am an upstanding citizen in this village."

"Norma, he still has the bag of coins that you gave to him and the bag belongs to you. I saw you carrying that bag one day at the bank. It is so unusual that it caught my attention. I have come here to give you a choice and I'll give you 24 hours to give me your answer. You can either serve one year in jail here in town or you can work at the village hotel as a maid and waitress for one year. Your salary will help pay for the damages to my property."

Norma couldn't believe what she had just heard. She would be humiliated no matter what decision she made. She had only wanted to get back at him for buying that ranch behind her back. She started shaking and looked like she was about to faint. Johnny said, "Can I get you a glass of water? Come back inside and sit down, Norma." He found the kitchen quite easily and brought her some water. The color still had not come back into her face. She could hardly hang onto the glass and had to use both hands.

"Sheriff, I couldn't face anyone if I was put in that jail. The other choice you have given me is almost as humiliating. Being a maid and a waitress! After the way I have been raised? How will I ever be able to hold my head up again?" Now the tears started trickling down her face but they were real. Norma softly said, "I have made my decision sheriff. I will work as a maid and waitress in the hotel, but does everyone have to know why I am doing this?"

Johnny thought about it and said, "I will not tell anyone about you and Jimmy. I have given him the option to work on my ranch for free for a year. I don't know what you can tell everyone in this village that asks you, but that is completely up to you. You will start work tomorrow at eight o'clock in the morning and Maude will supply you with a uniform. I'll see you tomorrow Norma. Good day and don't be late!"

From the moment Norma woke up the next morning, she knew that today was not going to be a good day for her. She had told Johnny that she would show up at the hotel at eight o'clock in the morning. *'Well, I can forget my days of sleeping in until noon or whatever time I want to get up.'* She had asked her friend Ada to loan her a plain outfit to wear to the hotel. She assumed that she would be given some ugly outfit to wear once she got there. *'How am I ever going to make it through this humiliation?'* She knew that Johnny would be checking on her quite often to make sure she wasn't just going through the motions of working. She and her friend were the same size so this plain outfit fit her perfectly, but made her feel like a washwoman. *'Why would any woman actually want to wear clothes like this?'* The skirt was a dark brown with no flowers or anything to make it look nicer. The blouse was a pale yellow that made Norma's face look washed out. She never wore yellow for that very reason. She drank some coffee and ate a muffin and reluctantly left the house.

As she entered the hotel, who other than 'Mr. Sheriff' himself was standing there waiting for her. He glanced at the clock, which was showing seven fifty-five and he nodded approvingly. *'One point for me',* thought Norma. *'He was probably shocked that I was actually on time.*

"Good morning, Norma. I appreciate your showing up on time. Maude is going to show you your uniform. You will be given two so that you can always have a clean one to wear."

Maude was walking down the hall, carrying the uniforms and she greeted her with a smile. "Good morning Norma. You may go into this room right here to get changed. When you come out, I will have one of the maids show you your duties." Norma didn't even acknowledge her friendly greeting; she just took one of the uniforms and turned to go into the room Maude had indicated.

"Well", Johnny said, "Your life will now be a lot more interesting. Are you sure you are up to this Maude?"

She laughed and said, "My life was a little too dull anyway and I've always welcomed a challenge."

A few minutes later the door opened and Norma slowly came out into the lobby. She held her head high but there were sparks of anger in her eyes. Johnny said, "Norma, I'd like a word with you in private before Maude takes you off to learn your new job. Maude smiled and nodded and Johnny motioned for Norma to follow him. When he had walked her far enough away that no one could hear them, he spoke softly and said, "Norma, I know you are angry about this, but it might turn out to be one of the best things that could ever have happened to you. Believe it or not! I just wanted to say that Maude is one of the sweetest women I've ever known and I don't want to hear about you doing anything to hurt her. The other young ladies that you are going to be working with are all nice and likable. I am going to be checking often to see if you are holding up your end of our bargain. Do I make myself clear?"

Norma looked up at Johnny like she would love to slap him across the face and she said very coldly, "Don't worry yourself about me sheriff. I can do anything these other girls are doing. In fact, I'll probably do the job a lot better. Check on me as often as you want to." At that, she walked off in a huff.

Maude introduced her to a mousy looking girl who acted like she wanted to be friendly. Her name was Ruthie and she was all bubbly and sweet and made Norma want to scream. "Norma, I'll be very happy to show you around and teach you what your job will be like. You and I will be working the same days and hours, so I'll always be around if you have any questions or need any help." Norma just stood there looking at her with contempt, but Ruthie didn't even seem to notice.

Norma followed her into one of the rooms, and she felt like she was in the middle of a nightmare. "Now this is how to make a bed so it looks very neat." It had never crossed Norma's mind how difficult it could be to make a bed look smooth. She had never made a bed in her entire life. After Ruthie had made the bed look attractive, much to Norma's horror, she messed up the bed again and asked Norma to try it. After several attempts, it actually managed to look worse. Norma wanted to stomp her feet in frustration but Ruthie came over and redid the bed correctly and she said, "Don't worry Norma, you'll catch on soon enough. Now I'll show you how to empty the chamber pots." Norma's eyes bugged out and when she saw Ruthie pull the pot out from under the bed, her face turned green. She rushed for a window and jerked it up quickly and was gasping for air.

Ruthie said, "Follow me and I'll show you how to dispose of it."

Norma dropped to her knees and was sobbing. "I can't do that; I just can't. I'll be sick and I'll never get used to it. Please, I'll pay you each week to do that part of the job for me, but you musn't let anyone know."

Ruthie went over to her and said, "I'll do it for you Norma and I won't speak of this to anyone. Are you feeling better now?" Norma shut the window and wiped her face and nodded. The next duty was to dust the room and Norma was actually relieved that this was something that she could handle without messing it up or getting sick.

Ruthie showed her where to find extra towels and toiletries and then handed her a list that she had made up for Norma. "Each room that doesn't have a guest staying in it, just needs a quick once over with the dust mop and then we dust the furniture and air out the room. If it is a room where we have a guest, the bed linens are changed every week and fresh towels every other day. I also wrote on the list approximately how much time should be spent on each room so we can stay on schedule."

Norma grabbed the list from Ruthie and didn't even thank her for going to that trouble. "What do we do next?"

Ruthie replied, "Now we can take a 15-minute break and get a drink from the kitchen and then I'll show you the rooms where the owners live and where Maude's room is."

When Norma got home that evening, she went straight to her room and fell across the bed, exhausted. *'This was only my first day and I have to do this for an entire year.'* Her housekeeper knocked on her bedroom door and asked if she were ready for supper. Norma asked her to bring it to her room on a tray and to help her undress. The housekeeper had heard rumors of where Miss Norma was actually working, but there was no way that she would ever bring that subject up. *'I wish that I could hide in the shadows and watch her for a few minutes, but that would be impossible. Maybe Miss Norma's eyes would finally be opened to what hard work it is to be a maid or a housekeeper. I can only hope!'*

Today was the day that Jimmy was moved out to Johnny's ranch and settled in the bunkhouse. So far there weren't many people living in there since Johnny was providing houses for Jacob and Bucky. He'd been told that Isaac would be coming out after school to show him around and tell him about what chores he would be responsible for. Jimmy put his few clothes away on a shelf and checked out his bunk. It was actually fairly comfortable for a bunkbed and that was a relief. He wouldn't have to deal with any of the men from Dwight's ranch who didn't like him. He knew that he desired the way they treated him but he was not going to make that mistake again.

A few minutes later, Isaac walked in and shook hands with him and introduced himself. "What kind of experience have you had, working on a ranch?"

Jimmy said, "I've only worked on a farm, taking care of the crops, but I'm willing to learn anything." Isaac hadn't said anything to Johnny but he had put two and two together about who had started the fire, and he was quite certain that it was Jimmy. He'd heard some of the workers at Dwight's talking about Jimmy being lazy and unpopular. Samuel had mentioned that whoever started the fire must have been young because he was running so fast and by his build. He intended to keep a really close eye on Jimmy.

"First of all, everyone who works at this ranch takes pride in their work. We take good care of all of the tools and always put them back where they belong when we are finished. All of the animals are treated with care and respect. Johnny won't tolerate any abuse towards any animals and neither will I. I'll show you around the ranch today and then tomorrow we can start on your responsibilities. You'll start off by cleaning all of the horse stalls, and cleaning the saddles. Do you have any questions?"

Jimmy could sense that Isaac didn't really trust him and how could he blame him? In a village this small, he had probably heard someone from Dwight's farm talking bad about him. Well, all he could do is prove to everyone that he had changed. "What time do I start work in the morning?"

"I'll be out here at seven o'clock and there will be plenty of time before leaving for school to show you what will be expected of you. You will hear a bell ringing when Rebecca has any meals ready. If you hear the bell and you are in the middle of a job, don't just drop everything and take off. Leave whatever you are working on neat, and always be sure that you have the gates locked so none of the animals can get loose."

Joshua had taken a walk every day for over two weeks, praying and asking God for some direction. He loved Albert like a brother and he wouldn't do anything to hurt him, so he could think of no other option, besides leaving Willow Bend. The village was so small, that he ran into Melissa all the time. He was so afraid that she or Albert would notice how he reacted every time he saw her. It didn't seem fair that he would have to make this choice. This village was exactly what he would enjoy living in for the rest of his life. He had experience keeping books for his uncle's company and when Johnny found out, he had offered him a job immediately. He was going to meet Albert in front of the hotel in a few minutes. He was going to have to come up with an excuse that Albert would believe.

"Joshua, I just heard the good news. Johnny told me about the job he has offered you. You would be perfect for the job. I'm so happy for you."

"Well, I haven't exactly accepted the job yet. I'm still thinking about it. In fact, I was actually considering the idea of moving on and finding a larger place to live in. Somewhere that has bigger stores and an opera house and fancier houses."

"I don't understand! You told me that you love Willow Bend and that it is exactly what you've always dreamed of. I know everyone who has met you has nothing but good things to say about you. Is there something that you're not telling me? I want the truth Joshua because this is really upsetting news to hear that you might move away. Will you at lease promise me that you will wait a month so that I'll know that this is not a hasty decision you are making?"

"Yes, I can promise you a month. I'd like to go for a ride out in the country by myself right now. I just need to be away from everyone so that I can think clearly. I'll let you know when I return later this afternoon."

Albert didn't say anything; he just gave Joshua a weak smile and nodded 'yes'. *'Something has definitely happened to make him change his mind and I am clueless as to what it could be. I saw his face when I showed him around the village and he was sincerely excited and happy with what he saw. I'm sure if he had an argument with someone, I would have heard about it by now. I just don't know what to think but at least he promised me to wait a month.'*

Rusty rode for several weeks, passing through Ohio and Indiana and then into southern Michigan. He found a ranch house several miles from the nearest town and he asked the rancher if he needed any work done in exchange for a place to sleep. The rancher shook his head and said that he was sorry but he didn't have any work for him. He did say that a man who lived down the road a peace had mentioned that he needed someone part time. Rusty thanked him for his time and rode on. He found the farm that he was looking for without any problem. For some reason, the farmer trusted Rusty and said that yes, he could use some help. His name was Ben and he lived alone. He showed him a place to put his saddle and saddlebags and where he could sleep at night. Then he took him to the stable and fed and watered his horse. The rancher gave him a brush and comb to take care of his horse. He asked Rusty when he had eaten last and Rusty said two days ago. The rancher invited him into his small kitchen and dished out some chili and crackers and a piece of cheese.

The next day Rusty decided to shave off his beard and moustache and cut his hair. He was hoping that he wouldn't be as easy to recognize. The farmer's name was Ben Lawson and as they walked around his farm, Ben pointed out where he needed help the most. He didn't question how Rusty's looks had suddenly changed. He was just so relieved to have some help and someone to talk to. A dog started following Rusty all over the ranch and his name was Shadow because he had always followed Ben so closely. Rusty offered to help with the cooking if that was agreeable to Ben and it sure was. Rusty's ma had insisted on all of the boys learning how to cook. Rusty was a fair cook when it came to stew and chicken and he could even make decent biscuits.

After his first full day of work, Rusty felt some pride for the first time in years. He had worked hard all day and rarely took a break except for a cup of water when he got thirsty. Ben had made sandwiches for both of them, to save time. Rusty had repaired a fence, cleaned out the stalls, fed and groomed the horses, put a pot of stew on to simmer, brought hay out to the cattle, milked the cows and fixed a wobbly step on the porch. It was now just about time for supper and he was tired, but it was a good feeling.

"Ben, exactly where is your farm located? I'm afraid I lost track of where I was a few days back."

"My farm is about ten miles from the village of Willow Bend. I will take you there in the spring, after most of the snow is behind us. I've lived here all of my life, but I am struggling to keep it up by himself. I was counting on my son to take over a lot of the physical labor. I lost him in the war and I don't know how I am going to keep my farm going."

"Ben, I'm sorry to hear about you losing your son. I'm a hard worker and I'm willing to do anything, if you have the patience to teach me. My parents passed away during the war and I've lost track of my two brothers. I am anxious to know if they are alright and where they are now."

"When we go into Willow Bend, there is a telegraph office there and maybe you can think of someone who might help you find your brothers. During the winter, it is mainly feeding the livestock and keeping the heavy snow off the barn and house roofs. I like to keep the horses groomed and get them out for a little exercise, when the weather allows. I am mighty happy to have you around Rusty, and I think we'll get along just fine. Do you happen to play checkers?"

"I think I can hold my own. I have a feeling that you won't be making it easy on me to win." Ben chuckled at that comment. They sat down to eat Rusty's stew and Ben was not shy about taking seconds. He had made a pan of cornbread and there wasn't a crumb left. *'It sure is good to have company again. I'm afraid I was getting pretty lonely.'*

Johnny made a point of going by Doc's office and waited for the last patient to leave. "Well Johnny, I'm surprised to see you in my office. You aren't sick, are you?"

"No Doc; I have a favor to ask of you. As you know, I've given Franklin one of my small cabins to live in. He insists on chopping firewood for me, on top of what he cuts for you to sell. Timothy has been really good about coming out to spend time with him, but I thought that maybe you might be willing to stop by and check on him. I know he is very close to you and I want to feel sure that he is adjusting to living out at my ranch."

"Well of course, I'll be happy to check on him. I was going to bring him out some more salve for his face. Thank you for being so thoughtful. Offering you the job of sheriff is one of the smartest things Pastor and I have ever done. You are doing an outstanding job, by the way. I have not heard one complaint, except for the occasional rowdy cowboys spending the night in one of your cells. I'll make a point of visiting with Franklin soon."

When Doc pulled up in front of Franklin's new home, he sat there for a minute admiring it. He remembered Franklin telling him that he had once considered taking his own life, but in the end he believed that God still had plans for his life. He was so happy to see that he wasn't living in the woods behind the hotel any longer. He knocked on the door and it was soon opened cautiously. "Franklin, it's Doc. I came to see if you know how to make a decent cup of coffee."

Now he stepped out of the shadows and put his hand out to shake Docs. "I'll let you be the judge of that. It's so good to see you. Can you believe what the Good Lord has done for me? One minute I'm living in the woods and the next thing I know, I'm in my own cabin."

Franklin poured a cup for Doc and himself. They sat around and talked about how blessed some of the villagers were with the wood being donated to their woodpile. Then the subject shifted to Johnny's ranch and how fast it was expanding. Finally, Franklin said, "Doc, I hear pain in your voice and I can see it in your eyes. Would you trust me to let me know what is hurting you? You must know that I would never repeat anything that you tell me."

This caught Doc off guard for a minute but then he collected himself and made a decision. "Well, you see son, there's been a fine lady in my life for several years. It seems like the entire village knew we were meant for each other, but I put up a huge wall. I knew that she cared deeply for me, but I ignored it and continued to hurt her, year after year. I gave her no hope, even when Pastor very bluntly told me that I would lose her if I didn't tell her how I really felt about her. The woman that I am speaking of is Maude, and everyone thinks the world of her. She and a friend planned this big dance in October and I know she expected me to be her escort, but I kept putting it off. Before I knew it, her old beau came into town and he ended up taking her. I attended that dance by myself and it almost killed me to see her there with this man, who seemed to make her smile so easily. I heard her laugh in a way that I've never heard before. He came to visit for a month and then has to go back to Indiana on business soon. How could I have been so heartless, Franklin? I'm driving her away even though I know that she is so perfect for me."

As Doc was speaking, Franklin hadn't interrupted even once and now he only said, "Something happened to you in the past that has made you afraid of loving someone; isn't that true?"

At that, Doc leaned over and just started sobbing his heart out. After a few minutes, he stood up and started pacing the floor, tears pouring down his face. "My father was always finding fault with me. I couldn't wait to leave home. I had no idea that after all these years, this would still be crippling me like it is. You are right son; I am afraid to love and be loved. It terrifies me, but so does the thought of losing Maude. I've actually had the thought that I'd be better off dead. Do you know what stopped me from doing anything about it? You, Franklin! You've been through more pain than I could ever imagine. You told Pastor and I that you too once thought about ending your life but you said, "I don't think God is finished with me yet."

"What right have I to even think about ending my own life when you set such an example of what God can do with broken heart like yours? You probably have no idea of how much you have affected Timothy or Johnny or Pastor and myself. We all look up to you for so many reasons. I am sorry to admit that I've pulled away from God for the past several years, right when I needed him the most. He didn't go anywhere; He has just been patiently waiting for me to call out to Him. He brought you into my life to save me. If I could even be half the man you are, I would be so happy. I am going back to the village and will ask Pastor James to pray with me, and then I'll try and see if there is even a small hope that Maude will even listen to me. I hope you can understand how important you are in my life. If you ever need anything, please let me know and I'll do my best to help you."

Franklin gave Doc a hug and patted him on the back and watched him walk out the door. As soon as the door closed, he started to silently talk to God. *'Please forgive me for ever wanting to take my own life. I was in so much pain and I felt so helpless. I couldn't imagine anyone wanting to be my friend or to look me in the face. Thank you for leading me to this village and back to Doc and Pastor. Thank you for using me to encourage him. God, I want to be used by you and I know it won't always be easy. I promise to*

*always do my best and never turn away from you.
Please put more people in my path that need to know
about you or need encouragement. Thank you, Lord.'*

How do you discourage a man? Annie wondered.
Introducing him to other girls obviously wasn't
working but something had to. Now she had a better
idea. She was going to make sure that he didn't like
her. She couldn't wait for him to show up today. No
sooner had that thought come to her, when here he
came. By now he had a special table that he sat at. All
of her customers avoided sitting at that table even
when Annie tried to steer them over to it. Pete sat
down and Annie brought him over a glass of water and
asked what he would like to order.

Pete hardly looked at the menu and said, "I think
I'd like a meatloaf sandwich today." When Annie
returned a few minutes later, she actually sat down
at his table. This was a surprise! Annie said, "I need
to take a break. My feet are killing me! My mother
died at a young age and I'm sure I'll follow along in
her footsteps. My health has always been poor."

Pete almost choked on his sandwich because it
was obvious what she was doing. He held back his
laugh and said, "I'm just the man you need Annie. I
love nothing more than to take care of someone who
is ailin'. I'll come by later today and will pick you up
in a carriage, to save your poor feet."

Annie sputtered "I don't need a ride home today;
I'll be fine. I'm just wearing new shoes. I was just
kidding about my mother." She couldn't get out of that
chair fast enough and stomped off as fast as she could
move.

Not only was Pete laughing hard but several of
her customers were also. "I see your feet seem to be
feeling better all of a sudden. I'm glad that you
recuperated so quickly."

She was getting so frustrated because all of her customers were rooting for Pete, especially Worley. *'No one seems to understand or care that I don't want or need a fellow in my life. My plans to own this café are all that I care about. A man would surely try to discourage me and that is not going to happen. Maybe if I went for a ride in the country, I could clear my mind and come up with a better idea to help Pete see that I'm not the girl he thinks he needs. Yes, that sounds like it might work. I'll go rent a small buggy and then I'll come back refreshed with a new plan.'*

Annie was enjoying the ride and the fresh air, rather pleased with herself for thinking of this idea to ride in the country. Her little trip had taken her out near the sign to 'Trails End' and she decided to turn around and head back to the village. She was definitely more relaxed, but she wasn't paying attention to the big dog who was chasing a rabbit. They both ran right in front of her horse, startling it. Before she could react, the horse took off running, and she remembered that a sharp turn was up ahead. She didn't know how to slow down the horse except to holler "whoa".

Pete was on his way to Johnny's ranch, to see if he could borrow some tools to repair the back steps of the saloon. He heard racing hoofbeats and someone yelling. Now he saw Annie flying down the road, obviously scared and helpless. He turned his horse around and timed it perfectly to ride up next to Annie's horse and grab the bridle, and calmly but loudly, said, "whoa now, whoa."

Annie's hat was hanging around her neck by a ribbon, her hair was completely undone and she did not look happy to see who had rescued her. Pete gave her one of his dazzling smiles and swept off his hat and said, "Oh my, a lady in distress again. I think you are coming up with ways to see more of me, Miss Annie and I'm right flattered."

She was trying to control her anger but wasn't doing a very good job of it. "I most certainly was not trying to get your attention. A crazy dog chased a rabbit right in front of us. I couldn't make the horse slow down but I would have eventually. You can go on your way now Pete."

"I wouldn't think of letting a helpless lady ride back to the village unescorted. I'll just ride right beside you and keep you company. I didn't know that you liked to go for rides in the country. I'll have to keep that in mind."

Annie was shooting darts at Pete, but it wasn't even phasing him. *This man is unbelievable. Of all the men to be on this road when I'm in trouble; it just had to be him. Now I'm more determined than ever to get him out of my life, but I need to calm down first.'*

The rest of the way back to the village, Pete was chattering happily away and Annie never opened her mouth. For some crazy reason, the more she rejected his company, the more he wanted to change her opinion of him. *'I have all of the cafe customers on my side and I'm not one to get discouraged easily. You'd better prepare yourself for the fact that you're going to be seeing a lot more of me in the future.'*

Harrison and Maude had spent the past few weeks catching up on the past 20 years that they had been apart. They were finding out a lot about each other that they hadn't known, and it was exciting. Maude knew that her first impression of him so many years ago hadn't changed at all. He was gentle and caring and yet strong at the same time. Harrison had always made her feel safe and special; that is, until he had suddenly vanished from her life. Now that she understood why he had done that, she admired him even more. There was a lot of laughter when they were together and he was even giving her painting lessons. She found out that she might possibly have some talent in this area and she was enjoying learning what Harrison was teaching her. His calm demeanor and his constant smile was so refreshing after being around Doc so many years, who rarely smiled at all.

"Maude, I'm afraid I'm going to have to come back to Indiana in two days, to take care of some business, but I want to return to Willow Bend, if you would like me to. I should be able to return sometime after Christmas, if the weather isn't too bad. Please tell me your honest feelings about this and don't be afraid of hurting my feelings. I only want the truth."

"Harrison, I would be very happy to have you return, whenever your business is taken care of. I've enjoyed these weeks, getting to know you again. I haven't been this relaxed or laughed so much, in such a long time. Would you please write to me to let me know how you are doing?"

"Oh, you'll hear from me all right. Probably more often than you would like to. I've tried so hard to go on with my life, after I left you, but my heart never managed to heal until now. You are the most extraordinary woman I've ever known and I cherish every moment that you've allowed me to spend with you. We have time for one more art lesson. It is so much fun to watch you doing something for the first time, that you enjoy. I will be expecting a painting that you have done, in the near future. It would mean the world to me to have something hanging in my home that was painted by you."

Maude stood outside of the hotel with Harrison, waiting for Worley to bring the stagecoach around. She knew that she wouldn't break down and cry but she did feel sad inside and was trying hard to hide it. Just one look from Harrison and she knew that he could read her thoughts immediately. He leaned down and touched her cheek with his fingers, so gently and his voice caught as he said, "Maude, as soon as the stagecoach takes the first curve, I'll start missing you. This is very difficult for me and I don't mind admitting it to you." He kissed her softly on her cheek and then she heard the stage coming around the corner.

"Harrison, please take care of yourself and come back as soon as you can. I can't imagine what kind of a painting I could do that you would want to hang in your home, but I'll do my best. I'll look forward to your letters and I'll write also. Thank you for coming to find me and letting me know the truth about what happened long ago. You are a special man and I will miss you."

Doc was standing in front of his office and saw the expression on their faces and his heart hurt all over again. *Maybe I can salvage our relationship enough that we can still be friends. I certainly don't deserve any more than that from her.'*

Harrison hadn't been gone for even an hour and he wanted with all his heart, to tell the driver to either let him out or turn the stage around. All of these years without Maude, he had managed to make a life for himself, but he was never truly happy. These past few weeks, seeing her again, had completely changed how he felt about his life. *'In a few short weeks, she has totally turned my life upside down. I feel younger and happier and I can feel hope welling up inside, that maybe we could be together. I have to be patient and let her make a decision about Doc. I don't ever want to be the cause for ruining their relationship. If I thought the past 20 years were difficult, that is going to be nothing compared to the next few months. Whatever she decides, I sincerely only want her to be happy.'*

Several new families had moved into Willow Bend after the war and Doc thought that he had met most of them. Today he and Elizabeth were going through all of the medical records, making a list of anyone they thought needed to be checked up on. They heard a horse come thundering up outside the office and that meant an emergency of some kind. Before they could get to the front door, a man they didn't know came bursting in.

"My wife is tryin' to have our baby and somethin's gone wrong. Please help her. I'm afraid I'll lose her."

Doc and Elizabeth reacted immediately and both of them grabbed their medical bags and Elizabeth threw on her long cape. There was no time to tell anyone where they were going but then Doc saw Sarah walking down the street and he yelled to her. He told her quickly what was happening and asked her to alert the Pastor.

The husband said, "My name is Donovan Childers and I live out past the sheriff's ranch, a couple of miles. There is a sign that says, *'Donovan farm.'* Sarah took off to find Pastor and Doc and Elizabeth followed Donovan in Doc's carriage.

When they reached the house, they heard his wife's screams. When they got to the bedroom, Doc could see she was in a lot of trouble. The baby wasn't coming out the normal way and this must have been going on for a long time. He washed his hands with soap and water and gently reached up into the birth canal to try to turn the baby. He knew that farmers often had to do this when a colt or calf was being born, but it wasn't always successful with babies. Elizabeth put a cold cloth on the woman's head and tried to sooth her and calm her down. The poor woman must have suffered for many hours. Doc tried twice to turn the baby and only made a little headway. The third time he was able to make some progress and now the baby was coming out the correct way. When the baby's head appeared, he was relieved, but by then the mother was too weak to push any longer. Doc had to reach in and help the baby. She was small and very weak but alive. He handed her to Elizabeth to get cleaned up and wrapped in a towel. When Doc turned back to the mother, it was too late for her. She lay so still in the bed and he knew they had lost her. Donovan understood what had just happened and he collapsed on his knees, sobbing and holding her hand. Doc put his hands on his shoulders and said "Donovan, I am so sorry for your loss. You are going to have to be strong for your new baby girl. She is going to need you since you are her only parent."

Donovan looked up at Doc through his tears and said, "I can't keep her Doc. I'd be no good to her. We've lost three babies and now I've lost my sweet wife. She was everything in the world to me and I'll never get past this. Please find a good home for my child. I'm leavin' here this week and I'm never comin' back. Have someone get the papers ready for me to sign 'cause I'm not changin' my mind."

Doc looked over at Elizabeth, who was silently crying, while holding the baby. They had to quickly find someone to nurse the baby and arrange for the burial. Right then they heard a carriage pull up and Pastor and Sarah came into the room. No one had to explain what had just happened. Pastor sat down beside Donovan and held his hand and spoke softly to him. Sarah went over to Elizabeth and asked for the baby. The baby had been crying but settled down as soon as Sarah held her in her arms. She sang a song that Elizabeth had never heard before, and her voice was beautiful.

Elizabeth told Sarah "We have to find a woman who can nurse the baby."

"I'm sure that Maggie would be happy to nurse her."

Sarah and Elizabeth bundled the baby up in a warm blanket and left in Pastor's carriage. On the way back into town, Elizabeth explained "Donovan wants someone else to raise the little girl and he is going to sign the papers to let her be adopted."

Sarah felt a strong tug on her heart and knew right away that she wanted to be that person. Now that she had the reward money, she could rent her own room and get it set up for this darling little girl. She was sure that she could find several women willing to watch her while Sarah was teaching school. No one was going to talk her out of this.

After Doc returned to his office, Sarah wasted no time talking to Doc and Elizabeth. "I want to adopt the little baby girl. I fell in love with her as soon as I held her in my arms. I have no problem with finances and will rent my own room at the hotel."

Doc advised her "Sarah, please take some more time to think about this. I know you mean well, but this is a very serious decision. Taking another week or so won't make any difference."

Sarah had never been so determined in her life about making a decision. The baby seemed to always know when Sarah was holding her and the contented look on Sarah's face was something to see. This bold woman who had ridden into town bareback a few months ago, now looked like the gentlest woman God had ever created. Doc decided to talk to Pastor about this because he suspected that Pastor was beginning to care about her, even if he hadn't realized it yet.

He walked over to the church and found Pastor alone, looking sad. "James, what has you so down this morning?"

Pastor tried to act like everything was fine but he wasn't fooling Doc. "I've just got a lot on my mind Doc. A lot of villagers have all kinds of problems that they come and share with me. I guess it just got to me. Are you here for a special reason?"

Doc thought that today didn't seem like the best time to bring up the subject of Sarah and the baby, but it couldn't be put off any longer. "James, you know the Donovan baby is going to be put up for adoption. Well, someone has come forward that wants to adopt the little girl."

"That's great news Doc! I mean, if it is a family that is loving and would take good care of her. Who wants to adopt her?"

"James, Sarah wants to adopt the little girl and she is quite determined about it. She has already rented her own room at the hotel so that she can fix it up for the baby."

"What? You've got to be kidding. Sarah's not even married and she has a job and, and...can't you talk her out of it?"

"She already loves the baby. Anyone can see that. She has asked three different women to watch the baby while she is at school and she has the finances. Sarah told me that her mind is made up and she doesn't want to hear anything more about it. She is ready to sign the paperwork."

Pastor jumped out of his chair and said, "Well, she is darn sure going to listen to me. Thanks for telling me Doc. I'll talk to you later."

He walked to the hotel as fast as he could and went directly to Maude and asked for Sarah's new room number. Maude said, "Pastor, let me go and let her know that you are here."

"No Maude, I want to see her right now. What is her room number?"

Maude had never seen Pastor upset like this and she suspected that she knew the reason. "Follow me and I'll take you to her room." They walked down the hall and Maude stopped in front of Sarah's door and tapped softly. When Sarah opened the door, she was holding the baby and her face lit up when she saw Maude, but when she saw Pastor's scowling face, her smile disappeared. "Sarah, Pastor insisted on talking to you right away. I didn't know what to do. Can I take the baby to my room while you talk?"

Sarah handed her the baby and Maude left right away. Sarah didn't invite the Pastor to come in and she didn't move out of the doorway. Pastor said, "What is this ridiculous idea that you have of adopting this baby? You aren't even married! There must be some loving couple that would love to adopt her. You need to stop and think about what you are doing Sarah. Use your head, for heaven's sake."

Pastor knew that the words flying out of his mouth were the wrong words to use on Sarah, plus the tone of his voice wasn't calming, to say the least. Sarah's face turned to stone and she had a redness creeping up from her neck. She was fighting for control; that was obvious. She finally trusted herself to speak and she said, "Pastor, first of all, this is no business of yours. I love this baby and she already feels like she is my child. She has had me in her life since the day she was born. I can take care of her and I don't need to be married to adopt her. Several women have offered to help me take care of her while I am teaching. I am even going to pay one of them because she needs the income. I think you had better leave now before either of us says something we might regret."

Sarah tried to close the door, but Pastor was not moving. "Sarah, I'm sorry for my tone of voice. I was just so upset when I heard what you were planning to do. I care very much about you and I don't want to see you do something that you might later decide was a decision made in haste."

This time Sarah used her arm and pushed him out into the hallway and shut the door. Pastor couldn't believe this was happening. First Sarah was about to make a big mistake and now she actually shoved him out of the doorway. He turned and walked away, almost in a daze. Now was the time for one of his walks and talks with the Lord. If anyone could convince Sarah that she was about to make a mistake, he knew that he could count on God to be on his side. At least that thought calmed him down.

Sarah went to Maude's room and asked "Could you please watch the baby a little longer while I run an errand?"

"Of course, I will. Has Pastor calmed down at all? I've never seen him like this before."

"No, he hasn't calmed down and I finally had to force him to leave. I won't be gone too long Maude."

Sarah bundled up and rented a horse from the stable and rode out to Johnny's ranch. She was lucky and spotted him walking into the horse barn and she yelled out and caught his attention. He was surprised but pleased to see her and walked over to her horse. She got down without his help, as he knew she would. He led her horse into the barn and put it in an empty stall and gave him some feed and water.

They both sat down on some bales of hay and it just seemed so natural. He knew she had to have a special reason for coming out. "Johnny, I needed someone to talk to that wouldn't be so quick to judge me. I trust you and feel like you are a special friend. I hope that you will hear me out before you say anything."

She proceeded to explain about the baby and how deeply she felt about adopting her. Pastor's outburst was also part of what she was confiding to him. She explained that she had the funds to take care of the baby and had already fallen in love with her. "I just want you to tell me the truth. How do you feel about what I want to do? Pastor just blew up at me and I don't handle being yelled at very well, as you can probably imagine."

Johnny was quiet for a few seconds, trying to pull his thoughts together. He cared so much for this woman and he didn't want to say anything to damage their special friendship. "I have always assumed that you would be marrying Pastor at some point and having your own children. I guess I never thought about you adopting a baby on your own."

"I don't want to have any children; I mean by a natural birth. My mother died in childbirth and I was only six years old. I can still remember her screaming and then she was gone and there was this little baby boy without a mother. That has given me nightmares all of my life. I just can't seem to get past that fear. This is an answer to prayer for me, Johnny. I love children and I know that I'd make a good mother. I don't need to be married to provide a loving home for a child."

"As far as your situation, I would say that you should do what you feel is right for you and the baby. Don't let anyone else talk you out of it. I will support you totally in whatever decision you end up making and I will help you in any way that I can. I have no doubt that you would make a wonderful mother to any child. Don't be too upset with Pastor. I'm sure this was a shock for him to hear. I know he cares a great deal for you Sarah."

"You always seem to know the right thing to say to me, Johnny."

"For years I have not wanted anything to do with getting married and having children. I thought I'd found the right woman twice in my life and both times they turned out to be the opposite of what they were pretending to be. I swore that women weren't to be trusted. Until, I mean, until I met you Sarah. You are the first woman that I know I can truly trust and you've managed to tear down that wall I've kept up. Julia and Timothy had a lot to do with that too, because they both look up to me, and I know that they want me to marry their mother. I love both of those children but I can't see myself married to Elizabeth. She's a wonderful person and a terrific mother but I don't think that I am the right man for her."

"Oh Johnny, thank you for what you just confided in me and for your support. I am afraid that I've started to lean on you too much lately. I feel much better now and I am going to go ahead and start the paperwork for the adoption. I know that several people will tell me that I don't know what I'm doing, but I do now. Regarding what you shared about Elizabeth, I have grown to love her like a sister. I know that she has had a hard time of it, having the sole responsibility for raising two children. Please try to be patient with her, Johnny." She walked over and gave him a hug and just stayed in his arms a little longer than he was comfortable with. *'I wish I only felt like we were good friends, but I'm afraid that it is going beyond that. I don't want to do anything to spoil our friendship.'*

A few weeks later, Sarah had finalized the paperwork. She decided to name the baby Clarissa, after a favorite aunt. She asked Richard to build her a crib and he had stopped everything to do this for her. Several of the ladies had a tea party for Sarah and each one had brought a lovely gift for the baby; most of them handmade. She was so touched by their thoughtfulness, especially when she knew that some of them disapproved of the adoption. Maggie had offered to nurse her for awhile until she could be weaned onto a bottle. Holding her in her arms felt like nothing in the world could ever feel this good. Maude took right over in the grandmother role and it suited her perfectly. Sarah was so thankful for her many blessings. *'I have a daughter, a job I love, wonderful friends and good health. The Lord has been good to me. All I want is to raise her up to love the Lord like I do and to shower her with love.'*

Johnny was doing everything that he knew to do to keep himself from falling apart. Each day that went by with no news about his child was threatening to increase his anger at God. *'I am trying to do something good for my child. To make sure the child is safe and loved and to let him know that I've been searching for years to find him. Why aren't you doing anything to help me? Rebecca told me that you are watching over my child. I am seriously having trouble believing that.'*

Robbie Anderson had been taught about Jesus in the orphanage he had been living in since he was a few days old. Now he was almost five and this was all he knew about being part of a family. He had problems reading because of his eyesight; he was partially blind. The teachers read to them every day from the Bible. He loved to hear about the miracles that Jesus performed, especially the one about when he healed the blind man. He had never been angry at God for his vision problems. He just figured that Jesus had a good reason for allowing it to happen. One of his best friends was Lucy Fredricks, who was six years old and totally blind. They would walk to their classes and meals together, hand in hand. He would try and describe the room, the teachers and the other children the best that he could. When they were allowed to go outside for fresh air, he would pick up leaves and put them in her hands and tell her what color they were and what the tree looked like.

It took several weeks before Lucy had begun to share things about her past. She told him that her parents were ashamed of her and she was never fed as much as her siblings. They always dressed her in old clothes that were torn, but everyone else was dressed in fine clothes.

One day she said, "Robbie, are you ashamed of me?" His first reaction was anger at her parents, but he calmed himself down quickly and managed to say, "I have no reason to feel ashamed of you Lucy. You have a beautiful smile and your hair is very pretty. All of us are wearing clothes in the same condition; clean and nice looking.

When she heard this, she had a wonderful smile on her face. "Robbie, I am so glad that we are friends and I hope we always will be. I would be scared if we were ever separated."

Pastor James had a few weeks to think about his outburst when he found out that Sarah was adopting a baby girl. He had spent each of those days, taking long walks and crying out to God for guidance. Whenever he saw Sarah, she was holding her baby and absolutely beaming. He felt ashamed of how he had acted, especially being her pastor and all. Today he had made a decision and he had asked Maude to help him to have an hour or so to talk to Sarah in private. He had promised her that there would not be any outbursts; only an apology. Maude had worked it out and Sarah was waiting at one of the small tables in the dining room. It was between meals and the room was empty except for the two of them.

"Hello Sarah, it was good of you to agree to talk to me."

"Good morning, Pastor. I must admit that I'm a little bit uncomfortable right now."

"Sarah, I want to give you my heartfelt apology for my attitude, when I found out about the adoption. Please believe me when I tell you that I was very concerned about you and mistakenly thought you were making a mistake. I know now that I was so wrong. I'm proud of you for sticking to what you knew in your heart was right. Please forgive me for hurting you."

"I'm relieved to hear you say that. I love my daughter so much and I could never regret my decision. She has already brought so much joy to my life. I do forgive you and I would like to put this behind us. Maude is delighted to be Clarissa's grandmother, since I lost my mother years ago. She 'borrows' my daughter every chance that she gets." Sarah had such a glow on her face and her eyes were so excited.

"Sarah, there is one more thing that I came to say to you and it is very important. I would like to ask you to marry me. I promise to always take care of you and your baby. I really believe that I will be a good father."

The look on Sarah's face was not something that he had expected. He was so sure that she would look pleased or excited; but he was not prepared for the look he saw now.

"Pastor, I don't understand. I know that you don't love me and why would you think I would want to marry you?"

"I may not love you at this moment but I do care about you, very much. This way you will have a father for your daughter and I will have a family like I've been praying about. Please give yourself time to think about this. Pray about it and talk to Maude, but don't turn me down without giving yourself time to realize how perfect this could be for both of us. I will leave you alone now, but thank you again for allowing me to apologize and to tell you that I'd like us to be married. I hope you will be able to give me your answer soon."

As Pastor walked away, Sarah sat there stunned. Knowing that Pastor was leaving, Maude came to her, holding Clarissa. "Sarah, you look so confused. Can you tell me what he said to you just now?"

"He wants us to be married. I know he means well but we don't love each other. I think part of the reason is so my child will have a father. He asked me to pray about it and to talk it over with you. After the way he reacted to my adopting Clarissa, I certainly didn't expect a marriage proposal from him. I really need your advice, Maude. Naturally, I want what is best for my child, and I want to do the right thing."

"My goodness, I am as shocked as you are. The only advice I can give you at the moment is to not make a hasty decision. A few weeks isn't going to hurt anything and you are right; you must make the right choice. There is no doubt that he would be good to you and your daughter, so that isn't the question. You need to find out what God would have you do. You'll have perfect peace when you know that. You know that I'll be praying often about this. I'm so happy that you came back into my life Sarah. You are like a daughter to me and now you have made me a grandmother. I've missed out on so much during the past several years, but now the wait was worth it. I hate to give her up, but here is your sweetheart. I need to get back to work."

Later that evening, Maude and Sarah and Elizabeth were in Maude's room, having tea. Usually they would never run out of conversation but tonight all three of them were thinking about their future. Maude missed Harrison but he had been faithful about writing to her, as he had promised. He was still planning on returning to Willow Bend, right after Christmas, depending on the weather. Elizabeth had just been told about Pastor's proposal to Sarah and for some reason, it was bothering her. She had grown close to Sarah and wanted the best for her. *'I'm not jealous of her receiving a proposal, so why am I having these misgivings about it?'*

Sarah was rocking her daughter to sleep and instead of thinking about Pastor, she found herself thinking about Johnny. *'He has turned out to be one of my best friends and I know that he always makes me so happy. I haven't told him this latest news, but I think maybe I'll find some time to talk to him tomorrow. Maybe he can say something that will help me make the best decision.'*

Dear Readers,

I was in Junior High when 'Gone With the Wind' came out and I hid out in the woods to read that long book. From that point on, I was always interested in the Civil War. Over the years I have read hundreds of books on this war, and I've never, in my heart, taken sides. The soldiers, parents, siblings and sweethearts back home all suffered equally, as far as I was concerned.

I have dedicated this book to my great, grandfather because I've always been sad that I never knew him. He passed away several years before I was born. When I started writing this book, my first character was 'Franklin' because I've always had a heart for any soldier, in any war, who has had terrible injuries.

I am hoping that when you read this book, you will sometimes laugh, sometimes cry and often, feel your heart being touched. I really do care about each of my characters and what they are going through. I've been through a lot of pain, rejection and depression in my life, which has given me a lot of compassion for others. Nothing would make me happier than to receive letters, card, emails or comments on my blog, that this book helped you in some way.

I'm already about 70% finished with the second book in this series, and I can't wait to get this out so you can see what new things are happening to the villagers in 'Willow Bend'. Thank you for purchasing my first book and I hope you will want to keep following my 'Willow Bend' series.

I would like to thank all of our soldiers for serving our wonderful country. I served in the Air Force from 1963-1967 and loved every minute of it.

Please check out my blog at:
http://willowbend.positive-imaging.com/

Hello to all those who have read the first book of my Willow Bend series. I am almost finished with the second book, which I am calling:

WILLOW BEND: Hearts Are Being Mended

Here are some of the things that will be happening in this second book of my series.

Austin: Jonas takes him to another village to pick up some feed and Austin sees someone he knows.

Annie & Pete: Annie gets herself in a lot of trouble with Pete and Worley.

Bucky: Johnny tells him that he's lost his job and home until he can make amends.

Charlie & Martha: They found out that Martha is pregnant, which is a shock to both of them.

Cynthia: She loves her job in Doc's office and is surprised to find a man who is interested in her.

Danny & Sadie & Mandie: Jonas receives a surprise that will affect him and Sadie in a special way.

Doc: His drinking has slowed down but he hasn't been able to stop completely.

Elizabeth: She asks Sarah to help her to be more exciting and interesting.

Franklin: He is now helping Johnny by taking care of several abused horses and he loves the job.

Gerard & Ellie: Shocked to find that Gerard is checking out of the hotel and taking a train back east.

Hank & Maggie: He is slowly getting rid of his anger at God for the loss of his wife and child.

Harrison: Trying to get back to Maude right after Christmas, his stagecoach is caught in a blizzard.

Isaac: Johnny teaches Isaac how to tie a slip knot, which he'll use to save someone in trouble.

Jacob & Emily: There little boy gets very ill but when they send for Doc, he has been drinking.

Jeffrey: He is furious when he finds out that his brother Rafe and Josh were both shot and are in jail.

Johnny: He is getting angry at God for not helping him to find his missing child.

Maude: She knows that she has to make a decision between Doc and Harrison.

Melissa: Two men who are best friends are both interested in her.

Millie: She befriends a man who is in Johnny's jail.

Murphy & Rocky: They are getting closer to finding Rusty. They are closer than they realize.

Norma: Johnny was about to release her from her job at the hotel but she makes him angry.

Pastor James: He always feels like he is not doing enough but then an emergency comes up and he responds, without thoughts of the danger involved.

Robbie & Lucy: Robbie is determined that he and Lucy will never be separated.

Rusty & Ben: Ben offers to let Rusty move into his son's bedroom and treats him like a son. He is only ten miles away from Willow Bend but doesn't know that is where Johnny lives.